Death in Enmity

SR Garrae

ISBN: 9798392921102

DEDICATION

To my family.

ALSO BY SR GARRAE

The Casey and Carval series
Death in Focus
Death in Camera
Death in Sight
Death in Frenzy
Death in Lights

CONTENTS

ACKNOWLEDGMENTS

Thanks go to Daniela, for all her help, support and encouragement from the very beginning, and for allowing me to use her name for a character. Joan has edited wonderfully and continues to correct my British English to American English.
I especially want to thank Mary, for allowing me to borrow her New York driver's licence for the cover (suitably amended); and finally the writers' group, for all their help and support.

CHAPTER ONE

Jamie Carval stood by an open grave, looking at a polished oak coffin, gleaming in the bright summer sun of June. For almost the first time in his adult life, he didn't have his camera with him, left at home. Today wasn't a day for taking photographs.

Today, Casey Clement was burying her father.

She stood beside him, dressed in plain, overwhelming black, small and white-faced, desperately dry-eyed. Despite the presence of her team and Carval around her, she could have been entirely alone; her gaze fixed on the officiant and the solitary lily on the coffin.

The service began: the old words, which Casey must have chosen.

"I am the resurrection and the life, saith the Lord: he that believeth in me, though he were dead, yet shall he live: and whosoever liveth and believeth in me shall never die…We brought nothing into this world, and it is certain we can carry nothing out. The Lord gave, and the Lord hath taken away; blessed be the name of the Lord."

He heard Casey muffle a sob; eyes still fixed on the pure white petals of the flower.

"O death, where is thy sting? O grave, where is thy victory?"

She took half a pace forward, and stopped: head up, spine straight, standing at parade attention. Her team came to attention with her as the coffin was lowered.

"We therefore commit his body to the ground; earth to earth, ashes to ashes, dust to dust; in sure and certain hope of the Resurrection to eternal life…"

Tears streamed down her face, but she stood erect throughout: unbending, unbreaking – unbreakable. The service finished, and the officiant left.

"Thank you all." She met each man's gaze, seeing the support and sympathy for her. "I appreciate it." Inadequate words were all she had. They understood. "I'll stay here for a while. I…" – she swallowed – "…need some time alone." *With my parents* choked in her throat, unspoken.

They filed away, and Casey was left alone between her mother's grave and her father's, her head now bent under the bright June sunshine.

It would have been a beautiful day, if only she weren't mourning her parents.

When the only remaining sounds were the soft rustle of the breeze through the leaves and the birdsong from beyond the headstones, she knelt down where she had stood, between the graves, and spent some time in silent contemplation, mourning, asking forgiveness of her dead. Finally, she rose, drying her eyes, and drifted, as silent as the dead surrounding her, towards the remains of the day. No hurry, now; no brisk commanding stride; no place to be. Only the quiet murmur of the wind and the gentle call of birds and insects; the light and warmth of the sun on her chilled body. This was how loneliness arrived, not suddenly, but garbed in unrelieved black, carried on the old words of the funeral service: *ashes to ashes, dust to dust.* Tears upon tears; solitude swelling and shrouding her as she passed through the cemetery.

It was a long time before she emerged, slow and dragging; drifting through the gates as if she trailed the ghosts of her dead behind her: as if she were half a ghost herself. She didn't, Carval thought, believe he was there until he moved to catch her. Sobbing in his arms, her small body seemed too fragile to bear the weight upon it; as if a careless touch would snap her; brittle and transparent as blown glass; cold despite the heat of the day. He held her close until her tears ran dry, while she leaned on him.

The team had waited too: Casey's partner and oldest, closest friend, O'Leary; the huge bulk of his six-foot ten bent protectively over her; Tyler's muscular black body behind her, silently supporting; Andy's slim Chinese form; his too-old eyes grieving for her loss. With them, part of them by some strange alchemy, Carval: famous, celebrated reality photographer, darling of the cultural elite and, previously, spoilt playboy – but now, Casey's lover.

Each detective wore full NYPD dress uniform, utterly spotless down to the pure white of their gloves: the only exception was Casey herself. He knew why. Her father, finally drowning from his abuse of alcohol, had told her she should never have been a cop. In her last farewell, she'd bowed to his feelings.

Carval wished she hadn't. She should have shown who she was: proudly worn the mark of her profession and her brilliance.

Perhaps she didn't want to be reminded of either. God knew, because Carval had put her in the centre of the media crosshairs, every headline in every tabloid the previous day had blazoned her loss across the page: *Tragic history of star NYPD cop*, they'd screamed, and advertised her father's death for everyone to read.

He hadn't told her about the publicity, but it hadn't mattered. The precinct bullies had been lining up to make sure she knew: Estrolla, Grendon, and their cronies, all gleefully vicious. She hadn't shown a flicker of interest or an iota of care…but she'd left exactly at shift end and refused to answer a single text, call or knock at her door. Even O'Leary had been blanked, and for once her titanic partner hadn't pushed his way in.

Before the exhibition had opened, before he'd made the four of them stars, before the media circus and the PR carousel; before any of those events, Casey had told him *it'll be rumours and ghosts*, and that was exactly what had happened. Whispers and sly glances, a snigger as someone ghosted past her, leaving press cuttings where she couldn't fail to see them: on the coffee machine, on the cups; on her desk when she returned from lunch with the team protectively around her.

He thought she could have dealt with the nastiness, if it hadn't been for the sympathy salting her wound. Feggetter, offering her a shot of Scotch; the officers with whom they'd worked on the previous case, never saying a word, but producing perfect paperwork so she didn't have to do a thing.

All the while, their eyes pitied her. Everyone knew the story, now. Everyone knew about her father's arrests, his death. She couldn't stand pity, but she'd worked her full shift the previous day without allowing a single hint of upset to show. Not to him, not to O'Leary, not to her team – not to anyone in the precinct. Especially not to Captain Kent and the ominous presence of Dr Renfrew, FBI profiler and shrink.

Still, he wished she'd worn her dress uniform.

He kept an arm around her, matching his stride to her shorter steps. O'Leary gestured to his SUV. "C'mon. I'll take you home."

"'Kay. Thanks." Casey stared up at him with drenched eyes. "Same as last time," she choked. Carval knew she was referring to her mother's funeral, more than eight years earlier.

"Not quite," Carval said. "I'm coming too."

"'Kay," she dripped.

She didn't argue when he pushed her into the back where he could sit by her and simply hold on; she didn't notice, though O'Leary did, Tyler and Andy following. She simply did as O'Leary directed, entirely passive.

She'd barely been anything other than disturbingly passive since she'd ripped into the hack reporter who'd tried to smear her as corrupt at the press conference on Monday morning, only two days ago: all her limited energy directed towards self-control in the face of her grief. She could – she *should* – have taken leave the previous day, but had refused outright. Even Kent hadn't wanted to force her.

Maybe now the funeral was over, she'd take some time.

Maybe pigs were lining up for landing at JFK.

***

Captain Kent's week had gone to hell before noon on Monday, thanks to the disastrous leak of Clement's father's arrests to the press conference. Although Clement had dealt with it perfectly, and the press office and Carval's prissy manager Penrith had shut down anything that might have smudged the NYPD, he now had three major issues on his overburdened hands. The first was Clement herself. She'd pleaded to be allowed to work, and he had, extremely reluctantly, permitted it. However, she looked like a truck had run her over, and if she wasn't any better on Thursday, he was benching her for at least a week.

Clement's state led him to the second issue: the leak itself, which had a couple of sub-problems. One, his suspicion that there was a nasty little campaign of reminders of her father's death going on; two: the need to involve Wetherly of the 112th, where Kent suspected the leak had begun; and three: the involvement of the FBI on a strictly unofficial – he might even have said personal – basis. Kent could see that Internal Affairs would be arriving pretty soon, because if it wasn't only his own precinct affected, he and Wetherly would have to pull IA in.

Worst of all, the final issue. The PR. Carval's goddamn exhibition was golden. It was the hottest ticket in town, the press office told him, and after the conference, every last headline had touted the wonderful team and the tragedy surrounding Clement. Kent's lips pinched. Yes, it was utterly brilliant. Yes, it was great PR for the NYPD. They wouldn't do better in a *year* of Sundays with five blue moons to boot. But it was all focused on Clement, and she hated photos, PR, and the media circus.

Kent glared at his desk, and waited for Dr Renfrew, a hugely experienced FBI agent and profiler, to call back. Wednesday afternoon, and all hell was breaking loose. Though he'd spoken to Renfrew on Monday as soon as the shitstorm had begun, Agent Bergen, Renfrew's sidekick and brilliant technogeek– *almost* as good as Detective Andy Chee – had been absent until today.

His fingers tapped impatiently as he worked through his in-tray and waited for the phone to ring, flicking glances towards his bullpen as he went. Everything was in order, as it should be. He didn't tolerate disorder, or inappropriate conduct – and if there was a covert campaign to rattle Clement, he would squeeze someone's balls in a vice.

Finally, his phone rang. "Kent."

"This is Dr Renfrew. Agent Bergen is with me. We wish to show you our findings."

"Why?"

4

"There are...complications," Renfrew said.

"How soon can you be here?"

"No more than fifteen minutes from now."

"I'll be waiting."

Less than fifteen minutes later, Renfrew and Bergen arrived in Kent's office, identically stern-faced. Bergen shut the door. Outside, the bullpen shivered. Kent's expression as he had met the agents presaged trouble.

"Sit down. You said there were complications?"

"Indeed. Agent Bergen, would you explain, please?"

"Sir. As you know, we've monitored access to the 112th's arrest records since Friday afternoon. As you'd expect, there were lots of accesses. However, we could easily discount most of them, since they didn't access David Clement's record. We were left with three entries. Captain Wetherly, almost immediately after you spoke to us. We consider his access isn't problematic. The other two, in order of access, were Officer Birkett, of the 112th, at six-fifteen on Friday; and Officer Henegan, of this precinct."

"Henegan?"

"Yes," Renfrew stated. "That is where the complication has arisen. Officer Birkett accessed the record for less than three minutes – long enough, in my estimation, to discover the details of David Clement's arrest. Officer Henegan's access, however, took place on Saturday, and remained open, as it were, for twenty-four minutes."

"Saturday?" Kent queried.

"Yes. Saturday, at seven twenty-two."

"Henegan wasn't on shift on Saturday. He's been working with Clement's team, and none of them should have been in the precinct on Saturday. Clement certainly wasn't – her father was taken to hospital on Friday afternoon. He died the same night."

"I had seen so from the press reporting on Tuesday. I am sorry," Renfrew offered, echoed by Bergen. "You say Officer Henegan was not on shift on Saturday?"

"I know Clement – and the rest of her team – weren't supposed to be here at any point on Saturday."

"How could Officer Henegan have accessed any NYPD information, still less data from another precinct?"

"A good question. Let me check if Henegan came into the precinct."

A few moments later, Kent sat back. "If Henegan did enter the precinct, he didn't use his access card, and he wasn't seen by the duty sergeant. Unless he developed invisibility or wings, he wasn't here. However, he's here today." Kent exited his office. "Henegan, my office, now."

Henegan followed Kent back in, white and shaking. When he spotted Renfrew, he shook even more. "Sirs?" he quavered.

"Where were you on Saturday?" Kent enquired coldly.

"Sir?" Henegan said blankly. "I wasn't on shift, sir. I watched the Yankees game in a bar. They beat the Orioles, sir."

"What time did it start?"

"Seven, sir."

"Which bar?"

"Kerry's, on Staten Island." He shivered at Kent's *You'd better be able to prove it* look. "Uh, sir, I got a receipt."

"Show me."

Henegan frantically searched his wallet, and eventually handed over a crumpled, greasy receipt which nevertheless showed a time stamp of seven thirty-three. Kent handed it back. "Thank you, Officer." Henegan recovered a little colour, which promptly drained to grey as Kent continued. "Since you were not here, how was your workstation used to access NYPD files on Saturday evening?"

Henegan gaped. "Sir?"

Renfrew took a hand. "Officer Henegan, we have traced an unauthorised access of NYPD files to your terminal. Who might have had access to your passwords?"

Henegan cringed. It was clear to the technologically average Kent and Renfrew, and blindingly obvious to technogeek Bergen, that the rules about not sharing passwords had been comprehensively ignored.

"I see," Kent pronounced. "Any of several people." Henegan nodded, pathetically incapable of speech. "Dismissed. You will not mention anything about this interview."

Henegan fled.

Kent turned to Renfrew. "We could identify two of those people," he stated.

"I expect you mean Officers Estrolla and Grendon," Renfrew replied.

"I do. However, I'd like to know what happened between Birkett accessing the file on Friday and Henegan's log-in being used on Saturday." Dr Renfrew raised his brows in query. "I don't see why logging in on Saturday was necessary. If Birkett tipped off the press, he didn't need Estrolla or Grendon – or anyone else – to access the file again. If he didn't, why tell Estrolla or Grendon? Or was there someone else in the mix? So, has someone been very smart, or very dumb?"

"It is possible," Renfrew agreed, "that Officer Birkett advised Detective Marcol of Mr Clement's arrest, and matters progressed from there. If Detective Marcol is protecting himself, he would have advised – or will say he advised, which may not be the same thing – Officer Birkett to take no steps. The question is whether Officer Birkett acted with malice; whether Detective Marcol took other steps; or whether some other act took place." He steepled his fingers. "Without access to phone records, we have no way of telling."

"Estrolla and Grendon have been trying to bully Henegan ever since I dropped him into Clement's pack of officers," Kent noted. "There hasn't been anything I could notice officially, but there's a lot of circumstantial evidence."

"You are suggesting they intended to implicate Henegan."

"Yes. Unlike some others, they're even dumber than you think they are."

"I had thought," Renfrew said aridly, "they could not be less intelligent than they had demonstrated by taking on Detective Clement and her team at sparring."

"I assure you, if they're the ones who tipped off the press, they are."

"Is it possible," Bergen suggested, "that Estrolla or Grendon found out by pressuring Henegan? We know they've been looking for an opportunity to, um…. Anyway, they could've gotten the reason from Henegan, and confirmed with Birkett or looked it up themselves. If they're as dumb as they seem, they might not have listened to anyone telling them to do nothing."

"I guess so," Kent assented. Renfrew beamed approvingly at his junior. "But," Kent continued, "we still don't know who. I'm reluctant to involve Internal Affairs: it always leads to unhappy precincts."

"Indeed," Renfrew agreed. "I suppose we do not know whether any of our miscreants attended the exhibition?"

"No – oh, what *now?*" Kent's phone rang. "Kent – Penrith? I thought you'd dealt with the press."

"It is," Penrith said irritably. "This is a different matter. The *Manhattan Daily Diary*, as a favour to me, told me their reporter was tipped off by a supposedly anonymous call, for which the caller forgot to withhold their number. When they searched the number, it came from the Thirty-Sixth precinct. The reporter followed up with a call to the 112th, to one Officer Birkett."

"I see. Thanks. Have you told anyone else?"

"If you mean Jamie, or Casey and the team, absolutely not. I don't want Jamie to go on another idiotic crusade like he did last time, and I'm sure you don't want your detectives taking their own steps."

"No. Thank you. We'll take it from here – would you e-mail me the number they gave you" – in the background, Bergen whistled softly – "please?"

"Sure. I'll leave it all to you."

"Thank you," Kent said with deep sincerity. Penrith ended the call, and Kent turned to the others. "Well. Now we have something to go on." His e-mail chimed. "And here's the number. They really, really are that dumb."

"You recognise the number?"

"No, but I have a list."

"Would you like me to match it, Captain?" Bergen offered. "If you e-mail me the list, I can do it in a couple of minutes."

"Okay." Kent flicked both the list and the number on.

"Not so dumb," Bergen said shortly. "It's Henegan's number."

"Which he couldn't possibly have used," Kent snapped. "So we aren't much further on."

"I do not agree," Renfrew pronounced. "We may not know who called the reporter, but we do know the reporter called Officer Birkett, who did not correct the reporter's misconception – which he both could and should have done, since he had known the truth since the day before. If, that is, he is permitted to talk to the press. I believe we have scope to interview Officer Birkett." His lips pinched coldly. "If you will permit a small deception, which would be that the FBI is interested in employing Detective Clement and her team, I consider that Captain Wetherly, you, and I would be justified in interviewing Officer Birkett. We might thereby understand both his views of Detective Clement and why he did not take heed of Captain Wetherly's warnings. We may proceed from there."

"I agree. Let's give Wetherly a call and set it up." He dialled. "Wetherly? Kent here. There've been some developments since we last spoke. I'll bring you up to speed, then let's discuss my proposal for dealing with the immediate problem." Kent laid out the whole situation, explained in more detail the FBI's unofficial involvement, and pointed out the possibilities of a three-way interview.

"Sounds good to me," Wetherly replied. "I'm not having double-dealing cops in my command. Birkett's off-shift today, but he'll be in tomorrow, starting at nine. I don't think we should let him get far into the day before we spoil it for him, do you?"

"No," Kent concurred. "When do you want us there? I have a relatively free day tomorrow. Dr Renfrew?"

"I can easily re-schedule any commitments."

"Can you be here at eight-thirty?" Wetherly suggested. "We should do it on my patch, to avoid tipping Birkett off. I want him to be surprised. If he *is* involved, I want him to have no doubt that his career in the NYPD is *over*, along with anyone else who helped him."

"If anyone else is involved, we must know about it. I suggest Agent Bergen makes a final copy of the arrest record, today."

"Fine by me," Wetherly approved.

"Sure," Bergen agreed.

"We'll root it out," Kent said. "Thanks. See you tomorrow." He studied Bergen, who appeared a tad dejected at being excluded from the interrogations. "Bergen, if Dr Renfrew agrees, I've got a job for you." Renfrew made a permitting gesture. "I'd like you to brief Clement and her team – and Carval, if he's there, but don't contact him specially – on where Dr Renfrew and I are, tomorrow morning. *After* we've left, please."

"Yes, sir." Bergen was unwontedly cheerful at a task which would undoubtedly result in some excitable commentary.

CHAPTER TWO

Casey's neat, cosy apartment was overfull with her team and Carval all squashing in, but it had been crowded several times over the last, horrible week. She was leaning hard on the support they had unstintingly provided from the moment she had told them of her father's death. Alcohol had killed him: messily and horribly, leaving blood coating his apartment. She had only crossed its threshold once since: had instructed cleaners and let them in, locked up after them, collected his will, and handed everything over to a probate attorney. Anything more would have been too much. She couldn't bear to go inside again. She knew she had to...just...not yet.

"You don't have to do anythin' today," O'Leary pointed out, reading her mind. "Leave it for now."

"Take some days," Tyler added. "Break."

"Take your bereavement leave," Andy suggested. "We closed the theatre case, and we could all do with a break."

"I don't want to," Casey replied. "I don't want to think about it and if I'm here I won't have anything else to do. I told you that. I don't care what you four think, I can't sit here alone. I'll remember all the blood." She stared down at her knotted hands.

"We better find you a nice murder," O'Leary mused. "Lots of suspects an' motives an' mebbe some action. You c'n try to be soup again, iffen you like."

"You can be the sandwich to go with it, since you got sliced up," Andy pointed out. Casey didn't react.

"A new case," she said slowly. "Yeah. That'd do. Keep my mind off it till I can...process. I only need space for a few days. That's all. Then I'll deal with it." She looked around. "I shouldn't be wishing for murder. Haven't I had enough of death in the last few days?"

"Mebbe it'll be some lowlife who deserves to get dead," O'Leary offered. "We don't mind if they get popped."

Casey shrugged. "I still don't want to wish people dead."

"Not a good look," Tyler said. "Want us to stay?" he continued, and was reassured as Casey considered it.

"No," she eventually decided. "I'll see you tomorrow in the precinct." Her hand slipped into Carval's and squeezed.

"Guess he's stayin'," O'Leary teased, and beamed at her faint blush. "Let him look after you," he added more seriously. "Someone should, tonight." He lumbered up and out of the door, shooing Tyler and Andy along with him.

Carval drew Casey closer, petted, and suppressed the insanely inane urge to ask *are you okay?* Of course she wasn't: how could she be? He drifted off into considering photographs, in which pursuit he could, and did, spend hours – when he wasn't out with his camera taking shots. Today was the first day he could remember when he hadn't taken a single photograph, and he wouldn't be taking any later today either. With sudden shock, he realised consoling Casey was more important.

Nothing had ever been more important to him than taking photographs.

He startled, and Casey *oofed*. "Sorry."

"It's okay." She wriggled back into place, tucked against him. She wasn't crying, but she was still pallid, face drawn, eyes dull. "He's gone." She sniffed soggily, and reached for a Kleenex. "They're gone." Abruptly, she began to cry in short, gulping sobs, trying to stop herself but failing. He turned her into him and let her weep, helplessly unable to soothe her shuddering or warm her to stop the shivers.

Eventually, Casey's tears stopped, and she slumped, silent, against Carval. "I'm sorry," she whispered. "I shouldn't…"

"Don't try to block it. When my father died, I spent weeks trying to be strong, but it was a huge mistake. It all hit me a couple of months later, and I didn't resurface for a week." He didn't say *because I took sleeping pills every night, and if I'd known any dealers, I'd probably have added other stuff to the booze. Carina and Mario slapped me out of it, almost literally.* "I couldn't take a decent photo for weeks, either. I completely lost it. I was lucky I could afford not to work for a while, but looking back I should have grieved from the beginning. I thought I had to be strong for Mom. She needed me…" He called up the memory. "She needed me," he repeated quietly.

"What happened?" Casey asked. Carval had never mentioned his parents, and a flicker of interest distracted her from her own misery. She'd never heard this slow, unhappy tone from him before.

"Dad – Dad was older than her. I was a late surprise – she was almost forty, and Dad was five years older than her. Dad wasn't exactly fit, but…" He hitched. "You don't expect it. I was twenty-eight. Almost six years ago.

One moment he was there, the next…" He stopped again, and swallowed. "The next he was gone. Heart attack." Another pause. "Gone in an instant."

"Not like Dad," Casey breathed, and thought, bitterly, *you had the easier one.*

"No. But Mom was."

"What? You never said – you said you didn't have an alcoholic parent."

"She wasn't. No booze, no drugs. She just…faded. Slowly. She didn't eat enough; she didn't look after herself. She…eventually, she had no reserves. A year after Dad passed" – Casey heard the falter in his voice – "she caught flu. It turned into pneumonia. She never came out of the hospital."

"Like Dad. He didn't care enough for who was left to stay sober or alive." Casey curved an arm around Carval's middle. "I didn't know you knew…" *how it felt* hung silently between them.

"I don't like to remember." Carval never liked thinking about anything unpleasant, and rarely did so, preferring by far to live in the moment. "So mostly I don't."

"I don't want to remember. But I can't forget."

"I have an idea to take your mind off it." Carval caught Casey's horrified face. "No, I don't mean that! I'm not an oaf." She mumbled something that might have been *sorry*, in translation. "You have to eat, and even if you're not hungry, something nice would be better than takeout or microwaved ready meals. Let's go to Villa Venetiana and Carina and Mario can give us good food and a glass of wine if you want one. They'll leave us alone. You won't have to talk or think or do anything. It's after five, so if I call them now, they'll fit us in."

Casey dragged her brain out of its miserable fog. She didn't want to eat, but she knew that if she was to make it to work the next day – and having fought off Kent's earlier attempts to bench her, she couldn't give him more ammunition – she would need to eat something. Why not have good food that someone else had cooked? "If they won't fuss at me," she conceded. "I can't deal with being fussed over today. I need to be quiet." On previous visits, Carina had fussed, not to say treated her as a long-lost, beloved daughter. Today of all days, Casey didn't want to be reminded of how a parent should love their child.

"I'll tell her," Carval agreed. "She won't…she'll…anyway, I'll make sure she doesn't." He contemplated Casey, still in her funeral garb. "Do you want to change first?"

"I guess," she dragged. "What about you?"

"I'll take my tie off." He rolled it up and stuffed it in a pocket, opening the button at his collar. "You go change, and I'll call Carina."

Casey trudged to her bedroom.

While she changed, Carval dialled Villa Venetiana, "Carina?" he opened. "Carina, I want to bring Casey to dinner tonight, now?"

"Jamie! What did I tell you last time? You should plan!"

"Casey is upset," he began.

"What have you done? If you have made her unhappy, I will be angry."

"Not me. Listen. Her father died" –

"Ah, poveretta! I shall take care of her" –

"That's exactly what she doesn't want. She needs to eat a nice meal, but the funeral was today and if you fuss over her" –

"I do not *fuss*," Carina declared with massive dignity.

"She'll see it as fussing. Could you give us one of your wonderful meals," he wheedled, "and not treat her any differently from everyone else in the restaurant? She needs to have peace."

"If you are sure." Carina added a sceptical noise.

"I am."

"Of course we shall do so."

"Thank you," Carval said with heartfelt gratitude.

A few minutes later Casey emerged in jeans and a cotton button-down.

"All arranged," he told her, took one searching look at her, hauled her in and cossetted until he thought she'd be able to make it through dinner.

"I'm *fine*," Casey insisted into his shirt.

"Sure."

"I. Am. Fine." Her words were ruined by the sniff in the middle, on which Carval, not being stupid, didn't remark.

"Let's go."

Twenty minutes later, they walked into Villa Venetiana, to be greeted by Carina.

"Piccola!" she greeted Casey. "Come, sit down." She ushered them to an out-of-the way table, neatly set with a red-checked tablecloth and a cornflower in the vase in the middle. "We are sorry," she condoled. "We shall not talk tonight. You will both eat and drink and have peace." She bustled off, to be succeeded by Mario, bearing a bottle of red wine and a carafe of water.

"I have chosen a wine," he announced to Carval, who made a *what-can-I-do* gesture. "You need not drink it if you do not want to," he added to Casey.

"No, that's fine, thank you. A glass of wine" – she stopped, and altered her next words – "would be nice."

"Do I get to choose our meal?" Carval asked.

"It depends," Mario joked. "If I do not think you choose correctly for my wine, I shall change it."

"Choose for me." Casey tried to make it light, but both Mario and Carval could tell that deciding was too much effort.

"Choose for both of us," Carval decided.

"Bene." Mario poured the wine for him to taste.

As he sipped, he raised his eyebrows, but on catching Mario's glance at Casey's bowed head, didn't comment. "Lovely," he said instead. Mario poured for both of them, and whisked away, to whisk back again with grissini and olives. Carval was more relieved than he'd have admitted under torture when Casey took a bread stick and nibbled, sipped her water, and afterwards the wine. It might not have been a large enough sip to quench a mouse's thirst, but it was something, even if Casey stared at the cheerfully chequered cloth rather than raising her gaze. He didn't try to talk, but slid his hand across the table to cover one of hers.

His hand was still there when Mario brought their appetisers: a small, delicately arranged assortment of bite-sized bruschetta for Casey, carpaccio with shaved Parmesan and salad leaves for Carval. He applauded the decision – and the tact that had given Casey only a small amount, easy to eat without noticing.

"Those were nice," Casey said, a few moments later. "I'm hungry."

"Did you get lunch?"

Casey coloured uncomfortably. "Uh…"

"No," he concluded. "I know you wouldn't have had breakfast; you never do. You'd better eat now, or Kent'll bench you." It wasn't what he wanted to say, which contained the phrase *eat or you'll collapse*, but it was far more likely to work.

"I am eating," Casey pointed out irritably, and munched down on her final miniature bruschetta, following it with another few sips of wine.

"Good. Don't upset Mario or Carina, or they'll scold you."

"No, they'll scold *you*," Casey retorted, with the first flash of spirit he'd seen all day.

"Probably," Carval conceded. "Carina always scolds me and it's not fair."

"Maybe you should plan, like she wants you to."

"Spontaneity is good. I wouldn't get my best shots if I planned them." *I wouldn't have my centrepiece of you if I'd planned it.*

Casey muttered something uncomplimentary about photos. Carval chewed the last bite of his delicious carpaccio, and ignored it. Irritated Casey was a whole bunch better than passive, miserable Casey.

Mario removed the appetiser plates, and replaced them with entrées: roast deboned rabbit with polenta speckled with Parma ham and radicchio for Casey; breast of guinea fowl with truffle and carrots for Carval.

Casey, discovering she was not merely hungry but starving, dug in. She couldn't remember eating dinner on Tuesday, never mind eating earlier today. Even though she hadn't wanted to move from her couch, Villa Venetiana had been a great idea. Her plate was cleared before she knew it, and she had another small mouthful of wine. Even the wine had been a good idea.

She looked across at Carval, savouring his food, and managed a weak smile. "You were right. I did need to come out and eat."

Carval smirked. "I'm always right." Casey pulled a face at him. "That's not nice."

She shrugged. Casey didn't believe in being nice, as it generally meant not doing things which were necessary to do her job. Being nice wouldn't pull answers out of criminals, suspects or witnesses. Being nice wouldn't keep her at the top of her game. Being nice, in fact, would rapidly result in her becoming a doormat and being walked upon. Being nice was a waste of time.

She'd been *nice* to her dad, and look where that had ended. If she'd been less nice, maybe he'd have sought help earlier, when it might have worked. If she'd only...

Only what? Threatened him? Told him he'd never see her again if he didn't stop drinking? Arrested him herself and hoped that would shock him sober? Marched him to the rehab centre?

None of it would have worked. None of it could ever have worked, because her father had wanted to drink far more than he'd wanted to do anything else. He'd wanted to have his wife back, and nothing else would ever have done.

"Casey?"

A tear dripped on to her empty plate.

"What's up?"

"He wouldn't ever have stopped. He only wanted Mom. It didn't matter what I did, did it? I wasted years trying to help him and I really believed it had worked the last time. Right up until it didn't." Another tear dropped. Carval took her hands, then applied some common sense and provided a Kleenex to one of Casey's small hands while holding the other. She scrubbed at her eyes. "Sorry."

"Don't be." His thumb smoothed over the back of her hand.

"What is wrong?" Mario's soft accent slid across the table. "It was not the food, no?" He stood to block the rest of the room, and patted her shoulder. "Do not try to stifle your crying, piccola." Casey snuffled, and wiped her face again. "Grief is natural. Take a sip of wine, and do not worry. No-one shall come for a few moments." He cleared the empty plates, and slipped away.

Casey hunched into herself and pressed the Kleenex to her eyes. "Sorry," she repeated, muffled by her hand. "I shouldn't have come out."

"Sure you should. Staying alone won't help either – you already said so. You might as well have a good meal, quietly, and we'll go back to your apartment." He regarded her dark curls. "There's a chocolate assortment for dessert."

Casey's drenched eyes peeked over the Kleenex. "Chocolate?"

"Well known to help. I'm having orange souffle, though. If I have chocolate, you'll eat all of yours and half of mine."

"Wouldn't," Casey humphed.

"I'll tell Mario, otherwise you might not have your chocolate. Coffee's a given." Carval stood, flicked a glance around, and ambled off in search of Mario.

As soon as he'd gone, Carina bustled up, pristine white apron covering her dress, hair in a knot at her nape. "I shall not talk," she announced. "I shall sit with you and make sure you are not upset." As Mario had done, she patted Casey's shoulder. "You will eat chocolate dessert and drink coffee," she pronounced.

"Carval went to tell Mario."

"Jamie is a silly boy." Casey snorted soggily at Carina's words. "Of course you will eat chocolate dessert. You have done so on each visit. Why should you change? Our chocolate assortment is the best in New York. You shall have espresso afterwards, which is the proper drink for evenings. Jamie will not listen to me when I tell him he is uncivilised, but at least he does not ask for latte!"

For someone who had said she wouldn't talk, Carina was emitting a lot of words. Strangely, Casey didn't object. Carina's volubility and briskly maternal description of Carval was cheering her up.

"If he asked for latte, I would scold him. He knows better. He will not drink proper coffee, but at least he does not ask for *milk!* Milk is for babies." She giggled mischievously. "And even babies should taste coffee."

Casey's second snort was a lot less soggy.

"Bene. Now, I shall bring you dessert and send Jamie back. He should not leave you alone. Ragazzo idiota! Some handsome young man will annoy you and there will be noise and fuss. I shall not have noise and fuss." She bustled off, leaving Casey more cheerful and looking forward to her dessert.

Shortly, Carval returned. "Carina told me off for underestimating them," he pouted. "She told me off for leaving you alone, too. She's always telling me off."

"I like her even more now." On Carval's pained squawk, the desserts arrived, after which Casey concentrated only on her dessert until the last molecule of chocolate hit her stomach.

After ambrosial coffee, Carval took Casey home, without a peep of protest. Truthfully, she had never intended to protest, except for form's sake, and she was too drained to manage even that.

"You'll be comfier in your ratty robe that looks like it was made for O'Leary," Carval said – and watched the red rise in Casey's face. "It was?"

"Not exactly. He gave me it as a joke when I told him they didn't make robes for giants." Carval grinned. "So I kept it. It's cosy," she added defensively, and dropped on to the couch, kicking off her shoes and yawning.

Carval sat beside her, didn't pause before wrapping her in, and thought she'd be asleep in around, oh, five minutes.

She curled into him, yawned again, leaned on his shoulder and let her eyelids fall. It didn't take two minutes before she fell asleep, though Carval waited for a good quarter-hour before moving her to her bedroom and leaving her on her bed. He'd tuck her – and himself – in later.

CHAPTER THREE

Thursday morning, the team lined up, neither bright nor early, in the precinct. If there wasn't a hot case, they wouldn't put in overtime, which would only result in being castigated by Kent. Casey sat, pallid and silent, studying a cold case. She would have come in early, but she'd been left in no doubt that Kent would be watching her, which made it doubly irritating that he wasn't present. Instead, she'd stayed huddled under the sheets and against Carval, who, sleeping, had nevertheless been warm and solid: a place to rest. The memory almost made up for the copy of one of the articles about her, which had been left on her desk. It had hit the trashcan at light speed. Tyler, especially, was ready to have pointed discussions with some members of the bullpen, and she suspected Andy was considering a tiny camera focused on her desk to help Tyler along.

She flipped cold case pages throughout the morning, failing to find any untrodden trails to follow. At close to ten-thirty, Agent Bergen approached: the world's most forgettably average man: mid-height, mid-size, light coffee-coloured skin, features shared with around a million others within New York.

"Hey, guys."

"Bergen? Nice to see you," Andy said, "but what's brought you back?"

Bergen wriggled, and his forgettable face coloured slightly. "Uh, can I talk to all of you together?"

"Sure. I'll collect them. Carval too? He's messing around somewhere."

Casey hadn't noticed Carval arriving, but she wasn't surprised. Whether his attention and his focal length had turned to theatres or construction sites, he'd made it clear he'd be sticking close for the next couple of days. She didn't *need* to be cossetted, but it was comforting.

"Might as well. You'll only tell him anyway, so he can get it from me too."

Andy cast him a sharp glance. "That doesn't sound too good." He surveyed the bullpen. "One of the conference rooms? Or outside the precinct?"

"Conference room."

"Okay."

Andy put Bergen in a room big enough for everyone, and corralled the rest of the team, eventually finding Carval in the entrance hall. Dragging him out of there wasn't easy, since he was absorbed in the ebb and flow of humanity.

"What's this about?" Casey asked, not particularly pleased to be disturbed from her work.

"I'm sorry for your loss, Casey."

"Thanks," she replied tersely, and blinked hard. "Now, what's up?"

Bergen smiled sharply. "You'll like this. Right now, Dr Renfrew and Captain Kent are at the 112th precinct with Captain Wetherly, interrogating Officer Birkett."

"*What?*" Four voices rose.

"After your father's arrest on Friday, Kent and Renfrew asked me to monitor all accesses to his arrest record – did you know I'd kept a time-stamped copy of the record from a while back, in case anyone tried to mess with it?"

"No," Casey said blankly.

"Kent ordered it. Anyway, the reporter who went after you; the one you slapped down, he 'fessed up to his boss, who's a pal of Penrith's, that the tip had come from here."

"*Here?*" chorused four cops and Carval.

Carval went on, "A pal of *Allan's?*" Everyone ignored him as Bergen continued.

"Specifically, Officer Henegan's phone."

"What the" – rasped Tyler.

"Henegan not only wasn't on shift when the call was made," Bergen interrupted, "he was verifiably in a sports bar in Staten Island, watching the Yankees. It wasn't him. He didn't look at the arrest record, either, but it was done from his workstation. Birkett got a call from the reporter, and obviously didn't correct him, though he'd also seen the arrest record – right after you picked up your father, Casey."

"Waal, ain't that somethin'," O'Leary pronounced. "So, the brass've gone to talk to Birkett?"

"Yeah. Birkett's shot himself in the head." Bergen rubbed his hands with satisfaction. "He'll have to explain why he didn't tell the reporter the truth, and why he's rubbed mud on the good name of an outstanding detective *and* the NYPD, in direct defiance of his captain's orders and 1PP's instructions. I'd love to listen to their chat."

"Estrolla," Tyler offered, which everyone in the room understood.

"Most likely," Andy agreed, "but we don't have any proof and, more importantly, Kent will have our heads if we get involved."

"Yeah," Casey said bleakly. "We won't do anything. Understood?" She caught each of their gazes. "You too, Carval." She didn't say – but he heard – *I don't need a hero.* They nodded. When Casey laid down the law, they listened. "We'll leave it to the brass. Let's get on with the cold cases." She managed a nod of thanks for Bergen. "Thanks for telling us. Want to stick around and come get lunch with us?"

"Sure," he replied. "You guys are always fun." His expression turned mischievous. "I've got the afternoon free, so I'll go see this show that's caused all the fuss."

"Enjoy," Carval smirked. "You're in it."

"Say *what?*" Bergen gasped. "Me?"

"You. And Renfrew, and Kent."

"Me?" Bergen repeated. "Wow! I have to tell my mom." He almost danced out of the conference room, pulling out his phone as he went.

"That's how you should react to being in my exhibition."

The rest jeered at Carval's smug comment. Before anyone could comment further, Casey's phone rang.

"Clement? Okay. Where? Okay."

"Guess we got a body," O'Leary told the others. Unusually, Casey was still listening to the dispatcher. The team, Carval, and the returning Agent Bergen waited. Finally, she cut the call.

"A body?" Andy asked.

"Yes. It's complicated, though."

"How?"

"Drive-by shooting. Two guys dead, and one woman in the hospital. Sounds like she was a bystander." Casey's mouth twisted. "We need to split this. Who'll go to the scene, and who'll go to the hospital?"

"You 'n' me'll go to the scene," O'Leary said instantly. He knew Casey's memories of her father's death in the hospital last week would be raw. "Tyler an' Andy c'n do the sympathy bit. We all know you don't do sympathy."

"I'll have lunch with you some other time." Bergen accepted reality. "I guess I'll go see this exhibition."

"See you," the team chorused. Bergen was welcome any time. Dr Renfrew, not so much.

"We better get going. Where are these bodies?" O'Leary asked.

"Riverside Drive, around 120th. The woman's been taken to Mount Sinai Morningside with gunshot wounds."

"On it," Tyler said.

Carval didn't want to photograph murder today. He considered his newest theme – theatres, which reminded him that Allan, his manager, hadn't arranged for him to see the Finisterres, huge funders of experimental culture and debuting performers. Now was the time to remind Allan, he thought. Allan had spent most of the week ensuring that the PR stayed blindingly clean and there were no more attempts to smear Casey, but he was flying to Pittsburgh on Tuesday to supervise Carval's small exhibition, *Hands*, which was touring. Carval decided to return to his studio, waving a generic goodbye which none of the detectives returned. He didn't mind. Casey, especially, needed to lose herself in a case. Since Allan hadn't fixed up theatres for him, he'd go find some construction sites to play with, and reappear at the precinct near shift end.

***

"Here we are." O'Leary parked next to the crime scene tape. "McDonald's already here. How he manages to get here so fast I dunno."

"He turns into a vampire bat and flies," Casey griped.

"Now, that ain't kind. I never heard anythin' meanin' vampire bats deserved you bein' mean like that."

Casey's lips curved briefly, before she relapsed into seriousness. "Drive-by shooting," she mused. "What do you bet we find at least one of them has a record?"

"No bet," her huge partner replied. "Anyways, it'll be both."

"Most likely. I hope there are witnesses" –

"Manhattan on a Thursday mornin'? We'll have witnesses an' passers-by comin' out of our ears, but none of 'em will have the same story, an' half of 'em'll make it up so's they get on TV."

"The last thing we want here is the media," Casey growled.

"Waal, we'd better hope they ain't monitorin' Dispatch 'cause it's a slow day."

"Too damn right."

Casey ducked under the tape, which O'Leary stepped over, to approach ME McDonald. His thin, angular form didn't turn when she greeted him; his skeletal fingers continuing to examine one of the two corpses sprawled on the sidewalk. A crowd was kept at bay by the tape, but there were phones raised all around. Casey did her best to keep her back to them, crouching down beside McDonald.

"Do not block the light," he snapped.

She stood and moved a fraction. "What can you tell me?"

McDonald glared. "Until they are autopsied, very little, as you should know. They were shot at medium range with a large calibre handgun. I shall confirm the exact type when I extract the bullets. Do not ask me now, as I cannot answer."

"Witnesses say the shooting took place less than an hour ago," one of the CSU team said. "There are officers taking statements from everyone they can."

"Thanks," Casey said. "They can report to me when they're done. What about the woman who was caught up in it?"

"She was alive. They took her to the ER, but I don't know anything more."

"Thanks. Dr McDonald, is there anything else I should know immediately?"

"No. The gunshot wound is the cause of death in both cases."

"I'd like to check the bodies when you're finished." She turned to the CSU tech. "Are you done with them?"

"Yes." The tech hesitated. "Uh, Casey?"

"Yes?"

"I'm sorry for your loss," he rushed out. "We all are."

"Thank you."

"Your loss?" McDonald queried, rising to his feet.

"My father died," Casey bit off.

"I am sorry." McDonald managed to infuse his words with enough sincerity to indicate a modicum of humanity, which surprised Casey. McDonald never normally exhibited any humanity, and gave the impression that he would be quite content if humanity disappeared. He glanced at the tech. "I am finished. The bodies can be taken to my morgue as soon as Detective Clement has completed her work." His brief excursion into sympathy had evaporated, and he pecked off without farewell.

"I guess he don't read the papers," O'Leary muttered.

"Good." She knelt beside the body again, and ignored the sudden pang of the memory of kneeling between her parents' graves only the day before. Her gloved hands checked the first victim's pockets, finding a driver's licence in the name of Tomas Wiedecz. The name didn't appear to belong to their victim, since he was of mixed heritage and had no hint of Slavic features, unlike the photo on the licence. However, they'd run it anyway, and visit the address. She probed further, and found a small bag containing white pills. She didn't open it, but summoned the tech to bag and tag it for testing.

"Anythin' else?"

"Not on this one." She moved to the other dead man. White, brown hair, no distinguishing features. The driver's licence she found bore the name Carlos Herencia, with a picture of a Latino man. There was another small bag of pills in the pocket of his pants, which was likewise bagged and tagged.

"Waal, those ain't their licences."

"Nope. The question is, did they steal, forge or borrow them?"

"An' the second question is why? It wouldn't take two seconds to know they were fake. Seems pretty dumb to me."

Casey pulled a face. "Me too, but there has to be a reason. We'll have to hope their prints are in the system." She beckoned the tech over. "We're done for now. Will you get the prints over asap?"

"There's a line – but I'll see what I can do," the tech added quickly, before Casey could protest.

"Thanks."

"Better get back," O'Leary said. "Find out how Tyler an' Andy got on. Mebbe we c'n pick up some lunch on the way?"

"Okay," Casey acceded.

"That way I'm sure you're eatin'."

"What? I have eaten!"

"Somethin' other than chocolate?" O'Leary asked.

"Yes! Carval took me to Villa Venetiana last night and I ate plenty. Stop fussing, you overgrown *nanny*."

"Where is he, anyways?"

Casey stopped. She hadn't thought about Carval's movements when they'd gone out. "I don't know. He didn't come with us, and he didn't go with Andy, so I guess he went back to the studio."

"He waved bye-bye," O'Leary pointed out. "Waal, you c'n go see him later."

"Yeah."

"You don't sound too happy 'bout it."

Casey said nothing for a moment, as she pretended to concentrate on scrambling into O'Leary's SUV. "All I've done for the last two weeks is mope and cry down his shirt. I'm sure he could use a break."

O'Leary paused in his turn. "I don't think he sees it the same way," he countered, losing his bucolic drawl. "Seemed to me like he was happy to be there. Don't you assume. Go see him after we're done."

"Yes, mommy," Casey snarked.

"So long as you take my advice," O'Leary said. "Now, do I need to tell you to eat your greens an' go to bed early?"

Casey spluttered, O'Leary chortled, and they pulled out.

***

"We don't even know who we're looking for," Andy grumbled.

"Won't be hard. Woman shot in a drive-by."

"I guess they'll be expecting us."

Tyler nodded, words being an unnecessary extra in his world.

They parked beside the entrance, and, as Tyler had predicted, there was no difficulty in finding the woman. Unfortunately, she was in surgery, and, naturally but annoyingly, the doctors couldn't release any information about her injuries and condition until that was done.

"Mrs Tania Hercliffe." The receptionist provided an address and social security number: the only information permitted. "You'll have to wait to speak to the doctors, I'm afraid."

"I'll call Casey," Andy said. "She can tell us if there's anything else, or send one of the officers to wait instead of us." Tyler nodded again. Andy made a quick call. "She'll send Adamo. She gave him the name. The others are busy. We don't need to wait for him. We'll go back."

***

In the precinct, Casey glared at her vacant murder board, containing only a timeline. "How'm I supposed to identify the victims, if CSU won't send me prints?"

"We know the injured woman is Mrs Hercliffe," Andy pointed out. "I put her name into the databases, but they're not spitting anything out yet."

"Call Adamo, and tell him to find out if her husband's been informed."

Tyler, who was taking Adamo under his wing, did so.

"Is there *anything* we can start?" Casey asked.

"Not yet," O'Leary said.

"At least Kent's still out," she noted. "I don't want him or that pompous ass Renfrew anywhere near me."

***

"Tell Captain Wetherly that Captain Kent and Dr Renfrew are here, please," Kent said to the desk sergeant at the 112th precinct.

"He told me you should go right up, sir. Top floor, first office to your right as you exit the elevator."

"Thanks."

A couple of minutes later Kent and Renfrew greeted Wetherly, who shut his office door firmly and invited them to sit.

"Birkett doesn't know you're here – he's not on shift for another half hour. I thought we could use the time to work out how to play this." He grimaced. "I don't want to involve Internal Affairs, but I don't see what else we can do if he's deliberately trying to smear your detectives."

"I don't want IA all over us either, but like you, I don't see what else we can do." Kent and Wetherly exchanged identically irritated looks.

"What's your role in this, Dr Renfrew?" Wetherly asked.

"As an FBI agent, I have none. As an expert in psychiatry and profiling, I am studying Detective Clement's team in order to research team dynamics. I hope to use my work to improve team selection in law enforcement agencies." He smiled avuncularly, and steepled his fingers. "Unofficially, I was most impressed by Detective Clement's abilities – and those of her team – and I do not wish to see those lost to the NYPD. Unless, of course, I could persuade the team to join the FBI."

"Not happening," Kent countered. "They're my best team and you're not stealing them."

"I am jesting," Renfrew said calmly. "They would be most unlikely to join the FBI. I am perfectly well aware that, although they like Agent Bergen, they would prefer not to work with me unless necessary."

A full twenty seconds later, Kent managed to retrieve his dropped jaw.

"I do not mind. I frequently find I have that effect on people, until they know me better."

Kent snorted, then recovered himself. "Let's work out what we'll do with Birkett," he said. "Wetherly, he's your officer – what do you want to do?"

Wetherly considered. "To summarise where we are," he began. "Last Friday, you implied Birkett had a motive for smearing Clement. I hauled him in and left him in no doubt whatsoever that 1PP and everyone from the top down wanted good PR, so anyone spoiling the press conference would regret it. I did some checking of my own over the weekend and found he'd read Mr Clement's file, but I didn't do anything about it – then. Now, it seems, Birkett *did* speak to the press, and, at best, didn't correct their misunderstanding." His narrow face turned cold and stern. "Time to do something about it. We'll put him in Interrogation and question him ourselves – Dr Renfrew, I appreciate your expertise, but on reflection, I don't think we can justify your presence in the interrogation to IA later. Would you stay in Observation, and after the first round of questions we'll take a break so you can add your thoughts or any further questions."

"Certainly." Dr Renfrew's mouth thinned. "I shall be delighted to assist."

"Kent, I'll start – he's one of mine, however much I wish he wasn't – but you come in any time you like. I won't stand on ceremony here. We both know how to do this."

"We'd better Mirandize him and record everything."

"Yes. I'll do that." Kent and Wetherly regarded each other with bitter satisfaction. "We'll get to the bottom of this," Wetherly said.

"Yeah. We will, but it means we're starting a massive shitstorm. I'm pretty sure we'll find Detective Marcol somewhere in this mess, so I hope you put your big boots on this morning."

"I did. I don't care who we find, I'm not having this behaviour in my precinct."

"Me neither," Kent agreed. "Let's get started."

"I'll take you down to Interrogation, install Dr Renfrew in Observation, then I'll – myself' – Wetherly bared his teeth – "take Birkett in."

CHAPTER FOUR

"Tyler," the man himself said into his phone. "Got it. On the way." He swiped off. "Adamo. Surgery done. They haven't located the husband yet."

"You an' Andy go," O'Leary instructed, before Casey could object. "Talk to the doctors. When she wakes up, Casey c'n have her turn."

Tyler nodded, and they left.

At Mount Sinai Morningside, the receptionist paged one Dr Chernosk, a lanky, brown-eyed, dark-haired man of around forty.

"Officers – sorry," he instantly corrected, "Detectives."

"Detectives Chee and Tyler," Andy confirmed. "You operated on a Mrs Tania Hercliffe this morning – gunshot wound."

"Yes." He squirmed. "Uh, I haven't had time to report it."

"That's okay. Reception gave us her details. She's most likely a bystander who got hurt, and we'll want to take her statement when she's able to give it. Can you tell us about her injuries?"

Chernosk's face twisted. "She took a bullet to the lower abdomen," he began. "It caused" – he braced – "a miscarriage. She was a few weeks pregnant. The embryo is so tiny early on… The shot ruptured the uterus. We couldn't save the baby."

"Shit," Tyler breathed.

"We don't know if she knew yet, and we can't contact her husband."

"We're trying," Andy offered.

"Good. He should be here. She's made it this far, but she's in ICU and he should know." He blinked. "The prognosis is good. She's young – thirty – and all the indications are that she's healthy. You could say she was lucky. The amniotic fluid stopped the bullet going further, and the ambulance got to her fast."

Tyler stepped away and made a quick call to Casey. "Our partners'll go," he confirmed.

"Do you have the bullet?" Andy asked. "We'll run ballistics testing, and we want to make sure it matches the other two victims."

"Sure. We kept it for you. I'll go get it."

"Can I come too? I have an evidence bag to keep it safe."

"Okay."

Andy and Dr Chernosk disappeared into the bowels of the hospital, while Tyler waited. His phone rang. "Tyler."

"It's Casey. We'll go to the Hercliffes' apartment to find Matthew, her husband. He's not at work."

"'Kay. Getting the bullet. Ballistics run." He didn't mention the miscarriage. It wasn't a matter for an open corridor.

"Later."

***

"What's this about?" Birkett asked, adding "Sir," at Wetherly's icy glare.

"Sit." Birkett did, with a sheen of insolence which neither captain, nor Renfrew, observing, missed.

"Present, Captain Wetherly of the 112th and Captain Kent of the Thirty-Sixth Precinct," Wetherly noted. "We are recording this interview, and I will read you your rights, Officer Birkett."

"What?"

"You will address us both as *sir*," Wetherly bit, and read the Miranda warning. "This interview is being conducted so I can decide when" – he stressed the word – "to involve Internal Affairs."

Birkett paled.

"To set the scene, and for the record," Wetherly continued, "last Friday I received a call from Captain Kent, informing me that officers from my precinct had, for the second time, arrested David Clement, the father of Detective Katrina Clement, under his command." Kent nodded; eyes fixed on Birkett. "He assured me that Mr Clement would be treated exactly like any other drunk. Detective Clement had previously insisted on that, as I had also done. I had no doubt she would do so again."

Birkett's complexion greyed to ashen.

"Following his call, in which Captain Kent informed me, with masterly understatement, that you might not understand that the NYPD – right up to the top of 1PP – supported the major exhibition currently on display, starring Detective Clement's team, I spoke to you. Do you recall our conversation?"

Birkett said nothing.

"Do you recall it?" Wetherly cracked out.

"Yes, sir."

"Repeat what I told you."

Birkett hesitated.

"Do you not remember my orders? If not, you are clearly unfit for duty and will be suspended immediately, pending a full health assessment and an investigation of all of your behaviour, cases, contacts and actions."

Kent remained entirely silent. Wetherly was doing an excellent job, and he didn't want to get involved until he absolutely had to. Wetherly's man, Wetherly should lead.

Silence stretched out.

***

Casey and O'Leary pulled up at an elegant West Side block close to, though not overlooking, Central Park. They buzzed the number, and, when there was no immediate answer, the button marked *Tradesmen*.

"Yeah?"

"Police."

"Okay." A bored voice opened the door. A face appeared over the banister. Casey and O'Leary held up their shields. "No problem."

"Sloppy," O'Leary disapproved. "Should'a come down an' inspected."

"You can do community instruction later. Right now, let's go find Mr Hercliffe."

O'Leary thumped on the door of the Hercliffes' apartment. No answer. He thumped again, harder, and the well-made frame rattled. Casey heard a noise inside. "Another knock," she suggested, "but don't break it. We don't get paid enough to mend it."

"Aww, okay." He thumped for a third time, and this time they both heard someone inside. The door dragged open.

"Mr Hercliffe?"

"Yeah," he yawned. "Whassup?" An odour of whiskey ghosted past them. Casey flinched. Unobtrusively, O'Leary touched her back, steadying her.

"Mr Hercliffe, I'm sorry to tell you your wife is in Mount Sinai Morningside. She's been shot, but she's come through surgery. The hospital has been trying to contact you for hours."

She saw the moment the news cut through the hangover and residual alcohol. "Tania? Tania! What happened?" Panic blazed across his face. "Tania! I have to get there" –

"We'll take you," O'Leary said. *You're not fit to drive* flashed between the cops. Casey stiffened her spine and shoulders, putting all extraneous memories away. *Do the job*, she thought. *Do the job*. "Get your keys an' wallet so's you c'n get home again."

"Yes. Gimme a moment."

They followed him inside, to a pretty, country-style décor, pictures on the walls, a wedding photo on a small side table – and, on another small table beside one of the two plump, old-fashioned armchairs, an empty crystal glass on a coaster. Casey determinedly looked everywhere but at it. Hercliffe emerged from, presumably, a bedroom, slightly less second-hand and holding keys and wallet. He shrugged into a jacket.

"Can we go?" he asked desperately. "I gotta see Tania. How can she be shot? She doesn't have any enemies. Everyone loves her."

"There was a drive-by," O'Leary said compassionately. "We don't think she was a target."

"No! This doesn't happen to people like us. She – this isn't the movies. People don't get shot on the sidewalk for no reason." His words tumbled out.

"Try to calm down. I know it's a shock," Casey said, "but Tania needs you to be with her now, and if you're too upset or angry, you might have to wait. She needs you," she repeated, clinging to her own composure. She hadn't needed her father. He'd needed her – but not enough to live, not enough to stay sober – *stop*. Do the job.

O'Leary stopped outside the ER, and decanted Casey and Hercliffe to find Mrs Hercliffe, while he parked more considerately. Hercliffe ran inside to demand his wife's location from the receptionist, so panicked he couldn't ask coherently. Casey clarified, told the receptionist O'Leary would follow, and escorted Hercliffe to the ICU, where they were met by Dr Chernosk.

"Mr Hercliffe?"

"Yes. Where's Tania? I want to see my wife!"

"Before you do, let me explain. Your wife has come through surgery well, but she's asleep now." Casey recognised the use of *asleep* as meaning *unconscious, but you're scared enough already*. Hercliffe sagged with relief.

"The cop said she'd been *shot*."

"Yes. She was shot in the stomach." Dr Chernosk stopped. Casey noted the sudden increase in the doctor's tension. "She'll want to see you as soon as she wakes up. I'll take you to her room."

"Mr Hercliffe," Casey said, "once you've had some time with your wife, we'd like to ask you some questions to help us find the shooter."

"Sure, sure. Anything. Lemme go to her."

"Come with me." Dr Chernosk swept him off.

"Somethin's up," O'Leary speculated.

"Yeah. Chernosk's not telling him everything."

"She's pregnant."

"How'd you get there?"

"When I was a rookie – before we were partners – I saw a bit of domestic abuse. Trigger was oftentimes pregnancy – you know that. You did the course too. Anyways, the good doc wouldn't be sayin' so in case there were complications, as you might say."

"Like he didn't want it, or maybe thought it wasn't his?" Casey winced. "Nasty. Do we need to think this wasn't a random accident?"

29

"Mebbe, though I ain't seein' it. Here comes the doc now. Let's ask." O'Leary halted Chernosk in his stride. "Is Mrs Hercliffe pregnant?"

"She *was*," he corrected. "But she's lost the baby because of the shooting, like I told your colleagues."

"They wouldn't have mentioned it on a phone in public."

"I see." He sighed. "She wasn't more than a few weeks along."

"Thank you. We won't mention it to her husband," Casey confirmed.

"'Kay."

"We need to know when she wakes up and can give us a statement. Can we put an officer outside her door?"

"Up to you. She won't wake up for several hours, and honestly, I'd wait till tomorrow. She isn't getting out of ICU for at least two days."

"Okay. We'll call tomorrow. Thanks." She turned to O'Leary. "We'll wait for Hercliffe, then we'll go back to regroup with Tyler and Andy, and see what we have."

"Statements," O'Leary drooped. "Hundreds of statements."

"While we're waiting, why don't we think about which gangs this might be? McDonald should be looking for gang tattoos."

"Okay."

***

"What orders did I give, Birkett?"

"No-one was to say or do anything to damage the NYPD." Wetherly glared at him. "Sir."

"Yes. I did. So, Birkett, why did you access Mr Clement's arrest record? You were not the arresting officer."

More silence.

"I believe, Birkett," Kent said coldly, "you attended the Academy at the same time as Detective Clement?"

"Yes." Pause. "Sir."

"And also Detective Marcol, with whom you were, and are, close friends."

"Yes."

Kent raised his eyebrows.

"Sir."

"Forget it again," Wetherly bit, "and you'll be on a disciplinary. Your friendship with Detective Marcol won't excuse you."

Birkett jerked.

"Your Academy record is undistinguished, at best, and your work since has not been notable. Detective Clement, however, graduated top, setting several unbeaten records, and has had an outstanding career to date."

Birkett's face twisted.

"Her success is the reason why she is at the centre of the best PR the NYPD has had in years. I am therefore," Wetherly bit, "entirely unaware of *any* reason why you would not have corrected the misapprehensions of the tabloid journalist Jared Margoly." Birkett failed to preserve a blank face. "He attempted to smear Detective Clement by accusing her of corruptly excusing her father from charges of drunkenness, in the press conference following the opening of the exhibition centred on her team."

Birkett kept his mouth shut, but guilt blotched his face.

"Perhaps you have forgotten you spoke to him before the press conference? Specifically, on Saturday." Wetherly waited. "Or perhaps you were continuing the campaign of persecution you began at the Academy?"

"We'll leave you to think about your answers – and your exceedingly limited career options with the NYPD," Kent said.

"Kent and Wetherly, exiting Interrogation," Wetherly said for the recording. The door locked shut behind them as they left.

"Observation?" Kent suggested.

"Oh, I think so. I'm interested in your Dr Renfrew's take."

"Not my Dr Renfrew," Kent said quickly, a moment before they entered Observation. "Still, he might have a giant redwood trunk up his ass, but you can rely on him."

"Most interesting," Renfrew commented as they entered Observation. "Officer Birkett is, as they say, as guilty as sin." He smiled self-deprecatingly. "I expect he will admit it. He is a weak reed." His fingers steepled on the ledge in front of the one-way glass. "The question is how long it will take him to 'give up' his co-conspirators."

"You have some names in mind, don't you, Kent?" Wetherly said.

"Yes. Let's talk about who – and how."

***

"Mr Hercliffe," Casey said to the devastated man stumbling from his wife's room, "can we get you anything?"

"My Tania," he wept, thudding down into a chair. "How could they?"

"We're goin' to do our best to catch 'em," O'Leary told him. "Sit with us, an' tell us about her." His homely face attempted to be comforting. Casey let the big man lead. The distinctive odour of hospitals wasn't helpful: too close to the ghastly night when she'd sat with her dying father, less than a week ago. She couldn't have waited outside the ICU room if she'd been offered a million dollars. She concentrated on Hercliffe, and tried, almost successfully, to block out the memory of last week.

"Your wife was injured at Riverside Drive, around about 120th," O'Leary told him. "D'you know why she'd gone there?"

"I don't know. She didn't say yesterday she was meeting anyone, but she might have gone for a walk."

31

"Does she work?" Casey asked.

"She'd taken a couple of days off. She wasn't feeling so good yesterday, but I guess she felt better. Stomach trouble."

"Not fun," Casey said.

"No. I felt pretty bad this morning, so I called in sick, but she must've been better..." He trailed off. "If I'd felt better I'd've maybe gone with her and maybe..."

"Or mebbe it would've been you in that bed, an' we'd be talkin' to your wife," O'Leary comforted. "Mebbes ain't no help."

"What does your wife do?"

"She's a fashion consultant."

"What's that, exactly?" Casey asked. Fashion didn't exactly pass her by: she liked nice, flattering clothes as much as anyone, but she wasn't into designer labels or the latest thing. She knew what cuts and colours suited her and were practical for work, she had a couple of summer dresses and even two sexier, evening-type ones – but she didn't spend her free time haunting the stores for new, trendy clothes or shoes. "Is it like personal shopping?"

"A bit, but she's more up-market than that. Colour consultation, brands, how to be on-trend without being ostentatious, guidance on what suits her clients best, hairstyles, and make-up for women. I don't exactly get it but she's really successful." Pride shone from him, and died. "Now she's in an ICU bed and I don't know why."

"We'll do our best to find out," Casey reaffirmed. "What do you do?"

"Me? I'm with Parmentir and Quigley – architects. I'm a partner there." Casey forced her face to mild interest. Her father had been an architect, once. "We mostly do commercial work – nothing up by 120th."

"Thanks." It was sounding more and more like Mrs Hercliffe had been desperately unlucky.

"Can I go back to her now? I want to sit with her." His eyes flickered back down the corridor to ICU.

"Sure. Leave us your details, and here's my card. Could you call us if she wakes up today? We don't want to disturb you or her unnecessarily, but we want to talk to her so we have the best chance of finding whoever did this."

"Yes, yes. Whatever you need. Find them and put them away. Tania didn't deserve this." He hurried back towards his wife.

"Let's go." O'Leary led her to his SUV. They got in, but he didn't start the engine. "You okay?"

"Yeah," Casey tried. She swallowed back a sob. "No. I'll be fine in a second."

"Naw, you're not okay. Take a few moments, an' let it go." He handed her a Kleenex. "I know you said you had to work, so's not to think about thin's, but are you sure this is a case you wanna stick with? Nobody's goin' to blame you for steppin' back. Hospitals, ICU, architect who might be a drinker – this ain't good for you."

"I can do it," Casey gulped. "I can't sit at home thinking."

"An' you can deal with this guy iffen you have to? 'Cause I'm not seein' it yet."

"I can. I have to." Damp, dark eyes lifted to O'Leary's. "I can't run away from it. There are always" – she sniffed hard – "drunks. I can't avoid them."

"I'm not sayin' as I agree with you, but I get it. You still don't have to start now. An' if Kent sees you, he might have some second thoughts, so you better think up some good answers for him. He won't be happy iffen you're all messed up."

"I know," she admitted. "I know all that, but I don't know what else I can do. Sitting at home won't help me."

"Casey," O'Leary said softly, "ain't nothin' goin' to help but time. You're tryin' to get past somethin' in a week that'll take months, an' even then there'll be moments when it's there afterwards. You can't fix this, all you c'n do is roll with it. You know that. You been through it before." He pulled her half out of her seat, and hugged her. "Now, fix yourself up, an' we'll go back an' talk gangs with Tyler an' Andy."

Casey sniffed, and dabbed at her eyes. "Let's go," she managed. "I'll be fine by the time we're back." O'Leary made a sceptical noise, but drove off.

Ten minutes later, they were back in the bullpen. Astonishingly, Casey's desk was as clear of paper as it had been when she left. Studiously blank looks on Andy and Tyler's faces told her they'd monitored her desk. She didn't comment. Thanks were understood from her look.

"What did you get from the husband?" Andy asked, ignoring the slight redness around Casey's eyes and nose.

"She's a fashion consultant. He implied she was pretty high end, so Tyler's got someone who'll dress him up for his next date night." Tyler grunted. Fashion was even less his bag than Casey's. "He's an architect – commercial projects. He was hungover when we picked him up." Her fingers interlaced, knuckles white. "He sobered up pretty fast when we told him his wife was hurt. He was desperate to see her."

"Ripped apart," O'Leary added. "I don't think he's involved. He doesn't know she was pregnant, neither."

"Ouch," Andy said.

"He went back to stay with her. I asked him to call if she woke up, but the doctor said she'd be in ICU for a couple of days minimum, so if he doesn't, we still know where she is." Casey paused to take a slow, deep breath. "We have two dead guys with obviously wrong ID. It looks like they were the targets. Has CSU come back with their prints yet?"

"Nope."

Casey humphed. "This looks like a gang hit to me." The team nodded. "The bystander getting shot makes it nastier. Let's get something to eat and drink and talk about gangs."

CHAPTER FIVE

"Kent and Wetherly returning to Interrogation," Wetherly said. The door closing sounded unpleasantly final. Birkett sat, pallid and sweating, where they had left him. "Why did you access Mr Clement's arrest record?"

"To make sure it wasn't amended. Sir."

"Why did you think it might be amended, and by whom?"

"To protect Clement" –

"*Detective* Clement," Kent snapped. "Show respect to her."

"Detective Clement," Birkett sneered. "Everyone knows she's protecting her father."

"Everyone?" Kent queried, dangerously quietly. "How is she doing so?"

"She's been erasing his arrest record."

"How do you know this?"

"He's been arrested three times but he's still walking around."

"Really? How does that show she's erased his record?"

"She must have. Any judge would have put him in jail by now. There's no record of him being in jail or even a hearing for the third arrest."

"She only took the desk appearance ticket on Friday," Wetherly noted, tapping Kent to indicate he should wait before cutting Birkett into shreds. "Normally it takes a few weeks for a hearing."

"Anyone else would have been kept in jail. She did favours for whoever booked him to keep him out."

"What *favours* has Detective Clement provided? To whom were they given, and when?" Wetherly demanded.

"Why did you not report this *immediately* to the correct authorities, with proof to back up your assertions?" Kent followed.

"You'll have ample opportunity to do so. Internal Affairs will want to know every detail."

"You can tell us what you have. Remember, we are on record, so IA will hear you reporting to us."

Dead silence. In Observation, Renfrew gently applauded.

"Where is your evidence, Officer Birkett?"

"I…"

"Surely you have evidence?" Kent pressed. "These are serious allegations. I can't have anyone corrupt in my precinct. Has the record of Friday's arrest been erased? Or the one before it?"

"Yes," Birkett exclaimed. "I'll show you, sir. Give me a few moments."

"Certainly," Wetherly said. "I will see you in my office in fifteen minutes, when you can show me the erasures."

"Thank you, sir," Birkett oozed. He departed.

Wetherly and Kent made their way to Observation, to meet Renfrew there, smiling thinly.

"I see your officer has swallowed the bait."

"Yes." Wetherly's lips were equally thin. "The more interesting part of this interview will come shortly."

"Yeah," Kent agreed. "Shall we have a small side bet on how long it takes him to roll on all the other weasels?"

"Why not?"

"I see no harm," Renfrew added.

***

"So, gangs." Casey took a bite of her sandwich. "Will McDonald look for tattoos or identifying marks?"

"Yeah. Spoke to him, and CSU. Prints later – there's a line."

"There's always a line," Casey grumbled. "We don't know who they are. Do we have the statements yet?"

"I told Fremont to collate them," Andy said. "He and Larson went off to get them. They should have them all pretty soon."

On the word, Fremont arrived, bearing a pile of paper approximately, to Casey's jaundiced eye, as tall as she was. "Ma'am, detectives, this is everything so far. We're still canvassing the area to catch anyone we might have missed."

"Thanks," she said. "Any highlights we should know before we read?"

"Everyone agreed a vehicle pulled up and a guy shot at the two dead guys, but that's about it. Sorry, ma'am."

The team sighed. "I guess there's a lot of reading in our future," Casey drooped. "We'd better get started."

***

"Allan," Carval called, bounding up the stairs to Allan's neat office below Carval's studio and apartment. "Allan, did you talk to the Finisterres already?"

"Jamie." Allan sighed. "Why aren't you at the precinct like you said you would be?"

"They caught a case but it's a drive-by shooting so there's nothing there for me. Even Kent's missing – oh. Oh, yes." Carval's expression shifted to vengeful. "Agent Bergen – the FBI technogeek who's almost as good as Andy – dropped by to tell us Kent, Renfrew, and whoever runs the precinct that Casey's dad was arrested in..." He thought. "Uh, it doesn't matter. Anyway, they've gone to interrogate Birkett, who's been Marcol's technoweasel since the Academy. He's likely the one who found my photo originally so Marcol could steal it."

"They have?" Allan displayed a notable lack of surprise.

"You knew," Carval realised. "You know something, and you aren't telling me. That's not fair."

"I didn't tell you so you didn't go off on another unhelpful crusade and get in Kent's way," Allan retorted. "We don't need to get involved."

"That's" –

"Accurate. Kent and Renfrew have this well in hand. You can't help. But," Allan added, holding up his hand to stop Carval's babble of indignation, "I can. Remember you promised Casey not to go after Marcol for anything except the copyright issue?"

"Yes."

"Our PI has managed to prove Marcol and Birkett came into possession – as he puts it – of an electronic copy of the poster. I was about to pass the information on to Kent. After I do that, I'll call the Finisterres."

"Great – both things."

"In return, you go find some construction sites. If you can manage a small exhibition, I have several spaces that would like it. I don't want you breathing down my neck while I'm talking to the Finisterres. You'd be in the way and you'd interfere. I have everything under control."

"I don't" – Carval began.

"You would. Go find your camera and go play."

"I don't *play*," Carval complained, offended.

"You don't think of it as work, either. Go do it, whatever you call it. Shoo."

Carval shooed.

Left to himself in blissful peace, Allan called Captain Kent, but reached only his voicemail. He left a brief message and moved on, dialling a number he hadn't used in some time.

"Claudia Finisterre?"

"Claudia, it's Allan Penrith."

"Allan! Henry darling, it's Allan! Let me put you on speaker. We haven't heard from you in *eons*. What have you been up to? You must come around. Have you reconsidered our offer? I know it's been ages, but we would still adore it if you would work with us."

"Allan," a tenor voice chimed in. "How delightful to hear from you. You must visit. In fact, why don't you come now? Can you?"

"I can come later this afternoon – say at four?" Allan conceded, "though I can't stay for long. Are you still in the same apartment?"

"Of course we are. We'll see you at four. Goodbye."

For all Allan had told Jamie that the Finisterres were sharks – and they were, where business was concerned – he'd known them for a long time. They'd offered him a role as their general business manager, but he'd chosen Jamie instead and never regretted it, as chaotic and childish as Jamie could be. He didn't think they knew he worked with Jamie Carval, although they'd met and chatted at various cultural events. Anyway, he wouldn't change his employment at any price.

He heard Jamie loping down the stairs and out; the door slamming shut behind him, and smiled fondly. Jamie might be a photographic superstar, but behind every great talent was an even greater manager.

***

"Sir." Birkett knocked on Captain Wetherly's door, where Wetherly, Kent, and Renfrew were discussing team selection and man-management.

"Birkett. Show us the deletions." Wetherly turned the computer on his desk so everyone could see it. Birkett tapped rapidly, requesting the arrest record.

"See, sir? It's gone."

"Yes, it is." Wetherly regarded Birkett. Kent shut the office door. "Officer Birkett, you are under arrest on suspicion of falsifying arrest records. We will be returning to Interrogation. If you disobey, you will be cuffed and perp-walked through the bullpen."

"I didn't! She did!"

"Walk." Birkett walked, back into Interrogation. This time, Renfrew joined the two captains. "Allow me to introduce to the record Dr Julian Renfrew, a senior agent of the FBI."

Birkett hunched as he was re-read the Miranda warning.

"Officer Birkett, you have been arrested on suspicion of falsifying the arrest record of this precinct."

"I didn't! I told you about Clement falsifying it!"

"When did she do so?"

"On Saturday, after he was arrested, so he didn't have to go to prison."

"How do you know?"

"On Friday he was arrested, on Saturday it wasn't there."

"How fascinating," Renfrew said coldly. "How did Detective Clement achieve this? One of the few Academy trophies she does *not* hold is for electronics work."

"That little Chinese rat in her team did it for her. They're all in it. She's corrupted them all, her and that monster she's paired with."

"You refer to Detectives Chee and O'Leary."

"And the Army vet. Tyler."

"To be clear, you are accusing Detective Clement of conspiring with Detective Chee to falsify her father's arrest record, which falsification took place on Saturday?"

"Yes!"

"Mm. I see," Wetherly said. "These are extremely serious allegations." He, Kent and Renfrew exchanged glances.

"Your man." Kent sat back.

"Indeed," Renfrew agreed.

Birkett eyed one man, then another, evidently surprised that they weren't falling on his neck with joy at his exposure of alleged corruption.

"You're lying," Wetherly said flatly. "Don't say a word. I know you are lying, because Dr Renfrew's FBI technical expert has been taking certified downloads of the arrest record since January. The most recent download was yesterday evening, and I have inspected it. Both arrests were on the record when it was taken. They were not deleted on Saturday." He flicked a glance at Kent.

"On Saturday," Kent continued, "Detective Clement was arranging her father's funeral, which took place yesterday. In my experience, judges are extremely reluctant to summon corpses to appear in court, and prisons are reluctant to jail dead men. I assume you have not seen a single news article since Monday, since the story of Mr Clement's death has been all over the media."

Birkett gasped. Kent passed the baton to Renfrew.

"My involvement, with my technical expert, was requested because we were concerned that someone would try to falsify Mr Clement's arrest record. However, we did not suspect at any stage that Detective Clement, or any of her team, would do so. On the contrary, we expected, if such a heinous action were taken, it would come from those persons who had attempted to smear her reputation at the Academy. You stand very close to the top of that list."

"We gave you an opportunity to do it, and you took it," Wetherly said. "The FBI will be taking another download – they had my consent, incidentally – and investigating the access data immediately. Dr Renfrew, would you please arrange it?"

"My pleasure." Renfrew exited Interrogation.

"Before we hand you over to Internal Affairs, Birkett, talk. Why were you going after Detective Clement now? The Academy was nine years ago. What put a burr up your ass – or who? Who else was involved?"

"Officer Henegan at the Thirty-Sixth!"

"Lie two," Kent stated flatly. "We have conclusive proof that Officer Henegan could not possibly have been involved."

Birkett slumped. "That bitch," he muttered. "She only graduated top 'cause she spread her legs."

"Lie three. But let's start there. Recruit-Officer Clement graduated top, and your long-time pal Recruit-Officer Marcol graduated second. He wasn't pleased about it. He wasn't pleased that Clement knocked him back, either. And quite recently he tried to harass her."

"Her team harassed him."

"You mean, Detective Clement refused to date him, as is her right, and the team supported her decision."

"No. They threatened to sue him."

"Lie four. They had nothing to do with it," Kent stated. "The owner of the photo used to slander her at the Academy is suing. It turns out, Birkett, that stealing photos can get you sued. Especially when the person taking the photo has substantial resources, cast-iron evidence, and a top-notch lawyer."

"Tell the truth, Birkett," Wetherly commanded. "You'll be telling it all again to IA."

Birkett broke.

***

"My eyes hurt," Casey complained, halfway down her pile of statements. "Can't CSU hurry up?"

"Let's take a break an' see if any of us has anythin' consistent," O'Leary suggested. "I got a few common themes."

"Me too," Andy said.

"Yeah," Casey said. Tyler simply nodded.

"Ev'ryone I got agrees it was a car or SUV, not a flatbed. Most of 'em say it was black, all of 'em say it was dark."

"Same here," Casey agreed, as Andy and Tyler both nodded. "I have part of the plate – and we need to get our canvassers to go back to all these bystanders to ask if they took photos or videos on their phones." She stopped, and whisked across to Fremont. "Fremont, did you or the other officers ask about photos or videos?"

"Sure did, ma'am – at least, me 'n' Larson did. Don't know about the others. We're trying to organise what we have."

"Good. I'll go ask Sergeant Tully for some help. I'll try to get you, Larson, Adamo, and Henegan on it. I want you to put together a list of all the witnesses we have statements from, but where we don't know whether they took photos."

"Yes'm," Fremont said. "We'll list who gave us photos or videos so we can check them off."

Casey hurried off to see the sergeant.

"Sir?" she asked Sergeant Tully, "can I get some officers?" She regarded him hopefully. "Fremont, Larson, Adamo – and I'll take Henegan too, if you still want us to keep him around."

"Sorry for your loss, Casey," Tully began, and to her relief left it there. "Yes, you can have those four." He cast her a sly glance. "You're taking Henegan? Voluntarily?"

"You'll only make me take him," she humphed, "but he found some spine and he didn't do badly. Maybe this time he won't shudder every time we speak to him."

Tully snickered. "That'll take a bit longer. I'll send them over – you can tell Fremont as you pass him."

"Thanks, sir." Casey swung off back to Fremont. "You're with us. The other three'll join in a moment, but you start a list of the ones you got photos from."

"Yes'm." He touch-typed the list, focusing on his scrawl. "My handwriting isn't so great."

"You'll fit right in with us," Casey said dryly. "When the others arrive, all four of you come over." She returned to her desk. "Okay, we got the same officers as last time."

"Good," O'Leary said amiably. "We don't have to mess around teachin' 'em what we like."

"Even better, Fremont and Larson already asked for photos or videos. They'll check off the ones they have statements from, then the four of them can chase down more. Larson with Henegan, Fremont can take Adamo." She sighed. "It'll be slow."

"Yeah," everyone agreed.

"Let's go back to these statements. Dark vehicle, not a flatbed, most people said it was black, maybe an SUV. My witnesses mostly say it was a small gun." The others nodded. "Likely a handgun, which fits with McDonald's initial take."

"Semi-automatic rifle or machine-gun would've hit more bystanders," Tyler pointed out. "Didn't stop."

"Same," said Andy. "Slowed right down but didn't fully stop."

"We're lucky there weren't more people hurt or dead."

"Yeah," O'Leary said heavily. "Could've been a helluva mess."

"Pro," Tyler added.

"Professionals? Okay." Casey wrote on her board. If Tyler called it professional, the shooters were professional. "It's feeling more like organised crime gangs, suddenly, not street gangs." She grimaced. "Drugs, anyone? Fake ID to hide who's dealing? Goes with the pills on our dead guys."

"No bet." Andy flicked over a page. "Moving on, I'm not getting any clear call on ethnicity, size, features: anything like that."

"Naw," O'Leary said. Tyler shook his head.

"Nope. We'll have to hope some of the photos or videos can help us out there."

"Anything else?"

"Not yet."

"Second half," Casey instructed. "Anything that contradicts what we have, tell us all."

Another hour later, the team resurfaced. "Anything more?" Casey asked.

"Nothin' contradictory, but nothin' new either. Coupla thoughts on the plates, so we c'n add them all together an' see if we got a whole one."

"Same," Tyler said. "One says tinted windows."

"I've got one saying that too," Andy noted. "That's illegal, but criminals don't much care for obeying the law."

"I don't have anyone saying tinted windows," Casey and O'Leary said in harmony.

"Not a lot further on. I want my prints, and the analysis of the pills," Casey complained for at least the tenth time. "I'll call CSU."

"Translation," Andy said dryly, "Casey'll harass Evan."

Fortunately, before the unfortunate Evan could be harassed, Casey's e-mail pinged with the arrival of the dead men's prints and the identification of the pills as opioids – oxycodone, to be precise.

"Our dead guys are both in the system – we'll get to their records in a moment – and they're Beau Resorge – aka Buster – the mixed heritage guy – and Carson Williams, aka Crusher – the white guy."

"I guess Buster is 'cause he busts thin's," O'Leary suggested. "Goes along with Crusher."

"Judging by their records, you'd be right. They each have a long trail of damage, assault, possession, and general troublemaking. Imagine our surprise to find out they're associated with the Yarrabees."

"This is my astonished face," Andy said sarcastically, with no expression whatsoever. "So we've got a drug war between the Yarrabees and, most likely, the Tarticcas. They're always facing off. But now they've got real trouble, 'cause they hit a bystander *and* she was pregnant and lost the baby. That won't go down well anywhere."

"The Tarticcas need to know what they've done," Casey growled. "I think the Yarrabees already know what's going on. Let's hope there isn't an open war already." She refocused, only too glad to have something to pursue. "Can we find next of kin?"

42

"On it." Andy tapped rapidly. "Running." He returned to his pile of statements. "If our officers would hurry up, we could sift through video."

"O'Leary and I'll take still photos. You and Tyler can do videos."

"Suits me."

"If the Tarticcas were mixed up in this, can anything tell us who the shooters might be? Anyone got an insight into the gangs?"

"Waal, we could ask Kent," O'Leary suggested.

"If he was here," Andy pointed out.

"He's not back?" Casey gasped. "That's…oh, crap. If he's been down at the 112th all morning and half the afternoon, the shit is really hitting the fan."

"You're reachin'," O'Leary said. "Most likely he's got meetin's here an' there. Stop borrowin' trouble."

"I guess," Casey conceded, but it wasn't agreement. Tension gathered in her stomach to join the sick grief she'd been repressing all day, making her wish she'd skipped lunch.

"Does anyone else know anything about the gangs?"

"I do," Feggetter said. Casey jumped. "Sorry. Overheard. I know something about them. What's up?"

"Two dead Yarrabees, one bystander put in the hospital and lost her baby, and it might be the Tarticcas."

Feggetter, a stocky detective claiming Scottish ancestry and therefore prone to drinking whisky and, unfortunately for the eyes of those around him, wearing a luridly, unrealistically patterned kilt on Burns Night, hummed thoughtfully. "Which Yarrabees?"

"Beau Resorge" –

"Buster" –

"And Carson Williams."

"Crusher," Feggetter identified instantly. "Couldn't happen to two nicer guys."

"I won't argue with you," Casey said. "The best we have right now is that two guys carried out a drive-by shooting. McDonald says it's a large-calibre handgun, but we don't have any more details. They didn't stop, though they slowed right down. What's your guess who'd do it? We're waiting for the canvass to bring back photos and videos from interested passers-by, so we might catch a break there."

"I'll check for street and building camera coverage, now that we've worked through the statements." Andy was already tapping.

"Financials," Tyler added. "Last big jobs."

CHAPTER SIX

Feggetter hummed. "The Yarrabees are aggressive – always fighting and starting trouble. They've crossed everyone, one time or another, but they've butted heads with the Tarticcas more often than most. It's not a bad starting point."

"What are each of them into? We've got oxycodone pills on the dead guys."

"They're both – allegedly," he added with a bitter twist, "into drugs. Crack, heroin, moving into opioids. Yarrabees are more street cut, Tarticcas are more into medical grade."

"Both as bad as each other, in my book," O'Leary rumbled disapprovingly.

"You're not wrong. Narcotics have been trying to pin them down for years, but they haven't had a lot of traction."

"Narcotics?" Casey rapped. Detective Mark Marcol, who'd tried to ruin her at the Academy by stealing and misusing a photo Carval had taken, was in Narcotics.

"Yeah. C'mon, Casey, you know they'll be in there." Feggetter shrugged. "They got a job to do too."

"Yeah. It complicates things, though."

O'Leary flicked a glance at her. They both knew what she wasn't saying, but Feggetter didn't need to know any of it. Kent, unhappily, would need to be informed when he returned, in accordance with his order to do so if there was anything that potentially crossed with Marcol.

Feggetter missed the interchange. "Anyways, up till now they've never done anything this public, and they sure haven't been injuring innocent bystanders. Now we'll have an excuse to make their lives hell."

"They're confined to the Tri-State area?" Casey asked.

Feggetter wriggled. "They *were*. There've been some hints they were expanding."

"How do you *know* all this?"

"I have pals. Not as many as O'Leary, but plenty, and I did some time in Narcotics back in the day. They keep me posted."

Casey stared at him. "Would you sound them out for us? Up to date info would be great. Do you know anyone who's in with those two gangs – confidential informants, maybe?"

"Or any other gangs," O'Leary put in. "We can't rule 'em out yet. Just 'cause the Tarticcas are most likely, don't mean they're the only suspects."

"Yeah," Feggetter agreed.

"True, but we don't have anything yet and if we go scattershot, we'll waste time." Casey tapped her short, neat nails on the desk. "Do any of these gangs have identifying marks – tattoos, scars, even bandanas?"

"I'll ask." He gave her an interested look. "Checking all those videos for gang marks?"

"Yep." She managed a flicker of amusement. "Though Andy'll have some matching program to do most of it for us."

"You guys have all the smart tech," Feggetter said enviously.

"You guys don't ask us iffen we c'n help," O'Leary mused.

Feggetter coloured slightly. "Okay, okay. If I come ask, you guys won't freeze me out?"

"We'll only be like Hudson Bay in winter, not the North Pole. How'll that do?"

Feggetter laughed. "Okay. I'll bring my snowshoes."

O'Leary chortled. "Sounds good."

"Can you get us the info?" Casey asked, having paid no attention to the two men's joking.

"Sure," Feggetter said cheerfully, and rose. "Uh, Casey?"

"Yes?"

"I know I said it already, but I'm sorry about your dad."

"Thanks."

Feggetter scurried off to make calls and question people. Casey excused herself, and spent a moment leaning against the cold porcelain tiles of the restroom, allowing the silence to calm her. The restroom smelt of industrial cleaners, with an undertone of bleach, the same as the hospital had.

The same as her father's apartment.

She plunged into a stall and lost her lunch; sat, heedless of any dust or dirt, on the floor. It took several minutes for her stomach to settle, after which she rinsed her mouth and cooled her skin on the tiles, again. She told herself she could push through the final two hours of shift. She simply needed to focus, go home, curl up against Carval, and try to forget.

Nine months ago – hell, five months ago – she'd never have taken that option. She'd have gone home, struggled through another insomniac night alone, shut out the world. When had that changed? When had *she* changed?

She rinsed her mouth again, and re-entered the bullpen, to discover O'Leary, dark-faced with unusual anger, at her desk: his immense paw gripping the arm of a uniformed officer.

"Now you c'n explain to Detective Clement exactly what you were doin' at her desk, Bartlett," O'Leary menaced, seeing her approach. "Then you c'n explain it to Sergeant Tully an' to Captain Kent."

"I wasn't doing nothing," Bartlett argued.

"That means you were doin' somethin'," O'Leary pointed out. "You were leavin' another of those press cuttin's on Detective Clement's desk. I watched you. You wanna explain to her an' me why you're doin' somethin' you know real well is goin' to upset her? You wanna tell her an' me why you're remindin' her that her father's dead when his funeral was yesterday? You wanna tell her an' me why you're a miserable li'l cowardly weasel who's a disgrace to your family an' the precinct?"

Casey, along with the rest of the bullpen, stared at the rare sight of an infuriated O'Leary. Unnoticed by Bartlett, Andy and Tyler ghosted up to stand with Casey. Behind them, Fremont and Larson arrived, followed by Adamo and, more slowly, Henegan. Spotting trouble, the rest of the bullpen tried to hide.

"Andy," O'Leary growled, "go get Sergeant Tully. We ain't allowed to take this piece of shit on the mats to teach him manners, so mebbe he'll learn them from the sergeant."

"Sure." Andy departed. Less than two minutes later, he arrived with Tully in tow.

"What's this?" Tully demanded.

"Officer Bartlett thought he'd leave another cuttin' talkin' about Casey's father's death on her desk, sir," O'Leary boomed, reaching every corner of the bullpen. "To go along with the ones that've been left there every day since the press conference." He hulked over Bartlett. "Seems to me like someone's deliberately harassin' her, sir."

"Release him," Tully ordered. "Open your hand, Bartlett, and show everyone the paper you're holding."

O'Leary released Bartlett. The team stood in a circle around him, blocking any exit. Casey, a good six inches shorter than Bartlett, nevertheless projected enough anger and menace to leave him unable to meet her accusing gaze.

Tully waited until Bartlett dropped a crumpled clipping on Casey's desk.

Tully picked it up, smoothed it out, and read it, slowly, face darkening with every line. "Bartlett, you come with me. We'll discuss this now, and we'll discuss it when the captain returns, too. Clement, I'm sorry about this. Leave it to me." He dragged Bartlett away.

"How long've people been pulling this shit?" Fremont grated.

O'Leary flicked him a look. "Didn't you hear me? Ev'ry day since Monday."

"Not any more, they won't be."

Casey scowled. "Don't cause trouble. I can deal with this."

"We won't, ma'am," Fremont soothed.

"We're simply gonna…adjust a few attitudes," Larson added. The two big officers smiled down at her. "It's not right."

"Leave it to the sergeant and captain," Casey ordered. "We have a murder to solve. Tell me you've got videos?"

"Photos and videos."

"Okay. Videos to Andy and Tyler, photos to me and O'Leary. I don't think there's anything else you can do right now – oh. Put these licences through the database." She handed over the Wiedecz and Herencia licences. "See if they're real. They didn't belong to the dead guys we found them on."

"Yes'm. Uh, ma'am?" Fremont said.

"Yeah?"

"Could we, um, help with interviewing again?"

"If there's something suitable, yes." Casey regarded the four officers her team had accidentally adopted. They all – even Henegan, still cringing from her – looked back with hopefully puppyish expressions. "We'll tell you if there is."

"Thank you, ma'am!" The four of them practically bounced off, even Henegan.

"Now they're gone, how's about you tell us the truth?" O'Leary instructed. "You're green, again, an' you scooted off right quick when Feggetter was done. You're not copin', Casey. You say you're fine, but you ain't. You should go home now. Nobody's goin' to quibble."

"I can do this," she insisted. "I'll leave at shift-end, and I won't do any overtime today, but I'm not going home now. I'll look at photos and wait for Tully to turn Bartlett into ground beef."

O'Leary frowned at her. "An' tomorrow?"

"Depends on the case. Can we move that along now, instead of picking on me?"

O'Leary's frown turned to a pout. "Pickin' on you's entertainin', though. Now what'll I do?"

"Look at photos," Casey snipped. "As if we haven't all had enough of looking at photos in the last two weeks."

"Now, that ain't nice." O'Leary shut up at Casey's fulminating glare.

"Photos and videos. I'll take the first half of the photos," she snapped, and opened her computer to review them.

Forty-five minutes later, she had a small pile of printed photos, all of which showed the shooter, the car, and/or the gun. "Andy?"

"Yeah?"

"Can you enhance any of these photos?"

"How'd you mean?"

"Sharpen them up, get rid of the fuzzy bits, that sort of thing?"

"Sure I can. Why?"

"I could," Carval said from behind her, before she could answer.

Casey jumped, and squeaked. "What're you doing here?"

"It's nearly shift end."

"No, it's not. There's over an hour to go."

"Only an hour," Carval said cheerfully. "Can I help? Why do you want the photos enhanced?"

"To sharpen up these images so I can get something useful from them. Better clarity on the plate, the shooter...but you can't do it."

"I can!" Carval objected.

"Technically you're able to, but you're not a cop, so you aren't allowed to. Leave it to Andy. You can watch over his shoulder and make suggestions, if you like, but you're not allowed to do things."

Andy wandered over. "Let's see." He collected her pile of printouts. "Send me all the others."

"They're in the file. Pick them out from there – the references are on the prints."

"Organised Casey strikes again," Andy teased. She simply stared him out.

"Ma'am?" Fremont said.

"Yeah?"

"Those licences...They're both registered to the same address." He read it off.

"They're real?"

"Well...they're in the DMV, but I ran the names and Tomas Wiedecz was found dead – stabbed – in the Bronx a week ago."

Casey cursed. "And Herencia?"

"He was picked up the next day and charged with possession with intent to sell. He didn't make bail."

She swore more vehemently. "Dead end, then. Dammit!"

***

Carval followed Andy to his desk, and tugged up a chair. Fortunately for him, Casey didn't see his concerned glance. "What happened?" he murmured.

"O'Leary caught an officer leaving press cuttings on her desk. He's being disciplined, but Feggetter condoled with her and she came back from the restroom green. She shouldn't be here, but you try telling her that."

"Nope. I like living." Carval met Andy's gaze. "I'll make sure she's not alone tonight."

"Good enough. I like living too. O'Leary already tried to send her home and she shut him down."

"Surprise."

"Yeah." Andy caught a glance from Casey. "What do you use to clean up photos?"

"Noise removers, mainly. What've you got?"

"Watch and learn." Andy opened a program of which Carval had never heard.

"What's that?"

"Proprietary."

"You wrote it, didn't you?"

"Yep."

"Technogeeking has some advantages."

"Yeah," Andy agreed. "I wrote one for day trading, too." He smirked. "It does pretty well."

Carval, who knew even less about the stock market than he did about murder, and didn't care, stared. "Day trading?"

"Keeps me in theatre tickets." Andy failed to mention that his tech skills provided a substantial second income. "You take photos. I like culture."

"You and Allan. A match made in heaven."

"He's good company."

***

Allan, being good company, didn't even have to knock on the Finisterres' door before it opened and Claudia fell upon his neck with joy.

"Allan! My dear," she fluted, "come in. Where have you been for the last few years? You haven't told us anything when we've met you."

"Do bring us up to date," her husband added. "Will you take tea?"

"Of course." Allan entered. "Thank you."

"Come and sit down, and tell us what you've been doing since you turned us down. Please tell me you are improving New York's cultural scene?"

Allan smiled sweetly. "I am, and attending it as often as possible. It's not always appreciated, though."

"We would appreciate you," Henry tried.

"I'm sure you would, and I do have an ulterior motive for seeing you."

"Which," Claudia deduced, "is not accepting a post with us." She poured scented tea into delicate Chinese porcelain cups, and handed them around.

"No. I'm afraid, lovely as you both are, you can't tempt me away from my current employer."

"Who is this paragon?" Claudia sniffed.

"Jamie Carval."

Claudia and Henry both choked on their tea. "Jamie *Carval?* My dear Allan! We are seeing his latest exhibition tomorrow. We enjoyed *Hands* enormously, and before that *New York's Ugly Underbelly.* Can we persuade you to produce him at our next soirée?"

"It's possible," Allan ventured, "but you'll have to do something for him too."

"What?" Henry asked, equally cautiously.

"Jamie took some shots of the theatre while they were rehearsing for Heyer's *Dream.*"

Claudia shuddered. "Darling, don't talk about that dreadful affair. Our protégée was murdered, and two others were arrested."

"Not that Cordell is any loss to the profession," Henry said cynically. "However, how on earth did Jamie Carval manage to enter the theatre while they were rehearsing?"

"Ah. Well. *Murder On Manhattan* is based on a team of NYPD Homicide detectives" –

"Allan! Do you mean the pretty young detective who *asked me for an alibi* and her Titan of a partner are the subjects of Jamie's exhibition?" Claudia's fluting voice rose to a glass-shattering soprano pitch.

"Yes, with their other two team members and the rest of their precinct. The *Hands* exhibition is mostly their hands, too."

"Had I known that, I should have ensured they were invited to our next soirée when they interviewed us. I shall have to arrange it."

Allan considered Casey's likely reaction to the invitation, and hoped he would see it. From a safe distance, naturally, which might mean Connecticut. Or possibly Alaska.

"I still have their cards, my love," Henry offered.

"Perfect. I shall invite them as soon as we have seen the exhibition."

"You might include the rest of the team," Allan suggested. "Detective Chee is highly cultured. We've had a few interesting discussions. And Detective Tyler, the fourth member, is involved with Alejandra Despero – whom I'll be assisting in her career when she graduates, if she needs any assistance."

Claudia's tea went down the wrong way. When she had recovered from her choking and spluttering, she stared at Allan. "You must tell us the story. How do you know Alejandra?"

"It's Jamie who knows her. She did a little modelling to help with tuition costs, and Jamie shot a portfolio for her. When Casey – Detective Clement – needed a model to help with an investigation, Jamie suggested her. She performed brilliantly, and Detective Tyler was smitten."

"How romantic," Claudia breathed, clasping her hands.

Allan considered Tyler's likely reaction to being termed romantic, and hoped once more he would be there to see *that*, preferably up close.

"So, Jamie asked me if I would protect her interests. Is there something I should know?"

"We are intending to support her," Claudia declaimed.

"In which case, I shall be delighted to make sure everyone is suitably protected," Allan said smoothly.

"And we shall be delighted to include her in any invitations. Now, did you mention that Jamie Carval might be persuaded to attend the soirée?"

"He might, if you allow him to shoot inside your theatres. Not performances, but rehearsals, interiors, lighting – he'll know it when he sees it. He won't get in anyone's way – he's managed not to get in the detectives' way, so you can trust him not to interfere or disrupt anything."

Claudia and Henry exchanged speaking glances as they sipped their tea. Allan relaxed into the comfortable armchair, and contemplated the purple wall with gauzy midnight blue curtains. It wasn't to his taste, which ran to clean cream and light woods, but it suited the Finisterres.

"I do wish you would work for us," Claudia lamented, "but that ship has sailed. We will facilitate Jamie's entry into any theatre or production in which we have an interest, if he will attend our next soirée. Of course, you are invited too. We should be delighted if you would attend."

"Thank you," Allan replied. "I'll do my best. I'm taking *Hands* to Pittsburgh on Tuesday, but here's my card so you can let me know when it is, and I'll talk to Jamie."

"Thank you."

***

"Have you cleaned up those photos?" Casey asked, ten minutes before shift end.

"The first few, yes. Not the rest. It takes time. I'll leave it running tonight and it should be finished by morning. O'Leary added another bunch." Andy tutted at O'Leary's demands. Casey made a face. "Instead, you can look at the videos. I merged them all together and we have some clear pictures." He clicked. "Here's the car. Black, or too dark for anyone to spot the difference. Here's part of the plate – New York plate, Empire Gold, H."

"So, no older than 2015? What model of car is it?"

"Ford. Specifically, Ford Edge – an SUV."

51

"Any better pictures of the plate?"

"Not yet, but let's see what the clean-up manages in the morning."

"I want your program," Carval decided. "Will you license it to me? Allan'll deal with the legalities and payment, but I want it. I need it."

Andy blinked. Casey stared. "What program?" she asked.

"The one Andy wrote to clean up photos. I need it. It's brilliant."

"I thought you said your photos were so good you didn't need to mess with them?" Andy noted, grinning.

"There's always something you can clean up. Noise, dust in the air, whatever. I'll get Allan to call you to fix it up."

"If you've finished your business discussion," Casey snipped, "perhaps we could go back to the case?"

"An' perhaps not." O'Leary lumbered up. "It's shift end, we've done all we c'n for tonight, an' you promised you'd go home without doin' any overtime today."

Casey's face turned sulky. "Feggetter" –

"Naw, Feggetter would'a told you iffen he had anythin' back. We're all goin' home. Pete's back, an' he's cookin'. I gotta get a nice bottle of wine on the way."

"I thought you didn't drink wine?" Carval queried.

"Sure I do, just not the vinegar in the Abbey."

"Bottle of wine," Carval mused. "That's a good idea."

"Enjoy it," Casey said. "I'm going home, since our oversized nanny won't let me stay and work."

Carval, watching her expression move from sulky to stroppy, didn't say a word. Under the stroppiness, Casey was exhausted, and home was the best place for her.

The team left a mere five minutes before Kent returned.

CHAPTER SEVEN

Kent was in the worst mood possible when he entered the bullpen, hoping the only task left would be a five-minute check of his in-tray to ensure it contained nothing earth-shatteringly urgent. At least, he thought blackly, he'd gotten rid of Renfrew, whose profiling skills had helped immensely with the takedown of Birkett and his removal to an Internal Affairs cell, and simultaneously fired Kent's deep desire to punch hell out of something, preferably Renfrew's pompous profile.

He made it into his office, noticing in passing that his misfits had left. For once, he hadn't had to order them out. He'd speak to them tomorrow.

His backside hadn't hit the chair when Sergeant Tully came in and shut the door. "Tully. What is it now?"

"Sorry, sir. We got a problem with Clement."

"Clement?"

"I should say, we got a problem with Bartlett trying to mess with Clement's head about her dad dying. O'Leary caught Bartlett leaving a press cutting about the death on Clement's desk."

"Bartlett did what?" Kent's jaw hit his desk.

"Tried to put one of those tabloid rag cuttings – you know, *Tragic story of NYPD star cop*" – Tully's mouth twisted – "on Clement's desk. It's not the first time. It's been happening since the press conference."

Kent's square face turned scarlet. "Where is Bartlett?"

"At his desk, with orders not to move until you returned."

"I did not need this today," he snapped. "Give me five minutes, and don't let him out of your sight."

Tully safely gone, Kent swore bitterly and repetitively, then picked up the phone. "Garrett," he said heavily, "it's all gone to shit. Come out for a drink, and listen to the latest disaster. I need to talk to another friendly captain to sort out my thoughts."

"Sure. When and where?"

"Stick with O'Lunneys," he told his old pal. "Six-thirty. I've got another mess to clear up that links into today's disaster. See you there. Thanks."

"No problem."

Kent put the phone down with extreme care, opened his office door, stepped into the middle of the bullpen and bellowed, "Officer Bartlett! My office, at once!" As he had intended, every person present, and possibly the entire building, heard him. Kent, who hadn't lost one jot of his investigative skills while moving up the ranks, watched Estrolla as Bartlett obeyed. Estrolla, Kent noted, appeared nervous. Grendon, his crony in unpleasantness, was more overtly worried. Both facts gave Kent considerable satisfaction.

"Sir?" Bartlett questioned, though Kent was sure he knew why he'd been publicly summoned.

"Close the door." Kent reached into his desk drawer, took out a copy of the NYPD's disciplinary rules, and placed it on his desk. Bartlett followed his movement, and swallowed. "I see you recognise this document."

"Sir."

"Explain to me why you were placing press cuttings on Detective Clement's desk."

Bartlett sagged. Kent allowed the ominous silence to stretch out, extending for longer and longer. Finally, Bartlett broke it.

"It was just a joke," he tried.

"A joke." Kent's contempt could have cut steel. "How, exactly, do you conclude that the death of a parent is a joke, or something to joke about?"

Bartlett turned an ugly crimson, dropping his eyes.

"Have you suffered the death of a parent?" Kent jabbed.

"No, sir."

"I see. Why did you think Detective Clement would regard a reminder of her loss as a *joke*?"

"Everyone knows he was a drunk," Bartlett mumbled. "He's no loss."

"Are you such close friends with Clement that you would know her thoughts and feelings?"

"No," Bartlett mumbled again.

"So why did you think she'd take it as a *joke*? You're not leaving this office till I get some clear answers, and I'll keep going all night if that's what it takes. I do not tolerate harassment or bullying in this precinct, whatever others may do."

"It was a *joke*, sir."

Kent's growl could have split granite. "No, Bartlett, it was not a joke. You deliberately harassed and bullied a fellow cop, who buried her father yesterday."

"But he said" – Bartlett stopped dead.

"*Who?*" Kent's question scythed through the air.

"Estrolla. He was told by Clement's friend, Birkett. They were pals since the Academy – Clement and Birkett, sir. He'd know she'd think it was a joke, 'cause they were pals."

"Are you rethinking that information yet?" Kent asked wearily. More goddamn complications, as if he didn't have enough to worry about. "Who else has been told Clement would regard it as a joke?"

"I don't know, sir." Bartlett's brain finally caught up. "Wasn't it true?"

Kent sighed. How had he acquired a precinct of dumbasses? "No, Bartlett. It wasn't true."

Bartlett drooped. "But..." *Oh, shit* suffused his face as he realised his mistake.

"I'll deal with your idiocy later. For now, get out, and consider how you'll make amends for your behaviour."

***

Carval followed Casey to her car, though she was shadowed by her team. "Can I hitch a ride?" he asked.

"Thought you were buying wine and going home." Her words implied *don't care if you do.* Her tone oozed disappointment.

"Buy wine, sure. Go home, nope. Go home with you, yep. If you want me to." He slid into the passenger seat, only then realising that Casey hadn't switched on the engine and was sitting with her face in her hands, unmoving. "Swap places, and I'll drive?"

"I'll be fine." Shaking fingers turned the key, puddling eyes checked the mirrors before she pulled out. "Where will I drop you to get wine?"

"Fairway. I'll walk to your apartment from there."

"'Kay."

She dropped Carval outside Fairway. He swiftly found a bottle of a light Californian white wine, a can of whipped cream, thought about Casey's preferences and added a substantial quantity of good chocolate, then went upstairs to the café and ordered two slices of apple pie to go. Whatever dinner might prove to be, wine, apple pie with cream, and chocolate were unlikely to be wrong.

He strolled along to Casey's block, deciding there was no point in planning what he might do, when he'd only change it on the fly, depending on what instinct told him.

It took a couple of moments for Casey to open the door, and when she did, she looked washed out and defeated.

"Chocolate." Carval pushed it at her. She took the candy bar, and stared at it. Since Casey normally fell upon chocolate with the same enthusiasm as a velociraptor on its prey, her hesitation didn't reassure Carval. He gently encouraged her out of the doorway, and shut it behind them. She plumped down on the sofa, stared at the chocolate bar, and put it aside. "You don't want *chocolate?*" he gasped.

Casey sniffed once, blinked hard several times, and gave up, scrubbing at her leaking eyes. Carval dropped down beside her, handed her a Kleenex in an unusual display of practicality, and hugged her. "It's okay."

"It's *not* okay," she cried. "It's not fucking *okay* that half the cops in the precinct are twisting the knife and the other half are ignoring it 'cause they're scared to call them out. It's *not okay!*"

Carval hadn't expected her outburst. He abruptly realised that her tears arose from sheer anger, not grief – or not entirely. Grief might be at the root of it, but the emotional explosion had been building since the press conference.

"You think I didn't want to wipe Bartlett across the floor? You think I didn't want to leave him in so much pain he couldn't move?" Her hands formed fists. "He deserves it. He deserves all of it, and so do the rest of them. But I can't do any of it because *I'll* be the one who's reprimanded or demoted or fired." She surged up, and paced across the floor, feet slapping down hard on the wood. "We can't do anything. Rumours and ghosts and no evidence Kent can act on." She stared out of the window. "I thought when he was dead it would all stop. No calls, no bailing him out, no going to court with him, no worrying about what he'd do." She turned back to the room. "Even when he's dead, he's ruining my life."

"He isn't. Whoever's behind all this is." Carval stayed on the couch, not daring to go to her.

"Marcol and Birkett, Estrolla and Grendon? They're behind it, but if Dad hadn't been a drunk, they'd have nothing. They can't make anything out of the exhibition, so they're using Dad instead. Why can't they let it go?"

"Because I dragged it all up again." Carval swallowed. Casey wouldn't like the next bit. "Allan's found proof that Marcol and Birkett stole my photo, as part of the copyright investigation. He's passed it on to Kent."

"You said you wouldn't" –

"Do anything about any of it except the copyright violation," Carval broke in. "This is about the copyright, and I don't want Kent blindsided when we pursue it. I *said* I wouldn't do anything else, and we haven't."

"Okay." She sighed, and collapsed back on to the couch. "I guess Kent has to know."

"And" – Carval had a flash of insight – "if Kent didn't come back all day" –

"He didn't" –

"He must have been dealing with Birkett. He'd have come back otherwise. If it took him all day, there must have been some proof."

"He had something, or Renfrew did. Bergen told us they had Dad's arrest record, and they could prove Birkett didn't correct that hack reporter – they pulled something on Birkett," Casey exclaimed. "They must have." Her eyes lit up. "They got him. A full day – they got him, and took him to IA."

"How do you know?"

"I don't, but it fits the facts. Kent wouldn't have been out all day for anything minor." She breathed slowly in and out. "If they got Birkett, he'll roll on everyone. Yellow-bellied cowardly dickweasel," she spat. "He'll try to save his own skin. He always did. Nothing was ever his fault in the Academy: it was always someone else. This'll be an absolute disaster." She smiled coldly, with no humour at all. "For them."

"Couldn't happen to a nicer bunch," Carval agreed viciously. Casey was still horribly pale, but there was fire in her dark eyes, and she'd recovered her spirit.

She really had recovered her spirit. He hadn't registered her movement before she'd hauled his head down and kissed him hard, raiding and invading in a way she hadn't since before her father had left rehab. It fired him up, but Casey was faster: small hands slipping under his t-shirt and pushing it up so he could either shed it or be trapped in it; while he was taking it off, she'd already opened his belt. She'd never hesitated to go for what she wanted, but this frantic haste, almost desperation, was new. If it was what she wanted…it was still scorching. He flicked open her cotton button-down, pushing it off her shoulders while she was still busy at his belt, and took an instant to admire the cream lace beneath. Casey's underwear might be practical, but it was always pretty, which Carval appreciated as often as possible.

He rapidly stopped thinking about her underwear as she kissed him hard again, touching him in a way that left him mindless. Instinct allowed him to murmur "Bed"; instinct left their remaining clothes strewn across the floor; and instinct kept him responding to her haste and aggressive desire. This was Casey's show; and this was what she needed. He'd give her what she needed, he thought, before he didn't think at all.

Afterwards, when he would have cuddled her in, she didn't snuggle as she usually did. He had an instant's worry, until he realised she'd buried her face in her pillow. Her shoulders shuddered. He put a hand on her bare back, noting the knotted muscles, the rigid spine.

"I can't forget," she whispered. "I thought you'd…but I can't forget." She pulled away. Carval pulled her back again, and tucked her small form in.

"It's okay," he soothed, and held her close.

"It's not okay. Nothing's okay."

"We're okay," he reassured. "We're okay, whatever else is going on." Suddenly she turned and hid her face in his chest. He expected to feel dampness, but he didn't. "You don't need to hide," he comforted.

"All I've done for weeks" – *hardly, Casey*, he thought, *you've been holding all this inside till about two weeks ago* – "is blubber and snuffle all over you. It's pathetic." She tried to turn away.

Carval, far bigger and heavier, simply hauled her up so he could see her tight, tense face and the pain at the back of her eyes. He opened his mouth, but something told him reassurance wouldn't work. "Don't be ridiculous," he shot back instead, and hoped he'd called it right.

Casey's eyes flared. "You" – she started.

"You don't *blubber*. You barely say anything when you're upset and you do your best not to tell anyone, even us. Your team. You're not some fragile little flower who spends all her time fainting and crying over dumb things like being bumped on the subway – you're more like a Venus flytrap: armed and snappish."

"You" – she started again, and once again was run right over.

"If you think you blubber and snuffle, you're *wrong*. Your dad just died, for Chrissake, you're allowed to be upset and *I'm* allowed to comfort you."

Casey stopped her infuriated noises and made a strange *gleep* sound. Carval seized his opportunity. "If I was irritated by you *grieving your dad*, I wouldn't be much of a partner, would I?" She *gleeped* again. "This isn't a fling. You know it and I know it so stop hiding and let me look after you!"

In the horrible silence following Carval's outburst, he had plenty of time to think that he'd royally screwed up. He might as well have hit her with a sledgehammer, her eyes wide, shocked speechless.

"Look after me?" she eventually managed. "Uh?"

"Yes!" Carval bit, utterly exasperated. "Like, hug you when you're upset, listen to you when you vent, take you out for dinner when you let me, the usual things."

"Oh." Casey slid off to one side and stared blankly at the ceiling.

"Oh? Is that all you can say?" Carval's irritation boiled over. "I tell you I think I love you and all you can say is *oh?*"

"You *what?*"

Carval's brain caught up with his mouth, rather too late. "Uh…" he mumbled, which didn't add anything to the conversation.

"Uh? You say you're in love with me and now it's *uh?*"

"How come I'm being interrogated here? You're the one who doesn't seem to get it."

"You're the one backtracking."

"I am *not!*" Carval yelled. "You're the one interrogating and disbelieving and not caring what I just said."

"I do *so* care!" Casey yelled back.

"About me or about what I said?"

"Both!" Her own words hit her ears, and she dived under the comforter, blushing furiously.

Carval hauled her back out again, and stared at her. "You mean it?"

"Uh…"

"Now who's saying *uh*?" Carval gave up on any idea that words would help, pulled Casey over him and simply kissed her. She relaxed over him, and kissed him back, her hands around his face, his locked at the small of her back. Their kiss turned from tentative to assured, then exploded into heat.

***

"Pass the beer, Garrett," Kent requested as he dropped heavily into a chair. He slugged the first bottle back in one long draught.

"Guess it hasn't been a good day," Garrett said dryly.

"Let's see now." Kent scowled. "One thoroughly corrupt officer in Queens, who rolled on two of my officers and blamed it all on Marcol Junior, leading to a long afternoon with IA. When I got back to my precinct, I found one of those officers had been orchestrating Clement's harassment. Enough dumbassed officers believed him that I'll be supervising around six months of apologies. How am I supposed to run a precinct if they're all benched without pay?"

"Ouch," Garrett offered.

"And worse, that damn pompous-assed profiler, Renfrew, was in on the whole damn mess."

"Ouch."

"He wants to poach Clement's team," Kent growled.

"It might simplify your management."

"Shut up, Garrett. You're not helping."

"Have another beer, and tell me what you want to bounce around." Garrett pushed another bottle into Kent's hand.

Kent leaned forward. "We set Birkett up, and he swallowed the bait whole. He scrubbed Clement's father's arrest record. Shame the FBI had made verified copies with Wetherly's consent."

"Wetherly was in it with you?"

"All the way. Good man, Wetherly."

Garrett nodded.

"So, we arrested Birkett for falsifying records. He squealed like a piglet and blamed it all on Marcol. Now, here's the problem. Birkett's dirty, and he'll pay, but he's the only evidence we have that Marcol instructed any of this, and he's about as reliable as a lump of dogshit. I had a message from that prissy-prim manager of Carval's saying *he's* found evidence Marcol and Birkett stole that photo, but he's not exactly disinterested either."

"I saw those photos." Garrett smirked. "You were right – and didn't you look lovely" –

"Leave it," Kent harrumphed.

"Anyway, your Carval is six feet under for Clement."

"He's not *my* Carval, thank God." Kent scowled harder. "*If* we could get back to the point?" Garrett nodded, still smirking. "I've got nothing for IA to go on as far as Marcol's concerned. His family'll close ranks – and God knows enough of them *have* rank – to protect him, though they'll make sure he doesn't rise any further. They don't want scandal."

"So, what's the problem?"

"Marcol. I don't think he'll take this well."

"You don't say."

"I've already told Clement and Chee not to leave the precinct alone."

"What? You think" – Garrett's eyes goggled.

"I think one or two officers with connections to Birkett would go a long way to provoke Clement or Chee into doing something dumb, especially after those officers' forthcoming, unpleasant interviews with me and IA."

"Ah." Garrett pulled on his beer, and thought. Kent pulled on his beer, and tried not to think, since all his thoughts irritated him more. "I don't suppose Clement has a case? A new case would keep them all out of the way."

"I don't know." Kent suddenly cursed vehemently. "I didn't want Clement out on a new case for a few days. She won't take bereavement leave and she's right on the edge, but I can't bench her because I don't have any evidence that she isn't fit for duty. Even if she wasn't," he added bitterly, "the team would hide it." He swore again. "I forgot to notify Dispatch not to call her. I guess I'll find out tomorrow."

"If they have a case, I'd leave them on it."

"Yeah. If they do, when it's done, I'll insist the whole damn lot of 'em take their accumulated days and overtime, and don't come back for at least ten days."

"And if they don't, I'd insist they took it now."

"Yeah. That'll work." Kent eased himself in his chair. "Thanks."

"I don't see what you can do about Marcol. His career prospects aren't going to be as good as he'd like, but unless you or IA find hard evidence, that's it."

"I'll make sure that jumped-up Travers suffers right along with him," Kent promised. "I warned him to put a leash on Marcol, and he didn't. Well, there's another man who won't be rising higher."

"Shame," Garrett said with immense insincerity. "Another beer, and now I've solved all your personnel problems, we can talk about the exhibition."

"No way. We can talk about the ball game."

CHAPTER EIGHT

Carval bounded upstairs, utterly delighted with the direction of his life, calling for Allan.

"Out all night again?" Allan disapproved.

"I was with Casey." Carval whistled a happy, off-key tune, still high on Casey's admission that she cared.

"Good. I've gotten you into the Finisterres' productions" –

"You have? Great! Can I start now?"

"Let me finish. They had a condition."

"I'm not paying them," Carval squawked. "People would pay *me* for good PR."

"Not monetary. Do you think I wouldn't have made that point?"

"What is it?"

"They're visiting your exhibition, and after they've seen it, they want you to attend one of their elegant soirées. They entertain a group of cultured people and talk about the latest thing, with good food and better wine."

Carval, unusually acute, regarded Allan. "You've been to the soirées," he said. "You never told me that!"

"Don't be such a baby. It was before I worked with you – they offered me a job too, and I chose yours. I occasionally see them at cultural events, and they occasionally try to recruit me again. Since I'm sitting here, obviously they failed."

"Oh." Carval dismissed the idea that Allan might work for someone else. Allan was his manager, and he wasn't letting him go. "So I go to this soirée, and they let me shoot in their productions however I want?"

"Yes."

"Allan, I love you. Can I start now?" he repeated.

"Not till I've spoken to them and gotten a list of productions."

"Oh." Carval remembered something. "You need to talk to Andy."

61

"Why? I'll happily talk to him – unlike the rest of you, he's cultured and interesting – but why?"

"He's got this photo program" –

"We can't use NYPD programs, Jamie!"

"No, no. It's not NYPD property, it's his. He wrote it to clean up photo and video, and it's better than anything I've seen commercially. I want you to license it so I can use it. Fix it for me, Allan, please?"

"I'll try. There's something else."

"What?"

Allan chuckled. "Claudia wants Casey and the team to attend."

Carval stared for an instant, then doubled up with laughter. "You're kidding. I have to see this."

"No, you have to tell them this," Allan said. "Otherwise Casey will blow up, and temper tantrums won't help Allie Despero or you."

"Did you tell them you were representing Allie?"

"Yes. They were a bit surprised, but they didn't quibble. She's invited to the soirée too, with Tyler." His mirth bubbled up again. "Claudia thinks it's" – he made air quotes – "'so romantic'."

Carval doubled over again. "I wanna see Tyler's face when she tells him he's romantic. Oh boy." He squeaked as he tried to recover his breath. "Oh boy," he repeated, and refocused. "Tell them I'll go to the soirée, and if it's not the one the team goes to, I'll go to that one too, just to see how it all plays out – with my camera."

"Okay. They'll call me with dates, so I'll organise it."

"That's your job. If I can't have theatres today, I'll go shoot construction sites, like I did yesterday. I got some great shots and I'll get more today."

"No access problems?"

"Nope. Why would there be? Everyone wants me to shoot them. They know they'll be famous, and they love it. We'll have another exhibition before you know it."

"Don't forget your hard hat and hi-vis jacket."

"Yes, Mommy."

Carval loped off, and shortly Allan heard him clattering down the stairs and out.

***

Casey, sure that Kent would be keeping a stern eye on her, hit her desk a few moments before shift started, rather than the hour or so earlier she'd have preferred. The extra time for coffee had allowed her to settle her frazzled brain, still shaken up from Carval's admission the night before, still squashing down her grief and gnawing guilt at her relief that it was all over. For the first time that Carval had stayed, she hadn't slept well, pursued by

62

nightmares and waking frequently, though his large, warm presence had been comforting even in her insomnia. She yawned, then firmly put Carval's words aside, shoved them away again as they sneaked back and nibbled at her – how could it have *happened?* Famous photographers who sported arm candy models didn't fall in love with cops. Except, it seemed, they did.

She glowered at her murder board and at her desk, then approached Andy. "Where are we with the photo clean-up?"

"I'm looking at it now." He waved at the screen. "Pull a chair up and you can look too."

They looked through the photos, all now clearer and sharper. "I can run facial recognition from some of these, but let's see if we get anything better from the videos," Andy said. "I'll do some manual work first."

"Look!" Casey exclaimed. "There's almost all the plate. I'll run it – chances are it's fake, but we might be lucky, or they could be that arrogant or dumb."

"I vote for dumb," Andy said, "with a side of arrogance. They might think we won't care, 'cause it's all between the gangs."

"They'll be wrong," Casey stated flatly. "Not only because they injured an innocent woman and killed her baby, but because they're not killing people – *any* people, no matter how criminal – on our patch."

"We can try," Andy replied cynically.

"I'll start with the plate. You do the videos."

Casey put the plate into the database, and made herself a coffee while the tech chugged. When she returned to her desk, she was amazed to find the ownership listed. "We got something." She promptly put the owner into the databases too. "The plate was legit."

"Wow." O'Leary clumped up to her. "Didn't expect that."

"Me either. I put the name into the databases, so maybe we'll have someone to interview."

"I always like some terrorisin' in the mornin'."

Casey smiled wanly.

"You look a bit better today," the big man went on.

"Mm," Casey hummed. "Clues always make me feel better."

O'Leary waggled his eyebrows. Casey glared, but blushed. O'Leary smirked knowingly. Before the silent conversation could devolve into an argument, her computer pinged.

"Oh, wow."

O'Leary lumbered around to see. "Oh, boy. Waal, ain't that somethin'?"

"Shall we go terrorise?" Casey bared her teeth. "I want to meet Pieter Wiedecz."

"Didn't we have a licence for Tomas Wiedecz?"

"We did – at the same address."

"Int'restin'. Where're we goin' to terrorise?"

"Registered at Tarticca HQ. Gangs are doing company cars these days."

"Oooohhhhhh," O'Leary strung out. "I'm shiverin' in my shoes. You'll protect me, won't you?"

Casey almost laughed, chopped off short as Bartlett approached them.

"You," she bit. "Get lost."

"Leave," O'Leary growled. Andy and Tyler casually wandered over.

Bartlett shuddered. "I... Look, I'm sorry, okay, but I was told you'd see the joke!"

"That ain't even close to an apology. *Who* told you Casey'd take it as a joke? Not many people think death's a *joke*."

"No," Tyler added. "Guys in my rifle sights didn't."

Bartlett glanced at Tyler, and didn't see any hint of a joke in his expression. "Estrolla said she was pals with Birkett since the Academy and he said" –

"You're as stupid as a stump," O'Leary cut him off.

"Estrolla loathes me," Casey said coldly. "Since we took him on the mats, which the whole bullpen knew about, he's been vocal about his feelings. Either you're even dumber than I thought, or you're trying to cover your cowardly ass. Either way, get out of *our* way. I don't have time for dumbasses or assholes and right now you're both." She stood up, and Bartlett jerked back from her projected intimidation. "Move." He *ran*.

"Waal, that explains a lot. Andy, how about you an' Tyler keep your eyes on Casey's desk while we go terrorise, an' we c'n see who else is in on this?"

"Sure," Andy agreed. "After your little show of menace – seriously, Casey, can't you do better?"

"Huh?"

"He's still in the bullpen. If you'd been trying, he'd be out the door and halfway to Arizona."

Casey managed a half-lift of lips. "Kent might object if I did."

"Practisin' moderation," O'Leary suggested. "Waal, I'll be damned."

"Let's go, before I stop it."

"Before you go anywhere else," arrived the unwelcome tones of Captain Kent, "go to my office."

Protesting that they had a lead wouldn't work, they knew. They trudged through the door to discomfort and terror, otherwise known as Kent's office, and waited.

"Why did you not report the press cuttings left for Clement to find?" Kent challenged.

"They weren't important, sir."

Kent harrumphed. "Someone trying to harass you isn't important?"

"No, sir. It's not relevant. We have a new case, and that's what's important."

"Indeed. Summarise the case." Casey did. "Gang on gang violence."
Kent pondered. "But innocent people have been hurt. Keep me informed.
If there is anything indicating a wider issue, I need to know about it."

"Yes, sir." The team turned for the door.

"Close the door."

O'Leary did. The team huddled together.

"Some days ago, I ordered you to inform me of any matters which
might damage the NYPD's reputation. Yesterday, I interviewed Officer
Birkett, who has been suspended and is assisting Internal Affairs with their
inquiry into the fiasco of the press conference on Monday. You will keep
this information strictly private – you may inform Carval, since his manager
knows about Birkett already, but you will not discuss it with anyone else
except me, Dr Renfrew or Agent Bergen. I expect this will produce some
disquiet. You will all take extreme care to avoid any involvement with
anyone or anything to do with the investigation. Any attempts to involve
you, or approaches from Internal Affairs, are to be reported to me
immediately." He scowled. "Keep your noses clean. After this case, you are
all taking at least ten days' leave. No exceptions. No excuses. Dismissed."

"Let's get out of here," Casey said instantly to O'Leary.

***

O'Leary parked as close as he could manage to the entrance of the
Tarticcas' HQ. Naturally, it was disguised as an ordinary bar and restaurant,
but every cop on Manhattan knew where their local gang leaders hung out
when they weren't engaged in maturing their felonious little plans. A quick
look around disclosed no sign of the vehicle from which the shots had
come. Neither cop was surprised.

"Ready?" he asked.

"Born ready," Casey replied, with an edge indicating to her enormous
partner that she was ready to use her ire to best effect.

"Federico Tarticca," Casey snapped at the bartender as soon as she
entered.

"Who?"

"Don't give me that bullshit. Take me to Federico."

"He no – hey, stop!" The bartender's faked accent gave way to pure
Bronx as Casey stomped past him, flung open a door marked *Employees
Only*, and marched downstairs to an office.

"Federico Tarticca."

A slight, dark man in chinos and an open-necked shirt looked up. "This
is an unexpected pleasure," he oozed – then saw O'Leary. "Cops," he said
flatly. "Shame. I thought you might be someone interesting."

"Oh, you'll find me interesting, Federico. Do the Tarticcas normally
shoot pregnant women and kill their babies?"

Federico's face showed a moment of shock, then blanked. "What are you talking about?"

"A vehicle of yours was used to shoot two members of the Yarrabees yesterday. The shooters also hit a pregnant woman, resulting in the loss of her baby."

"My vehicle?"

"Yes. Registered to Pieter Wiedecz, whose record shows he's a paid-up member of your mob. We have some clear photos and videos of the shooter and driver."

"My mob?" Tarticca queried. "Surely you mean my business associates and employees. I don't recall a Pieter Wiedecz as either." He spread his hands. "The vehicle must have been stolen." He acquired a patina of fake worry. "I'd better report it. Thank you for letting me know," he dismissed them.

"We're not done here. Since a bystander was shot, we have a nice clean bullet for ballistics testing. We have videos and photos. We have your plate. Cut the crap, Federico. You're in this up to your pretty white collar and we'll prove it." Casey put both hands flat on his desk and got right into his face. "Tell your boys we're coming for them. If we find you had anything to do with it, we'll take you down too, and I'll be right there to see it." Her face twisted. "Baby-killer," she hissed. "You'll pay." She spun on her heel and stalked out.

"Bitch," Federico spat.

"She's *Detective* Bitch to you." O'Leary strode out after Casey.

The bartender cast Casey a filthy look, which only stoked her temper higher. "Name!" she demanded.

"None of your business."

"Name," she repeated harshly.

He backed down. "Jeff. Jeff Tarrant."

"Where's Pieter Wiedecz? His car was used in a shooting. He's an accessory to murder."

"Dunno who he is."

"Liar."

"Dunno. We didn't shoot anyone."

"Sure you did. You shot two Yarrabees. Shame you shot a woman too."

"Don't know anything 'bout that."

"Did you know your mob is killing babies?" Casey menaced. "You boys kill babies for kicks in between dealing opioids and shooting up the Yarrabees?"

"Fuck you. We don't kill kids."

"You sure? 'Cause I got one in the morgue. You shot a pregnant woman and her baby's dead. I'll destroy you all for that."

She strode out, leaving the bartender staring after her. "It's not true!" he yelled.

"It's true," O'Leary threw back. "You boys kill babies. That'll go down well with the other gangs around here." He left, then turned back. "We'll make sure they know."

"It's not true!" Tarrant yelled again.

Casey didn't say a word until they were safely back in O'Leary's SUV. "They know something. Didn't you see his shock?"

"I saw you losin' your temper, too, an' scarin' them silly."

"Acting. You know we fake it."

"Mm. Actin'. Right. More like takin' out your feelin's on them. Don't let bein' angry with your pa spill over, Casey, 'cause you ain't far off it."

"I'm fine." She blew her nose. "Pollen," she bit at O'Leary's glance.

"Iffen you say so." He backed off, pulling out. "Guess we'll go see if we can find this Wiedecz."

"We should find next of kin first. They might be lowlifes, but they have someone. We didn't find them yesterday because of Mrs Hercliffe, but the databases should've spat it out by now."

"Okay. Back to the bullpen an' hope the databases co-operate."

***

Andy and Tyler reviewed videos until their eyes bled, then stuffed the best stills of the shooter's and driver's faces into facial recognition programs.

"Casey said the car was registered to Pieter Wiedecz, but I already checked his mugshot, and he's nothing like either of these guys. I hope the videos throw up something better."

"Yeah." Tyler dropped his voice. "You set up a camera?"

"Yeah. Didn't you spot it?"

Tyler shook his head.

"If you didn't, no-one will." Andy laughed softly. "Some people won't be delighted."

"Think they'll carry on?"

"Yeah. Bartlett won't – Casey chopped his balls off – but the others will."

"Dumbasses."

"Too dumb to live."

"Be dead if I catch them." Tyler might have been joking, but he wasn't smiling.

"You won't be any good to the team if you're in prison."

"Guess so." He glowered. "Serve them right, though."

"Yeah."

Andy's phone cheeped. "Chee – oh, hi, Allan. I'm busy – tonight? Sure. I'll call you when I'm done."

"Allan?"

"Carval wants to use my clean-up program."

"'Kay." Tyler's brow furrowed. "He looking after her?"

Andy shrugged. "If she lets him. You saw those photos same as I did."

"Should've taken leave."

"Kent's pushing all of us out. She'll have to take some."

"Mm."

"What's up?"

"Not dealing. Needs to deal, not hide."

"I'm not going there. Leave it to O'Leary. She won't kill him. You and me...not so much." The computer beeped demandingly. "We got something." He stared at the output. "That's weird."

"Huh?"

"The shooter's popped up – as" –

"Yarrabee?"

"Nope. Not a Tarticca, either. Crap. He's a Pagliacci, from Chicago. Andrew Grappano."

"Fuckit. FBI. DEA. Feds all over us."

"So, we know who did it, but how will we find him? What are the Pagliaccis doing in a Tarticca car shooting Yarrabees in Manhattan?" Andy wondered aloud.

"Good question," Feggetter said.

"Hey." Andy smiled at him.

"Casey asked me to talk to my pals in Narcotics about the Yarrabees and Tarticcas. There are rumours that both of 'em were expanding out of the Tri-State area."

"Fuckit," Tyler swore again.

"I had a chat – is Casey here? You all oughta hear this."

"The car belongs to one of the Tarticcas," Andy explained, "so Casey and O'Leary went to talk to them."

"And now we're back," Casey announced. "They know something."

"She got right in Federico's face and told him she'd let every gang in NYC know they were killin' babies."

"Ballsy," Feggetter, Tyler and Andy all said together.

"He was shocked, but only about the bystander."

"We came back to see iffen we had next of kin yet," O'Leary said, "but it sounds like you gotta story to tell. I like stories."

"Yeah," Feggetter answered. "I have some stuff. I put in a few calls."

"Thanks." Casey made a *tell-us-all* gesture, and sat down.

"Both gangs are trying to expand out of New York. My pals tell me they're going towards Chicago" –

"Pagliaccis," Andy put in.

"Yep. They don't like it, rumour says. They're allegedly responsible for most of the opioids around."

"But the Yarrabees are the ones who got shot – oh. Yeah. Get the two gangs to take each other out, and move in."

"Bit tenuous," Andy suggested. "How did he get his hands on a Tarticca car?"

"Yeah." Feggetter frowned.

The team exchanged unhappy glances.

"I need to see Kent," Casey said. "If it's potentially across state lines, he has to know." The glance she sent O'Leary added *and if Narcotics are involved, he needs to know.* O'Leary nodded, out of Feggetter's sightline. "I guess I'd better see him now," Casey dragged. "Give me some good news. Did we find next of kin?"

Tyler nodded.

"One for you, one for us?" Andy added.

"Sounds good. Are they in New York?"

"Yes."

"We'll go tell them after I've seen Kent."

Casey marched off to Kent's office to tap on the door.

"Come in." He removed his attention from a pile of papers. "What is it, Clement?"

"Sir, we've received information indicating our gang case might extend across state lines, and might have Narcotics implications. Both gangs are well known to be involved with drugs, but it seems like they've been moving in on Chicago gang territory. We ran facial recognition on the shooter, sir, and though he was in a car belonging to a known Tarticca member, his record shows he's a known Chicago Pagliacci member."

Kent sighed. "State lines and Narcotics. I see. I will contact the FBI – Dr Renfrew, since you've worked with him before, and he can liaise with DEA. I will speak to Narcotics myself. Rest assured, Clement, that Detective Marcol will not be involved in this case."

"Thank you, sir." Casey fled before Kent could ask her any questions or suggest she should take immediate leave.

Kent, putting aside his shock and worry at Clement's haggard state, reluctantly lifted his phone. "Dr Renfrew, Captain Kent here. Clement's latest case crosses state lines and involves criminal organisations and drugs."

"I see. I shall attend on the team this afternoon. Do I infer there may be an involvement from Narcotics and DEA?"

"Yes. I'll talk to Narcotics – there's no way I'm allowing Marcol near Clement or the team – but would you liaise with DEA?"

"Naturally. Tell Detective Clement I shall be delighted to work with her team again, please. I will bring Agent Bergen, who has also enjoyed working with them."

"Thanks." Kent swiftly ended the call. Talking to Renfrew made his boot itch to kick some pompous profiler backside.

CHAPTER NINE

"We'd better go see next of kin." Casey added an unfavourable mutter about Renfrew's appearance. "Andy, Tyler, you take Crusher's, and we'll take Buster's."

Tyler and Andy made their way to Morrisania in companionable silence. Andy was quite happy with Agent Bergen's arrival, and since Casey would suffer most of the pain of both Renfrew's psychiatric profiling of the team and the case-related interaction, they were relatively sanguine about the situation. Casey had left trailing an entire thunderstorm's worth of black clouds, so both men were content to leave her to O'Leary's amiability – and invulnerability to anything short of a nuclear missile.

"We're seeing Crusher's father. No mother – died of a heroin overdose when he was a young teen. Dad's a bruiser, thought to have been linked to the last generation of Yarrabees. Family business, no?"

"Yeah."

"You lead. He might respect the muscles and the hard edge where he sure won't respect the badge."

"Know that," Tyler pointed out.

"I know you know. I'm making sure you know you'll have to use your words." Andy smirked. Tyler grumbled.

They pulled up outside a dilapidated apartment building. Two floors up, Tyler rapped hard on the peeling blue paint of the wooden door.

"What?" A big man, run to seed, red-faced and jowly, opened and stood foursquare in the doorway, blocking it.

"Mr Williams?"

"Who wants to know?"

"Detective Tyler, and Detective Chee."

"Whaddya want?"

"Can we come in? We've" –

71

"No."

Tyler scrapped any thought of persuasion. "I'm sorry to tell you, your son, Carson, was shot yesterday."

Williams rocked, then recovered. "Junior's dead? Shot?" He stood straight. "Dumb fuck." Tyler could see the shock and the sheen in his eyes. "Why'd the dumbass hafta get dead?"

"I'm sorry for your loss," Tyler tried. "We'd like to ask" –

"Fuck off outta here." Williams stepped back and slammed the door in their faces.

"I don't think he'll be answering any questions today," Andy said.

"Nah."

"Back to the bullpen. We can try again when he's less angry."

"Yeah."

"We can set Casey on him."

"Mean."

"Effective."

Tyler laughed, and they started back.

***

"Beau Resorge," Casey said. "His sister is next of kin. Parents deceased." She scrolled down. "Illnesses, not accidents or violence. They didn't have a record. His sister has a couple of teen smudges on file, nothing serious. Nothing since, and no indications she's mixed up in the gang world." She moved further down. "Married. Let's have a look at him later – I'll give Fremont a call and he can start the search." She did so, as O'Leary rolled into the district of Laurelton, in Queens – well away from the 112th, to Casey's relief.

Buster's sister – Leselle Farage, Casey's data told her – lived in a two-story house with a yard out front, well-kept and in good condition. A small, clean car was parked tidily outside. Casey rang the doorbell, while O'Leary fell in behind her.

"Yes?" A woman dressed in a rainbow t-shirt, ripped, stonewashed jeans, and with bare feet, opened the door on a chain.

"Ms Farage?" Casey held up her shield. "I'm Detective Clement. I'm here about your brother, Beau. May we come in?"

"Yes." She shakily closed the door to undo the safety chain, ushering them swiftly in and replacing the chain after them. "This way."

"I'm sorry to tell you" – knowledge and grief bloomed in Ms Farage's face – "Beau was killed yesterday."

"Dead?" she gasped, and tears puddled instantly. "Oh, Beau. You dumb boy," she sobbed. "I told you not to get involved."

The family room was full of small-child toys, in the centre of which sat a barely-toddler age child. O'Leary waggled his sausage-fingers at it.

"Ma-ma," it squeaked, and pointed at O'Leary. "Da! Da-da-da!" It heaved itself up, wobbled on its chubby little legs, and toddled straight into the redwoods masquerading as O'Leary's legs, holding up its hands to be picked up.

"Lissy," Ms Farage warned to her infant, which identified the tot as female.

"Aw," cooed O'Leary, who liked small children and enjoyed playing with them, much to Casey's relief since she did not, "she's cute. C'mere, poppet." He lifted her and, hands safely around her middle, swung her gently up and down.

Beau's sister's tears escaped her rapidly blinking eyes. "Beau."

"While my partner's entertaining your daughter, could I ask you about Beau?"

"Sure," Leselle Farage sniffled, and blew her nose. "How was he killed?" She wiped at her eyes.

"He was shot." Casey couldn't soften the blow. Leselle buried her face in her hands, while O'Leary made sure small Lissy couldn't see her mother cry, bouncing her up and down, bending over to walk her to the window and pick her up again. Casey thought, cynically, that if he walked the tot much more he'd be stuck with spinal issues, but she wasn't offering to take over.

"Tell me about Beau," she invited.

Leselle snuffled. "He's my brother. He's not very smart, but he was kind to me – he's three years older. Big but dumb, our mom used to say, before she passed." She began to cry again, remembering her brother was dead. "He would do anything for his friends, but he doesn't make good choices – didn't. He wanted a nice life."

"Did you know he was involved with the Yarrabee gang?"

She hesitated. Casey waited.

"It wasn't his fault," she snuffled.

"Mm?"

"He had" – she'd finally moved to the past tense – "the wrong friends. Bad choices," she repeated. "They were in with the Yarrabees so Beau went along, and he was big and fit so…anyway, I told him he shouldn't get involved but he didn't listen and now he's *dead*." She dissolved in tears. "If he'd only listened. Walked away. He never walked away from his friends."

"Do you know who his friends were?"

"I don't know their real names. Beau used their nicknames. Stupid names, some of them. Crusher – he talked about him a lot." That wasn't any help, seeing as Crusher was also in the morgue. "Jacker." She thought, brow furrowing above the damp eyes and pinched, pained mouth. "Roo." She shook her head. "I can't think of anyone else."

"If you do, let me know. Thank you for your time." She handed over her card. "Will your husband be back soon?"

"Yes." She turned to O'Leary. "Give me Lissy." He brought the toddler over, and plopped her in her mother's lap. Leselle cuddled her in, face in the child's soft, light hair. "He loved Lissy," she wept. "He loved her and now he'll never see her grow up. He would have been a good uncle."

"I'm sorry for your loss," Casey said, echoed by O'Leary.

"Now we've got some names to try on Feggetter and the databases." Casey stared out of the windshield of O'Leary's vehicle.

"Yeah. She cared about him. She'll be blamin' herself for not savin' him, even though she couldn't."

Casey declined to comment. O'Leary's words punched her in the stomach, but she didn't want to talk about it. "We'll have the joy of Renfrew when we get back, and likely DEA arriving too. Great."

"JFK's a coupla miles over there, iffen you wanna take a vacation," O'Leary teased gently.

"Maybe when this case is done. We'll have to take leave, so…somewhere else. Away from here." She thought again of Carval's suggestion of visiting San Francisco. She loved the city, but she hadn't been back since she'd graduated from Stanford. Maybe she should go. Maybe *they* should go. Think about everything…somewhere else. Maybe elsewhere she'd be able to clear her head.

***

Kent picked up the phone without enthusiasm, and dialled Captain Travers, whom Kent considered to be a jumped-up, ambitious pain in the ass. Making Travers' day unhappy wouldn't please Kent, but it sure wouldn't upset him either.

"Captain Travers."

"Travers. It's Captain Kent of the Thirty-Sixth here." Travers inhaled sharply. "Detective Clement's team has a case with possible Narcotics implications and involvement from the FBI and DEA."

"You want a liaison? Marcol's my best man."

"I want a liaison, but I don't want Marcol. I don't want Marcol anywhere near Clement or any of her team."

"You can't interfere with my staffing decisions, Kent."

"If you assign him, I'll ensure he is removed. The FBI, who will be working with DEA, will back my call. I warned you that if there was *any* attempt to make bad PR out of the photo exhibition, I'd ensure it was known, all the way to the top of 1PP, that Marcol harassed Clement, both at the Academy and when he was liaising on a case."

"So?"

"So, Travers, there was such an attempt. It was only averted due to Clement's quick thinking, the death of her father, and the exhibition manager's close relations with the media. 1PP are delighted with the PR to date, and with Clement and her team. Keep Marcol away from them."

Kent didn't mention, though he desperately wanted to, that Marcol would shortly have his hands full with IA's questions. The momentary satisfaction wouldn't make up for messing up an IA investigation.

"Your team is getting too big for its boots."

"My team doesn't know about this. I told them I would deal with Narcotics. This time, I suggest you pay attention to what I tell you. You're already on thin ice. Don't let arrogance break it beneath you."

Kent slapped the phone down. He had no confidence that Travers would listen to him, but if there was any attempt to inflict Marcol on his team, there would be blood in the Hudson.

**

"We've got some more names." Casey nibbled unenthusiastically on her lunchtime sandwich, back in the bullpen. "It's only nicknames, though. Is Feggetter around? He knew about them last time, so maybe he'll know these ones." She swallowed another morsel, and gazed around. "There he is." She left the rest of her sandwich, which she hadn't been enjoying, and marched over to ask. A few moments later she returned with a list of names. "Is one of our officers around to feed these into the databases? I can't see any of them."

"They should've gone to get lunch," O'Leary pointed out. Casey humphed. "But…"

"But what?"

"Bartlett's missin' too. Fremont an' Larson said somethin' about attitude adjustin', we gave them some trainin'…an' they'll've taken the lesson from us trainin'" – he smirked – "Estrolla." The smirk dissolved. "They might be doin' a li'l attitude adjustin' of their own."

"Crap. They shouldn't be intimidating other officers. They'll be in the shit, and we'll end up there with them." She bit viciously through the sandwich.

"Think we should go see?"

"Yeah. Before there's real trouble."

The team didn't draw attention to their exit towards the gym, Casey departing before Andy followed, Tyler and O'Leary leaving together. They gathered at the gym entrance, couldn't hear any sparring, and listened for a moment.

"You don't disrespect Detective Clement," Larson growled. "She doesn't hold grudges" – three of the four detectives listening tried not to choke: Casey cuddled a grudge as if it were a teddy bear – "and she gave me an' Henegan second chances, but you've been a total dumbass."

"She didn't let me explain," Bartlett whined.

"Your explanation stank like a crock of week-old shit," Fremont snapped. "Everyone knows Estrolla hates her. I don't believe you could've missed it, so why the *fuck* d'you think he'd tell you the truth?"

"Cops don't lie to cops," Bartlett tried.

"How dumb *are* you? Sure they do. There's bad cops just like there's good cops, and Estrolla's downright bad. He's already tried to fuck up Henegan, by getting him to spread lies, and now he's done it to you. The difference is, Henegan tried to apologise properly. You didn't. You tried to justify yourself. Don't come whining to us to fix your mess, 'cause we aren't interested."

"You need to adjust your thinking," Larson grated.

"It's time for us to intervene," Casey whispered. The others nodded, and the team marched in as one, Casey slightly ahead of the three men. O'Leary smacked the door shut, and the five men inside jerked in horror – and to attention.

"Ma'am," Fremont said. Larson, Henegan and Adamo echoed it. Bartlett simply stared.

"Sparring practice?" Casey asked, with an inflection that conveyed she wouldn't believe it if they agreed. The team waited a few beats. "Or attitude adjustment?"

"Just pointing out some facts, ma'am," Fremont tried. Casey surveyed him cynically. "With a little adjustment."

"Hm. Don't you think we're able to deal with our own issues – if they need to be dealt with?"

"Uh…" Fremont worked his way through the syntax. "Yes'm, but you shouldn't have to deal with dumbasses."

"Don't," Tyler stated. "Leave 'em to it." He turned his thousand-yard stare on the five officers. "No sparring. Use your words." The team preserved straight faces, at some cost to their breathing. Tyler fixed his gaze on Bartlett. "Don't like assholes," he noted.

"When your *discussions* are finished," Casey said, "we've got some work for you." Her look at the officers omitted Bartlett. "See us."

"Yes'm."

Safely back downstairs, the team regarded each other. "Do we need to have defenders?" Casey enquired.

"Naw, but iffen it makes 'em happy an' they don't get us into trouble, do we care?"

"Nope," Andy said. "It's nice to have people who don't automatically hate and fear us."

"Good to be hated and feared," Tyler contradicted.

"That's Casey's bag," O'Leary said. "I like bein' liked."

"Everyone likes you. They're too scared not to."

"Waal, that ain't fair. I'm likeable."

Further banter was interrupted by the arrival of Adamo, presumably because he was the least likely of their four victims to be eaten alive. "You had something for us to do, ma'am?"

"Yes. Run these names. We think they're members of the Yarrabee gang, but they might not be. Bring back the results as soon as you get them." She turned to her chirping phone. "Clement? I see. Can we come now? Okay. Thanks." She looked up at O'Leary. "Mrs Hercliffe's awake."

"What about the FBI?"

"Andy and Tyler can start them off."

"Casey!" Andy wailed.

"And you can try to track his car on street or building cameras while we're out. Bye," she cast over her shoulder, already halfway to the exit, O'Leary striding after her.

"That's not fair," Andy grumped.

***

"How convenient." Casey plonked down in O'Leary's SUV, exuding satisfaction.

"Yeah. You're goin' to have to talk to him later."

"That's later. Now, we have to go see if Mrs Hercliffe can tell us anything useful." Casey shut down that line of conversation in a hurry. She had no desire to talk to Renfrew about anything other than the case, and if he tried it, she'd shut him down too. She didn't need to have therapy; she didn't need to see a shrink. She only needed to solve her case, then take a vacation.

They reached the hospital and asked for Mrs Hercliffe's room. Oddly, she was alone. Casey had expected her husband to be there. They studied the room and corridor, but not only didn't they see him, there was nothing to indicate he was there – no jacket, or cup, or dent in the chair where he might have sat.

"Mrs Hercliffe?" Casey murmured to the small, defeated form in the bed, still hooked up to monitors and an IV.

"Who is it?" The eyes opened, showing only grief and overwhelming pain. "I don't want to see anyone." Her gaze dragged across the room, and, finding it empty of anybody except the cops, her lashes fell again; not soon enough to hide the whip of agony.

"I'm Detective Clement, and this is my partner, Detective O'Leary. We're investigating the attack on you."

Tania Hercliffe's eyes sprang open. "They *killed my baby!*" she howled. "My baby's dead." She burst into gulping, sawing sobs, each gasp ripping through her chest and the air. "I don't even know if my baby was a girl or boy. They couldn't tell me. She was too small...I thought...I felt she was a girl but now I'll never know, and *they took her away from me!*"

Casey moved a chair over to the bed, sat down and took the furious, grieving woman's hand. "I'll do everything I can to find them and make them pay," she promised. "I know it doesn't help. Nothing can ever help this, but I will do my best to find them."

"It won't bring my baby back," Tania spat bitterly.

"No." Casey made a swift decision, and made a gesture to O'Leary which told him *shut-up-and-stay-out-of-this.* "Nothing brings back your loved ones. I lost my dad last week. Nothing'll ever bring him back. He shouldn't have died either." She let Tania see her grief. "I keep thinking I could have done something to stop it. You're thinking the same: I can see it. There wasn't anything you could have done. Nothing."

"I could have gone somewhere else."

"You couldn't know," Casey consoled her. "You couldn't ever know. It's not your fault. It's on the shooter. No-one else." She let a momentary silence fall. "Is your husband here?"

"Matthew had to go home. He'll be back. He's only been gone a few minutes. He's devastated." Something moved through her eyes, a flash of evasion that Casey recognised.

"Okay." Casey murmured, and didn't probe any further. She was already horribly suspicious of Matthew's absence, based solely on the waft of whiskey yesterday, and she couldn't afford to open her own wounds. "Are you able to answer any questions? If it's too much, say so. It can wait." It couldn't wait long. The sooner they got as much information as possible the better, but Casey wouldn't pressure Tania, and she wouldn't guilt-trip her either, not while she was still crying hopelessly.

"I want them *dead*," she cried. "I want them dead and *buried*." The tears streamed down her cheeks, but her mouth suddenly set hard. "Ask," she said. "I don't want to" – the tears fell faster. "I want it all to go back to how it was two days ago. I want my baby. I want this never to have happened." She failed to calm her voice. "But it did, and all I want - I want them *gone*. Ask your questions," she said desolately. "It's all I can do for my baby."

"Thank you. If you want to stop at any time, say. We'll stop right away. If you want, O'Leary can bring your husband, so he's here to support you. We'll wait for him. Take any time you need to, any breaks you want. You're helping us."

"Can we just do it?"

"Yes. Why had you gone up there?"

Tania gulped. "I went to see my ob-gyn. I'd taken a home test but, before I told Matthew, I wanted confirmation. I was finished and I was delighted. I was going to tell him when I got home..." She trailed off, burying her face in the handful of Kleenex that Casey passed her. It took several minutes for her to recover her voice.

"So, you were on your way home?"

Tania nodded.

"Can you describe what happened?"

"I was coming down Riverside. It was such a nice day, and I wanted to walk. I was thrilled, and if I got tired I could hop on a bus or the subway, but I felt good. Then this car – big, black – came screeching by and I thought *what an asshat* because I thought he was trying to run the light or something but then there were gunshots and it hurt so bad and I blacked out."

"Thank you." Casey still held Tania's hand. "Are you okay to carry on?" Tania nodded. "Do you remember if they said anything, or yelled?"

"No. I don't remember them saying anything. Only the shots."

"They shot two men. Did you see that?"

Tania's brow creased. "Yes…then they turned the gun towards me." Her face went deathly white. "I've never done anything. I help people look good and feel great. There's no reason to shoot me."

"Was there a third person with the two who were shot?" Casey asked suddenly.

"I didn't see."

O'Leary exited the room. Casey knew he'd be calling Tyler or Andy to look for a third gang member in the videos and photos.

"Is there anything else you remember?"

"No. It hurt so bad, then I woke up here, and Matthew was here with me but he had to go home." She began to cry again, almost silently. "Will you please get Matthew back? I have to tell him about our baby."

"We will. I'll call him for you now."

Casey went out to make the call, but somewhat to her surprise, given her jaded view, Matthew Hercliffe picked up immediately.

"Mr Hercliffe, this is Detective Clement. Your wife agreed to talk to us, but now she wants you to come back, please."

"Of course. Tell her I'm on my way already. Is she okay?" Casey heard a slight slushiness on the *s*'s.

"She'll be better when you're here."

"Can you stay with her till I get there?"

If you don't want her left alone, why did you go home? Casey wondered acidly, but said only, "Yes, of course."

She went back into the hospital room, where Tania was lying, eyes shut, tears still leaking out. "He's on his way already," Casey said softly. "He's asked me to stay until he gets here, if you want me to."

"Please." Tania caught Casey's gaze, and held it, sodden blue eyes meeting Casey's liquid brown. "How did your dad die?" Casey gasped. "Please. You're there too."

"He" – Casey swallowed hard. "He drank himself to death after my mom passed. Cancer."

"How do you carry on?"

"I don't know," Casey admitted. "I haven't – I put one foot in front of the other and try not to think about it. I can't... I'm not dealing with it yet. I can't." She turned her head away, and blinked several times, turned back, face forcibly calmed. "I don't know how you do it. I'm working, and trying not to think."

"Thank you." Tania took a deep breath, but let it out without speaking. Casey watched something go through her face, but she didn't explain, and Casey didn't ask. She thought she knew, and – oh, hell. She couldn't let Tania go through the hell of an alcoholic partner alone, if she could point her to help.

"If you need to talk, here's my card."

CHAPTER TEN

They sat in silence, Tania's eyes having closed once more, until Matthew turned up. Casey slipped out, collected O'Leary, and walked down to the SUV.

"You told her," O'Leary charged, "an' you gave her your card so's she could call you."

"Yeah?"

"That's…" O'Leary tried to find a word other than *dumb*, and failed. "Don't get yourself too involved. You gotta look after yourself. Put your own oxygen mask on first, don't they say?"

"I know what I'm doing."

"Didn't say no different." O'Leary's hayseed amiability was on full display. "Time to go face the music – or the shrink."

"Ugh," Casey replied. "Did you find out anything about a third target?"

"Naw. I left it with Tyler an' Andy to see what they could find." O'Leary hummed. "You know, I'd'a thought the Yarrabees might've taken some revenge already."

"Yeah," Casey agreed. "You'd think. They could simply be planning, and we'll find out about it in a few days." She smiled nastily. "Let's go scare their leader, and see what shakes out."

"There's a cheery thought. Terrorising Frank Auster'll give us a nice boost, an' here's another cheery thought for you."

"Yes?" Casey said suspiciously.

"You c'n tell Renfrew about the Yarrabees' revenge, an' the third man."

"Revenge was your idea," Casey pointed out. "You tell him."

"You're in charge of the team, you get to tell him." O'Leary snickered, exposing elephantine teeth. "Perks of office."

Casey grumbled and groused all the way back, to which O'Leary remained impervious.

***

"Kent."

"Travers. I have assigned Detective Daniela Handjiev to liaise between your team, the FBI, and DEA."

"Thank you. What's her number, so Detective Clement can call her as soon as possible?"

Travers read off a number, which Kent read back to him. "Next time, don't interfere in my staffing," Travers snapped.

"If there is a next time, Travers, I hope you won't be dumb enough to try to assign a man who's already tried to harass a female detective, and who's managed to irritate a senior FBI agent, the best team in the NYPD, and me. Before you go any further, consider your position as a junior captain. I have many years' seniority and experience on you. What'll the press do if they find out you're deliberately forcing the harasser on the victim? I'll tell you. They'll have your guts, and nobody'll help you." Kent took a deep breath, and controlled his temper. "We've had this discussion three times, and it hasn't sunk in. Either you're a fool, or Marcol has something on you. Fix it, because I'm tired of you trying to mess up my team."

Kent slammed the phone down on Travers' infuriated squawking – but not denial – and sighed. He picked the phone up to IA, who could investigate Travers. A short conversation later, the Travers problem had left Kent's desk. He sighed with relief, and poked his head out of his office to see Clement at her desk. He still didn't like her haggard pallor, but he'd deal with that problem after the case was closed.

"Clement," he rapped.

She hurried over. "Sir?"

"I have the name of your Narcotics liaison, and a number. Detective Handjiev. Make contact. Dismissed."

Casey returned to her desk and put in a call, without any enthusiasm.

"Detective Handjiev," a crisp, no-nonsense, female voice answered, which made Casey happier at once.

"Hey. This is Detective Clement at the Thirty-Sixth. We're working on the murders of a couple of Yarrabees, and my captain told me you were the Narcotics liaison."

"Hey. Nice to hear from you."

A few moments of civilised conversation later, Detective Daniela *call-me-Dani* Handjiev had agreed to meet Casey around shift end, for what they agreed should be a getting-to-know-each-other chat – without any other team members or agents of any description present. Adding anyone else to

82

the conversation would be unhelpful, they agreed. They also agreed that Dani's presence at the Yarrabee interview would be unhelpful, mostly because Frank Auster, their leader, would recognise Dani instantly. Casey was pleased Dani had agreed, because she hadn't intended to wait for her.

***

Renfrew and his sidekick, Bergen, had installed themselves in a handy conference room, though Bergen was sitting with Andy discussing the video footage and likely candidates for the third target. Casey couldn't see Renfrew, which made her happy.

"Detective Clement." Renfrew greeted her from behind, which made her extremely unhappy. She cleared her face before turning around.

"Dr Renfrew." She didn't bother with any pleasantries such as *how nice to see you again*, since they both knew she would be lying outright.

Dr Renfrew had not met Detective Clement since the end of March. He unobtrusively examined her face, and was shocked by the tiredness, grief and guilt therein, all of which she was failing to conceal. He would have liked to offer help, but Detective Clement had evinced no desire to benefit from his substantial abilities, and indeed had previously rejected them in the most cutting of terms. Dr Renfrew was not sufficiently unwise to offer his assistance again, especially when it was patently obvious that Detective Clement and, to a lesser extent, the rest of the team, were using the extant case of gang homicide to suppress any inconvenient manifestations of emotion.

Dr Renfrew decided to suggest to Captain Kent that the team should be made to take vacation, if Captain Kent had not instructed them to take leave. He expected it would already have been contemplated, but one should never assume.

"I am sorry for your loss, Detective."

"Thank you," Casey clipped. She didn't need to receive sympathy from Renfrew, and she sure wouldn't open herself up to another offer of *therapy*.

"Detectives Tyler and Chee have summarised the status of the investigation. I understand that your interview with Mrs Hercliffe has indicated the possibility of a third target. Agent Bergen is assisting Detective Chee to identify that person. Is there anything else of which I should be aware?"

Casey gritted her teeth. "O'Leary and I are surprised the Yarrabees haven't already retaliated." Renfrew nodded. "We surmise they're planning something bigger, but it's not clear whether they know their men were targeted by a member of the Chicago Pagliaccis. Either way, someone's starting a gang war, possibly across states, most likely for drugs."

"When you identified both these issues, you reported to Captain Kent, who quite properly involved the FBI and the NYPD's Narcotics division. I understand Detective Marcol will not be a part of their work, with which I am entirely in agreement." Renfrew's expression hardened. "His involvement would be unhelpful on many levels, but in any event, I believe he will shortly find he has other concerns."

Casey blinked. Renfrew seemed to be hinting that Birkett had rolled on Marcol's involvement. What a terrible shame. She waited for Renfrew to say something useful about the case.

"Narcotics will liaise with DEA. Your concern is the homicides, and the collateral damage to Mrs Hercliffe and her pregnancy. I do not think it will help anyone if you are distracted from your goal by the drug issues, although naturally if you, or we, uncover information in the course of your work we will collectively ensure it reaches the correct destination." Renfrew gazed over his pince-nez and down his nose, which made Casey's trigger finger itch. "What is your preferred next step?"

"I want to interview Frank Auster, who's the leader of the Yarrabees. I've already contacted Detective Handjiev of Narcotics, and we'll have a discussion later. She's happy not to be there, so he doesn't know about the Narcotics involvement."

"Mm," Renfrew approved. "Your reasoning for interviewing Mr Auster?"

"Overtly, to find out if there is any non-gang related reason for two of his men to be shot and a third targeted. Under that," Casey clipped, "to inform him he's partly responsible for the injury to an innocent woman and the death of her baby, and to use his reaction to find out if there's any information on the incipient gang war and the involvement of the Pagliaccis on the Tarticcas' side." She stopped. "Can you find out if there's any existing connection between the Pagliaccis and the Tarticcas? I'll ask Narcotics too, but you might find something different from your search."

"I shall inquire. You hypothesise they may be linked, perhaps by family or marriage?"

"Marriage, or in-law relationships. Not family, or they'd likely all be the same. Near enough to be pals but not near enough to merge. I can't see how the Tarticcas would be lending cars to the Pagliaccis otherwise – I don't buy that the Pagliaccis are trying to take them out."

"I concur. Who will go with you?"

"O'Leary. He's big enough so nobody'll try anything dumb."

"Mm." Renfrew steepled his fingers. "Would you take Agent Bergen with you as well?"

"Why?"

"So the FBI has direct contact with the leader of an organised crime group." Renfrew smiled thinly. "You may call it a hunch. Agent Bergen is exceedingly adept at remaining unnoticed and unmemorable, but he is also adept at seeing connections in seemingly random information." His expression became proud, almost paternal. "He is an excellent agent."

"Okay, he can come too."

"Thank you." Renfrew regarded Casey slightly oddly. "I attended Mr Carval's exhibition on Tuesday evening. I found it most interesting."

"How nice," Casey said insincerely.

"I should like to discuss it with him. Will he be visiting the precinct today?"

"I guess. He might be here at shift end."

"I would appreciate a conversation with him. Please let him know."

Casey, much as she disliked Renfrew, didn't intend to open another front of hostilities. "I'll tell him."

"Thank you."

Casey texted Carval, and descended upon Andy. "Any news on tracking the car?"

"All the requests for footage and for warrants for building footage are in. Nothing's back yet."

"Ugh," Casey gloomed. "I'm supposed to take Bergen with us to see the Yarrabees – Renfrew requested it."

"Okay. I'll carry on trying to work out who the third target is."

Casey collected O'Leary and Bergen, who happily agreed to join them in a trip to meet the Yarrabees.

"Where do they hang out?" Bergen asked.

"Near the waterfront," O'Leary rumbled happily. "Just what I like. Sunshine on the river."

"We'll be in a corrugated iron shed with no natural light, talking to a major criminal who should be in prison, if only Narcotics or DEA could pin anything on him."

"Let's have a go," Bergen enthused. "I bet we can do better than them." Casey stared at him. "What? We took down those people traffickers, and we wouldn't have done that without your team." He grinned, in a *listen-to-this* way. Casey came to full, suspicious attention. "Dr Renfrew never works with outsiders twice, because they expect him to do all the thinking and the work. You, um...well...you shoved it back in his face and made it clear *you* were in charge, and he was an optional extra you didn't want around. He's not a bad guy, honestly, but he's used to being the smartest guy in the room by a long shot. You don't care and I don't think you believe he's smarter than you. So" – his grin wrapped around his head – "he respects you four. And Carval, for other reasons. He doesn't respect many people."

"Oh," Casey squeaked out. She had no idea what to say. Even O'Leary failed to find a comment. The rest of the drive took place in stunned silence from the two detectives and smug amusement from Bergen.

Fortunately, by the time they reached the shabby, corrugated-iron roofed building in which the Yarrabees made their home, Casey had recovered her composure. She marched in, flanked by O'Leary and Bergen, and glared at the scruffy man lounging on a chair, a few feet inside the door.

"Where's Auster?" she demanded.

The man ran a slow leer over her. "Who's asking? He already got a girl."

"Ain't it lucky we're not offerin' him a girl?" O'Leary asked the air. The man, who'd been too busy ogling Casey to pay attention to the two men, looked up, and gulped. "Mebbe you should take us to Auster. We got business with him." He took two huge strides, and plucked the man up. "Now."

The man would have scuttled off, but O'Leary's ham hand had descended on his shoulder before he could flee. "Auster," he rumbled. "You c'n lead us there."

He did. When he tapped on a door, the three investigators rearranged themselves so Casey, temper fired by the unpleasant leering and assumptions of the door guard, was in front of the two men.

"Frank Auster," she said to the greying, heavy-set older man behind a desk. "We want to talk about Beau Resorge and Carson Williams – though you know them as Buster and Crusher. They're dead. Shot, yesterday. Along with an innocent bystander whose unborn baby died."

Shock flashed in Auster's face. "Who are you?"

"I'm the detective investigating their murders. All *three* murders."

"I can't tell you anything."

"That's a sweeping statement when I haven't asked you anything yet." Casey produced an expression bearing a tangential relationship to a smile. "You don't have to help me with my investigation, but if you don't, I might accidentally let it drop that you don't care your men are dead – and you don't care that a pregnant woman was shot, losing her baby along the way – as long as you can say you don't talk to the cops."

Auster stared at her, then surged to his feet, his face suffused with anger. "You dare" –

"Sure I dare. I solve murders. You stand in my way, and I'll arrest you for obstructing me. Wanna try me?" Casey held his furious gaze. "I don't back down from a fight."

Auster's eyes dropped first, and he sat down again. "You'll investigate the murders of my boys?"

"I said so. And *when* I find the killers, they'll be charged, tried, and, if found guilty, sent to prison." Her face set hard. "Who else will try to find them? It's me, or nobody."

"Who're they?" he asked, gesturing at O'Leary and Bergen.

"My team." Casey annexed Bergen without a second thought. "Are you going to co-operate by answering questions, or are you going to obstruct me?"

"What d'you wanna know?" he capitulated.

"Did Beau or Carson have any enemies within the Yarrabees?"

Auster blinked at the unexpected question. "Nah. Beau was pals with everyone – too dumb to make enemies: everyone liked him. Getting mad at him was like kicking a puppy. Carson – not that I know about."

"After we're done, I'll talk to Jacker and Roo. I'm informed they were Beau's closest friends. That won't be a problem, will it?"

Auster shook his head. He appeared confused, possibly because Casey was following (albeit without any sympathy or preliminaries) the normal course of questioning and entirely ignoring the gang or drug aspects. She wanted Auster off-balance, and off-balance was precisely where he was.

"So, you're not aware of any enemies within the Yarrabees. Any bad break-ups?"

"Dunno. I don't get involved with my boys' personal lives. They work here, they don't live here. They're grown up."

Casey made a mental note to send an officer back to both men's next-of-kin to ask about break-ups. It was vanishingly unlikely that the murders had anything to do with vengeful exes, but it would be best to rule it out.

"What about 'business rivals'?" she asked.

"I don't know what you mean."

"Don't give me that crap. I mean the Tarticcas. Your feud with them is well known. What's going on there?" Behind her, Bergen's barely noticed presence went on alert.

"We don't get into arguments with nobody."

"Really? Okay, why would anyone shoot your boys?"

"I dunno."

"Let's try again. You say you're not fighting with the Tarticcas – which is weird, since it's the best-known feud in gangland – but let's go with that for a moment. Do you know anything about Beau or Carson which would make someone want to shoot them?"

"Nah."

"A third man from your 'business' was targeted, but the shooter hit a bystander instead." Casey watched closely. Auster's fingers clenched into fists. As soon as he saw she'd noticed, he dropped them from his desk. "Something ringing a bell? We're looking into who the target might have been. Got any ideas?"

"No." Everyone in the room knew he was lying.

"Okay," Casey dismissed. "If you've got nothing more to tell me, I'll talk to Jacker and Roo. Where can I find them?"

"They're out."

"Oh?" Casey raised her eyebrows. "You'd better give me their contact details. We'll be happy to interview them at the precinct. Or," she said easily, "you could tell us where to find them, and we'll take them in from there. We'd hate to inconvenience your 'business', or disturb your on-site employees."

Auster acquired an expression that indicated he was looking for his lower legs, since Casey had just cut him off at the knees. He had an unhappy choice. Call his employees in, which meant admitting he'd lied when saying they were out; give Casey and the cops free rein to pick them up, which even as witnesses meant he had no control over the interviews *and* they'd know where his men had been; or give Casey their contact details, which would allow the cops to trace their movements or, if he changed their phones, show there was something to be traced. Auster, in fact, had no good options. Casey waited, with an unpleasant smirk clearly conveying that she knew Auster had a problem.

"Surely they'd want to help find Beau's killer." Casey's words improved Auster's shining hour not at all. "They were good friends of his." She waited another half-minute. "Contact details, or location. Or you can come with us."

"I don't have to," Auster argued.

O'Leary took three giant strides and arrived beside him before Auster could blink. "Now," he rumbled. "Let's not have anythin' dumb happen. You don't want trouble an' nor do we. So, instead of reachin' for that gun I reckon you got nearby, how about you put your hands on the desk, an' we c'n continue havin' this nice li'l chat. You c'n give us the details, or come with me."

Auster contemplated the long way up to O'Leary's implacable face, and saw the future. He didn't seem to like it, but he also wasn't totally dumb. There was no way he could get the drop on O'Leary, and he could also see Casey's hand on her Glock. Bergen was making himself invisible, but Casey was pretty sure his fingers were on the grip of his own gun. Auster's man was outside the room, and couldn't enter without causing a serious escalation.

"Well, Auster?" Casey pressed, after another few seconds of silence. "What'll it be?"

"I'll call them in," he said bitterly. He made one call. The implications weren't lost on Casey. Not five minutes later, two men arrived. One was small and rat-faced, with an oily complexion and something that, with a vat of hair growth serum, might eventually become a moustache; the other could have usefully applied some depilatory cream in order to see his face under the thatch of beard, moustache, and over-long hair. He resembled an overgrown Shih Tzu.

"Which of you is Jacker?" The rat raised his hand. "Full name Pete Jackman?" He nodded. "So, you must be Roo, aka Jared Reuben." The Shih Tzu nodded. "We have some questions for you." They both looked at Auster.

"Answer them," Auster ordered.

CHAPTER ELEVEN

"Yes, boss," Jacker and Roo chorused.

"Sit down," Casey commanded. They regarded her sleazily, until they noticed her icy glare and O'Leary's unsmiling face. They hadn't registered Bergen.

"You're friends of Beau Resorge – Buster?"

"Yeah."

"He was shot yesterday, along with his pal Crusher." This didn't seem to surprise Jacker or Roo. "You knew?"

"Course we knew. Everyone knew there'd been a shooting."

"How did you find out?"

They eyed each other. "Uh…"

"It wasn't on the local news, before you try saying so," Casey said coldly. "Who told you?"

"Boss," Roo answered.

"How did you know?" Casey addressed Auster.

He cast his underlings an annoyed glance. "One of my boys was there."

"Who?"

"Paddy Hocking."

"We'll want to talk to him next. Why don't you call him now, so we don't waste time trying to find him?" Reluctantly, Auster picked up the phone.

"While we're waiting, tell us about Beau."

"He was a good guy. Dumb, but friendly. Reliable."

"Did he have a girlfriend?"

Jacker and Roo exchanged glances, sending a slightly worried look at Auster. "Naw," they tried.

"Don't lie to me. Who was the girlfriend, and where do I find her?"

"Maria Montelucci."

Auster drew a sharp breath.

"You know her?" Casey asked.

"No…"

"Know of her?" she followed up. Auster didn't answer. "We'll find out who she is, so you might as well tell me what you know."

"I don't know anything."

Casey turned back to Jacker. "Where does she live? I want to talk to her about Beau."

"Dunno." He finally caught his boss's signals. Casey raised her eyebrows, but left it. They'd find her through the databases.

"What was Beau's job?"

"He did the heavy lifting. Boxes, that sort of thing."

"Heavy boxes?"

"Yeah. He was a big, strong guy."

"Anybody object?"

"Naw. If he wanted to do the heavy work, it was fine with us. He sure couldn't do the thinking."

"Thinking?"

"You know. Accounts, sales, customer relations."

"Oh?" Casey enquired. "Where do you sell? Stores?"

"Nah. Word of mouth." Roo smiled, obviously thinking he'd gotten away with it.

"What did you say your products were?"

"Medic" – Auster whistled – "Herbal products," Roo corrected.

"Oh? What type of herbals?" Casey smiled sweetly back. "I'm sure you can produce all the relevant permits. Lots of herbal products require FDA authorisation now."

"How's this relevant to Beau's murder?" Auster interrupted sharply, hoping to divert Casey's attention.

"That's the question, isn't it? We don't know what might lead us to the shooter if we don't ask questions." She turned back to Jacker. "Did anyone have a beef with Beau?"

"Naw."

"Okay. What about Carson – Crusher? Did he have a girlfriend?"

"Not so's we knew."

"Boyfriend?"

"Fuck, no. He don't swing that way."

"What was his role in the business?"

"Logistics."

"What aspects?"

"All of them."

"So, deliveries of stock to – where's your warehouse?"

"Here."

Auster winced.

"Mm. And providing stock to your customers – you said you didn't have stores, so do they come here?"

"Why're you askin'?"

"To see if your customers might have met Beau or Carson and taken exception to one of them," Casey explained blandly. "If Carson met customers, one of them might have had an argument with him. Or Beau might have dropped a box on their foot, or banged into them. Do you know of anyone who was upset with him?"

"No," Jacker said. Roo shook his head.

"Are we done yet?" Auster asked.

"We'll talk to Paddy now. Eyewitness testimony is always helpful."

"He's not here yet," Auster said. "You could come back later."

"We'll wait. How long will he be?"

"Not long." Auster's face revealed his desperation for Paddy to show up. Jacker and Roo hadn't distinguished themselves by their intelligence. Casey could sense Bergen's delight at the revelations.

Fortunately for Auster's blood pressure and the continued survival of Jacker and Roo, Paddy walked in only two minutes later.

"Yes, boss?"

"We're investigating the murder of Beau and Carson," Casey rapped. Paddy's attention whipped to her. "Your boss says you saw it."

"Sure did." Remembered terror crossed Paddy's face. "Some guy in a big black vehicle with a handgun shot them both and fired at me too. Missed me, but got some woman. Paramedics came and took her away."

"Fired at you? Why?"

"He was a fucking Tarticca, that's why," Paddy blustered. "He didn't have no reason to shoot at us."

"I'm confused. First you say he was a Tarticca, then that he had no reason to shoot you."

"Those Tarticcas shoot anyone. They don't need no reasons, they just shoot. We didn't do nothing to them."

"They're a bit unfriendly?"

"You fucking said it, lady. But they'll get theirs."

"Oh?"

Paddy suddenly realised his comment could be, um, *misinterpreted*. "We'll be successful and rub their fucking noses in it."

"I see." Casey changed tack. "Can you describe the shooter?"

Paddy thought. "White. Maybe Italian-American." He added an insulting term. Casey ignored it. "Arm was tattooed – full sleeve. T-shirt. Big guy."

"Hair colour, style?"

"Brown, but nothing a million other guys don't look like. Short but not a buzz cut, you know? Didn't see no glasses or anything like that."

"Do you think you could identify him if we had a photograph?"

"Sure I could. He fucking tried to shoot me!"

"Okay. If we get a photograph, we'll ask you to come in and look at it. It'll make it a lot easier to arrest him if there's a positive ID."

"Okay."

"Let's have your contact details."

Paddy, oblivious to Auster's despairing look, wrote them down.

"Thank you for your co-operation," Casey said. "If you remember anything else that might help us find the killer, let me know. Here's my card. We'll talk to you again if anything we find relates to Beau or Carson's work here."

"I'll show you out," Jacker offered at a glare from Auster, which positively shouted *don't let the cops go anywhere alone for fear of what they'll find.*

Outside, the three investigators beamed at each other, and tucked themselves into O'Leary's SUV before saying anything.

"How do they remember how to breathe if they're that dumb?" Casey turned round to grin widely at Bergen. "Does that give you something to go on?"

"Sure does, and now we can track Paddy via the cell towers." Bergen hummed happily. "I see a search warrant arriving."

"I have to meet our Narcotics liaison – Detective Daniela – Dani – Handjiev," Casey said. "Drop me at the subway, please, and I'll see you tomorrow. I'm hoping Dani'll come and join us at the precinct."

"It'll make everythin' easier," O'Leary rumbled, "an' she ain't Marcol, so that's a good start."

"Sure is," Casey agreed. "Bergen, will you brief Dr Renfrew? O'Leary'll catch up with the rest of the team. O'Leary, see if you can spot Paddy in Andy's videos. Sounds like he was the third man."

"Yeah," the big man rumbled.

Casey slipped out of the SUV at the subway, leaving her car safely at the precinct.

***

Carval trudged into the precinct a little after five, not pleased at having to stop shooting to talk to Renfrew, and still less pleased to find a text from Casey telling him she had to meet some Narcotics cop and would go straight home. He decided, sulkily, that he'd go to Casey's from the precinct, which at least was a pleasant thought.

Instead of finding Renfrew, he spotted Andy, and ambled over. "Hey," he greeted him. "Allan'll talk to you about your program."

"I'm meeting him later," Andy replied, "so we'll do it then."

"I have to have it," Carval insisted. "It's superb."

"Allan won't be happy you're telling me you're keen. I'll jack the price up if you're desperate," Andy scoffed at Carval. "Don't you know anything about negotiating?"

"Sure, but if you license it to me the rest of the photography world'll be screaming for it, so Allan's still got a good chance." He changed the subject. "What are you doing?"

"Pulling camera footage, but while I'm waiting, I'm looking for a third target. The shooter hit this woman" – he tapped on the shot – "but she wasn't a target. Someone else was, but the gunman missed. I'm trying to work out who."

"What's Tyler doing? He's usually good at this."

"He is, and he's looking too."

"Can I play? I'm supposed to be seeing Renfrew" –

"Why?"

"He saw the show, and he wants to talk to me." Carval pouted sulkily. "I was having a great day shooting construction sites, then Casey texted me to say I had to see Renfrew."

"There's always tomorrow," Andy said unsympathetically. "It's not like you need to hurry with the next show." Carval scowled at him. He carried on. "If you want to have a look, you can. Here are the shots, here are the first two victims, here's the woman."

"Where's the shooter?"

"Car, here – look at the video. The car never stopped."

Carval ran the video five times, stopped it and tapped a figure. "Him."

Simultaneously, Tyler strode up. "Got him." He looked at Carval. "You?"

"This one," Carval replied, and tapped it again.

"Same." They bumped fists.

"Sightlines," Carval said.

"Yep."

"Ah, Mr Carval." Renfrew appeared. "Thank you for attending. I wish to discuss some matters of team bonding arising from my visit to your exhibition, which is an outstanding advertisement for the professionalism of the NYPD."

Carval's face acquired a hunted-down expression. Andy and Tyler made no move to take Renfrew's attention away from him.

"Perhaps we could avail ourselves of the coffee machine before we begin?"

"Okay." The coffee, however excellent, was no consolation as Renfrew swept him off. Sitting in Renfrew's annexed conference room, he felt unpleasantly as if he had been sent to the principal's office for an examination for which he was completely unprepared.

Renfrew steepled his fingers. Carval picked up his camera, smiled seraphically at Renfrew's less-than-impressed expression, and took a few shots, more to irritate Renfrew than for any desire for more shots of his skeletal fingers.

"I visited your exhibition on Tuesday," Renfrew opened.

"Mhm? I'm delighted. More visitors are always a good thing. Tell all your friends to visit as well."

"Dr McDonald attended with me." Carval gawped, before he recovered himself. Renfrew preserved a bland face. "We agreed it was outstanding. I believe Dr McDonald to have been overwhelmed by the portrayal of his work."

"Oh," Carval managed. "I guess he won't come after me with scalpel raised."

"He would never do such a thing," Renfrew chided. Carval wasn't nearly as sure. "However, that is a side issue. I wish to continue our discussion of some weeks ago about your identification and portrayal of the team's structure and bonds. Before we discuss that, I also wish to understand the team's reactions to your photographs."

"Shouldn't you ask them?" Carval snipped.

"I shall," Renfrew replied calmly. "However, 'the onlooker sees most of the game', as they say. I expect that you were observing the reactions of your subjects."

"Do you?"

"I do. I note that you are evading my question, which leads me to think that your subjects were unhappy with your photographs. Since those shots are technically outstanding, and show Detective Clement and her team, together with Captain Kent and others, in a highly favourable light, something else must have occurred." Renfrew peered at Carval. "Did Detective Clement's father attend?"

Carval choked on the dregs of his coffee. "How did you know?" he exclaimed. He only realised what he'd inadvertently admitted after he'd closed his mouth.

"Ah. I take it he did not react well?"

Carval declined to answer for a moment. "I don't see what that has to do with the team bonds. I showed the strength of the team. It's what I do. How other people react is nothing to do with me: it's all down to them. Kent and the team were perfectly happy with the show, and I'm delighted with the public's reaction."

"Describe to me your view of the team's structure, if you please. I recall your previous commentary, but I wish to start there once more."

Carval didn't please. Renfrew, despite the prim, pompous manner, was acutely perceptive, and Carval didn't want to betray any secrets. On the other, equally displeased, hand, if he refused point-blank, Renfrew would draw conclusions, which were only too likely to be accurate.

"Casey and O'Leary have been partners for years," he began, "so they know how each other operates and they don't have to think about it. It's automatic. When one of them's with Tyler or Andy, it's nearly as smooth. Tyler and Andy shouldn't work, but they do. They fit into each other's spaces, like a jigsaw puzzle." He interlaced his fingers. "Casey and O'Leary are more like a continuum." He undid his fingers, and put his hands side by side. "They work. They know each other's strengths and weaknesses, and they use it."

"I see. Do you consider that the team would adapt if one of its members required extra support?"

"*If* they did, it would. I haven't seen it."

Renfrew scrutinised Carval with an expression that made it perfectly clear he knew Carval was outright lying. Carval met his eyes steadily, and refused to squirm or blink. "I see," Renfrew repeated. "If I were to say to you that your shots place the team, and in particular Detective Clement, upon a pedestal from which any ill-intentioned person would wish to remove them" –

"I already said that how people react to my shots is up to them. I don't invent or pose my shots, so anything you see is what I saw and what your own prejudices bring. Are we done here? I have commitments this evening and I need to leave now."

"We are finished for now," Renfrew said smoothly. "Good night."

"Bye."

Carval fled both Renfrew and the precinct, thoroughly irritated. Renfrew had exposed something he didn't wish to discuss with anyone beyond Casey and *maybe* the other three, and, though he hadn't said so, Renfrew had been dancing around discussing Carval's feelings for Casey, which wasn't a subject for discussion until he and Casey decided how strong those feelings were.

***

Casey acquired a double espresso in the coffee bar where she was to meet Dani, and sat down. Shortly, a tall woman with a smart blonde bob entered, glanced around, and waggled fingers at Casey. She waggled hers back. The woman collected a coffee, and joined her.

"Hey. You must be Dani. How'd you know it was me?"

"You're wearing a gun," Dani pointed out. "Your face was all over the media Tuesday, too. Sorry for your loss."

Casey wrinkled that same face. "Thank you," she clipped. "Let's talk about this case."

"Okay, but afterwards," Dani added seriously, "there's some stuff you need to know."

Casey stared. "What?"

"Case first."

"Sure. This is what we've got," she began, and laid out everything she knew, including the afternoon's visit to the Yarrabees. Dani listened attentively until she was done.

"Okay. What you got from your Feggetter is accurate, as far as it goes. Up till now, the Yarrabees have stuck with street stuff – heroin, crack, Ecstasy, et cetera. And meth. Lots of meth. The Tarticcas moved into medical drugs – opioids – a while ago, and so did the Pagliaccis, so DEA tells me. What you don't know is we've largely cut the Yarrabees off from most of the street drugs – we hit their meth labs hard a few months back, and between us, DEA and the Coast Guard we've blocked a lot of incoming shipments, so they're looking for something new. They're trying to move into opioids, and the Tarticcas don't like it."

"What's the Pagliacci connection? I thought it might be marriage, or in-laws."

Dani nodded. "Yep. Good guess. God knows how many generations back, they were related, and they do the gang equivalent of student exchanges. Some Pagliacci bright young spark comes here, learns a bit, goes home to Chicago, and vice versa."

"Pretty close ties?"

"True partners in crime," Dani said aridly. "I'm not surprised by what you've told me about the shooting. It'll be one of their exchanges. You said you'd tell the criminal world they were killing babies?"

"Yeah."

"Nice. Good threat. They won't like that."

"It wasn't a threat. It was a promise." Casey met Dani's eyes. "But let's close the case first."

Dani relaxed. "Right answer."

"I don't let personal get in the way."

Dani blinked. "Okay," she drawled. "I was told to liaise between you and DEA."

"Fine with me. I have to keep the FBI in the loop. I don't want to deal with DEA as well, and you know them all anyway." Her mouth twisted. "One federal agency's more than enough for me. D'you want the liaison role with the Feds as well? You can have it."

"No, thanks. How'll we play this?"

"Come along and join us. We can find you a desk, you'll know everything we do right away, and it's better if we're all in the same place."

"Agreed. I'll check with my boss, but unless there's a problem, I'll be there tomorrow morning. I'll get my shifts matched to yours." She gulped at her coffee.

"Sounds good." Casey had rapidly decided she liked Dani. "Let me give you the rundown on the rest of the team and the Feds." She described her team, then went on to Renfrew and Bergen. Dani laughed. "Not your favourite guy."

"Nope."

"I hear your favourite guy is the photographer," Dani tossed out.

"Do you?" Casey snapped, hackles instantly rising.

"Yeah. That's the second thing we need to talk about. What's your relationship with Mark Marcol?"

"None."

"Weird."

"How?"

"He wanted this assignment."

Casey choked on the last sips of her espresso. "What the *fuck?*"

"I heard him arguing with the captain about it. Why'd he want to be in on it?"

Casey thought fast. "About six months ago, we had a case where some guys were doping girls and raping them on-line." Dani flinched. "Then killing them. We were trying to get a line on the drugs they were using, and Marcol was sent along. Couldn't tell us anything useful, and hit on me. I wasn't interested. I guess it hurt his pride, and he thought he'd have a second go."

"Hm. Some guys just can't take rejection."

"Nope."

Dani drained her coffee. "Okay, see you tomorrow. What time do you start?"

"Shift starts at eight-thirty. Our captain's hot on not doing overtime unless he approves it, so I'll be there just before then." She grinned. "We've got our own coffee machine, too."

"Sounds great. Seeya." She swung off.

Casey wondered if she should have warned Dani about Carval, then thought that if he showed up in the precinct, they could have a discussion. Why borrow any more trouble? Thinking of Carval, she tapped out a text. *Going home. Come around?*

CHAPTER TWELVE

O'Leary and Bergen ambled cheerfully into the bullpen and made straight for Andy. "We think we got your third man," O'Leary rumbled. "C'n we see your video?"

"Tyler and Carval think they've spotted him too," Andy replied. "Let's see if it matches up." He ran the video slowly.

"That's him." O'Leary tapped on a figure.

"Nice. It's the same guy."

"Paddy Hocking. We better run him now. Mebbe the databases'll tell us somethin' before tomorrow."

"I'll go report to Dr Renfrew." Bergen wandered off.

Andy set the run going. "So, what happened?" he asked. O'Leary provided a full download. "Let's put Maria Montelucci in too." He did. "Now what?"

"Waal, Casey went off to get to know the Narcotics detective, we've done everythin' we can, an' it's shift end. I'm goin' home."

"I'm seeing Allan – oh, Renfrew summoned Carval. I don't think it went well. He came out looking pretty pissed."

O'Leary drooped. "Gotta mean more researchin'. I'm goin' before he spots me." He left, hurriedly, evading Dr Renfrew by only a few seconds.

"Detective Chee?" Renfrew tried.

"I have an appointment," Andy excused himself, entirely truthfully. "I have to leave."

Only Tyler was left to Renfrew's tender mercies. However, Tyler hadn't been in the Army for nothing. He'd spotted the others' tactical withdrawals, and when Renfrew scanned the vicinity, Tyler had also beaten his retreat.

Dr Renfrew determined to speak to each of them as early as possible, and instead conducted a thoroughly satisfying debrief with Bergen.

**

"Hi, Allan."

"Hi." Allan looked up from his glass of Sauvignon Blanc. "Wine?"

"Sure."

Allan poured. "Jamie tells me you've written a brilliant photo clean-up program, and he wants it."

"So he said." Andy sniggered. "No negotiating game, your boy. None."

"That's why I do it," Allan agreed, "but if Jamie wants something, he doesn't care what he says, as long as he gets his own way. Toddler," he added affectionately.

"He pushed hard for it. Does he know what he's doing?"

"When it comes to photos and photography, yes, he does. Sure, most of his shots are taken on instinct, and he has immense natural ability, but despite what he pretends, he does a lot of thinking, a lot of studying up and a lot of work."

"I guess – he spent a long time with the one-way glass."

"Same thing. If he says your program is better than anything he has or anything he's seen, you can take it to the bank – and if you do," Allan added, "I'll be happy to introduce you to a specialist lawyer who can make sure your rights are fully protected and you're able to monetise it properly. Jamie'll endorse it, and you'll make money."

Andy sipped his wine thoughtfully. "What you're actually saying is: 'License it to Jamie Carval on reasonable terms, and he'll make sure everyone knows it's the best program on the market so you can license it to everyone else for more'?"

"Yes." Allan smiled. "You knew all that already, didn't you? You already have a plan, and you worked it out as soon as Jamie saw it and wanted it."

"Yes." Andy sipped his wine again. "I don't *only* do cop work and culture. I day trade, and I do pretty well, and I've been programming in the background for a while now."

"Why don't we stop dancing, you make me a proposal, and, as long as it's reasonable for both of us, we can agree on terms and sort out the legalities later – do you have a good intellectual property lawyer in your pocket, or shall I suggest one?"

"I retained a good lawyer – I had it protected before I started using it at the precinct, so the NYPD couldn't get their paws on it. Your proposal sounds good to me. You won't cheat me, and I won't fleece Carval, so let's agree now and talk about something more interesting instead."

A brief discussion, memorialised in Allan's phone and e-mailed to Andy, later, they were happy to move on to a discussion of cultural events.

"There's some other news for you," Allan trailed.

"Yeah?"

"You'll like it."

"Why am I suddenly suspicious?" Andy wondered to his wine.

"You know on your last case you came across the Finisterres?"

"Oh, God." Andy's head hit his hands.

"They didn't know you were the subjects of Jamie's show. Now they do" –

"What? Why did you tell them?"

"Because they were visiting the show this morning and they'd have recognised Casey and O'Leary straight off the bat, so there wasn't any point hiding it. However, they have soirées, full of interesting, cultured people talking about interesting cultural things...such as Jamie's exhibitions."

"You're kidding." Andy caught on immediately. "When will you tell Casey she's invited to a cultural soirée as the main attraction?"

"When I'm at a safe distance. I'm flying to Pittsburgh Tuesday. That should be far enough."

"I wouldn't bet on it," Andy said mordantly. "I'd try Hawaii." He thought for an instant. "Why were you visiting the Finisterres?"

"Jamie wants to shoot their productions, and I told him I'd fix it. I also wanted to tell them I'd be helping Allie."

"Know them well?"

"How'd you guess?"

"Detective, remember?"

"Yes. Anyway, if Jamie wants to shoot, he has to turn up at a soirée." Allan smirked evilly. "They're going to invite you – not just Casey, the rest of you too – and Jamie wants to shoot all of you at it."

"Has *he* told Casey?"

"Is he still alive?"

"Yes, as of six this evening."

"Probably not." Allan raised his glass to Andy, who toasted him back, and they passed on to a discussion of theatre.

***

Casey dragged herself home. Not fifteen minutes after she'd arrived, Carval rapped on the door. He wrapped her in immediately, which was stupidly comforting and wholly necessary.

"You're tired."

She supposed Carval's comment covered the fact that now, with nobody to interrogate and no leads to chase, she had nothing to take her mind off her grief. "Yeah."

"Dinner?"

"I'm not hungry." She had no desire to eat – not even chocolate.

"I am," Carval said. "I'll order for me, and if you change your mind we'll share."

She shrugged. There was ice cream in the freezer – there was always chocolate ice cream in her freezer – and coffee, and those would do if she wanted to eat anything. Right now, she only wanted to curl up and forget everything.

"Renfrew interrogated me," Carval complained, after he'd ordered enough dinner to allow Casey to eat if she changed her mind. "He said he wanted to talk about the team bonds, 'cause he'd seen the show, but I think he's looking for something else. I don't know what, but I can't tell him anything more because it's all right there in the photos. I'm not wasting my time analysing those when he can go look again. But he'll probably ask you pretty soon."

"Great," Casey muttered. "At least we didn't have Marcol pushed on us," she added.

"Why would you have him?"

"Narcotics involvement. The dead guys were gang members, and their gangs deal in drugs."

"New people to shoot?" Carval enthused. "I'll be at the precinct in the morning. Who is he?"

"*She* is Detective Dani Handjiev. She'll be sitting with us, but hopefully she'll deal with DEA so we can ignore them and the FBI. God knows what Renfrew will make of it. Anyway, she seemed sensible. We'll get along fine – we *got* along fine."

"Who'd be dumb enough to force Marcol into this case?" Carval's brow wrinkled as he returned to the important point.

"Marcol himself, according to Dani."

"What the actual *fuck?*" Carval yelped. "What's he up to? I have hard evidence Birkett and Marcol lifted *my* photo and the PI proved months ago Marcol misused it. Why does he want to be within a hundred miles of you?"

"I don't know and I don't care. It's not happening so I'm not wasting time on him. I'd rather think about the case. I sure don't want to think about other things. But…" She peeped sidelong, uncertainly, from under her lashes. "Um…Kent ordered us to take vacation after this case is done."

"He did?" Carval waited, largely because he couldn't see where Casey might be going.

"Yeah. I'm sure he's thinking about benching me, but he hasn't – yet. Anyway, he ordered us all to take at least ten days." She peeped at him again; deep pink colouring her cheeks, a tiny tremor in her voice. "I thought maybe we could go away?"

Carval gaped at her, utterly dumbfounded. Her face fell as he failed to find words, so instead he hauled her in and kissed her until she squeaked and shoved at him.

"Air!" she gasped.

"Sorry. Did you mean that?"

"No, I meant let's find tadpoles and fry them for dinner."

"Ugh." He refocused. "Go on vacation? Together?"

"Don't you want to?" She shrank.

"Of course I want to! I never thought you'd suggest it. Where do you want to go? San Francisco, like we talked about a couple of months ago? Somewhere else? Hawaii? Outside the USA?"

"San Francisco," Casey decided. "Or anywhere, so I won't be here, moping."

"Sure," Carval bounced, and kissed her some more. "I'll fix it up and all you'll have to do is solve your case and meet me at the airport."

"I'll" –

"You won't pay. I'll take you on vacation. All you'll do is say *yes I'll go* and turn up with a suitcase of summer clothes and a pretty dress for dinner. Otherwise you'll fuss and fret and disagree with me." He pouted theatrically. "I don't like it when you argue. Leave it all to me and enjoy it."

Suddenly she conceded. "Okay. You fix it." It sounded more like exhaustion than enthusiasm, but he didn't care if it meant he could do what *he* wanted to set up their vacation. He'd include a good boutique hotel in central San Francisco, ice cream at Ghirardelli's, and general tourist behaviour. Sunshine, relaxation, and a long way from NYC.

"I will," he agreed smugly. "We'll have a great time." He tucked her in, and plopped a few casual kisses on her hair. She gave a funny little noise, and snuggled in, closing her eyes. Carval petted until her breathing had evened out into sleep, which took at least three minutes, realigned her to lean on the couch, then stood, picked her up, and deposited her on her own bed. He barely had time to sit down before his dinner arrived.

Casey woke, heard Carval having dinner, and decided not to join him. She didn't want to eat. She stripped, tugged on a sloppy tee, and slid under the bedcovers, smothering her face in the pillow and muffling her misery. If she were lucky, Carval wouldn't notice. She was exhausted, now that she'd stopped moving. Her work had held her together all day, but now that its pressure was gone, the fractured fragments of her composure were free to fly apart. She closed her eyes tightly, but salt water still leaked from them, no matter how hard she struggled to keep them dry. She tugged the covers further over her head, and gave up.

On the other side of the closed bedroom door, Carval half-heard an odd noise. He stopped wolfing down his dinner (he'd forgotten to eat lunch, submerged in his construction shots), and listened. Silence. He returned to sating his stomach, but the odd noise whispered across his ears again. He put his empty plate down, and waited. Suspicion wriggled its way into his mind.

Ah. There it was again, and this time Carval recognised it – after all, he'd heard Casey crying far too often as her father finally, fatally, fell, and afterwards. His first impulse was to burst into the bedroom, haul her up and cuddle her, while berating her for not turning to him for comfort. Berating was high up his list. She'd ignored everything he'd said the previous night about *wanting* to be there for her, and run off to cry on her own.

Fortunately, common sense intervened before Carval could discover how it felt to be turned into a colander, and shortly thereafter how it felt to be dead. While it stung – oh boy did it sting: it *hurt* – to watch her run away and hide her emotions, once he engaged his brain, not merely his feelings, it simply wasn't about him.

It might not be about him, but that didn't mean he couldn't get involved. He could still hear faint, half-suppressed sobbing. He gave Casey another couple of minutes while he cleared up his dinner, then softly entered her bedroom. All he could see was a mound under the covers, with a dark curl or two escaping. He sat down beside the lump, and gently patted it.

Casey's unhappy face emerged, still dripping tears. "It was okay when I was at work," she mumbled. "I didn't have time to remember." She sniffed damply, and rubbed already red eyes. "I let him die. I can't get past it."

"You couldn't save him. You did *more* than enough," Carval pointed out, trying and failing to hug her.

"I let him die," she wept again.

"You're talking complete fucking *nonsense!*" Carval snapped, instantly out of any patience with Casey's unwarranted guilt. "What were you supposed to do, lock him in a cell for the next thirty years so he couldn't drink? You couldn't stop him drinking because he didn't want to stop drinking, and that's the *only* reason he died. He knew – the doctors *told* him outright – if he didn't stop he'd die. He didn't stop."

"He wouldn't have kept drinking if I hadn't disappointed him."

"That's complete bullshit too. You didn't disappoint him and you didn't disappoint your mom. The only reason you think so is because your dad said a whole lot of drunken crap to you. He never said any of it before he drowned himself in a bottle, did he? Your mom never said any of it ever, did she?" He gulped in an infuriated breath, and hauled her to sitting. "I can take one look at the photograph of your Academy graduation and see they were both totally proud of you, so *stop* believing the drunken lies and start believing the truth!"

"He *said* I should've been a lawyer!"

"Yeah, he did. Right when he needed a lawyer for the court hearing, when he was still drunk! How don't you get it? He was too drunk to know anything about anything. He couldn't have added two and two, never mind known what he actually meant. It was all about that moment and him, and he was too drunk to care. If I'd been in front of him, he'd've said *I* should be a lawyer because that's all he could think about."

"You barely met him, so how do you know?" Casey flashed straight back.

"Because I met plenty of alcoholics shooting *Underbelly* – I told you that. They were all a mess. They couldn't think, they sure couldn't reason, and every single fucking one of them would have done or said absolutely anything so they didn't have to blame themselves for their own bad choices. Every. Single. One. No exceptions." He drew in air, and tried, not successfully, to calm down. "Sometimes one of them would say that's what they did. All of them blamed others, all the time." Another gulp of air. "Just like your dad blamed it on your mom dying and on you." His hands gripped her shoulders, consciously not shaking her back to her senses. "It's on him. It's *not on you* and you have to get it." He hesitated. "Your mom dying wasn't on you either. You said it was an accident."

"If it was an accident. Sure, she had a car crash. But..." Casey's words were lost in terrifying tears. From the storm, enough words emerged for Carval to understand that Casey was more than half convinced her mother had committed suicide, not had a fatal accident. "Dad was never the same again..."

"That's not down to you either!" Carval exploded. "She had cancer. You didn't cause it. You weren't responsible for her decisions *or* whether it was an accident or not. How could you be? You aren't responsible for other people's choices, and if you don't stop thinking you are, I'll get O'Leary to shake sense into you on the mats. Sure, you're grieving and miserable but that's *okay* because it's been a *week*. One fucking *week*. You shouldn't even be at work, you should take time off, but you won't because you never, ever, cut yourself any slack. None of this was your fault, but if you don't stop thinking it was, Renfrew'll spot it and you'll be analysed whether you like it or not, 'cause he'll go to Kent and insist."

"He can't force me."

"Kent can. He can bench you. He's already told you all to take ten days as soon as this case is done. Do you want to be pushed out for longer? You sure don't want to see Renfrew – or any other shrink."

"He can't force me," she repeated.

"Renfrew's already suspicious. He asked me if the team would – quote – 'adapt if one of its members required extra support'. He's watching. He knows – God knows how he guessed – your dad showed up and made trouble."

"He what?"

105

"He went to see the exhibition – you know that – and was stunned – so was McDonald," Carval boasted, distracted from his irritation by his success.

"McDonald?" Casey was equally distracted. "McDonald *approved?*"

"Sure did. Anyway, Renfrew asked me about the team's reactions, and I tried to be vague. He wasn't having it. He guessed your dad saw it and didn't like it. He's already on your case."

Casey bit out a short, pungent, and extremely vulgar comment about Renfrew. She had stopped crying, though, since tears had been replaced by anger, Carval wasn't sure the atmosphere would improve. Her normally cosy apartment currently felt cold and unwelcoming.

"I'm not talking about this any more." Casey slid down and pulled the covers over her head, turning away from Carval.

Well, her action was pretty clear. Carval took the brick applied to his head, and left Casey to herself, closing the door to her bedroom with a decided crack and not sorry about his display of temper.

CHAPTER THIRTEEN

Casey, having achieved precisely what she'd thought she wanted, immediately found she didn't like it. Shoving Carval away hadn't made her less miserable, and now she was alone with only her unpleasant, unwanted thoughts. She buried her face in her pillow, pulled the quilt further over her head and ears, and tried to shut out the world – and especially Carval's words. She didn't want words.

She wanted comfort.

And dumbass that she was, she'd pushed it away. Well, she'd stay here under her quilt and sleep.

Twenty-five restless minutes later, in which sleep receded further and further, and grief and guilt pushed into her roiling mind, she rose, wrapped herself in her oversized robe, drooped out into the main room – and stopped.

"You're still here?"

"Yeah."

Casey blinked hard for a second, trailed over to the couch and curled herself up beside him. Carval, disarmed by her bedraggled state, cuddled her, and didn't talk. Since Casey was doing her best to burrow into his ribcage, he wasn't sure she'd have heard. Anyway, he knew talking hadn't worked half an hour ago, and he wasn't inclined to provoke a further argument if Casey had come out to find comfort with him.

"Will you stay?" finally emerged from the folds of his shirt, in a vaguely apologetic, but wholly uncertain, wobble.

"Sure." He hoisted the bundle of Casey and robe into his lap, and left it at that. Shortly, he became aware of a dampish patch of t-shirt over his collarbone, though there was no sound. He petted, and cossetted, and let Casey deal with her grief as she preferred – silently, and without demands or attention-seeking company.

107

But not – shouldn't it be *no longer*, he thought – alone.

Casey remained still and silent against him for some considerable time, taking warmth and ease from Carval's broad body and faint aroma of cologne, determinedly not thinking about anything. Not Carval's words, not her own misery, not the strange, soothing feeling of being *taken care of*. Thinking wasn't her friend, tonight. It wouldn't be her friend tomorrow either, but that was another day.

"Bed time," Carval murmured. "You'll want to work the case tomorrow."

"Yeah…" She didn't sound convinced. "Stay?"

"I will, unless you want me to go." He stroked softly over her tangled curls and down her back. "You don't need to be alone."

***

When Casey reached her desk, before the rest of her team arrived, there was another copy of one of the press articles. She crumpled it up and fired it into the trash, made herself a double espresso and started with the database runs.

Well, well, well. Maria Montelucci was originally from Chicago. Hmmm. Casey didn't think that was coincidence. She read on, and found, to her complete lack of surprise, Maria was related to the Pagliaccis. The last thing she needed, she thought bitterly, was another Shakespearean tragedy. *Romeo and Juliet* should stay firmly on the stage and a long way away from Casey.

As should Renfrew, but that mercy was denied her. What was he doing here so early? She'd only wanted a little bit of time to ponder before Dani showed up, and here was Renfrew ruining her day before it had begun.

"Detective Clement, good morning."

"Hey." Sadly, Renfrew wasn't deterred by the unwelcoming tone.

"Before you work on your case, I should like to discuss your views of Mr Carval's exhibition."

"That won't be possible. I'm expecting Detective Handjiev in a moment. We've got a lot to do today." Casey tapped her screen. "Buster's girlfriend was connected to the Pagliaccis, and it was a Pagliacci who shot him, Crusher, and Mrs Hercliffe – though he was almost certainly aiming at someone else."

"Paddy Hocking," O'Leary put in from behind her. "We stuffed him into the databases last night too. Anythin' come out?"

"I haven't checked, 'cause I didn't know you'd identified him as the third man and were running him."

Renfrew coughed. "When might either of you have a free moment?"

"Let's see how the case goes. That's my priority." As Casey spoke, Tyler and Andy appeared, followed by Detective Handjiev, who made straight for Casey. "Hey, Dani. Come meet the team." Casey introduced her, and found

108

her a conveniently close desk. Renfrew, thwarted, retreated to his conference room after being introduced, trailing Bergen (who seemed a tad disappointed to be removed) behind him.

"Overnight," Casey told Dani, "the databases have told us Beau's girlfriend, Maria Montelucci, was related to the Pagliaccis."

Dani swore, mostly under her breath. "*West Side Story?*" emerged from the dark muttering.

"I thought *Romeo and Juliet*, but it's all the same thing."

"Same story," Andy pontificated. "*West Side Story* was an updated musical version, but anyone cultured would go to see Shakespeare." On meeting Casey's glare, he retreated.

"Andy does high culture," Casey explained. "He's boring about popular culture."

"I can hear you," Andy said. Casey made a face at him. Dani grinned.

"Instead of complaining about my lack of culture, did you get the street and building footage to try to trace the shooter's car?"

"No. I'll chase up that before I start anything else."

"Okay." Casey turned back to Dani. "One more person you should meet – Feggetter. He's the one who gave me all the background gossip."

"Sure."

Casey introduced them, then gestured across the bullpen. "Those four there are the officers we're using. They're pretty good."

"Okay. I'll leave them to you, though – they're yours. No treading on toes here," she smiled.

Casey smiled back. "What about DEA?" she asked. "Who's your contact there?"

Dani thought for a moment. "Best option is Agent Glencross, who's been after the Pagliaccis for months, but I'll see who's available and talk to Dr Renfrew."

"There was one weird thing," Casey said, "they both had ID that was obviously not theirs. Have you seen that before? As soon as we put their prints in we got their correct ID, so what was the point?"

"No, I haven't seen it. Weird," she agreed. "I'd better go suggest to Renfrew we should try for Agent Glencross." Dani strode off, not noticeably enthused by the prospect of talking to Renfrew.

While Casey had been introducing Dani to Feggetter, Andy and Tyler had been examining camera footage, to which they shortly summoned O'Leary's attention. His huge form stiffened as he watched.

"Casey know about this?"

"Nah."

"I'm not telling her."

"Good plan," O'Leary said. "What'll we do with it?" He waited expectantly. "I get it," he grumbled. "You want me to decide, 'cause Casey won't shoot me an' Kent won't throw me out."

"Yep," Andy said.

"Waal, an' what if I won't?" he teased, edged with acid.

"I will." Tyler stepped up.

"Aw, I guess I'd better. Gimme it on a thumb drive? Or, better, get Bergen to take it off an' confirm you ain't been messin' with it. I'll go see Kent. You doin' the same all the time?"

"One little camera."

"Sneaky," O'Leary approved. "Very sneaky." He noticed Casey returning. "How long'll those cameras take?"

"I'm chasing," Andy said irritably, "at least if you stopped chattering and let me work."

"Okay, okay." O'Leary lumbered off to have a word with Bergen, who blinked, bared his teeth, and shortly received a thumb drive from Andy, which he bore off before Casey could spot it. Andy emitted happy noises as he received footage, which he shared with Tyler.

"Waal, I'll look into Hocking, iffen you're lookin' at Maria," O'Leary suggested to Casey.

"Okay. I'll find out where Maria hangs out, and we'll go talk to her. Dani can come if she wants, though she might want to brief her DEA contact." Casey's face twisted. "Renfrew wants to talk about the exhibition."

"Good time to be elsewhere."

"Yeah." Casey remembered something. "Maybe Dani can track down Pieter Wiedecz."

"That'd help. You go talk to her."

Casey did, coming back to find that the databases had spat out Maria's address. "Dani'll look up Wiedecz, but she'll liaise with DEA and Renfrew this morning. She'll text me anything she finds."

"Who will?" asked Carval, appearing as if by magic.

"I thought you were shooting construction sites?" Casey queried.

"Not today. It's raining and I don't like getting wet."

"That's why they invented raincoats."

"I can't shoot with a hood up!" Carval argued. "So I'm here."

"Okay. We're going witness chasing. You can come, if you like." Casey didn't say *because it'll help me*, so Carval couldn't have explained why he heard it.

"Yep. I still haven't had anything from the Finisterres," he sulked. "I wanna shoot in theatres too."

"Ain't we enough for you?" O'Leary teased.

110

"The more I do, the more I can do," Carval said. "I like having more than one project on the go." He looked around. "Who's that?" He gestured.

"Our Narcotics liaison. Detective Handjiev."

"She'll be a total contrast," Carval mused, raising his camera. "Yeah…yeah…that'll be good…. Yep."

"Don't you think you should ask her first?" Casey suggested. "Like, get her permission before you shoot her?"

"I guess." Carval agreed, and instantly approached Dani. Casey followed, to smooth over the likely difficulties – more accurately, to make sure he didn't upset Dani. "Hey. I wanna shoot you," he announced.

Dani gaped. "What?" *The hell* was clearly bitten off the end of her exclamation.

"I wanna shoot you," Carval repeated impatiently. "You'll be a total contrast to Casey and I wanna shoot it."

"Have you been smoking something?"

Casey thought she'd better intervene. "He's Carval. Little things like introductions don't always occur to him. He's the one who photo'd us for the exhibition – *Murder on Manhattan*. You don't have to let him shoot you, though."

"You'd be famous. I'm the best."

"Not at humility," Dani pointed out, and she and Casey smirked at each other.

"Can I shoot you or not?" Carval returned to his point.

Dani shrugged. "Sure. Doesn't matter to me. I don't do undercover work."

Carval's camera clicked immediately. Dani flung a harried glare at Casey, who simply smirked more widely. "You agreed," she said. Carval flicked around and caught the smirk. Casey glowered. "We're going to find Maria," she snipped.

"I'll catch up with Agent Glencross."

"I'm going with you," Carval said to Casey.

"Okay."

Half an hour later, O'Leary pulled up at a small apartment block, in which the cops hoped to find Maria Montelucci and Carval hoped to find some good shots. He'd hoped for a chance to hug Casey, but that wasn't a possibility when she was working. He hunched his shoulders against the driving rain. June shouldn't be rainy, he decided. Though if it was still raining tomorrow, maybe he'd get some interesting shots of water on the rising steel frames of his chosen sites.

Casey rapped on the door, not expecting an answer. Maria could easily be out meeting friends, shopping, or simply out. To her astonishment, the lock turned over, and the door opened as far as its safety chain would allow.

A tiny, dark, mid-twenties woman peeked around the door. "Hi?" she questioned.

"Detectives Clement and O'Leary, NYPD." Casey showed her shield. "Maria Montelucci? Can we come in, please?"

"Uh, sure." She peeked again. "Who's he?"

"He's the photographer, but he'll only take shots if you're okay with it."

"Can he take a couple of good ones?" Maria didn't register that he might have been a police photographer. "I'd like them for my boyfriend."

"Could we come in, please?" Casey repeated. Maria opened the door fully, and waved them in, barely registering surprise at O'Leary's size.

"Why are you here?" she asked.

"Miss Montelucci, do you know Beau Resorge?"

"Oh, sure. He's my boyfriend," she disclosed happily. Casey suddenly realised Maria wasn't the sharpest chisel in the toolbox, and that she had no idea Beau had been killed. Well, *hell*. The next few minutes wouldn't be any fun. "We're going out to the movies tonight. We haven't decided what to see. Maybe Transformers, or the Mummy, but I'd like to see Wonder Woman and I think Beau would like it too." She smiled innocently, looking close to sixteen, not twenty-something.

"Miss Montelucci" –

"Call me Maria," she interrupted.

"Maria, I have some bad news for you. I'm sorry to tell you that Beau was killed on Wednesday."

"Killed? No! Not Beau. He – everyone loves him. He doesn't have a mean bone in his body. He's so sweet. He's not dead." Her eyes filled. "You're – you're not cops. You're from my family, trying to make me think he's gone so I won't see him any more. Well, you're *lying*. I don't believe you! Beau'll be here to pick me up at seven like we agreed."

"We really are NYPD detectives," O'Leary rumbled. "I'm sorry for your loss."

"I don't *believe* you!" Maria almost stamped her foot.

"Maria, we can take you to see Beau's body" –

"No! It's not true!" she howled. "It's not *true!*" She burst into hysterical weeping. "It's not! Tell me it's not true…"

Casey, less likely to break fragile household items such as kettles and coffeemakers than O'Leary, went to make hot, sweet tea to cushion the shock – and calm Maria enough that they could question her. The reference she'd made to her family was clue enough for them to investigate a line of feuding families, and Maria didn't have the smarts that Tarticca did.

As she waited for the water to boil, raiding the pretty china jars on the counter for tea or coffee and sugar, her phone chirped, providing Pieter Wiedecz's address and, unusually, a phone number. Dani's accompanying note said that DEA had run across his phone number in a previous case, and now passed it on with their compliments and a request to interrogate if Casey brought Wiedecz in. She could arrange it. Favour for a favour.

A moment or two later she took through hot drinks, with plenty of sugar in Maria's, and sat down beside her. Maria was still sobbing uncontrollably, but she took the tea and drank some. Her shock and tears ebbed a little.

Casey consciously adopted a soothing, older-sister tone. "Tell us about Beau," she encouraged. "He sounds like a nice boy."

Maria snuffled, and drank another gulp of tea. "He's totally sweet. He looks after me really well. He doesn't let anyone be nasty. He's big, but he's never scary. Nobody bothers me when he's around."

"Sounds great," O'Leary rumbled in a similarly soothing fashion, from a chintz-covered armchair. "Like a better big brother?"

"Much better than a big brother," Maria dripped, wringing a Kleenex in her fingers. "My brother's a pain in the butt. Always telling me what to do and how to do it. Beau never did. Gio didn't like Beau, either. Always saying I shouldn't date him and how it was" – her face scrunched up – "disrespecting the family."

"What did he mean?" Casey asked. "Beau made you happy. Didn't they want you to be happy?"

"They wanted me to go with some nice boy Uncle Federico thought would be good for me." Maria pouted. "I don't want some nice boy who'll never do anything the family doesn't want. I want my own life, not their life! Beau and I can have a nice life of our own where everyone isn't telling us what to do and where to be." She started to sob. "We got it all planned out. Lots of places use big guys to fetch and carry, and I can work in day-care, and we'll get married and have a family, somewhere out of the city." She sipped her drink defiantly.

"Why would any of your family object?"

"Beau wasn't one of them. Uncle Federico" –

"You mean Federico Tarticca?"

"Yes. He's not exactly my uncle but he's some sort of relative and I've always called him uncle – he said I should stick to our own kind and Beau wasn't one of us."

"What did he mean?" Casey matched Maria's sips, establishing rapport.

"Oh, he was always trashing anyone who wasn't our family or our cousins in Chicago. He was real big on family, but I don't get how family included Pieter or Sasha or the other guys. They aren't Italian-American either, so I don't see how they're family and anyway I like *Beau!* I don't like any of them."

"Who's Pieter?" O'Leary picked up. "He sure don't sound Italian-American to me either."

"He's Uncle Federico's assistant."

"Do you know his last name?"

"Wiedecz. I call him Wiedick, because he is. He's a total asshat. No way I was dating him. Beau's much nicer and he's totally sweet to me."

Both Casey and O'Leary noticed that Maria hadn't once referred to Beau in the past tense.

"Pieter wanted to date you?"

"Only because it would get him in good with Uncle Federico," Maria spat. "I hated him."

"What did he think of Beau?"

"Hates him, but he never says why. I don't think he has a good reason."

"Maria, did you know Beau was a member of the Yarrabees organisation?"

"Who?"

"The Yarrabees," Casey repeated. Her opinion of Maria's intelligence hadn't been high, and was currently passing through mediocre on its way to low. How could she be this naïve? "They're a" – she abruptly changed her word choice to match Maria's apparent level of understanding – "gang."

"Beau? Beau doesn't work for a gang. Why would he? He moves boxes. He doesn't run drugs or beat people up or anything like that. He's a good guy."

"Do you know what your uncle Federico does?" O'Leary asked.

"He's in business. I think he supplies medical stuff. He doesn't talk about it."

Casey and O'Leary exchanged glances. Telling Maria her uncle was – allegedly – another organised crime boss wouldn't improve anything.

"And Pieter's his main man?"

"Yeah."

"Where were you on Thursday morning?"

"I was at the day-care centre, working. It's on 144th Street. I love working with tinies. I do the baby room. I've been there for five years."

"Nice," O'Leary agreed. "Babies are cute."

Casey didn't comment. Babies were not cute. Babies bawled, vomited, and created dirty diapers. Babies, in her view, were someone else's problem until they became adults. However, Maria had an alibi, which Adamo could go check on Monday.

"Can you tell me a bit more about Pieter?" she asked. He was coming up in conversation relatively often – his car, Tarticca denying all knowledge, and now he'd wanted to date Maria, who had passed him over for Beau despite Tarticca's support for Pieter.

"I don't like him." Maria's miserable face twisted. "He's mean. Uncle Federico thinks he's so great because he ass-kisses him every day, but he's mean. He's always picking on younger employees. He hassles all the girls, too."

"You?"

"Beau won't ever let him, but Uncle Federico never left us alone anyway." She managed a tearful smirk. "I never let him."

"Would Pieter have tried to beat up Beau?"

"He might've, but he'd never manage it," Maria said proudly. "Anyway, Pieter likes guns. He's always playing with his gun, and threatening to shoot anyone who looks at him wrong."

Behind them, forgotten and unnoticed, Carval tried not to burst into inappropriate laughter.

"What gun does he have?" Casey asked.

"Oh, he was trying to impress me telling me about all sorts. I didn't listen."

"Try to remember," O'Leary encouraged.

"Will it help Beau?"

"Yes."

Maria finally caught the tone in Casey's voice. "Is he really dead?" Maria whimpered, fat tears trickling back down her cheeks.

"I'm afraid so," Casey said. "I'm sorry."

Maria fell apart again. Casey basely left O'Leary to console her under the guise of making more tea, and when she returned found that, from O'Leary's wiggle of eyebrows, he'd extracted some more information.

"Sure," O'Leary wound up. "Gimme your cell number, an' I'll make sure you get to see him to say goodbye."

CHAPTER FOURTEEN

"What did you get?" Casey asked as she scrambled into the passenger side of O'Leary's SUV.

"Waal, she wasn't too sure, but it sounds like he has a coupla handguns an' mebbe a rifle."

"Let's get Tyler checking." She paused, thinking. "Should we call Wiedecz and ask him nicely to come in for a chat?"

"Pretendin' he ain't a good suspect?"

"Yeah. If this was about Beau" –

"You don't think it is" –

"No, but if it was, why shoot Crusher and especially why aim for Hocking? It wasn't even Wiedecz who did the shooting."

"That's no problem. He could just've asked a pal to do it for him."

"We still need to talk to him. Should we try a call first, soften him up a little?" she asked again.

"Naw. He'll already know. Tarticca'll've called him ten seconds after we left his office yesterday, so it ain't goin' to be any use to try 'n' be soft an' cuddly."

"You're right."

"Course I am," O'Leary said smugly. "So, we're goin' over? You got an address?"

"Yep." She read it off, and O'Leary turned towards it. "While we're getting there, we ought to make sure he doesn't sneak out the back while we're at the front. I'll get Fremont and Larson to cover the fire exit."

"'Kay."

***

"O'Leary didn't go see Kent," Andy complained. "Guess we better."

"Bergen checked it?"

116

"Yeah." Andy regarded Tyler with dispirited cynicism. "He'll shoot the messenger, won't he?"

"Likely."

"Bergen told Renfrew about it, didn't he?"

"Likely."

"Toss you for seeing Kent?"

Tyler grimaced, but produced a quarter from his pocket. "Heads," he chose, and spun.

"Tails it is. You get to be executed." Andy sighed in relief. "You're better at it anyway." He passed the thumb drive to Tyler, who stared at it with all the enthusiasm he would have had if it were a live, slimy slug. He marched off in perfect dress-parade style, every inch of his ramrod-straight spine indicating his absolute loathing of the next few minutes.

"Come in," Kent rapped. "Detective Tyler." He frowned. "Close the door." Tyler obeyed. "I assume this is yet another issue relating to Detective Clement. Does she know you're here?"

"No, sir."

"Why are you here, and why have you not told her?"

"You ordered us to report any trouble, sir."

Kent didn't appreciate the barrack lawyer answer, but didn't pursue it. "What 'trouble'?"

"This, sir," Tyler said tersely, and handed over the thumb drive.

"Expand."

Tyler didn't squirm, but only because he'd spent years in the Army preserving perfect blandness in the face of authority.

"After Bartlett, rigged a camera. Caught someone."

"You did *what?*"

"Bergen confirms it's not altered." Tyler ignored Kent's bellow.

"You rigged a camera *inside* the bullpen?"

"Harassing Casey's not acceptable, sir." Tyler didn't say *and you won't let us take them on the mats*, but his face conveyed it.

"This is useless as evidence."

"Confirmatory. Could have sat there with body cams, sir."

"You'll do no such thing. Dismissed."

Tyler executed a smart parade turn, and marched out, noting that Kent had not ordered him to remove the camera.

Kent was infuriated by the implication that he couldn't find out who was harassing Clement without the assistance of some frankly unreasonable methods of discovery. Surreptitious footage couldn't be relied upon and most likely wouldn't pass the union rep. He was, nevertheless, content to let the camera run, now he was aware of it. Had the team asked him first, he might even have approved it.

He watched the footage, swore vilely at his laptop, checked the staffing roster, then summoned Dr Renfrew and Bergen for a brief discussion.

**

Casey and O'Leary briefed their officers at the base of Wiedecz's utilitarian block.

"Fremont, you and Larson wait at the fire exit. If he's in, we don't want him getting away." They took up their positions.

Carval had slipped out of the SUV without comment, ready to follow Casey and O'Leary, taking a few shots of their set, hard faces. He'd never followed them to a hostile witness before, but now he had the chance for a new set of shots.

Wiedecz's apartment was on the first floor: the hall, originally painted cream, greying with age, dull under the harsh fluorescent lighting. Casey took one side of the flimsy door, out of sight of the spyhole, O'Leary in front. Carval stayed well out of the way, and shot their positions, their increasingly harsh visages. O'Leary stretched out a ham-hand and thumped.

Shuffling behind the door indicated someone was home. The footsteps came closer: there was a pause while someone peered through the spyhole, then walked away again without opening the door. Casey thought grimly that Tarticca had described O'Leary's size, and silently swore.

"He knows it's us."

O'Leary thumped again. "Pieter Wiedecz! NYPD! Open the door! We have some questions for you." Still no answer. He flicked a glance at Casey. "Force it open?"

"Yeah."

"Okay. You go low."

"You have to go high."

O'Leary grinned sharply at her. "Vest tight?"

"Yep. You?"

He nodded.

Carval lifted his camera to shoot continuously.

"Okay," Casey whispered. "On my signal." She raised her hand with three fingers extended, counting down silently. "Three…two…one" – they hit the door together, guns raised, and it tore like perforated paper. She saw Wiedecz, gun in hand, aiming right at them: time slowed as she yelled, "Police! Drop the gun." He didn't. She could see his finger tighten on the trigger: she went left, O'Leary right; Wiedecz tracked O'Leary, who swore vilely as a bullet scored his bicep. Casey fired as Wiedecz shot at her and missed by an inch.

Wiedecz fell, dead.

Carval captured the whole sequence and, without thinking, took shots of the dead man too, then spun away and exited precipitately. Casey hadn't flinched from firing: focused only on Wiedecz, even when O'Leary had yowled and cursed.

He'd never seen a kill shot before.

He never wanted to see one again. All their training, all their expertise…and here and now it led only to death. He stumbled out of the building. He'd watched – he'd *shot* – life leaving the man, and now all he wanted to do was forget.

Casey hadn't hesitated, and there Wiedecz was, dead on the floor. She stared at the body, and sat down hard, back against the wall. In her nine years on the job, she'd never shot someone dead before. She *wouldn't* throw up. Vomiting was for rookies. Acid burning crawled up her throat, but she swallowed it.

"Thanks," O'Leary gritted out, distracting her. "C'n you tie up my arm? Sonofabitch creased me."

"ER for you." Casey pulled herself together and called Fremont. "Can Larson bring some padding and a bandage? One of you needs to take O'Leary to the ER to get checked out. I'm fine" – O'Leary regarded her dead-white face sceptically – "but I need to call this in. Wiedecz's dead." She looked around, and didn't see Carval. Right now, she was relieved.

"Yes'm," Fremont said. Within three minutes, he and Larson had arrived and bandaged O'Leary. "We're getting good at this. Last time it was a knife." O'Leary muttered darkly at the officers, who simply smiled at him. "Eight stitches, wasn't it?" O'Leary muttered some more.

"One of you take him to the ER, one of you stay here with me."

"I'll take him, ma'am." Larson helped O'Leary to his feet and propped him up until his dizziness receded. "Where are your keys?"

"Pocket." O'Leary winced as he pulled them out. Larson shepherded him away.

"Take Carval with you," Casey called. "He can stay with O'Leary in the ER." She didn't want Carval here. If he were here, she might give in to her terrifying need to lean on him, and if she did…she might fall apart. She'd *killed* a man. Lawfully and on duty – but she'd *killed someone*. It was nothing like training, nothing like the movies. Death was swift and ugly, at the muzzle of her gun.

"What do we do, ma'am?" Fremont asked.

"I call Kent." Casey dialled. "Sir, it's Clement. Pieter Wiedecz – a witness in our case – shot at us, creased O'Leary – and I shot him dead."

"I see. Where are you?"

"At Wiedecz's apartment" – she gave the address – "and Fremont is with me. Larson is taking O'Leary to the ER, sir."

"Wait there until the shooting team arrive, Clement, then do exactly what they tell you. Don't disturb anything."

"Sir." She swiped off, and sat back down on the floor, not looking at the trickle of blood spreading from Wiedecz's unmoving chest, his eyes dull in death, body lax. "We can't do anything till the shooting team get here." She stared into space. "Why'd he fire? That was plain dumb. He knew we were cops. How'd he think he could get away with it? Was he just that trigger-happy? We know he didn't shoot the Yarrabees, so why'd he act like he did?"

"Maybe he didn't think the same."

"Obviously," Casey retorted. Her eyes fell on the corpse, and the blood, and she swallowed convulsively. *So much blood.* That had been her father, not Wiedecz. "Don't move," she snapped at Fremont, and dashed out of the apartment, gulping in air, desperately trying to blank the memory of her father's blood-splattered apartment, the night he'd died. She leaned on the windowsill at the end of the corridor, and forced herself not to throw up.

She could deal with this. Breathe in, breathe out; breathe in, breathe out. Her heart rate slowed. She forced herself to go back into the apartment, but her hands still trembled. Fremont glanced at her, opened his mouth, then shut it firmly. Not another word was spoken until the shooting team turned up, took Casey's gun, secured the scene, breathalysed her, and sent her back to the precinct to write her statement. O'Leary, they told her, could have his turn when he'd finished in the ER.

***

Casey walked in and went straight to her desk, not exchanging a word or glance with anyone. Tyler and Andy swapped concerned looks, but when she started to type at machine-gun speed, didn't interrupt. On catching their gestures, nor did Dani.

Twenty-odd minutes later, she saved, printed, and trudged to Kent's office with her statement.

"Sir?"

"Clement. Come in, and close the door."

"Sir," she said dispiritedly.

Kent flicked through the pages. "Nice and clear. There should be no trouble." He examined her. "Have you ever shot a man before?"

"No, sir." She swallowed, memory rising on a tide of bile.

"Contrary to popular belief, most cops haven't." Kent examined Clement again, noting her green-tinged complexion and the strain underlying it. "You've dealt with a lot in the last few weeks." He frowned at her. "You are ordered to see Dr Renfrew to discuss the shooting and *any*" – his emphasis was profound – "matters which pertain to your present state of mind."

"But" –

"Ordered, Clement. And as soon as this case is over you are taking ten days' vacation, as I previously ordered." He saw mutiny rising in her eyes, and condescended to explain further. "If you talk to Dr Renfrew, you don't have to leave the precinct and you won't lose any time. I'm sure he takes medical confidentiality extremely seriously. He won't disclose anything that any other therapist wouldn't."

"Sir," Casey surrendered.

"Dismissed."

She went straight past her desk to the restroom, where she retched from her empty stomach until she thought her toenails would appear. When the spasms finally ceased, she sat back on her heels, leaning on the cubicle wall, and wondered if it wouldn't be easier to ask Kent for leave starting right now. It was almost irresistibly tempting.

However, she remembered Tania Hercliffe's devastation, Maria's utter misery, and the bullet that had grazed O'Leary. She wouldn't let them down. She wouldn't pass her responsibilities off. They deserved better from her, and thoughts of quitting were pathetic. She wouldn't let herself down.

She didn't consciously think *like I let my dad down*. If it had been conscious, she might have noticed it. Instead, it coiled poisonously in the recesses of her mind, waiting. She washed her face, swilled out her mouth, and was ready to face the bullpen.

"Casey?" Dani said from the door. "What the hell?"

"I'm fine," she replied reflexively.

"Like a cow is fine when it's ground beef? You're green. It doesn't suit you."

"I don't need make-up advice."

"You need something. I guess you don't want to talk about it, but I don't want to hit any sore spots without knowing."

"Shot someone earlier. First time I've taken the kill shot. He was shooting at us. O'Leary's in the ER – winged," she added quickly.

"'Kay."

"So now I've got no gun till they decide if it was justified."

"Sucks."

"Yeah."

"When I did it, I went home and cuddled my partner for a while."

Casey blinked.

"I only had to take the shot once, but once is enough." Memory flashed painfully through Dani's face. "I saw the shrink, after. It helped." She met Casey's eyes. "Don't turn it down. It comes back at unexpected times. I took a while to get to the shrink. When I had the shakes and bad thoughts, I knew I should've gone earlier." Her lips pinched. "Don't be dumb. Waiting didn't help. Time didn't help."

"I hear you," Casey said. Both of them knew it wasn't agreement, but Dani had the sense not to push the point. "Let's get to work."

Casey had barely finished giving Dani the full download on the morning when O'Leary lumbered in, a little pale and lacking the sleeve with which his right arm had started the day. The sleeve had been replaced by packing and gauze. "Got winged. Casey put him down."

"How many stitches this time?" Andy asked. "I thought we'd agreed you wouldn't get sliced up for sandwiches."

"None," O'Leary growled. "Pete's goin' to kill me anyways."

"Pete?" Dani asked.

"His husband," Casey explained. "Did you bring Carval back with you?"

"Naw. He took a million shots in the ER, but he went home to download an' likely take a coupla antacids. He was green." O'Leary examined Casey's complexion, and didn't say *so are you* aloud. The team heard it anyway. "C'n we go get lunch?"

"We got ours, with Bergen." Andy's gesture encompassed Tyler and Dani. "You two go eat."

"Red meat," Tyler gibed. "Replace the blood."

"C'mon, before I die of not laughin'," O'Leary flicked out, and was instantly flipped the bird by Tyler as he and Casey left.

"Food truck?" Casey asked.

"Naw. Let's go sit down at Kitchenette. I'm starvin' an' they do good food."

"Okay, but don't walk too fast."

"Bit shaky-like?" O'Leary looked down at Casey's crumpled form.

"Yeah," she admitted.

"Talk about it when we're there," he reassured. "We could call your boy, too?"

"No...not yet," she amended. Her face twisted, but she stayed quiet until they reached Kitchenette and were seated by a bored server. "Coffee, please." O'Leary raised his eyebrows. "I want coffee," she clipped. He shrugged, almost knocking into a wall light.

"I'll have coffee too, and c'n we get the lunch menu? I know we're a li'l late, but it's been a busy mornin'." He smiled cheerfully at the server, who considered the risks of refusing a Bigfoot and brought two menus along with water. O'Leary tipped down a full glass, followed by two more refills. "ER said I had to," he explained.

"You were lucky," Casey said. "Where'd I find another partner if" – she stopped, and clutched at a napkin, hiding her face.

"Nobody else'd have you," O'Leary joshed. "Proper li'l spitfire, you. Nobody'd dare."

Casey's damp eyes flashed. "Nobody'd have you if I wasn't around, you big lump."

"I ain't no lump. I'm a marvel."

"Yeah. Marvel's Hulk."

"Now you're not as green as the Hulk, an' you're not goin' to cry all down my stylish clothes. Havin' one sleeve's goin' to be a fashion statement before you c'n blink. Think you c'n eat? You looked rough before we came out."

"Okay."

They ordered briskly.

"Now," O'Leary said, "that wasn't no fun for either of us. We'll go to the Abbey tonight, drink beer an' be the team – Carval too, before you make faces at me – an' you 'n' me c'n talk about it iffen we want to, an' not iffen we don't."

"Kent *ordered* me to see Renfrew," Casey emitted. "As a shrink."

"Waal, *that's* no fun either. Why're you bein' therapized?"

"Shooting." O'Leary merely looked at her. "And likely Dad."

"Huh."

Their lunches arrived. Casey hadn't ordered much, and ate slowly; O'Leary, awkwardly one-handed, packed away a huge lunch, and perused the dessert menu.

"C'mon, there's choc'late here," he enticed. Casey paused. "Settle your stomach. I know you been throwin' up."

"I never shot anyone dead before," Casey mumbled.

"An' I ain't never shot anyone dead ever, but iffen he'd aimed at you 'stead of me I'd'a been you an' you'd'a been me in the ER. Though you're so li'l, he'd likely have missed you." Casey regarded him soggily. "Now ain't no time to be talkin' about it, like I said. Have some dessert, an' drink your coffee, an' we'll go back an' do somethin' useful with your Dani from Narcotics."

"Only if we can avoid Renfrew," Casey bit. "He'll be chasing us all about the exhibition too."

"Waal, there's a Duane Reed practic'lly on our way, an' I'm sure they sell emetics…" O'Leary waggled his eyebrows and smirked.

"I don't think so." Casey cheered up under O'Leary's nonsense and teasing. "We're not in high school now."

"Naw," O'Leary agreed with an evil grin. "C'mon, time to pay the check an' go."

***

Back in the bullpen, Dani, Andy and Tyler hurried to tell Casey and O'Leary that they'd managed to trace the shooter's car – Wiedecz's car – to a parking garage close to Wiedecz's apartment.

"So that's what set him off," O'Leary suggested. "He thought we'd already found his car."

"Sent Larson and Henegan to search it."

"Okay. CSU joining them?"

Tyler nodded.

"Should be interesting," Andy said. "Wonder what they'll find to start someone shooting without even saying *hi*."

"Yeah. It doesn't seem enough." Casey turned to Dani. "What did DEA say?"

"Nothing about Maria. They don't think she's in the business – she doesn't have the smarts."

"That tracks. She didn't seem too bright. We'll check her alibi, but she said she worked at a day-care centre. What else?" Casey cocked her head with interest.

"Wiedecz was a real bad guy. Second-in-command to Tarticca, and the main liaison with the Pagliaccis."

"Light dawns," Andy opined. "He lent his car to the Pagliacci who fired." He consulted his notes. "Grappano. Mm. I feel a request for Wiedecz's phone records arriving."

"Okay, we know Grappano shot them," Casey said, "so we know who our perpetrator is, which is a nice change. Can we track *him*, instead of the car?"

"We can try," Andy said. "We *are* trying. But after he left the parking lot, he turned into an alley and disappeared. We've put out a BOLO for him, and we've requested more camera footage, but it's a long shot."

"Have we tried for cameras near the Tarticcas' hangout?" Casey asked. "He might have gone back there."

"On it." Andy tapped his keyboard.

"None of this gives us any idea *why* Grappano was shooting. I don't believe it was about Maria, or someone would have taken Beau out neatly, not in a messy drive-by."

"I agree," Dr Renfrew said.

CHAPTER FIFTEEN

Nobody obviously winced at Renfrew's entrance, but nobody was pleased to see him. "I have, together with Agent Glencross, communicated with the FBI and DEA offices in Chicago." He steepled his fingers. Casey, filled with a desire to shoot them off, touched her belt – and remembered that her gun had been taken by the shooting team. She shivered. Renfrew, of-freaking-course, noticed. She *knew* he was storing it up for later.

"What did you conclude?" Casey asked.

"We have not concluded anything," Renfrew chided. Casey bristled. "We hypothesise that Mr Grappano is 'on retainer' to the Tarticcas, giving them plausible deniability."

"We already got that far," Andy muttered. Tyler made a *shut-up* gesture, though his expression agreed.

"We further hypothesise that the Tarticcas are attempting to execute a take-over of the Yarrabees' business, by stoking a 'gang war'." Renfrew's lips pinched at the colloquialism.

"We thought that too," Andy grumbled.

"I am sure you did," Renfrew said. "This team is perfectly capable of logical reasoning."

The team didn't take it as a compliment: if Renfrew had meant it as such, the patronising tone robbed it of any measure of praise.

"However, while you are understandably focused on the two murders" –

"Three," Casey corrected. "Tania Hercliffe wanted to keep her baby. Grappano killed her hope."

Renfrew made a peculiar face, but didn't comment. Casey expected that *yet* was the correct suffix to his lack of comment, judging by his tight lips.

"Three. While you focus on those crimes, the FBI, DEA and Detective Handjiev must take a far wider view." Dani didn't look flattered to be included in the federal group. "If a hostile takeover of the Yarrabees is indeed planned, we must aim to prevent it, and to 'throw a wrench in the works' of as many of these organised crime groups as possible." He pushed up his pince-nez. "Should you discover information which might assist us, I should be obliged if you would share it with us at the first opportunity, as in previous cases. I shall, of course, ensure that all relevant information is shared with you equally rapidly, and, if you wish any profiling to be done, I will be delighted to do so." He smiled avuncularly. "It is a pleasure to work with you all again."

Casey mumbled something in response, which couldn't have been said to be enthusiastic reciprocation.

"Now, to exchange information, Detective Clement, I should like to talk to you about Pieter Wiedecz."

"Sure," Casey replied with commendable coolness. "I'll join you in a couple of minutes."

"Certainly." Renfrew retired to his conference room. Dani went to her borrowed desk.

Casey looked at the team, who closed in around her. "Abbey, at shift end," she said.

"Good." Tyler nodded once. "Carval?"

"Him too. Call him for me? Renfrew won't wait." She made a quick restroom stop, and went to beard Renfrew in his den. Behind her Tyler, not wasting his limited supply of words, texted Carval, noting that Casey had asked him to.

***

"Allan? Allan?" Allan heard Jamie trudging up the stairs and poking himself into Allan's tidy office below the studio. "Are you here?"

"Yes." He emerged from his chair. "What is it – Jamie, what's happened? You sound dreadful and look worse."

"Casey killed someone, and I was shooting. Allan, I saw everything and it was *awful*" – Jamie dived for the bathroom. Unpleasant noises arose, followed by the faucet running. Allan drew the obvious conclusion, and waited for Jamie to emerge. He didn't look any better when he did.

"Sit down. Coffee or a stiff drink?"

"I don't want anything. It" – Jamie stopped, and Allan heard *wouldn't stay put*.

"Okay," he soothed. "Wanna talk about it?"

"No. Well, yes. Um, maybe?"

Jamie's vacillation didn't help Allan. He put a glass of water near Jamie, and turned back to the last few arrangements before he left for Pittsburgh on Tuesday, supervising the now-touring *Hands* exhibition.

"It was horrible," Jamie wavered. "I didn't think about it till I'd stopped shooting, but it was horrible. Not like the movies at all. He *shot* O'Leary – I

126

went to the ER with him and one of their pet officers and he's okay, but he could have been badly hurt or *dead*." He stopped. "Casey could have been shot and what would I do then?"

It was clear to Allan that Jamie didn't mean *without her to photograph*.

"She didn't hesitate. As soon as he fired at O'Leary, she had her gun up. He aimed at her and she shot him but the blood didn't run out of his mouth. I thought it would, but it didn't, and his eyes went dull and you could *see* him die." He swallowed several times. "But I shot and shot and shot."

Despite the adult voice, Allan thought Jamie sounded exactly like a small, scared boy witnessing a bad accident. "It's okay," he reassured. "You didn't know they'd have to shoot him."

"I couldn't stop shooting. What if Casey had been hit? I'd have shot it too."

Allan didn't like Jamie's shocked state, but he had an answer for him. "If Casey had been hit, you wouldn't have *Murder Two*."

"I don't fucking care about *Murder Two* if Casey gets shot!" Jamie yelled. "What the hell do you think I am?"

A lot more adult than a year ago, Allan thought. *And head over heels in love. Do you know that yet? Everyone else does, if they've seen your exhibition.*

"Good. Now, have a drink of water. I'm delighted Casey and O'Leary aren't badly hurt, but Casey'll likely want to see you later" –

"She sent me to the ER with O'Leary" –

"Yes, because she'll have to follow procedures. You aren't a part of the NYPD, and you wouldn't be allowed to be there. You could help O'Leary." Allan wagged a finger at Jamie. "As I was saying, Casey'll likely want to see you later, so you need to be ready for her. I bet she'll be upset, and she's had to go through whatever they do when a cop shoots someone."

"I wanna go see her now."

"No, Jamie. Wait till she calls you. You can't see her if she's giving a statement. She'll call. Now, show me these shots you took, and maybe admiring your own work will cheer you up. It usually does."

"I don't want to look at them."

"Who are you? You're sure not Jamie Carval."

"I don't want to throw up again."

"You won't," Allan encouraged, certain this was the only way to restore Jamie to his normal arrogant self. "You'll be so caught up in telling me how brilliant you are, how wonderful the photographs are, and how only you could do it, you'll be fine."

"You think?" Jamie's voice still wobbled.

"I'm sure. Show me."

They went up to Jamie's studio, where he connected his camera to the computer and his huge screens, then downloaded before showing the photographs to Allan.

Four shots in, Allan sat gaping at the screen. Jamie was muttering in the background about technicalities, but Allan couldn't get past his astonishment.

"Even raw, these are *fabulous*," he exclaimed.

"What?"

"They're amazing. You've done it again."

"Keep looking," Jamie said acidly.

Allan did. "Oh. Oh my God." He had known…but this was brilliant, outstanding – and, as Jamie had said, horrible. He gulped. "It's still utterly amazing. If this doesn't show people that the cops don't open fire for no reason, nothing ever will. Look at their faces."

"Look at the *corpse*," Jamie bit. "He's *dead*."

"Yes, and it's awful. But what you've shown" – Allan deliberately diverted into technical matters of exhibiting photographs – "is how terrible violent death is, and how seriously the cops take shooting. Nobody's done that before."

"Nobody?" Jamie was instantly distracted by the thought of being the first.

"Not that I've heard of."

"You've heard of everything."

"That's my job. And see, now you feel better, too. All you needed was a little flattery and you bounced right back."

Allan watched Jamie meditating a response when his phone buzzed, and he grabbed it. "Oh. It's Tyler," he said disappointedly, and read it. "Oh!"

"Do I need to know?"

"Tyler says Casey wants me to join the team at the Abbey after shift." He managed a feeble smile.

"Told you so," Allan pointed out. "Go do something and let me get on with things. I fly out Tuesday, remember? I'll chase the Finisterres before I go, and I should have the list of productions and dates for the soirées early next week."

"Great."

Jamie bounced off, restored to equilibrium by Allan's unusually early praise. Allan remained at his desk, pondering. The shots were indeed brilliant, and they'd form a great section of *Murder Two*. He only hoped Jamie wouldn't mess up with Casey. Every emotion Jamie felt showed in every photograph he took, and while Allan had to admit Jamie was more productive than he'd ever been, if Casey were to be upset with him, his productivity would come to a shuddering halt. Still, Jamie had done a lot of growing up in the last few months, and he seemed to be providing whatever

Casey needed in the days since her father's death. On balance, Allan decided, it would be okay.

He picked up the phone to call the Finisterres, and after a short, fruitful and civilised conversation, they promised him a list by Monday. In turn, he promised to produce Jamie at their next soirée, later in June, and to remind him to tell the detectives, since Claudia intended to call Casey early next week.

***

"Would you like coffee, Detective Clement?" Dr Renfrew asked when she arrived in his conference room. He hoped to establish a less formal atmosphere. His hopes were immediately dashed.

"No, thank you." She sat, without waiting for an invitation. "Pieter Wiedecz. Federico Tarticca denied all knowledge of him, which we know is a lie, and most likely warned him about our investigation as soon as we left. I guess he provided a description of us, because when he saw O'Leary through the spyhole, he didn't open the door, and he was ready with a gun when we broke it down."

Dr Renfrew noted Detective Clement's stern control while referring to the gun, and added it to his list of matters to be raised with her at a suitable time. Captain Kent, while he had undoubtedly thought he had concealed his concern, had unknowingly suggested that there was considerable reason to worry about Detective Clement. Repressing perfectly natural grief rarely ended well, but adding the stress imposed by the appalling behaviour exhibited and encouraged by certain other police personnel would give concern to any moderately well-qualified psychiatrist. Dr Renfrew knew himself to be considerably better qualified than the average.

Dr Renfrew wished most earnestly that it had not been Detective Clement who had shot and killed Pieter Wiedecz. The shooting had been unavoidable, but he did not consider that would relieve Detective Clement's stress. Nor, he considered, would it subtract an iota of the guilt that she carried in relation to her father. Such a malign coincidence could not have occurred at a worse moment.

On the other hand, he reflected, he would also be able to observe some more aspects of the team's bonds. It would not substitute for the insights that he could and would provide to Detective Clement, despite the inevitable lack of co-operation he expected from her. For every cloud, there must also be a silver lining, although Dr Renfrew strongly doubted whether Detective Clement would regard his observations, or indeed his therapeutic assistance, as a silver lining.

"Describe, if you please, the circumstances of the shooting."

Detective Clement regarded Dr Renfrew with distaste, but calmly assembled her thoughts. "Wiedecz, like I said, recognised O'Leary. He didn't open the door, and I expect he used the time between our first knock and our second, where we identified ourselves as NYPD, to pick up a loaded gun. From Maria Montelucci's interview, we believe he had more than one. When Wiedecz failed to open the door, we broke it down. He already had a gun in his hand, his finger was on the trigger, and he didn't drop the gun when ordered to do so. O'Leary and I went in opposite directions. He tracked O'Leary, and he had already fired, hitting O'Leary's arm, before I did. When I saw him tighten his finger on the trigger, aiming at me, I fired. If I hadn't fired he would have shot again, likely with a worse outcome. My two shots to the chest killed him. Had he been wearing a vest; they would still have incapacitated him for long enough to allow us to restrain him."

Detective Clement's unemotional recitation conveyed all the relevant facts to Dr Renfrew. The words did not convey a single hint of her feelings; however, her mouth was pinched, and her fingers were interlocked sufficiently tightly to whiten her knuckles. Dr Renfrew considered her emotional control to be entirely unhelpful.

"How did you feel about the situation?" he asked.

"I thought," Detective Clement enunciated, "we were exchanging information relevant to the crimes."

Dr Renfrew despaired. "We are. However, Captain Kent has ordered you to discuss with me all aspects of the shooting of Pieter Wiedecz. I am enquiring about this aspect of the shooting."

"Fine," said Detective Clement, with a gesture which, from a different woman, would have been best described as a flounce. "I didn't want to shoot him, but I didn't have a choice. He'd have killed O'Leary and me without a blink. I don't want either of us to be dead. I didn't want Wiedecz to be dead, because I wanted to interrogate him and put in prison, where he belonged." She paused. "I wanted to know why he'd lent his vehicle to the shooter." Another pause. "I wanted to see his face when I told him he'd killed a baby." A longer pause. "Even if she was barely pregnant, *Tania* thought of it as her baby. I have to think of it the same way." She paused, and steadied herself. "Wiedecz was key to your investigation as well as mine. Having to shoot him has made both cases more difficult. I don't like that."

Dr Renfrew did not believe for one single instant that Detective Clement's feelings could truthfully be described as dislike. She was obviously concealing stronger emotions, but Dr Renfrew could not, to his irritation, discern their source. He did not think they had arisen solely from the death of Wiedecz. He decided to speak to Detective O'Leary, and abandoned any idea of discussing her father's death, Mr Carval's astoundingly accomplished exhibition, or the harassment to which Detective Clement was presently subject.

"Indeed," was all he replied. "How shall we adapt our investigations to this event?"

"It's crazy that he went straight to shooting," Detective Clement mused. "We've traced his car to a parking lot, and CSU are searching it with two of the officers working with us – Henegan and Larson. There might be something in it which would have set him off if he thought we'd found it."

Dr Renfrew steepled his fingers. "Yes. That does indeed seem likely. However, you have already identified the perpetrator, so it cannot only be finding the vehicle that caused his actions."

"No. We're trying to track Grappano himself, but it'll take some time to get more camera footage. When Andy gets it, maybe he and Bergen can go through it?"

"Of course."

"We could pull Tarticca in, so you and DEA could question him as federal agents, but he already denied all knowledge of Wiedecz – ah!"

"Mm?"

"The car. I need to call Larson – they need to process every bit of it, hunting for anything that might tie it to Tarticca himself." She tugged out her phone. "Larson? Casey. CSU needs to go over Wiedecz's car, inch by inch. Tell them I want them to search for *anything* – prints, hair, anything they can pull DNA from – that might come off any Tarticca, but especially Federico Tarticca. 'Kay?"

Dr Renfrew heard only, "Yes'm!" in reply, in tones more appropriate for addressing a head of state. He faintly remembered Officer Larson as having been less than impressive, and concluded accurately that, if he was working with Detective Clement's team again, he had improved with extreme rapidity. It was a narrative that he would like to hear, from the source. He decided to talk to Officer Larson, and, a sudden memory of earlier attempts to disturb Detective Clement's team intruding, also Officer Fremont. His brow furrowed. Had not Detective Clement said that Officer Henegan was working with her team? How had that arisen? Officer Henegan had been a major contributor to the previous disruption, and Dr Renfrew had observed that Detective Clement was not quick to give second chances. However, the others responsible for that disturbance had attempted, although had failed, to make Officer Henegan the scapegoat for their misdeeds. Dr Renfrew added Officer Henegan to his list of persons to interview in pursuit of his research into the bonds within the team.

"Okay." Detective Clement swiped off her cell phone. Dr Renfrew returned his attention to her. "They'll go over Wiedecz's car with a fine-tooth comb. If we can definitely link it to Tarticca, we can bring him in."

"Yes."

"Yesterday we interviewed Frank Auster – he runs the Yarrabees – and three of his men. One of them, Paddy Hocking, was the third target. He gave us his cell number."

"Agent Bergen so informed me. How astonishingly unintelligent."

"Auster wasn't too impressed either. Anyway, Bergen said he'd track Hocking's phone off the cell towers, which should give us a nice little map of where he's going and why he was targeted." Detective Clement made an unhappy moue. "The problem with it is: it could have been three random Yarrabees and any of them would have done…" She trailed off. "That can't be right. The shooter wasn't – couldn't have been – cruising upper Manhattan looking for three stray Yarrabees. He must have known where to find them."

"Indeed, it must have been so," Dr Renfrew agreed. It was a pleasure to work with such a fast-thinking detective as Detective Clement. Even he had not yet made that connection. "If he knew where to find them, it is most likely he was tipped off." He smiled thinly. "My next step is to consider on whom a wiretap would produce the most useful results. I now have good grounds to apply for one, which I shall discuss with Agent Glencross. I will inform him that the suggestion came from you."

"Thank you," Detective Clement said. Dr Renfrew observed that her teeth were gritted. "If your wiretap picks up anything we can use on these homicides, please pass it on to one of us at once."

"Of course. We shall continue to use Detective Handjiev as liaison, though her interests in these investigations march more closely with the federal interests."

"Fine. Are we done for now?"

Dr Renfrew would have liked to move on to Detective Clement's views of Mr Carval's exhibition, the team's behaviour around it, and the press conference. Her words, however, although posed as a question, had been a statement that they had finished. Glancing at his watch, he noticed that it was likely to be the end of the detectives' shifts, and he did not wish to delay Detective Clement's departure. In his opinion, she would benefit from rest.

"Yes. This has been most useful. We might resume tomorrow morning, if either of us discover further matters which should be discussed."

"Yeah."

Detective Clement rapidly vacated Dr Renfrew's room. He observed her departure, then made some private notes, relating firstly to Captain Kent's request to provide Detective Clement with counselling, and secondly to his research into the team dynamic. Once done, he capped his fountain pen with satisfaction, and requested that Detective Handjiev join him to consult with Agent Glencross. He noted that Agent Bergen had once again been absorbed into Detective Clement's team, and approved.

CHAPTER SIXTEEN

"End of shift." Casey had disposed of Bergen with instructions to construct his map. Despite Casey having even less authority over Bergen than the none that she had over any member of the NYPD, he obeyed her with alacrity.

"We're goin' to the Abbey like we agreed earlier," O'Leary reminded everyone, "an' I guess Carval'll meet us there?"

Tyler nodded.

"Let's go, before somebody thinks of a reason we can't."

Thirty seconds later, the team had gone. Dr Renfrew, who had wished to speak to any member of the team other than Detective Clement, regretted the missed opportunity, but concluded correctly that the team was closing ranks around Detectives Clement and O'Leary, following the day's events. He found their action to be thoroughly satisfactory, inasmuch as it confirmed one of his conclusions about the team.

None of the five people in the Abbey cared in the slightest for Renfrew's conclusions, or indeed for Renfrew. They cared for the drinks in front of them, which Carval, arriving first, had bought.

"I never had to shoot anyone before," Casey said bleakly.

"I never shot anyone," O'Leary commented.

"Nor me," Andy added. "Never yet."

"I have." Everybody knew Tyler's record. "In the sandpit and a couple on the job."

Silence surrounded the table for a moment or two. Unusually, Tyler took point, using his words without his normal brevity. "Want to talk?" he addressed to Casey. "Don't have to." He included the team's general caveat. They only talked if they wanted to. To everyone's amazement, he carried on. "Think you should. Helps. Talked to my unit." Tyler had *talked* to someone?

Carval unobtrusively put an arm around Casey, still shrunken into herself, though it was as much to help him as to console her. He remained, he realised, shaken up and distressed, despite Allan's briskly comforting actions and speech earlier, and *he* wanted to talk, to the one other person who knew what it was all about.

"Fremont came to me," Tyler continued. "Said you were wrecked. Didn't know why. Didn't want to ask. Good man."

"Tattling to you?" Casey snapped.

"Thought I'd know what to do. My past isn't secret. Told him to leave it alone."

Casey eased down, saying nothing more.

Carval met Tyler's gaze. "I watched them go in, and I shot it all." His voice trembled. "It was horrible. I did what I *do*, take photos. I can't *not* take photos when I see the shot, and they're great photos." He gulped. "But I threw up until I went to the ER with O'Leary and Larson. I've never seen anyone die before. Not even my mom. I wasn't with her…she waited until I was outside the room."

"They say that's how it happens," O'Leary rumbled gently.

"Anyway," Carval pushed out, "she was in the hospital. It wasn't" – he stopped. *Violent* hung in the air. "It was ordinary. Peaceful, almost," he managed, and drank his beer. Nobody commented on the tiny tremor in his hand, or the creases at his eyes and mouth; nobody commented on Casey's wince and twisting lips. One of her hands dropped from the table, and remained unseen below it, while Carval's arm around her tightened slightly. "This wasn't." He drank again. "But I shot it all like it happens every day, like it was the same as the theatre or the construction sites or the people walking through Sakura Park." He looked at each of them. "I didn't see the difference till I put the camera down," he said defeatedly. "I don't think I thought *he's dead* until I stopped shooting."

"Instinct," Tyler said. "Shoot – photos or bullets – by instinct. Don't realise till it's over."

"Shouldn't I have realised earlier, and stopped?"

The others stared at him. "You?" Andy choked on his soda. "Stop photographing? Not unless you stopped breathing, and even then you'd carry on till you fell over."

"He said it," O'Leary continued, nodding at Andy. "Snappin's what you do. You can't stop, even iffen you thought you wanted to. See picture, take picture. Tyler said it a second ago, it's instinct." He patted Carval's shoulder. "We don't judge. 'Specially when you're upset now, an' right after."

Carval smiled weakly, and drank his beer.

"Iffen you hadn't been upset, we'd'a been worried. It wouldn't be nat'ral. Seein' as you are upset, we're cool. I mean, you're talkin', an' we

134

ain't used to that happenin' in this team, but we'll cope, I guess." O'Leary grinned. "You even made Tyler talk, an' that's points to you."

Tyler made a disagreeable noise, and scowled at the big man. O'Leary smiled back sweetly. "So anyways, it's a big thin' to see. Give it time. Or take it on the mats. Sparrin' works for most of us."

"Works for Bigfoot," Tyler jeered, "'cause he throws everyone around, except me."

"An' you, mostly," O'Leary contradicted. "I don't often throw Casey around, 'cause she'll do somethin' mean to me, like put salt in my coffee."

"She did?" Carval squawked. "For real?"

"Yup. I took a swig an' almost choked. She's mean when she gets mad."

Casey, staring at her beer bottle, which she hadn't lifted once, didn't seem to hear her partner. Although Carval's arm was around her, and her hand on his knee, she felt oddly disconnected from everyone around her: cold, as if she were sitting in a thick sea fog.

"Still an' all, I'm glad she took the shot. I don't wanna be dead. 'Tain't no fun, an' Pete would kill me." O'Leary flashed a piercing glance at Casey, totally at variance with his hayseed drawl and black humour. "Not that Casey doesn't try, regular-like." O'Leary's teasing didn't register with her, though she heard the words.

"There was so much blood," she whispered, and stared at the plastic table top. Now she had nothing to distract her, the magnitude of her action had hit her like an Amtrak engine. She'd killed him, and the blood had soaked through his clothes on his chest, where her bullets had hit. It had been just like her father, somehow, even though it hadn't been the same because there had been far more blood from her father, all over his floor…They'd cleaned him up, in the hospital. There'd been no blood when he died. Only pain, and she there to see it. "Not Wiedecz. He died. I thought…I thought there'd be more blood."

"Not like the movies," Tyler pointed out.

"He's still dead and I shot him," Casey said. "I know we train for it, but training isn't reality. They get up after we shoot training guns." She gazed down at the table. "I killed him."

"Yeah," Tyler rapped. "You did." Casey jerked up, gaping at him. "First time I shot someone, wasn't sniping. Saw him fall, and not stand up again. Threw up, later. You don't forget." He surveyed the group. "Swap, Bigfoot." O'Leary was, as usual, on one side of Casey, Carval on the other. O'Leary shifted. Tyler sat down again next to Casey's huddled form. "Helluva thing. Changes you," he said quietly. The others simply listened. "I get it. Never the same again. Get how fragile we are. Shouldn't be easy, but it is." His voice fell further. "Don't get used to it. Sniping…from nearly a mile you don't see it clearly, even with the scope. On the job, you do. Don't push it down. See the shrink." He paused. "I did."

Andy and O'Leary exchanged astonished glances, and said nothing, hiding their surprise behind their drinks.

"After the Army?" Casey asked.

"After the first time as a cop."

"But..."

"Thought so too. Sniping's different. First time on the job he was ten feet away, not half a mile." His eyes searched backwards into memory, creasing up as if he were back with the Army, lining up his shot. "You see the blood, up close," he said remotely. "Didn't think it would be different. Thought I'd be used to it." His eyes returned to the present. "It wasn't the same. Saw the shrink, fixed it."

"Kent's ordered me to see Renfrew." Casey's tone was as remote as Tyler's. She spoke directly and solely to him.

"Must be good. Wouldn't send you otherwise."

"I don't need to talk to him or anyone, but I have to."

"Don't have to. Don't have to talk, or don't have to talk to anyone but us. Renfrew doesn't get it. We do."

"You do." She fell silent, thinking. "I want to see your shots," she suddenly said to Carval. "Even if they're raw. I need to see what I did."

Carval blinked. He only ever allowed Allan to see the raw shots – but this was important. "Okay," he agreed. "We'd better all go."

They drank up, except for Casey, who made a small *you-take-it* gesture to O'Leary, who didn't need to be asked twice, and arrived in Carval's studio a few moments later. Carval hadn't lost contact with Casey for more than a second in the journey, by dint of pushing her into the back of O'Leary's SUV and staying there with her. She hadn't objected, which was mildly worrying. He tapped one-handed at his computer, and brought up the sequence.

Casey did nothing, face and eyes empty. Carval wasn't sure she was even looking at the photographs she'd claimed she wanted to see. Suddenly, her eyes focused on the screen. Carval had put the first up: she and O'Leary counting down. He moved through the shots, the door splintering, the set expressions, the changes in posture and alertness as Wiedecz brought his gun up; Casey shooting; the light dying in Wiedecz's eyes.

"Waal," O'Leary gasped. "Waal, I never saw nothing like that."

"I hope it's not the next centrepiece," Andy whispered. "She'll never be off the front page. Every gun nut in the world'll want it as a pin-up."

Tyler whistled softly. "Caught it."

"I didn't hesitate," she murmured. "I didn't hesitate before I killed him."

"Waal, I'm glad you didn't," O'Leary said sternly. "Iffen you had; I might be dead. Or you might. Don't you go feelin' guilty about what you had to do to stop him. He wasn't goin' to stop shootin' an' neither of us could've put him down when he was shootin' at us."

136

Casey paid no attention. "I thought there'd be more blood. Dad's apartment…there was more blood there. There was blood everywhere." She shivered.

"Snap out of it," O'Leary instructed briskly. "You're bein' morbid an' it's dumb. The two thin's ain't anythin' like the same. You didn't do *nothin'* for your dad you c'n blame yourself for, an' you didn't have a choice about shootin' Wiedecz 'cause he was goin' to shoot us, like I said an' you didn't listen to. Waal, you listen now. This ain't your fault an' it ain't you who's to blame." He expelled irritation with a huff. "Iffen you don't straighten your head out; it'll be Renfrew doin' it for you. Iffen you do it yourself before you see him, he won't therapize you quite so bad."

O'Leary's size fifteen boot metaphorically applied itself to Casey's rear, with some force. His hands moved as if to shake Casey.

"He'll do it anyway," she said acidly, but the deadness had departed her face.

"Waal, don't you go shootin' him."

Carval inhaled sharply, but it seemed O'Leary had it right. Casey's face twisted, but she growled at the big man. "Bully," she grumbled. "See if I help you explain that bandage to Pete."

"You never do." O'Leary glanced around. "C'n I get a coffee? All this layin' down the law to Casey here's makin' me thirsty, but I gotta drive home."

"Sure." Carval put the coffee on. The team examined the shots he'd taken, then tugged chairs close together and sat, O'Leary and Tyler flanking Casey. Andy, too slow to reach a chair, perched on the edge of the desk. Carval leaned on the wall, supervising the coffee maker, which stopped him striding over and plucking Casey up from the chair and into his embrace. He wanted to, but it would wait for later, when the others had left.

He handed coffee around, and remembered something. "Allan told me to tell you something." He tried to find some words that wouldn't have him removed to a cell.

"Yes?" Andy said suspiciously. "Is this something you should have told us already?"

Carval wriggled. "Well, um."

"Do we have to do another press conference?"

"No!"

"Thank Christ," O'Leary muttered.

"It's about the exhibition, isn't it?" Andy surmised, knowing exactly what Carval was about to say and not scrupling to skewer him on his own discomfort.

"Um, you remember the Finisterres?"

"Yeah," O'Leary replied. "Teeny li'l people big into theatre, with a weird taste in interior décor."

"The Finisterres?" Casey said. "Why do we need to remember the Finisterres?"

"Uh, because…because-they-want-you-to-go-to-their-soirée because of the show," Carval blurted out.

"They want *what?*" three detectives chorused. Andy's voice was noticeably absent.

"They want you all to go to one of their soirées so they can show you off to their cultured friends. I *have* to go," Carval huffed, mostly muffled by the squawking and complaining. "Allan said so, otherwise they won't let me shoot in their productions. You all get a choice. I don't. They'll call you early next week."

"They want us." Casey wasn't asking a question.

"Yep. You because you're the stars, me because I wanna shoot in their theatres, Allan because they've known him forever and offered him a job when I did but he's mine and they're not luring him away now, and Allie because they're supporting her – and because they think it's so romantic about her and Tyler," he finished with a flourish.

O'Leary's guffaw shook the room, and Andy laughed. Even Casey smiled. Tyler's dark face acquired a tinge of dark red.

"Naw, Tyler ain't romantic," O'Leary gibed. "He'd have to make flowery speeches, an' we all know he ain't allowed to say more than two words at a time."

"Am."

"Waal, you must save 'em all up for Allie, 'cause you sure don't use 'em for us."

Andy caught Tyler's eye, and grinned. "We're not as pretty as she is. He doesn't waste words on us."

Tyler's blush increased. "Shut up."

"He don't even waste them on Casey, an' she's quite pretty when she scrubs up." O'Leary smirked at her. "Not that you scrub up often."

Carval opened his mouth, noticed Casey's expression and shut it rapidly.

"If I wanted to scrub up pretty, I'd have taken lessons from you, Bigfoot – in how *not* to do it."

"Aw, you mean you don't want coloured tips on your hair an' matchin' polish on your nails?"

"Ugh," Casey humphed.

"Have you *ever* put polish on your nails?" Carval asked. Casey glared at him. "No," he concluded.

"Let me get this straight," she snipped. "The Finisterres, fresh off being persons of interest and for a minute or two murder suspects, want the four of us – who suspected them – to attend one of their elegant soirées, plus Allie, plus Allan, plus you."

"Yep."

138

"Why?" The tone came straight from Interrogation. "And don't give me that crap about romance and Tyler."

"They said it."

"Why. Do. The. Finisterres. Want. Us?"

Carval acquiesced to the tone. "You're the hottest cultural ticket in town, so they want you. Showing you off."

"We're a circus act," she said bleakly.

"Bigfoot did his circus act as the strongman," Andy quipped.

"That's not the point," Casey growled. "We're not zoo exhibits."

"Actually," Carval intervened, "you're there as the guests of honour." He cast around for a similar idea. "Like if the model for the Mona Lisa or Ecce Homo was alive now, they'd have them."

"Oh, my God," Casey muttered.

"I always wanted to be a model," O'Leary said happily, "an' I'm happy to be the centre of attention if it means good food an' free drinks. C'n Pete come too? He's more into football, but he'll want to see me all popular an' cultural."

"I'm going," Andy announced. "Allan already told me about it, and, unlike you Philistines, I can talk about culture all day long. I'll enjoy it."

"Allie'll like it," Tyler said.

Casey said nothing, and continued not commenting on her attendance or otherwise while she drank her coffee.

The coffee drunk, the team departed, leaving Casey. Carval barely waited for the studio door to close before he tucked her close, trying to soothe her as holding her was soothing him. Talking to Tyler had helped, showing the photographs and the team's wonder and admiration had helped – sincere flattery always improved Carval's mood; but holding his Casey helped most of all. He nuzzled into her hair, smelling the faint aroma of shampoo and conditioner. Normality, in a day that had been anything but normal. He wondered when cuddling Casey had become a part of his normality, but swiftly decided it didn't matter. He nuzzled again, then straightened up. The difference in height cricked his spine.

"Let's go upstairs. Do you want to get some dinner?"

Casey unfurled herself, and glanced up. "I guess," she said unenthusiastically. "If I don't eat, tomorrow won't improve. I hate working weekends," she added. He thought she might have continued, but whatever it had been, she'd thought better of it.

Casey thought that working this particular weekend meant she couldn't feel guilty – guiltier – about not dealing with her father's possessions and apartment. She had to work, and she couldn't be in two places at once. It was barely a week since…anyway. Nobody would expect her to have done everything already, and anyway, since the probate attorney hadn't contacted her, there wasn't anything she could do.

She had no appetite, but she had to eat something, and she might as well let Carval take care of her. He claimed he wanted to, and right now she'd like him to.

He steered her to the couch and gently pushed her down. "Curl up there, while I find some menus."

"Lychee chicken," Casey said. "I don't need a menu." She automatically reached for her wallet, and was tutted at.

"I'm buying you dinner," Carval insisted. "You can pay next time if you must, but today I'm buying."

"But" –

"Nope. I hate what happened but they're another brilliant sequence and it's all down to you. I'm buying dinner." Carval called the order in, paid, sat down close to Casey, wrapped her in, and resumed his imitation of a small child with its favourite stuffed toy until dinner arrived.

CHAPTER SEVENTEEN

"I couldn't have had you there, after," she said out of nowhere, when they'd finished eating. "I had to deal with it all and if you'd been there I wouldn't have been able to."

"I guessed," Carval said, surprisingly. "It's okay."

Casey wriggled to move closer, and wrapped her own arms around Carval. "You had a pretty rough time too," she murmured. "We expect it. We know it can happen every time we go out. You...don't."

"It's never happened to you either."

"We expect it," she repeated, "or, well, we're ready for it. You aren't. We have vests. Guns. It's our protection – can you even shoot?"

"Only with a camera. I'm not interested in guns."

"Cameras don't usually kill people," she said sardonically, though she had to force the words to sound like her normal banter, "so you're better off with one of those."

"I guess." He forced lightness into his voice in turn. "Though I had the feeling you'd happily kill me for having one."

"I still might, but not today. One dead man's one too many for me." She didn't manage lightness, her voice cracking part way through her sentence. She hid her face in her sleeve, but it didn't conceal the quivers in her shoulders.

"Come here." He cuddled her. "It's one too many for me too." He tipped up her face, and dropped a kiss on her lips. "I don't want to think about it. I don't wanna think about anything."

"What a coincidence," Casey said bleakly. "Me either." She stopped. "Dani – Detective Handjiev – told me she went home and cuddled her boyfriend. It sounds like a plan to me."

"Sounds like a pretty good plan to me too – to start with," Carval said in a totally different tone. "Why don't we start there, and see what comes up?"

141

"If it's as old as that line, nothing'll come up," Casey snarked. Carval sniffed offendedly, and moved slightly – "You *rat!*" Casey squealed. "Stoppit! Stop tickling me. You know I hate it."

Carval grinned for the first time since the morning, and didn't stop for another moment. He dipped his head and kissed Casey, which somehow resulted in her shirt falling open. Sneakily, he'd unbuttoned it while she was squeaking and complaining and threatening to wreak revenge. He smiled slowly at her, running a hot, assessing gaze over the dark blue fabric, covering tantalisingly lush curves on a slim, toned form. Casey was, he decided, a complete cure for his unpleasant memories.

He hoped he'd be a cure for hers.

He began softly: light, teasing kisses, returned with interest and a determined effort to go further. If that was how Casey wanted to play it…they'd get there, but not yet. Seduction was the name of his game. Seducing the memories away, he thought, and kissed her again, flirting with her soft lips and a tiny stroke of tongue across the seam before drawing back. Casey made an irritated little noise, and a moue that still, most of a year since they'd met, reminded him of a cross kitten, all fluff, with teeth and claws. At times like this, he noticed how small she really was: in the precinct her personality expanded to make her seem far taller. Here and now, though, she fitted neatly into his clasp, happy to be soft and even snuggly. He needed that. From her behaviour, *Casey* needed that. Somewhere she needn't command, but could choose to be an equal, not a leader. Somewhere, with someone, she could be taken care of.

He kissed her again, pulling her closer, a big hand over her slightly-too-protuberant vertebrae, stroking soothingly up and down, under her loosened shirt. One of Casey's elegant hands slid under his t-shirt, petting in her turn –

She pinched and tickled with swift, evil movements until Carval was red-faced, breathless, and vowing vengeance on all sneaky little cops. Casey giggled at him, which didn't help, until he caught her hands and trapped them in one of his; used the other to pull her into his lap and took her mouth as passionately as she had wanted a few moments before. There was no more tickling, and no more giggles. His hand slipped back under her shirt; hers came up to his neck and held him firmly in place as she kissed him equally hard.

"Bedroom," she suggested. Carval was happy to comply. She stood, tugged him up, and led him through; stretched, wriggled, and let her shirt fall off. Carval took a step back, and admired. His fingers twitched, as if he wanted to focus his camera, his gaze changed to the intent stare that he otherwise only applied to his shots. The shots he'd taken of her on Valentine's Day were the best he'd ever done, but he'd never show them to anyone except Casey, and she'd never asked to see them. He looked her up

142

and down, reached out, drew her closer, and neatly undid her belt and pants, pushing them down. Her pretty underwear didn't match, but he didn't care. He only cared about the Casey inside the underwear, who was regarding him with a *what-are-you-waiting-for* expression. It lasted all of half a second before he took the hint and stripped off his t-shirt, flexing simply so he could see the heat rise in her eyes.

If only he couldn't also see the pain.

Still, if he could take it away…even for a night. Another night. And for as many nights as he could, or as she would let him.

Casey only wanted to forget, and Carval was a fine distraction. *And more than that*, her mind told her. Maybe. Probably. Oh, the hell with it. Why was she still trying to pretend to herself? He was. Right now, she didn't want to think about their relationship: she didn't want to think at all, and Carval was an extremely good remedy for thinking. She examined him: a slow, thorough perusal, carrying a command to lose the t-shirt. She couldn't reach to take it off, when he was standing. Fortunately, it hit the floor before she'd had time to speak. He flexed, showing off as he stripped his pants, a touch of his usual arrogance, but when she put out her hands to him he came to her grip and for a moment, simply held her, soft curves against the muscle and roughness of the hair on his chest.

She stretched up, rubbing over him, cupped his face and brought his head down so she could kiss him in an unmistakably sexual fashion which brought him to instant response. They fell to the bed, where they could finish undressing each other, and touch as they pleased. Gentle strokes became hotter, more demanding; slow burn and seduction turned to wet heat and hard force, and finally to swift movement and shattering release.

Casey, instead of curling up against Carval's side, pillowed her head on his chest and laid an arm around his midriff. He cuddled her in. "'S been a hell of a day," she murmured drowsily, and quietly, motionless, began to cry.

Carval let her cry. He didn't like crying women – he *hadn't* liked crying women; it always made him feel as if he'd done something wrong – but Casey had finally come to the end of her endurance, the stress of the day and the weight of her action spilling over. She *needed* to cry, and it wasn't about him.

Except it was, somehow. Carval, not a man who normally used his intuition for anything other than photographs, understood, suddenly, that Casey crying into his chest meant she trusted him not to use her weakness against her, exactly as she trusted her team. She'd said, a bare week ago, he was part of the team, and here she was proving it. This wasn't the broken-hearted grief for her father, which she could have shown to anyone without reproach; this was the burden of taking a life because she'd been doing her job, which she could only share with her team. They were the only people she could trust not to use it against her; not to say *see, too emotional to be a cop*; not to think *weak*. He held her closer, until the damp patch on his chest dried, then petted. "It's late," he said. "Stay?"

"I shouldn't. I don't have anything to wear tomorrow." She didn't move.

"Get up a little early and go home," he yawned.

"'Kay."

***

Captain Kent, hoping to enjoy a pleasant day with his wife, was thoroughly displeased to receive a call midway through Sunday morning. Unexpected calls were displeasing at any time, but Sundays should be sacrosanct.

"Kent," he snapped.

"Captain Kent, this is Captain Lewin from Internal Affairs. I'm patching in Captain Wetherly."

"Morning," Wetherly said. He didn't sound any happier to be called on a Sunday morning than Kent was. "What's this about?"

"Officer Birkett," Lewin said. The other two sighed. "He's crumpled like a wet Kleenex."

"Good," Wetherly rapped. "There's no place for him in my precinct."

"Or any other," Kent grated.

"That's not why I'm calling," Lewin continued. "Birkett has named several other names. I'll be speaking to several other captains today. We'll be interviewing some of their men – there aren't any women involved. I'm talking to you together because you teamed up to expose Birkett's behaviour. We intend to interview Officers Estrolla, Grendon, and Henegan from the 36th, and Fental from the 112th."

"I see," Wetherly said. "Thanks for the heads-up."

"Thank you. I'll let you know when we want to talk to him."

"Sure. I have to go. Family Sunday, you know."

"Kent," Lewin said.

Kent sighed again. "Yes?"

"I want your take on this whole situation, with the background. We can do it today, or we can meet early tomorrow, but I must have all the information you can give me as soon as possible. I've already arranged a meeting with Sergeant Carter of the Academy, and with Captain Garrett of the Third. After all those, I'll decide if I need to talk to Detective Clement, or anyone else from her team."

Kent hunched his shoulders. "No point waiting. I'll see you today at two, at your shop."

"Okay, thanks."

Kent went to explain to his wife. Many years of marriage to a cop had left her resigned to sudden changes of plan, but she was surprisingly unbothered.

"I'll go see this new artist, Katz, in Chelsea." She patted his shoulder. "You know you'd hate it."

"You shouldn't have to," Kent apologised.

"I'll enjoy it a lot more than whatever you're doing." She pecked him on his florid cheek. "Come help fix lunch. I'm guessing you'll want it early?"

"Thanks, honey." Kent privately rejoiced in his wife.

***

"Do we have the footage to find Grappano?" Casey asked.

"I got the warrants, I'm getting it." Andy scowled. "You've already asked me four times this morning. Stop."

"I want to find him," Casey complained. "We know he did it, we've got plenty of evidence. Why can't we find him and put him away?"

"You want to take vacation," O'Leary teased. "I do too. Pete wants to go outta New York. Mebbe we'll go see Niagara Falls."

"I have to deal with probate first."

"You got an attorney to deal with that. You c'n go on vacation an' take the occasional call iffen there's anythin' to worry about."

"I guess." Casey didn't say that there were unlikely to be any issues. She was the only legatee, the medical bills and maybe the rehab costs would need to be settled, and his apartment and any other expenses would need to be managed until probate and estate taxes had been dealt with. She wouldn't keep the apartment. She couldn't bear to, even if she hadn't had her own apartment, far more convenient than her father's. Disposing of his was a sadness for another day. She blinked hard, and turned to her work.

Two hours later, Andy had obtained most of his footage, though several offices had been shut till Monday. Still, he had enough to work with, and he was constructing a pretty map of sightings which he could use to refine the data from any further footage.

Unlike Andy, the others were getting nowhere. Casey glared at her papers, O'Leary sighed, Tyler tapped fingers.

"Did Bergen create a map of Paddy Hocking's movements?" she asked.

"He's running a program to build it." Andy raised his head, then went back to his own map. "He wanted to run it for a day or two to see if a pattern emerged."

"That means no," Casey said. She tapped her fingers, out of time with Tyler.

"Aha!" Andy celebrated.

Dani hurried over from her borrowed desk. "What?"

"Footage from around Tarticca's hangout. Look what we have here. Our boy Grappano, large as life and twice as clear, going in."

Casey smiled nastily. "Oh, dear. Looks like we have cause for a warrant. What a shame. I'll get on with it."

"Didn't you say the FBI were askin' for a wiretap?" O'Leary queried.

"Yep. By the time we've gotten this warrant, we'll know what they have. We won't execute it till we've worked it out together – DEA might have some thoughts as well. Likely we'll want to put a whole lot of things together and hit them in force – DEA might want to raid them and/or the Yarrabees, if Bergen finds something interesting."

"Mm," Tyler hummed. "Could be nasty. Firefight."

"Yeah," Dani agreed.

"We'll put DEA and the FBI at the front. I had enough of gunshots yesterday, and I'm damn sure you did, Bigfoot." Casey looked wryly at him. "What did Pete say this time?"

"Lots." O'Leary pouted. "He told me off all evenin'. He'd barely finished complainin' about the knife slash, too."

"Poor baby," Casey drawled with notable insincerity.

"Not as poor as you're wishing on the assorted Feds," Andy said dryly.

"They're not here. We are. Let's work out what we think. Dani," Casey said, "you know how DEA and Narcotics work, so can you add their views in?"

"Sure."

The team, with Dani an enthusiastic contributor, worked out a plan, to be discussed the following day with Renfrew and the as-yet-unseen Agent Glencross.

"How they got those drivers' licences worry me," Casey fretted. "I don't see why they wanted them."

"Let's get some lunch and think about why," Andy suggested. "Dani, you wanna come with us?"

"Sounds good."

***

Kent arrived at Internal Affairs, already irritable, which wouldn't help him with Lewin. IA had a perfect right to establish the truth, but Kent intended to ensure they heard it.

He was politely taken to a conference room, which was a good start, in which there was a recorder, which wasn't, though he'd have been astonished if there hadn't been one. Usefully, there was coffee.

"Thanks for coming in," Lewin said. Kent grunted. "Let's confirm the ground rules. I'd like you to tell me everything you know about the situation – when I start the recording I'll describe it in detail – including before Detective Clement joined your precinct. This isn't a formal interview, and

I'm only recording it – I'll say this for the tape too – so I don't have to take notes and slow the chat down. I want to establish the facts, but I also want your views and opinions. You're only one of many people we'll be talking to. I'd rather have more than less."

"I understand." Kent harrumphed. "I wish it hadn't come to this."

"So do we," Lewin agreed. "IA might not have the happiest reputation, but I assure you we don't like investigating allegations of corruption in the NYPD." He shrugged. "It's not often we have direct evidence collected by two captains and the FBI, though."

"I guess not."

"However, we'll get there. Let's start."

"Okay." Kent sat back and listened to Lewin's accurate summary of the situation.

"Captain Kent, does this summary reflect your understanding of why Internal Affairs has become involved?"

"Yes."

"Thanks. Please set out the background as you understand it, going back as early as you can."

Kent didn't have to pause. He'd been assembling his thoughts since they'd passed Birkett over to IA. "Some of this, you understand, is hearsay from other members of the NYPD." Lewin nodded. "I'll start with my understanding of the roots of this affair, which I've been told by others: specifically, Sergeant Carter of the Academy, Captain Garrett at the Third, and Detectives Clement, O'Leary, Tyler and Chee of my own precinct." He sipped his coffee, apparently relaxed. "I've also heard various comments from Captain Travers of Narcotics in Queens, Officer Birkett, and Officers Estrolla, Grendon and Henegan of my precinct." He sighed ruefully. "You're aware of the FBI involvement, and Dr Renfrew has discussed his thoughts with me. Finally, I've received information from Jamie Carval and his business manager, Allan Penrith." Kent sat back. "I'll start right back at the beginning, when Clement, Mark Marcol of Narcotics, and Birkett were all in the same class at the Academy."

"Mm?"

"Marcol's from a long line of cops, and expected to do well. He did. Clement did better, and his nose got put out of joint. I understand – third hand – he tried to ask her out, but she turned him down. Carter never noticed or heard anything, and they don't encourage dating."

"Quite right," Lewin commented.

"Marcol and Birkett were close friends at the Academy – I don't know if they had known each other before then. Anyway, Clement started to come out on top, switching it with Marcol. Marcol didn't like losing, but neither does Clement, so I guess they fired each other up. Here's where the mess began. Someone dug up a photo of her, taken when she was at Stanford."

Lewin blinked. "She was at Stanford?"

"Yes. I am told," Kent emphasised, "the photo was used by Marcol and Birkett to try to portray Clement as promiscuous, and only on top because she was sleeping with the instructors. Both Garrett and I investigated. It wasn't true, but I'm sure you'll ask Sergeant Carter about it. Clement kept herself to herself and worked harder, and after that no-one came close. As you'll know, she came top by miles." He had another gulp of coffee. "The stolen photo was taken by Jamie Carval."

Lewin choked on his coffee. "Dear God," he emitted. "The same Jamie Carval – there can't be two, can there?"

"I hope not," Kent said bitterly. "One of them's done enough damage – I know it sounds unfair, but if he'd never stumbled over my team we wouldn't be here now." He harrumphed. "Anyway, yes, the same Carval. The photo was taken as part of a marketing campaign for the wonders of attending college. Carval's manager, Penrith, tells me he has proof Marcol and Birkett copied it from there."

"He does?"

"He says so, and I have no reason to disbelieve him. Anyway, after the Academy, Clement was assigned to the Third under Garrett, and he paired her up with Detective O'Leary. They matched up perfectly." Kent sighed. "That's the next complication."

"Yes?"

"The whole world knows O'Leary's gay – now. Back then, he kept it very quiet indeed – even I didn't know he was married until late last year. He and Clement cooked up some scheme to cover up his preferences – I guess she pretended to be his girlfriend. There were rumours she was sleeping with O'Leary and some other guy."

Lewin choked again. "Together? Is this an episode of some late-night HBO show?"

"I surmise," Kent said dryly, "she wasn't sleeping with either, but O'Leary had met someone and she was helping them cover up the relationship."

"I see," Lewin managed. "You've got an interesting bunch there, Kent."

"You don't know the half of it, yet."

"There's *more?*"

"Yeah." Kent nodded. "Could I get another coffee?"

"Sure." Lewin, evidently shell-shocked, brought the pot over, and poured. Kent tipped half of it back in one go, and Lewin refilled it again.

CHAPTER EIGHTEEN

Kent refreshed himself, and started again. "So, there was a shake up, and Clement and O'Leary were transferred to me as a pair. I didn't want to break it up or change things because it's hard to pair up attractive women. I had a chat with Garrett, and there was no truth to the rumours and nothing to worry about. I added Detectives Tyler and Chee to them, and it worked out. They didn't mix with the others – Clement still keeps herself to herself, O'Leary's pally with everyone but close friends with nobody outside the team – and Carval, now, but I'll get to that. Tyler's ex-Army and you know how that goes down, and Chee's a technogeek. They've all got difficult histories – nothing bad, but they don't play well with others who can't keep up with them. They're incredibly smart, and competitive as all-get-out, and they don't suffer fools at all. They're not popular." Lewin nodded understandingly. "Still, they get the job done and they have the best record in the NYPD. That damn FBI profiler would steal them if he could," Kent added, not accidentally, "but he's not getting them."

Lewin blinked, entirely bereft of words.

"There'd been no trouble their whole time in my precinct. The photo never came up, there were no rumours, and no problems." Kent sighed loudly. "Then the damn photographer turned up. He'd found them at a crime scene – you wouldn't believe it, would you? – and took the shot that's the centrepiece of the exhibition" –

"I've seen it." Lewin winced. "Not my thing, but I thought I'd better see what the fuss was about."

"Yeah. Carval showed up wanting to shoot the team. I don't know what happened between him and the four of them, but Clement was seriously against it, O'Leary was for it, and the result was that I gave permission for him to shoot them and anyone else who agreed. It would have been fine, except once Carval found out that his photo from the college poster had been used to slut-shame Clement, he decided to go after whoever did it – without mentioning it to her. He and Penrith claim they have sufficient proof to file a breach of copyright case against Marcol and Birkett for stealing the shot."

"Oh."

"Indeed. Oh. Next, we had a case with models being used for snuff movies on line."

Lewin's face twisted. "Nasty business."

Kent nodded. "There was a Narcotics connection, and Travers sent Marcol. Marcol asked Clement for a date, she turned him down, and he lost his temper and accused the team – Detective Tyler told me – of suing him over the photo."

"You don't run a precinct, Kent, you're filming a soap opera." Lewin's eyebrows had met his hairline several moments earlier, and had stayed there.

"I'm beginning to think so, except nobody would believe it." Kent drained his cup. "Marcol tried to get back into my team, using Captain Travers, who wasn't aware of the story. None of my team had done anything wrong, but Travers didn't have the full facts. I interviewed my team, and made Travers aware of the real situation. He wasn't receptive, and indeed he tried to foist Marcol on my team last week, when I referred his conduct to you."

"Mm," Lewin hummed non-committally.

"I was sufficiently concerned by the situation, and by a persistent set of rumours, concerning Clement, buzzing around my bullpen, to ask the FBI to take a download of Clement's father's arrest record."

Lewin stared. "You what?"

"Nobody could seriously claim the FBI would fake it," Kent pointed out. "I and Dr Renfrew agreed that Marcol's suspected conduct at the Academy and in pursuing Clement when she wasn't interested was worrying. Still, if nothing happened, there would be no comeback." Kent's lips twisted. "Officer Birkett's one area of strength was electronic records."

Lewin's eyebrows rose again. "I see."

"Clement's father was arrested for the second time in Queens, at the 112th. She told the 112th to treat him like any other drunk, and I made sure it happened, by checking with Wetherly. Unfortunately, Officer Birkett was present when she collected her father. Nothing seemed to happen, though, apart from the rumours, and I thought we'd slid through the whole thing. The team, including Clement, had accepted Carval – if you've seen the show, you can't miss that he's head over heels, but he's not a cop, they don't let him do cop things, and I'm damn sure they're toeing the line. The minute they don't, I'll have their collective asses. I don't care whether they're dating," he added. "Anyway, Clement wasn't happy to be the star of the show, but she gritted her teeth and took it."

"Yes. And?" Lewin leaned forward.

"The exhibition opened. As you know, 1PP wanted the NYPD to benefit from any good PR, so they arranged a press conference for the Monday, after it was clear the show was an outstanding success. I was confident the team could deal with it, but Clement's father went on a bender and was arrested again, at the 112th. Clement came to me for permission to go and collect him. I spoke to Wetherly, with Clement's full agreement, to make it clear they weren't to go easy on him. I also warned Wetherly that Birkett might try to make trouble, and asked him to make sure Birkett knew it would be a bad idea."

"Yes. I guess that was a good precaution."

"Sure it was. We were trying to head off anything that could put the NYPD in a bad light. You'd have thought every cop would understand that."

"Yeah," Lewin agreed.

"Clement collected her father, but the following day, Friday, he was admitted to the hospital and died. At Monday's press conference, a reporter had been tipped off that Clement's father had been arrested. He had been allowed to believe she was corruptly assisting her father to escape charges."

"Tipped off?"

"Yep. The tip-off was from my precinct, but Birkett didn't correct the record. I strongly suspect Officers Estrolla and Grendon, who tried to scapegoat Officer Henegan. I haven't interviewed them yet."

"Can I ask that you don't interview them about the tip-off? I appreciate you want to deal with your own men, but if we take over it'll remove any question of bias."

Kent sat back. "Okay. I'm grateful: this is a huge mess." He relaxed. "You know the rest, except there's been a covert campaign of harassing Clement by constantly placing press clippings of the articles about her father's death in places where she can't miss them. I'm taking steps, but that's purely a precinct matter. Again, I suspect Estrolla and Grendon, but it may lead back to Birkett. He's already come up in conversation, but it's third-hand at best."

"Thank you. It's fine if you go after them about the harassment, but leave the rest to me. Let's take a quick break, then we'll go into more detail about some things." Lewin switched off the recorder. "Wow," he said. "You've laid out a hell of a situation."

"Yeah." Kent disappeared for a moment.

Lewin switched the recorder back on when he returned. "Let's go back to when you took on Clement and O'Leary. You said you'd made some investigations?"

"Yes."

"Tell me about them."

Kent opened his mouth, and his phone rang. "Detective O'Leary?" He listened. "I see. Proceed. I will speak to you later."

"Trouble?"

"No, a case."

"Let's carry on, but if you need to deal with it, tell me and we'll continue later."

***

When the team came back from lunch, O'Leary checked his computer. "The runs have finished. Let's see what we got." He read down. "Waal, waal. Int'restin'."

"What?"

"Tomas is a relation of Pieter" –

"Hell," Casey spat.

"– an' he's another Tarticca. Herencia – Carlos – is a Pagliacci. It's a mystery what their licences are doin' on two Yarrabees."

"We thought the licences were fake," Andy mused, "but they're real – could they have stolen them?"

"Yeah, but why?" Dani asked the key question. "What's the point of stealing a licence you can't use?"

"To make sure someone else can't use it?" Casey thought aloud, slowly. "What if they needed those licences for ID?"

"This is organised crime, though. They must know how to make a quality fake driver's licence." Dani frowned.

"Yeah. That can't be why they were stolen."

"Or maybe," Dani began, "there's something more to those licences." She smiled suddenly. "This sounds crazy, but hear me out."

"RFID chip," Andy exclaimed.

"You guessed." Dani humphed. "Stealing my thunder."

"An' for the rest of us?" O'Leary said.

"We're suggesting," Dani said, Andy nodding, "those two licences had a tiny little tracking chip – an RFID chip – for the other side of a transaction to identify, so they knew it was the right people."

"But," Andy went on, "you can track an RFID chip with a mobile scanner, though the range isn't huge" –

"That's how they found them!" Casey burst out. "I knew they couldn't have cruised Upper Manhattan till they found a stray Yarrabee – but what about Hocking? Is there a third stolen licence we haven't found yet? Or more?"

"And from my point of view in Narcotics," Dani added, "why did they steal them *now*? What's going down?"

152

"Must be something," Tyler said. "Big delivery?"

"We need to get the Feds in now," Casey decided. "If something's planned," – she cast a quick glance at Dani, who didn't mind her taking the lead – "we should brief the Feds asap. We can't wait till tomorrow. We'd better not do anything about hauling Hocking in before we co-ordinate with them."

"I'll call Glencross," Dani said, "if you get Renfrew."

"Ugh," Casey griped, "but okay. Andy, you call Bergen." She made a face. "O'Leary, Tyler, I guess you ought to brief Kent. He won't be happy about being disturbed on a Sunday."

They split up. Casey dialled. "Dr Renfrew?"

"Detective Clement? Has something transpired?"

"We've worked out how they found the Yarrabees." She explained the team's reasoning.

"I see. How ingenious."

"If there is a major delivery being planned," Casey said, "we should discuss immediately, so you and DEA have the best chance of stopping it."

"I concur. Thank you. I shall attend on you immediately. It will take me approximately forty minutes to arrive. I shall call Agent Bergen and Agent Glencross."

"Andy is calling Bergen, so we don't lose time. Detective Handjiev is speaking to Agent Glencross."

"Most efficient."

"We'll inform Captain Kent, too. He may or may not want to join us."

"Thank you. I will be there as quickly as possible."

At Andy's desk, the conversation was rapid. "Bergen, it's Andy. We caught a break. There are RFID tags in the fake licences. You got a scanner?"

"Sure I do."

"Great. Can you get it here stat?"

"On the way. Bye."

Dani was more formal. "Agent Glencross, I'm at the Thirty-Sixth precinct. Could you join us, please? We suspect the Tarticcas and Pagliaccis are planning a big shipment, and possibly taking out the Yarrabees along the way."

"Okay. I'll be there within the hour. Brief me then."

"Dr Renfrew and Agent Bergen are on their way too."

"Good. Later."

The team reconvened. "Everyone's on their way. What did Kent say?" Casey asked.

"Keep him posted, but he'll talk to us later. Funny, it sounded like he was in an office."

"Not relevant. We've got an hour. What can we find out in that time?"

"Bergen's bringing a scanner to check those licences. We need to find out if Hocking was carrying one."

"Prints?" Tyler queried.

"Unpack."

"Whose prints are on the licences?"

"Why?"

"Tie in others."

"Any other licences in the car?"

"I'll call CSU," O'Leary said. Casey wrote both on the to-do list.

"Autopsy report? We didn't get it yet," she said. "There's no point chasing McDonald. He'll send it as soon as it's done."

"What did they find at Wiedecz's apartment?"

"I was too busy gettin' shot to find out. Did we send in CSU?"

"I don't know. How do they interact with the shooting team?"

"I'll ask CSU that too, an' send 'em over iffen they haven't gone already."

"Okay. Any other thoughts? We need to keep on going through the cameras, too."

Andy didn't react.

"Andy!"

"Uh, yeah? I was thinking about the RFID tracking. Those tiny little chips don't have a big range, so I'm not sure how they found the Yarrabees. It can't have been luck."

"That's what I said."

"You can have a network of scanners – Dani, do you have a list of all the Tarticcas' hangouts around Upper Manhattan and especially near the Yarrabees' headquarters?"

"That's seriously sophisticated," Casey said. "Could they do that?"

"If they're smart enough to use RFID" –

"It's a step up, but the Tarticcas are smart," Dani interjected.

"– they could do this. It's not difficult, once you get started."

"Great. Does this help us find Grappano?" Casey asked. "'Cause we've still got a murder to solve."

"Mebbe he's carryin' one of these teeny li'l chips," O'Leary speculated. "We c'n wander around the Tarticcas HQ an' see iffen anythin' pings."

"Dodging bullets all the way." Casey made a sour face. "You're as inconspicuous as an elephant."

"I ain't insistin'," O'Leary said amiably.

"We could get some of our officers to do it," Andy suggested. "Swap them out for the beat cops on duty, and give them little readers to see what they find."

"It's a bit random," Casey said. "We only want Grappano."

"We might want all the others," Dani pointed out, "but it'd be better as a co-ordinated operation, rather than randomly picking up Tarticcas or Pagliaccis."

"Okay. We'll discuss when the others get here. Let's get on with the rest of the list, till they show up."

Precisely forty minutes later, Renfrew arrived, which Casey acidly supposed meant he'd waited outside to make sure it took him exactly forty minutes. Bergen was only five minutes behind. Agent Glencross, a sinewy, middle-aged man with the lean build of a long-distance runner and piercing grey-green eyes, made up the party.

"Thanks for coming here at short notice," Casey opened in the FBI's conference room, taking charge without a pause and bringing everyone up to date with their thoughts and conclusions. "We thought it was best to get everyone together immediately so we can work out what to do next."

"Most clearly delineated," Renfrew said. Casey caught Agent Glencross's tiny eyeroll, and decided he'd be a sensible guy. "Agent Bergen, with Agent Glencross, has arranged for wiretaps on the landlines and cell phones of Federico Tarticca and Frank Auster. I have copies of the federal judge's approvals should we need them."

"They were set up as soon as we had the judge's approval," Bergen said, "but that wasn't till early this morning."

"Nothing useful yet?"

"No. If there is, I'll be alerted at once."

"Before we plan any raid," Agent Glencross suggested, "let's listen in for a while. I agree something interesting is likely to happen, but I don't think it'll be tonight. Do you have the licences there? Let's see what Bergen's little toy shows us."

Andy brought the licences out, safely in evidence bags. "CSU'll run them for prints," he explained, "so I'm leaving them in the bags. It won't make any difference to the scan." He grinned at Bergen. "I'd like that scanner," he tried.

"I bet." Bergen grinned back. "If it disappears, I'll search you first." He worked his scanning magic, and his grin widened. "I don't know how you worked it out," he admired, "but there are chips in these licences. See these little dots? That's them."

"It was Dani and Andy," Casey noted.

"Team effort," the two blushing cops said.

"Yep." Casey closed that line off. "We could send our officers out as beat cops to find the readers. Dani's asked for a list of Tarticca hangouts. Agent Glencross, would you check in case you know of more? We want to put a map together. How do we spot the readers?"

"Likely they'll look like door security – same as where we put our passes to get into the precinct," Andy said.

"That's an RFID?"

Andy pulled his out and looked at it. "Yep. No magnetic stripe. Didn't you ever notice?"

"Nope." Casey shook her head. "Why would I?"

Andy sighed at Casey's complete lack of technological interest. "Never mind." He received a sympathetic glance from Bergen. "They look like door security. That's all you need to know."

"We'll show our officers some images, and they can map it out. Every time they spot one, they plot it. By the time they're done" –

"They'll have sore feet," O'Leary chortled.

"We'll have a map of how the Tarticcas found their missing licences and the Yarrabees carrying them," Casey finished firmly, scowling at O'Leary's teasing.

"Indeed. Will four officers, no matter how motivated, be enough?" Renfrew asked. "We shall need to achieve our map" – *our?* thought the team and Dani – "rapidly, in case we should discover from our wiretaps that the Tarticcas will be, as they say, 'making their move' shortly."

"If we put too many boots on the ground," Glencross pointed out, "they'll spot us."

"So we mix uniformed officers with some plain clothes officers," Casey replied. "We have to keep Fremont and our three in uniform – they've done a whole bunch of canvassing around there and they might have been noticed. This is work that rookies were invented for. All they have to do is amble around and note door security, in ordinary clothes."

"Brief 'em." Tyler smiled in best drill-sergeant fashion.

"Fine by me," Glencross, Dani, and Casey chorused.

"I'll go find the sergeant," O'Leary suggested, and didn't wait for agreement before clomping off.

"Do we have a plan for now?" Casey asked. "We're getting somewhere with your drugs and crime gangs, but I have a murder to solve, and I need to find Grappano. He was last seen going into Tarticca headquarters, but if there's a major DEA and FBI raid on it, it won't help if I storm in there with a warrant for Grappano without co-ordinating it with you."

"Indeed not," Renfrew agreed. Glencross nodded firmly.

"Grappano might be carrying one of these little chips too." She grimaced horribly. "How did the Yarrabees get their paws on these souped-up licences?"

CHAPTER NINETEEN

"Maria!" Casey exclaimed. "Maria Montelucci."

"Mm?" Glencross hummed.

"Miss Montelucci is connected to the Tarticcas," Renfrew expanded, "albeit she is reluctant to be so."

"She was dating Buster – Beau Resorge," Casey explained, "one of our two dead Yarrabees."

"Ah." Glencross made a gentle *carry-on* gesture.

"Maria isn't too bright, though neither was Beau," Casey said. "It's possible she let something slip to Beau, or to his friends if she met them – we can ask her – that a smarter Yarrabee picked up on."

"Talking to Miss Montelucci again appears to be a priority," Renfrew pontificated.

"Yes." Casey glanced at her slim watch. "Almost four, and she's supposed to be at work tomorrow." Her forehead creased for an instant. "I'd better talk to her today." She cast around. "O'Leary, have you finished your socialising? We need to go talk to Maria again." She turned back to Renfrew and Glencross. "If we do that now, and Tyler fixes up the uniforms – uniformed and plain clothes – will you still be here when we get back?"

"I will," Renfrew opined. "We have much to consider, and if all else fails, we shall plan how best to achieve our operation."

"Yes," Glencross said to Casey, which brevity was appreciated. "I'll want to know what you find out."

"Sure. Okay, O'Leary, let's go."

"CSU?" Andy asked.

"C'n you an' Tyler do it?"

"Sure."

***

"So," Lewin summarised, "Clement pissed off Marcol and Birkett at the Academy. Birkett was pretty outspoken about her. He asserted that she lied, cheated and slept with every instructor."

Kent turned purple, eyes bulging. "You give one *scrap* of credence to that evidence-falsifying *weasel?*" he bellowed. "He's lying through his teeth out of spite."

"You don't believe it?"

"Of course I don't! I told you, I investigated those rumours – as did Garrett, before me." Kent raked Lewin with a scarifying glare. "There wasn't a single word of truth in it. A recruit *might* – though I doubt it – be able to pull the wool over the instructors' eyes for a week, but not for the full course. They'd be found out. And if Clement were trying to get promotion by handing out sexual favours, she wouldn't only have tried it on the instructors. There's never been a single whisper."

"You said there were rumours about her and O'Leary."

"I *also* said he's gay, and I'm convinced they cooked it up together to protect him. Not her." Kent forcibly relaxed his fists. "Clement's team – all four of them – are so tight-knit you couldn't put a Kleenex between them. They're utterly loyal to each other, but there's never been a single whisper," he repeated, "of anything even a smidgeon out of order. Clement went in to bat against Dr Renfrew of the FBI, when she thought he was taking pot-shots at her team. Tyler made sure I wouldn't impose Marcol on them. The whole bunch of them took some of the dumber officers for some sparring training, but I'm dead sure it was a lesson in what happens when you try a little rumour-spreading." Kent harrumphed. "I ordered them not to do it again, but no-one'll go anywhere near them now. They fix each other, and I don't interfere unless I have to. Like now," he added acidly. "I don't want them upset. They've got a solve rate the rest of the NYPD would die for, and they don't take shortcuts."

Lewin sipped his tepid coffee. "How do four such different people get to be that tight?"

"They're known as the misfit team. Four misfits, who fit together, God knows how."

"I see." He drained his cup. "Going back to Clement's Academy period, the whole mess sounds like junior high. Are you sure about it?"

"There are Marcols right through the NYPD," Kent began, "all of 'em good cops. Bob Marcol is respected from the top of the force to the bottom, and I've never heard anything bad about any of the others – until this one. He's an arrogant guy, he's got a decent record, but he's not the superstar he thinks he is. He expected to be at the top of the Academy because he's a Marcol, and he didn't like someone taking the place he thought was his by right. Yes, it's something he should've grown out of in junior high, but he's sure as hell not the first person who's had some growing up to do. Birkett? I don't know. You'd need to ask Wetherly." Kent sighed. "Clement's record shows she's as good as the Academy trophy cabinet says she was. That tells you all you need to know about Birkett's lies."

"Mm. Look, Kent, this is all very helpful as far as it goes, but it doesn't exactly go far. Why *is* Marcol so set on taking Clement down?"

"The only reason I can think of is that damn stolen photograph. Carval – without Clement knowing, and that didn't go down well when she found out – went after it. He and his manager both told me they didn't care what I said, they had every right to sue, and they would. Now, *I* think Marcol can see his scheme being found out, and he'll look bad in front of his family, IA, and 1PP. Even if nobody takes any action, he'll look pretty poor. Like I said, he's an arrogant guy, and if this had never come out he'd've been aiming to be high up in 1PP."

Lewin sighed. "I see," he reiterated, in a tone which strongly suggested that he didn't see.

"You could," Kent said with gentle malice, "ask Dr Renfrew, who's been studying the team as well as working with them. He might have more insights."

"Involve the FBI?"

"He's a profiler and shrink. He's studying them for some paper he wants to write on team dynamics, but he's also been heavily involved in the affair." Kent's mouth twisted. "Try not to get riled by him. He's a pompous, patronising man, but he's top-class."

"Mm. Okay. Like I said, I'll be interviewing some of your officers. That won't be a problem, will it?"

"No. If you prove they're implicated, I don't want them. But if you intend to interview Clement or any of her team, I want to know first. You're not messing around with them."

"We don't" –

"You won't," Kent stated. "There's *nothing* that indicates Clement's team has done anything wrong, and I won't have IA implying they have."

"I'll tell you. But if I tell you not to tip them off, don't."

***

"Maria? It's Detectives Clement and O'Leary, again."

Maria looked around the chain, blinked damply, and opened the door. "Hey," she dripped. "Is this about Beau? Have you caught them?" Tears puddled in her reddened eyes. "Tell me you got them?"

"We have a likely suspect," Casey temporised. "Can we come in and talk to you? You're our best chance to put Beau's murderer in jail."

"Sure. Anything. We were going to be so happy…" She dissolved into desolate sobs.

"Thank you." Casey gathered her thoughts and dialled down her vocabulary to something Maria would understand. The words 'RFID chips' didn't figure in the list. "Maria, don't worry if this sounds weird, I promise it'll help us find Beau's killer."

"Okay," Maria acceded.

"When you were chatting to Beau, on the way to the movies or going for pizza, did you ever talk about getting your drivers' licences?"

"Oh, sure. He'd taken a while to get through the written test – he wasn't big on writing," she sniffed, then blew her nose, "but he was a good driver. Careful, you know? Not like some of Uncle Federico's friends. I don't know how they got their licences."

"I guess they drove better for the test?"

"They couldn't have driven worse." She blew her nose again. "Uncle Federico checked all their licences. He wanted everyone to give them to him."

"That's good," O'Leary approved. "We don't want dangerous drivers on the roads."

"No."

"Did your uncle keep the licences for long?"

"Oh, no. I guess he was making copies or something, so he had the information."

"Did he copy yours?"

"Yes, even though I didn't work for him, and I hardly ever drive anyway, 'cause it's so hard to park."

"Sure is. You told Beau about it?"

"Yes. I showed him my licence, but it was a couple of days later."

"When?"

"Uh…" Maria's pretty, juvenile face wrinkled. "Maybe a month or two ago – oh, yes. About a month, because we went to the movies."

"Thanks. That's great." Casey manufactured a gentle smile. "Could I see your licence?"

"Sure."

Casey examined the licence, finding a small dot on the back. "That's been really helpful. Did you show it to Beau?"

"Yes. There's this little dot – see, here? – and I was wondering what it was, but Beau's didn't have it, so I guess it's just a mark." Maria tapped the dot Casey had spotted.

"There's one more thing you can do for Beau. Could we borrow this licence for a couple of days? We want to make sure nobody's cloned it."

160

Casey was pretty certain Maria wouldn't understand cloning, but would co-operate.

"Yes. Will you bring it back or should I come get it? I can't come till after work."

"What's easier for you? You're helping us."

"I could come get it. It's only an extra couple of stops on the subway."

"Okay. Thank you."

Casey wrote her a receipt on a clean sheet from her notebook. "Just so there's no problem when we call you to come get it – if I'm not around, ask any of the desk officers. Someone'll find it for you."

"This'll help you?"

"Yes." Casey wasn't lying. It would help enormously. It simply wasn't the help Maria thought she was giving. "It will."

"Okay," she wobbled, trying to steady her voice. "You'll tell me…?"

"Of course we will."

***

"Waal, that was interestin'," O'Leary said.

"Sure was. It sounds like Tarticca was chipping all the licences." Casey frowned. "That's another way he could've been tracking Beau, though, by tracking Maria – but Beau had a stolen licence with him. My head hurts," she complained. "Why can't we find Grappano and put him away, and leave the Feds to it?"

"You need to finish your shift an' go home," O'Leary said. "If I was you, I'd go find your boy an' snuggle up."

"Yeah. Maybe."

"Where's he been?"

"Shooting construction. There's too many Feds around." *For him to be able to support me*, O'Leary heard. "Renfrew's already poking his nose in."

"There's another good reason to finish your shift an' go home. He can't talk to you iffen you ain't there."

"He'll go poking into Dad," Casey griped, "and Kent ordered it."

"Shame. Let's get back, get done, an' get out." O'Leary flicked a glance at her. "You oughta get a good night's sleep. Iffen them bags under your eyes get any bigger, you'll need to put 'em in the trunk."

When they returned to the bullpen, they gathered the team, the Feds, and Dani, and produced the licence together with a brisk download of the information they'd gained from Maria.

"So, Bergen," Casey wound up, "could you run your scanner over this and see if it pings?"

"Yep." Bergen grinned widely as his scanner did indeed ping happily, which matched the mood of the collective law enforcers. "There. One RFID chip. Smart guys."

"I prefer my criminals to be dumb," Glencross commented sardonically. "It makes my life easier."

"You should be happy with the Yarrabees," Dani replied. "They don't seem too smart."

"Smart enough to find out about the chips."

"I have a thought," Casey said. "We're mapping Paddy Hocking via his cell phone, and he was the third target. I bet he's got his hands on another of these chipped licences, and he's trying to find out where the shipment might come in. I'd also bet that every Yarrabee they can spare is trying to get hold of more licences so they can do the same. Dani, has anyone heard about more messing around and fighting between the Tarticcas and the Yarrabees than usual – say in the last month?"

"You think they might be going after them individually to steal chipped licences?"

"It's possible."

"I agree, and furthermore, it is likely. Such instances of individual argument might go unnoticed, whereas a more extensive raid or fight would have come to the attention of DEA and Narcotics division." Dr Renfrew pushed up his glasses, then steepled his fingers.

"I'll call," Dani said. "It's been a little more lively than usual, but I'll see what my colleagues know."

"How's the map going?" Casey asked Bergen.

"Slowly. It hasn't had long to build up a pattern, but by the time your officers have passed by the Tarticca properties and noted whether they have card readers on the doors, we'll have something that might be useful. We can overlay one on the other, and see what turns up."

"Okay. Should we bring Hocking in to see if he's got a stolen licence?" Casey suggested.

"I'd like to get a better map from him first," Bergen said.

"It might tip off the Yarrabees that we're on to something," Dani noted, one step ahead of Glencross.

"Okay," Casey conceded. "Can we do anything more tonight? Tyler, are our officers briefed?"

"Yeah. Start now, through tomorrow."

"Okay. Andy, any smart tech stuff you can do? What did CSU say?"

"They'll process Wiedecz's apartment tonight – Evan doesn't love you any more – they didn't find any more licences in Wiedecz's car, but I've asked the shooting team to give us Wiedecz's if they have it, or CSU if they find it, so we can check it for chips – and I'll send one of the officers over to Jamaica to the lab to hand in these licences to be run for prints." He smiled widely. "But."

"But what?" everyone asked.

"But there was a mobile scanner in the car."

"Aha! That's how they did the last bit. They tracked, and when they'd narrowed it right down, they went out with the scanner." Casey looked at the assorted Feds. "Is there anything more?" she asked.

"Not for your team," Glencross replied. "You've gotten us a lot further than we could've hoped for. If there's anything more tonight, one of us can call you. Tomorrow, most likely, we'll be hurrying up and waiting."

Casey regarded her team, who regarded her right back with *nothing-more* expressions. "Okay. If we're done for the evening, let's pack up and reconvene tomorrow." She stopped. "If we don't have anything more for your side of things, I'd like to interview Federico Tarticca about Grappano. I want to pick Grappano up as soon as I can without blowing up your wider operation."

"I do not think that should be an issue," Renfrew opined. "I am quite certain you can now pursue Grappano with the evidence you have without compromising our movements."

"Thanks," Casey answered, and repressed the desire to add a sarcastic inflection. "Good night, everyone."

"Wait for me," O'Leary said meaningfully. Casey shrugged, but dutifully waited.

Downstairs, O'Leary wiggled his squirrel-tail eyebrows at Casey. "You goin' to see your boy?"

"This is your business how?"

"Just lookin' out for you," the big man said pacifically, "like you'd look out for me." Casey made a disgusted noise. "You would." He patted her head, which he knew infuriated her. "Home you go. Eat somethin', snuggle up to Carval, get some sleep."

"I guess you're cheaper than hiring a nanny," Casey snipped.

"I am, but I do hear nannies get paid a whole bunch an' get to travel."

"Only if they're working for mega-rich people."

"Oh," O'Leary drooped. "That ain't us."

"Nope. See you tomorrow."

"Yeah."

Casey, watched by O'Leary, drove off. O'Leary shook his massive head, then texted Carval. *Casey done for today. If she's not at yours, go find her. Make her eat and sleep.*

***

Carval read O'Leary's text, smiled wryly, and waited to see what would happen. As he was wondering whether to go to Casey's apartment, his entry phone buzzed. He opened the door, and shortly Casey peeked around the door of his studio.

"Hey," she said.

Carval extracted himself from his desk and screens, and scanned Casey's tired form. "How were the Feds?" Casey made a horrible face, which was all the answer he needed. "Dinner?"

"I have food at home," she said. "I dropped by because I know O'Leary texted you."

Carval coloured slightly.

"I knew he would."

"Oh."

"So it was easier to pick you up than wait for you to show up at my door," Casey finished. Carval's jaw dropped. "I'm hungry. C'mon."

"Okay," he bounced. "Give me five minutes." He bounded upstairs and collected a small holdall containing a change of clothes and a small washbag, hastily purchased earlier as he'd realised he disliked borrowing a razor, toothbrush, or going out in the previous day's underwear. He loped back down, three steps at a time, picked up his camera bag, and grinned. "Ready."

"What's that?"

"My camera bag."

"No, the other bag."

"Change of clothes, if you want me to stay. I like to have clean clothes in the morning," he said pompously. Casey made a sound that might, had she not been so drawn and tired-looking, have been a raspberry. Without needing to think about it, Carval switched his bags to his other shoulder, and drew Casey into the side she preferred to walk on. "There."

Casey breathed in deeply, and let the day go. Once again, as soon as she had left the precinct, her energy had drained and her memories resurfaced. Carval put his bags in the trunk, and slid into the passenger seat, swamping her small hand on the wheel. She turned her hand upward to link into his, and took some comfort from the warmth before she withdrew to switch the engine on and move out.

Halfway home, her phone chirped.

"Do you want me to look, in case it's the team?" Carval asked.

"No. It can wait till we get there."

Shortly, Casey unlocked her apartment. "I've got some noodles," she began, and was stopped by Carval, turning her into him and simply hugging her.

"Don't worry about it for a minute. Have a hug. You'd better eat, because you look like a ghost."

"Who texted me?" She dug up her phone, and stared at the screen. "It's Kayla – you remember, Asher's girlfriend. The runner who was murdered by his aunt and uncle."

"What's she want?"

"She's suggesting coffee, or dinner and drinks." Casey put the phone away. "I'll think about it."

"You should go."

"Huh? Are you O'Leary suddenly?"

"No," Carval humphed. "You should go. Someone who isn't about murder. Different friends." She gaped at him. "Different friends," he repeated. "More than the team."

"But you" –

"I make lots of friends, everywhere I shoot. Some of them even genuinely like me," he added cynically. "But mostly I keep to a very few people, like Allan, and Mario and Carina, who've known me forever."

"Oh," Casey managed. "Uh…there are others?"

"Yeah. Sometime, you'll have to meet them. I'll set it up. For now, you should go meet Kayla and have a nice evening away from the job and…and everything. Even me, though I'm sure you'll miss me," he added conceitedly.

"Turn your ego off," Casey suggested. "It's doubling my electricity bill."

Carval hugged her again. "Mean," he complained. "Very mean."

"You'll live." She flinched at her own words.

"What's for dinner?" Carval asked hastily. "More microwaved morsels?"

"Lasagne," Casey said. "Not microwaved, so you'll have to wait."

"It'll give you time to reply to Kayla."

Casey scrunched her face up. "Don't push," she warned. "I…I don't need to be pushed." She unwrapped the lasagne and put it in the oven, silently. "Let me work it out."

"Okay," he said to her back as she retreated to her bedroom. *Well, that was a major fuck-up*, he thought, and wondered, before he heard the soft sounds of her changing from work clothes to something more relaxed, if she'd come back out. If she was changing, she'd come back. And if she wanted him to leave, she'd have yelled at him to go.

CHAPTER TWENTY

She came back out in comfortable sweats and a cotton t-shirt, minimal make-up cleaned off, found plates and cutlery, some not-dead-yet salad in the drawer of the fridge, and two sodas. She didn't say anything, but her silence didn't convey annoyance or hostility, simply exhausted sadness. He didn't push, merely respected her silence and set the table quietly.

He sat on the couch, and when she flopped down beside him, placed an arm around her shoulders. They stayed cuddled up until the oven timer beeped. There wasn't much conversation over dinner, nor after they returned to the couch. Casey had a small crease between her eyebrows, as if she was analysing a difficult problem. Carval kept his mouth shut by main force and an occasional bite of his tongue, and thought about construction sites and photographs.

His photographic reverie was interrupted by Casey wriggling out of his loose clasp; picking up her phone to text; pressing send with a sharp, *done* emphasis; finally coming back to curl up on the couch again. "Kayla." She didn't explain further.

"'Kay." Carval plopped a kiss on the top of her head. He *wanted* to say *wowowowow you took my advice!* Since he didn't want to be dead, he merely said, "C'mere."

"Okay." Casey was happy to snuggle back in. Telling Kayla she'd be happy to meet when the case was done had been enough. She was ebbing fast, and while Carval next to her was good for her sleeping, she had a vague idea that relying on him was both dumb and unfair. She couldn't expect someone else to solve her problems: she had to do it. She knew he'd support her – but there was support, and there was turning into a parasitic vine, clinging to him without even trying to do things herself. Regardless of what he'd said, *she* didn't want to be crying all over him every other minute.

166

It wasn't…well, it wasn't a good plan. She yawned widely, then kissed him. "I'll see you tomorrow?"

Carval took the hint, though he wished she'd told him before he'd brought the holdall. "I'll drop by the precinct at shift end, unless I hear from you."

"Okay." She half-smiled, and hugged him.

He hugged her back, and reluctantly left. He'd hoped she'd ask him to stay, but when he thought about it, he realised they'd spent quite a few nights together since her father died, and maybe she needed a little space. He ambled home, wondering, but downloading his shots put any discomfort out of his mind, and soon he was lost in working with them.

In her warm-toned apartment, curled up on her plump couch, Casey finally let the memories of her father's awful, final evening resurface. They punched through her as viciously as the first day afterwards: repressing them while she'd worked hadn't softened their pinpoint, painful precision. O'Leary's words haunted her. *You're tryin' to get past somethin' in a week that'll take months*, he'd said. She didn't want to take months. She didn't want to remember those last few terrible hours. She didn't want to remember how she'd told him she was done; how she'd only told him she loved him a moment before he had gone; how she might have been too late; how he might have died thinking she didn't care.

He must have heard her. He'd known she was there. She buried her face in her sweatshirt. He *had* known.

She had to believe he had heard her.

She shivered, and went to take the hottest shower she could manage; telling herself all the water running down her face was only the spray. She was still chilled when she wrapped herself in her robe, but tucking under her quilt didn't warm her. She wished she'd asked Carval to stay, but shook her head. She couldn't. They weren't *ready* for 100% togetherness.

She slid down, and tried to sleep. It even worked, for at least half an hour at a time.

***

Casey ignored every single one of Kent's decrees about unapproved overtime and, in particular, his requirement that she work her shifts and nothing more without his explicit authorisation. She bought coffee at her favourite coffee bar and hit the bullpen far too early on Monday, still exhausted but unable to sleep without nightmares. Prompted by a small piece of common-sense, she tipped back her double espresso and went up to the gym, where she could run on one of the treadmills until her brain had cleared.

Two miles later, her mind and limbs were eased; a mile afterwards, she thought, correctly, she could safely shower and reach her desk without Kent admonishing her. She was quietly considering the day ahead when her team filtered in, followed by Agent Glencross and Dani, deep in conversation; Agent Bergen, enthusiastically waving at Andy; and finally Dr Renfrew.

"We have something from the wiretap," Bergen said happily.

"We do? What?" Casey jerked to full attention.

"Well, it's not nearly conclusive, but they're discussing a potential delivery. Glencross, Dani and Renfrew are all trying to fit it into what DEA and Narcotics already know."

"Great, but how does it help me find Grappano?"

"The delivery sounds like it's in the next couple of days. Can we speed up your patrolling officers to get that map, and I'll see what Paddy's movements are showing up? When the officers come back, I can overlay."

"Okay. I can still go interrogate Tarticca, can't I?"

"I'd check, but it didn't sound like there was a problem."

Casey stalked off to see Glencross, and shortly returned. "Okay, we can go interview about Grappano, as long as we don't even hint about drugs and raids, and don't use our warrant – yet. And still no pulling Hocking in."

"Were we goin' to?"

"Nope, and I pointed that out."

"I bet," Andy whispered. "Should we check the room for corpses?"

O'Leary sniggered, swiftly smothered when Casey glared. "Are you coming?" she growled, "or are you visiting the Comedy Club to try out?"

"Someone ain't full of sweetness an' light," O'Leary chided, but followed Casey out. "You okay?" he asked in the SUV.

"I'm fine."

O'Leary rapidly translated her words to mean *I'm not fine but don't push me*, and diverted his conversation. "What're you planning with Tarticca?"

"Call him on his lies, demand Grappano, show him the footage of Grappano entering and a picture of Grappano and the driver to demand he produces the driver too, and generally make trouble, fuss and cause terror."

"Sounds good to me. Causin' terror's what we do."

"For criminals."

"Yeah. An' for troublesome types around the bullpen."

"What do you mean?"

"Waal," O'Leary said with unusual uncertainty, "I think thin's are hottin' up a bit, what with Kent bein' missin' an' weird echoes. 'T ain't like him not to want a report iffen one of us calls, but he didn't, an' I'd lay good green dollars he was in an office somewheres. I think he's had about enough of all this trouble an' fuss, and we know he was interrogatin' Birkett."

"We know Birkett got hauled in by IA," Casey recalled. "You're suggesting Kent's going after everyone?"

"Naw. I'm suggestin' IA's goin' after everyone. Didn't you notice Kent warnin' us to keep everythin' completely clean an' shiny white?"

"Yeah. Great."

"So you take care of yourself, okay? No goin' out on your own. Not even to the gym – I know you were up there runnin' this mornin', an' what would you've done if Estrolla'd come in? You'd've had your earbuds in, an' you wouldn't've heard him till he was right there. I know you c'n out-spar him, but iffen you have to, Kent'll have your ass in a sling, an' that's no fun."

"I needed to run," she explained unhappily. "It's not like the bullpen's a friendly place right now."

"When's it ever been? But you ain't as right as you'd've been a year ago. Year ago, no-one liked us" – Casey joined in the mantra – "an' we didn't care. Now...waal, Feggetter's quite fond of us, an' we got those four li'l officers – even Henegan's doin' better, an' they went in to bat when Bartlett got dumbassed, so...y'know, Casey, we're slippin'. Some people actually like us. We can't have that: we'll lose our reputation. You better go scarin' one or two of 'em before they think we're gettin' soft an' fluffy."

Casey's lips twisted bitterly. "Maybe we should go to a precinct quiz night? That'll do it. Or we could wait for Kent to scour the bullpen, because that'll make sure everyone hates us again."

"I don't think we'll have to wait too long," O'Leary said heavily. "I really don't."

"No." Casey yawned.

"Didn't you sleep?"

"Some. Thinking."

O'Leary leered cheerfully at her. "Should'a been snugglin' up to your boy." Casey didn't say anything. "Now, don't tell me you had a fight again."

"No."

"Good. Why wasn't he there?"

"I needed a night on my own. He was there earlier."

O'Leary made a *Puh!* noise, but didn't comment, loudly.

"Anyway, I agreed to go for coffee or drinks or dinner or something with Kayla when the case is done," Casey defended. "I wasn't going to, but Carval said I should think about it, so I did."

"You took someone's advice? Casey, Casey. What'm I goin' to do 'bout my career as the next Dear Abby iffen you take someone else's advice?"

"You'd've said the same." She peered out of the windshield. "Are we here already?"

"Yep. Time to go terrorisin'."

Both of them noted the ostensible security reader outside the door of the Tarticcas' main hangout. It was discreet, but it didn't belong on a bar.

***

Kent regarded his tidy desk with annoyance, largely caused by the knowledge that in the next few moments he would have to undertake two truly unpleasant interviews. However, the unpleasantness would be experienced solely by those unlucky officers to whom he would apply an enormous dose of reality.

He strode to the middle of the bullpen, stood foursquare, scowled blackly at the cringing cops, and spotted his prey.

"Officer Grendon!"

Grendon rocketed from his casual slouch to full attention. "Sir?"

"You will accompany me to Interrogation Two," Kent ordered. Grendon tried to disappear, failed; tried to catch Estrolla's eye, failed; tried to spot anything informative in the contents of the file Kent was holding – and failed again.

"Sir," he mumbled. Nothing in his sloppy demeanour indicated that he had the slightest idea of the unhappiness about to descend upon him.

To Andy and Tyler's deeply interested eyes, Kent appeared to be arresting Grendon.

In Interrogation Two, Kent closed the door with an ominous gentleness, the meaning of which was entirely lost on Grendon.

"Officer Grendon." Kent sat down. Grendon moved to the other chair, which Kent didn't prevent. Grendon hadn't worked out he was about to sit down in the suspect's position. He dropped into the seat. Kent, a man who knew the value of silence, waited.

"Isn't there someone else coming in?" Grendon asked. "Shouldn't there be a suspect, or witness?"

Kent produced a razor-thin smile. "There is, Officer Grendon. You."

"What?" Grendon gaped.

Kent pushed across a series of photographs. "These were taken from a camera placed to observe Detective Clement's desk. I note you are clearly visible. Why were you there? You are not working on any of her cases, or on any matter which would require you to be within ten feet of Detective Clement, her desk, or any of her team or their desks. So, Officer Grendon, why, *precisely*, were you there?"

Kent waited, to no avail. "In case your memory is at fault, Grendon, this footage is time stamped. Friday, at eight-forty-eight p.m. I have checked the staffing roster. You were on shift. None of Detective Clement or her team were, which, no doubt, explains why she was not at her desk." He let the words hang, icicle-like, over Grendon's head for a long, cold, sixty measured seconds. "So why were you?"

Grendon gaped some more, petrified. "I…" he started, saw his sentence unrolling in front of him and stopped, clearly realising he hadn't seen all the contents of the buff folder in front of Kent.

"I believe, Grendon, you experienced some sparring practice with Clement and her team recently?" Kent smiled again. It didn't reassure Grendon one iota. "While I applaud the dedication to duty that, no doubt, prompted Clement's team to practice with you, I should advise you that I have seen the shots of your sparring session, and it is perfectly obvious that you were completely outclassed by Detective Chee. Whose idea was the session?"

Grendon's petrified face remained stone silent.

"Answer me!" Kent bellowed. Grendon didn't, or, more likely, couldn't. "You will remain here while I interrogate Officer Estrolla. The door will remain locked."

Kent returned to the bullpen, stopped once more in its centre, and drew a deep breath. "Officer Estrolla, you will attend in Interrogation with me, immediately."

"Sir." Estrolla slouched to his feet, until he caught the look in Kent's eye, when he straightened up fast.

***

The same underling manned the bar masking the entry to Federico Tarticca's main hangout. This time, however, he recognised Casey and O'Leary, and a flash of fear whipped through his face. "You!"

"Us, Tarrant," Casey confirmed coldly. "I see you remember us. Good. We like to be memorable. We like memorable people, too. Especially when they kill babies. Where's Grappano?"

"Who?" Tarrant quivered. Casey's projected intimidation rose. O'Leary merely looked stern, which was intimidating enough. "I don't know him!"

Casey rammed a photo under Tarrant's terrified nose. "Him. And the guy driving."

"I don't know him."

"You didn't look." Casey's tone was solid steel. "Look at the photo." Tarrant did. "Now, *do you know them?*"

"No!"

"Have you seen them" –

"What's going on here?" Federico Tarticca had erupted into the room. "How dare you" –

"Federico." Casey exposed her teeth, which didn't express any pleasure. "How nice to see you. You've saved us the trouble of walking downstairs to find you. You'll have to wait, though. We aren't finished with Jeff yet." She turned away dismissively, and his face darkened.

"You can't" –

O'Leary's huge frame moved itself to stand between Federico and Casey. "We can," he rumbled. "We c'n ask him here or we c'n ask him

171

down at the precinct. We don't mind. You c'n come too. We got questions for you."

Casey ignored them. O'Leary would deal with Federico. "Have you seen this man?" she repeated to Tarrant, tapping Grappano.

He tried to look at Federico, but O'Leary's mass blocked him. "No." he eventually said.

"Were you here on Thursday?"

Tarrant's lips formed *No*, but under Casey's icy stare they didn't say it. He could sense the trap, but he couldn't see how to evade it. "Yes," he admitted.

"And you can't miss people coming in. You're a barman," she said sarcastically, "so you must notice them as you serve them drinks. In my experience, if they don't buy a drink you notice them even more." She smiled; stiletto sharp. "So I'll ask you again. Did you see this man on Thursday?"

"No. He never came in."

"O'Leary?"

"Yeah?"

"We're taking Jeff here in. Obstruction."

"What?" Jeff yelped. "Boss" –

"No," Federico ordered.

"Yes," Casey slammed back. "He's lied to me. He's coming with us."

"Now," O'Leary said, "take your hand off that gun you got in the back of your pants. We ain't goin' to have trouble." Since O'Leary's gigantic paw was on Federico's arm, pulling it forward, Casey didn't think there'd be any trouble. Federico stood down, recognising reality.

Casey pushed Tarrant into a chair and cuffed him to it – possibly unnecessary, but some more serious intimidation wouldn't go amiss. "We're not done," she said to Federico. "That'll keep your lying front man from doing anything dumb while we talk to you – here. I don't want him out of my sight." Her smile, impossibly, sharpened further. "I wouldn't want to mislay a key witness to conspiracy."

"I've no idea what you're talking about," Federico denied.

"Let's start with the obvious. Have you seen these men?" She shoved the photos into Federico's view.

"Why should I have?" He waved a hand, dismissing her query.

"Evasion. Answer the question. And this time, try looking at the photo before you answer."

Federico ostentatiously perused the photos. "I may have," he sneered. "I don't pay attention to every barfly who visits my fine establishment."

"Not even those who've borrowed cars from your second-in-command?"

"I'm sorry?" Federico said smoothly, but both Casey and O'Leary had seen him flinch for an instant. "Borrowed whose car?"

"Pieter Wiedecz's." Casey continued to smile. "Who's the driver?"

"What?"

"Oh, don't pretend. We know whoever it was works for you, like Pieter worked for you."

Federico visibly flinched. "Pieter?" he queried. "I suppose it's possible. I don't know everyone who works for me."

Scepticism settled firmly on Casey's face, but she let the obvious falsehood, since last time he'd told her explicitly that Wiedecz was nothing to do with the Tarticcas, pass. "Who drove it?" she repeated.

"I don't know."

"Hm. I don't believe you about anything you've said in the last five minutes. You're obstructing me too."

O'Leary had started moving before Casey had clipped out the *t* on *don't*. Federico found himself cuffed and held in O'Leary's monstrous grip.

"Federico Tarticca, Jeff Tarrant, you are both under arrest for obstructing a homicide investigation, or, if you want the full formal charge, obstruction of governmental administration in the second degree." She stared them both down. "I wouldn't want you to think I don't know what I'm doing."

***

"Arrested them?" Agent Glencross choked. "You *arrested* Tarticca?"

"I am sure Detective Clement had good reasons, but perhaps" – Renfrew turned to Casey – "you would share them with us?"

"Tarticca was lying through his shiny white teeth, and so was Tarrant. But if I hold them for twenty-four hours or so" –

"Paperwork c'n take a terrible long time," O'Leary smirked.

"– it gives you an extra twenty-four hours to listen for more information about your shipment. Nothing'll happen without Tarticca being available."

Glencross gawped, then laughed. "Marvellous," he complimented. "That's exactly what we needed."

"Indeed." Even Renfrew gave a short laugh.

"Where is he?"

"Processing. And they won't hurry." Casey smirked as nastily as O'Leary had. "If you'll excuse me, I want to see how our officers have been doing." She exited, before Renfrew could ask her to wait. O'Leary lumbered after her.

"That's helpful," Glencross said. "Does it often happen?"

"I believe so. I am told they have the best solve rate in the NYPD. Captain Kent has made it clear that he does not wish them to leave."

Renfrew briefly allowed regret to cross his face, in sympathy with Glencross.

***

"Officer Estrolla." Kent began, facing across the table in Interrogation, a laptop ominously open beside him. "Do you know why you are here?"

"No." He paused. "Sir," he finally added.

"I *could* start with your lack of respect for authority," Kent snapped. "However, that's a minor issue compared with the matters for which you are being questioned."

Estrolla's face went slack.

"You, Estrolla, may think your association with Detective Marcol and Officer Birkett will protect you from the consequences of your own stupidity, but I can assure you that they have no authority in this precinct. You will remember that *I* am the authority here, and you will show the respect my authority demands."

"Why am I here? I haven't done anything."

Kent waited.

"Sir."

"Remember it. I will remember each individual incident of disrespect."

Estrolla paled.

"Your co-worker, Officer Grendon, with whom you were stupid enough to go sparring with Detective Clement's team, is also under investigation. Explain whose idea it was to spar with her team."

Silence.

"Yours," he concluded. "Clearly intelligence – or even basic research – is not your strength. Nor is obeying orders. Did I not tell you to leave Clement's team – and anyone associated with them – alone?"

"I haven't been near them. Sir."

"You have been near Officer Henegan, who is working with Clement's team. I am not aware you had any authority to order him to inform you of anything." Kent's enquiring tone would have cut diamond.

"I don't know what you mean, sir." Estrolla's face was entirely blank.

"Don't you? Let me show you." Kent produced a thumb drive, which he inserted into his laptop, and played a video. "Is that you?"

Estrolla stared.

"The problem, Estrolla, with making your prejudices obvious, is that they will be noticed. As this was."

"It's a fake, sir."

"It has been thoroughly checked by an independent expert in electronic manipulation, from the FBI. Are you claiming the FBI would falsify evidence?"

Estrolla was silenced.

"I will continue."

Estrolla's knuckles turned white.

CHAPTER TWENTY ONE

"Where are we with the officers' patrols?" Casey asked Tyler.

"Some back. Andy's mapping."

"Andy?" she queried.

"Yeah?" Andy looked up.

"What does the map of security controls look like? We checked: there's one on the outside of the bar hiding Tarticca headquarters."

"Let me add it in." Andy tapped for a moment. "Okay, this is what we have." A second later, the printer whined and spat out the map. Casey glanced at it.

"Dani?"

"Yeah?"

"Come look at this."

Dani arrived. "That the map of where these security controls are?"

"Yep, so far. Do you have the list of Tarticca hangouts? Let's match them up."

"Okay, that's weird," Dani said, a moment or two later. "You've got more than me already. Let's bring Glencross over."

"Let's see." Glencross peered at the list and map. "Weird," he echoed Dani. "I have a couple more" – he checked them off – "but there are more here than we knew about. I'll see if anyone back at base has any more I haven't heard about yet."

Casey and Dani regarded each other, their list and their map in confusion. "Is there any chance your officers have picked up some extra places?" Dani asked. "You know, ordinary offices?"

"I guess. I'd prefer they had more, and some were wrong, than missed them, though."

"For sure." Dani frowned. "Problem is, I don't think your guys are missing things. I think they might be finding ones we didn't know about. Which is great, but...what else are we missing?"

"I don't know – that's Narcotics' business. I don't do drugs, I do murder."

Dani spluttered with mirth. "Did you mean that the way it sounded?"

Casey replayed her words, and laughed. "No, but maybe I'll make it my slogan."

"What?" The other three wandered up, interested in Casey's currently unusual laughter.

"New team slogan. We don't do drugs, we do murder."

"I don't think it'll catch on," Andy said dryly, "or if it does, we'll be sampling the cells downstairs before we can explain."

"Dani says we've found more sites than they know about." Casey reverted to the job. "What are the odds we've picked up a few false positives?"

"Reasonable. I'll run some checks on the ones Dani doesn't know about, to see if we can lose any of them. It shouldn't take me and Bergen long."

"Okay. Done by lunchtime?"

"Don't insult me. Of course we will be." Andy humphed, summoned Bergen, and began.

Casey ignored Andy's offended back, and went to make herself a coffee. Oddly, she noticed, neither Estrolla nor Grendon were in the bullpen. She took her coffee to Tyler's desk. "What happened to Estrolla and Grendon? We didn't have them on patrol for finding those readers, did we? I don't trust them not to mess it up."

Tyler smiled. "Kent. Interrogation. Separately."

Casey parsed Tyler's brevity. "Kent hauled each of them off to Interrogation – separately?" She shrugged. "Couldn't happen to two nicer guys. At least they're not on my murder case." She swigged back her coffee. "Not my problem."

"Here's your problem," O'Leary said cheerfully, waving at Carval.

"Hey," he bounced, camera already out. "I got bored of construction and Claudia Finisterre hasn't called me or Allan yet, so I came here to see what's happening." *And,* he thought, *to make sure you're okay.*

"Not a lot. We're waiting for our officers to come back."

"Come back?" Carval questioned. "You sent them out without you?"

"They're patrolling. Searching for security-controlled doors. One of our gangs has gone hi-tech, and they're using a little RFID tag on their driver's licences to identify each other. We sent a bunch of officers out to find the transmitters these RFIDs react to – we think they're disguised as door controls, but they send out a signal or something. That's how one gang

177

identified the other gang had stolen some of their driver's licences, then they went and shot the thieves." Casey's mouth twisted. "Maybe we should put one on you, so Allan knows where you are."

"No, thank you." Carval ambled over to Casey's desk and perched on the corner, scanning the bullpen for anything photographable. As he did, his phone and Casey's rang almost simultaneously.

"Hey, Allan," he said smoothly. "What's up?"

"You can go shoot the Finisterres' productions."

"I can? Great! When?"

"As soon as you like, from tomorrow."

"Starting tomorrow if I want? Will you send me the list?"

"Yes, Jamie. Please don't annoy them or the theatres."

"Sure, sure. Yes. I won't."

"And they want you to attend their next soirée."

"Put it in my diary, please?"

"Can't you even manage a diary entry?"

"Yes, I can, but if you do it, I won't forget. Please?"

"Okay. If only to make sure you show up and don't mess them around."

"Great."

"Okay. You remember I'm away for the next few days?"

"Yes, I *know* you're flying to Pittsburgh tomorrow. You've been reminding me for ages. Yes, I can manage without you for a couple of days. No, I won't get into trouble. Stop playing Mommy."

"I'll stop playing Mommy when you stop getting into trouble."

"*Okay*, okay. I'll be good. Bye."

"Detective Clement."

"Hello, Detective Clement. This is Claudia Finisterre. I'm sure you remember me?"

"Of course."

"Henry and I went to see Jamie Carval's exhibition centred on you and your team, and, my dear, it was utterly fabulous. We were dazzled. We want to invite the four of you, and Jamie, and Alejandra Despero – we understand your Detective Tyler is courting her?"

"Uh, yes." *Courting?* Casey thought. *Who says 'courting' in this century?*

"All of you are invited to our next soirée. It would mean such a lot if you were all to attend, and since you solved Isabella's murder" – her voice shook – "I don't think there can be any ethical issues in inviting you or you visiting. Please say you'll come?"

"Uh…" Casey remembered something. "Detective O'Leary would like to bring his husband with him."

"Naturally. That would be lovely. We'll look forward to meeting you all. I'll send you the dates – if you wouldn't mind passing them to the others? Thank you."

"But" – Casey realised Claudia had gone, without waiting for Casey to say she'd attend. Well, *hell*. Now she'd have to go.

"Was that Claudia?" Carval asked.

"Yeah. How did you guess?"

"Your stunned ox expression. Claudia has that effect on people."

"She snookered me into her damn soirée," Casey groused. "I don't even want to go."

"I'll be there too, or I won't be able to shoot in their theatres," Carval grumbled. "She always gets her own way. She's worse than Allan."

"Are we all goin' to be cultural icons?" O'Leary asked. "C'n Pete go too?"

"Pete can go." Casey humphed. "I don't want to be an icon."

"You're too li'l to be an icon, an' ain't they Russian anyways? You ain't Russian."

Casey muttered. "How's our map going?" she asked, ostentatiously changing the subject.

"Just the same as half an hour ago. Andy an' Bergen'll be back as soon as they're done. Stop frettin', it'll give you wrinkles." O'Leary smiled at her irritated face. "When they're back, we'll go have lunch."

"Detective Clement."

Oh, hell, Renfrew. What does he want?

"Yes, Dr Renfrew?"

"I wish to confer with Detective O'Leary." O'Leary's face fell. Casey concealed a hurricane-strength sigh of relief.

"Sure," O'Leary agreed with commendable calm.

"Thank you. Perhaps we could avail ourselves of some of your excellent coffee to assist our deliberations, before Captain Kent returns?"

O'Leary trudged off behind Renfrew.

Dr Renfrew had found, during his distinguished career, that the sharing of beverages, or food, relaxed his subjects. He was not, naturally, naïve enough to rely on such an action to ease the path of a difficult discussion, but he would utilise the available advantages. If only Detective Clement's team were less obdurately uncommunicative, his present path would be considerably simpler. He resolved to begin with a relatively easier route.

"Detective O'Leary, may I have your views on the exhibition that Mr Carval has put together?"

Detective O'Leary regarded Dr Renfrew with an unexpectedly speculative, intelligent gaze. His size was most deceptive, even to those who, as Dr Renfrew did, knew him to be far smarter than his assumed persona indicated.

"Waal," he hummed, "it sure is flatterin'. Lotsa good PR for the NYPD. I do hear as it's a stunnin' success. Carval's done a good job, an' I guess he'll be real popular."

"Perhaps," Dr Renfrew suggested irritably, "you would cease to pretend you are stupid and uncultured, and provide me with opinions that reflect your true thoughts?"

"Why would I want to do that?" Detective O'Leary's execrable accent vanished as fast as his amiability. Dr Renfrew was not, of course, intimidated. He was merely momentarily unnerved by the change. He noted that, when he wished to do so, Detective O'Leary could project as much menace as Detective Clement, though his greater size would ensure he appeared more threatening to any criminal.

"Because you wish to ensure Detective Clement does not suffer lasting damage from the cumulative effects of her father's death, the harassment she is suffering, and her fatal shooting of a gang member who was endeavouring to kill both of you," Dr Renfrew said sharply. "I shall be exceedingly grateful if you cease to temporise and instead assist."

Detective O'Leary slowly elevated his eyebrows, which did not diminish the impressive effect of his daunting size and demeanour. Dr Renfrew held his gaze, being entirely unwilling to show himself in any way moved, and maintained calm.

"Perhaps," Detective O'Leary suggested coldly, "you would cease to dance around the subject and simply ask what you want to ask?"

Dr Renfrew did not miss Detective O'Leary's repetition of his own phrasing. "How did Detective Clement's father react to Mr Carval's exhibition?"

"Why do you think he saw it?"

"I was so informed. Please tell me how you thought he reacted, as a relatively neutral observer." Dr Renfrew considered that Detective O'Leary might readily assume that Captain Kent had told him about Mr Clement's attendance, and therefore would be moderately forthcoming and accurate in his description.

"He didn't like it. He didn't like seein' Casey beat up, an' he laid into the rest of us – includin' Captain Kent – about protectin' her. He spent the rest of the show with me."

"I see," Dr Renfrew said. Only bluntness would, it appeared, serve him in this discussion. "Is it your view that Detective Clement was upset by this?"

"Yup."

"Is it also your opinion that Mr Clement's final episode of drunkenness was caused by his reaction to the exhibition? I infer that the views of his daughter therein contained contradicted his paternal view of her."

O'Leary remained silent, staring at his huge hands. Finally he met Dr Renfrew's eyes. "You're askin' because you think Casey's feelin' guilty about her dad. What's that got to do with her shootin' a lowlife who was tryin' to kill us both?"

"I am not, as I have already noted, solely concerned with the shooting of a criminal in the line of duty." Dr Renfrew consciously recovered his serenity. "I am concerned with the cumulative effects of a series of stressful events on Detective Clement. It is perfectly obvious to me, since I have not seen her since March, that she is under considerable strain, even allowing for her grief. You may not like me, Detective, but I can assure you I have only Detective Clement's best interests at heart. I do not wish to see her placed on medical leave, should the strain eventually prove too great. She is, as I am sure you know, presently at a point where a further traumatic – in the medical sense – event may exceed even her resilience."

Detective O'Leary's light eyes bored into Dr Renfrew's face, examining him in a way that he had not often experienced. In fact, he realised, the only other times in which he had been so scrutinised as an adult had been by Detective Clement.

"She has us." Detective O'Leary made a dismissive gesture. "We're her team, an' she's ours."

"I notice that you do not say you are enough for her. Should I assume that you consider she might benefit from external analysis?"

"I ain't convinced."

"That is entirely obvious," Dr Renfrew said wryly. "However, since you have resumed your unnatural accent, I can only conclude that you appreciate my point. Now, may we return to my original question?"

***

"Why, Estrolla, did you presume to instruct Henegan?"

"I've been helping him, sir." Estrolla was entirely bland.

"Do you not think Detective Clement and her team, who are far more experienced than you, can instruct him? After all, they're detectives – and you are not." Kent paused, to menacing effect. "You have no authority to second-guess their work or decisions – or mine."

"*Yours?* Sir," he added.

"Mine." It fell like lead. "I ordered Clement's team to take Henegan, in part to teach him." Kent didn't mention that he had intended to separate Henegan, who might prove useful, from Estrolla and Grendon, who were not. "You've second-guessed *my* authority. You are out of line."

"I" –

"Didn't know. No. You didn't. That's because *I* am the captain, and you are not. Now, whose idea was sparring with Clement's team?"

"Mine, sir."

"Why?" It scythed out. Estrolla, only brave when faced with people weaker than himself, shuddered.

"You can think about your answer. I suggest, Estrolla, you don't even consider lying. You're not good enough of a liar to deceive me."

Kent left, and made sure that the sound of the door locking was as loud as it could be. He had noticed all the signs of Estrolla's cowardice: the damp forehead, the patches under his arms, the scent of terror. Now for Grendon, who'd had time to stew in his own fear.

He opened the door on Grendon, whose expression displayed a pleasing degree of outright fright. "Before I left," Kent said coldly, "I asked you two questions. One, why were you at Detective Clement's desk on Friday night, and two, whose idea was the sparring session with her team? Have you found an answer yet?"

Grendon regarded Kent with the demeanour and intelligence of a mouse faced with a tiger.

"I shall add a third question. Why were you and Officer Estrolla instructing Officer Henegan to report to you after I had assigned him to Detective Clement's team?"

Grendon gasped. "We didn't, sir."

"Don't make this worse for yourself by lying. I have you on video."

"But..."

"Do you want to see the video? It has, you will be relieved to know, been checked for any signs of tampering. By the FBI," Kent added, and had the pleasure of seeing defeat crumple Grendon's face as the little weasel realised his first line of defence was dead.

"Yes, sir."

"Now. Whose idea was the sparring session?"

Grendon slumped. "It wasn't fair," he whimpered. "Those other officers were talking about how they dropped them, and they couldn't possibly be as good as their reputation, so Estrolla thought we'd try them out. We're pretty good."

"Or not," Kent pointed out, "since you were comprehensively thrashed. They are as good as their reputation, and their reputations are spectacularly good. In every possible way." He let the point sink in. "So it was Estrolla's idea. Was it also his idea to harass Detective Clement with press cuttings relating to the death of her father? Which occurred, I shall remind you, less than ten days ago. Is it your normal practice to be entirely insensitive to others' feelings? Should I ask whether that insensitivity extends to harassment relating, say, to race or sexual orientation?" Kent scowled. Grendon cringed. "Most likely. I shall make some other enquiries. However, we have now established that you are stupid, bullying and offensive. You will not return to the bullpen today. You will remain here until I return for you. Should you need anything, you may ask the officer who will be stationed in Observation. He will seek my approval."

He paused. "One more thing, Grendon. Clement and her team are the highest rated unit in the NYPD. They are also highly rated by the FBI. You picked the wrong team to mess with, and you picked the wrong Captain's bullpen. Your future is not bright."

Kent stalked out, perfectly satisfied with the effect he had had on that greasy little worm. He'd be even happier when he'd handed them over to IA, which was his next call. By the time Lewin sent men over to collect them, he'd have reduced Estrolla to a small pile of scraps too.

***

"We're done," Andy said. "We've managed to eliminate a few – didn't we think the Tarticcas might have put transmitters on other people's buildings?"

"Yes, but they'll be concealed," Casey pointed out. "These are all obvious, 'cause that's how Tyler briefed the officers."

Tyler nodded.

"So we still have more than I knew about," Dani grumbled. "I called my guys, and I'm waiting for them. Did Glencross find out anything more?"

"Not yet," the man himself said. "I'm waiting too." He frowned. "I loathe smart criminals. This is a whole new level of intelligent tech, and the Tarticcas can't be the only ones who've worked out that RFIDs can be useful."

"They'll have told the Pagliaccis as soon as they worked it out," Dani half-spat. "As if we didn't have enough problems here in New York."

"You can't keep a bad criminal down," Glencross noted cynically. "Bergen, did you hear anything more on the wiretaps?"

"A lot of complaining. Casey's messed up today very nicely for them."

"I'm good at messing things up." Casey's meant-to-be-a-joke carried more bitterness than it should have. "I love messing up criminals' days. It makes me happy."

"It's lunchtime." Carval noted her bitterness. "Where's O'Leary?"

"Renfrew snagged him."

"Oh. We'd better wait."

"So what have we found?" Dani asked.

"Here's our network of controls – at least, what we think it is, mapped on to the Tarticcas' key hangouts." Andy inspected it. "Bergen, how's the map of Hocking's movements coming along?"

Bergen pressed print, and produced it. "There. Still not great, but better – oh. Oh, wow."

"What?"

"I see," Andy said smugly. "Guess who's been trying to find the Tarticcas' warehouse?"

"Looks like the Yarrabees aren't as dumb as we thought."

"Not if they're sending out Hocking to get shot if they catch him. That'll improve their average IQ by around thirty points."

"Not the sharpest tool in the box," Bergen agreed.

"Isn't there a way we can find Grappano?" Casey asked. "He's the one who did all our murders, and I want him. I'm happy to *help* you along the way, but my job is solving this homicide."

"So you keep saying. I can help you," Bergen said. Casey's expression yelled *about time too*. "Our wiretap picked up a few words about him. We already knew he was borrowed from the Pagliaccis, but he'll be part of receiving the delivery. Guess the Pagliaccis are in this shipment somewhere too."

"Do we know when the delivery will be?"

"Not yet. We're still listening. You slowed it down." Bergen beamed at her. "Don't you have a couple of lowlifes to interrogate?"

"Not now. I want them to be suitably unhappy with me. Anyway, they'll barely have cleared Processing." She looked around. "Isn't O'Leary done yet?"

"Nah," Tyler said.

CHAPTER TWENTY TWO

O'Leary continued to meet Renfrew's gaze with his own acute assessment. "You're askin' if *I* think Casey's pa went on his bender 'cause of the exhibition?"

"Yes."

"Why? It don't matter what I think, just what Casey thinks."

"Because you have an opinion, and you do not have the same emotional reactions to the question as Detective Clement."

Detective O'Leary paused before making a decision. "Yeah. I think so."

"Thank you."

"Are we done yet?"

"Not quite. Do you consider Mr Carval accurately captured the inter-relationships between the four members of your team in his exhibition?"

"Yep. C'n I go now? It's lunchtime."

Dr Renfrew sighed. If only Detective Clement's team would *co-operate*. "I have one further question, to which I would appreciate an expansive, reasoned answer rather than the single word that I would receive from Detective Tyler. I am trying to help Detective Clement. Please do not hinder me."

Detective O'Leary remained apparently unmoved, but his hands had relaxed. "Ask." Dr Renfrew noted that it was not agreement.

"Does Detective Clement consider that she bears responsibility for her father's death?"

"We're done." Detective O'Leary exited.

Dr Renfrew concluded that Detective Clement did so consider, and further concluded that a short absence would be both prudent and desirable.

***

"What's up?" Casey registered O'Leary's angry face.

"Renfrew. Is it lunchtime? I gotta get outta here."

"Yes. I was only waiting for you. Let's go, before he comes looking for me."

They disappeared faster than a genie freed from a lamp, clattering down the stairs and arriving in the sunshine. Carval caught up. "Wait!" he called. O'Leary paused. "The others are coming too. They needed a minute."

"Oh."

"They know they'll be next."

"Oh," O'Leary repeated, less unhappily. "Team debrief?"

"Yeah."

"With food," Casey said. "If you don't eat, you'll be hangry."

"Yeah. I'm already a li'l bit cross."

"You don't say." Andy and Tyler hurried up. "You went without us."

"Thumpin' shrinks ain't no good for my career."

"Let's get some sandwiches, and sit in the sun," Andy suggested. "Sunshine's good for your chi."

"Renfrew ain't," O'Leary growled. "Pokin' an' pryin' and proddin'."

"It's not like you to get this worked up," Andy soothed. "Come on. Food, sodas, and sunshine, and you can tell us all about it and smooth your ruffled chi."

Sitting on the grass of Sakura Park, and variously staring at the cherry trees, General Grant Memorial and Manhattan School of Music depending on alignment and preference, they munched their sandwiches, drank their sodas, nibbled on sugary confections, and waited for O'Leary to recover his temper. Eventually, he stretched, flexed barrel-sized biceps, wriggled his shoulders happily in the warmth, and sighed.

"That's better," he said.

"So what's up with Renfrew?"

"He's worryin' about you, Casey."

"What?"

"He started with what did I think about the show, an' when I didn't say anythin' controversial, just I heard it was a success, he got ratty an' told me to help, not pretend I was dumb. He asked about your pa's views, an' about whether I thought your pa had gone drinkin' 'cause of seein' it." He heaved a sigh. "Yeah, I said."

Casey drew in a long breath.

"He asked me iffen the show reflected the team, an' that was easy, 'cause it does." O'Leary heaved another huge sigh. "Lastly, he asked me iffen you thought you were responsible for your pa's death, an' I walked out, 'cause that ain't my question to answer, whatever he thinks. He's claimin' all he wants is to make sure you don't break under all this stress –

186

your pa, the exhibition, those dumbasses in an' out of the precinct, the shootin'…"

"That's up to me," Casey snarled. "How does he think he'll help? I'll know if I've had enough." Four men looked disbelievingly at each other, over Casey's dark head. "I *said* I'd take vacation."

"Naw, *Kent* said you – an' all of us – had to take vacation."

"Not the point, O'Leary!"

"Anyways, *I* think iffen Renfrew wants to know that sorta thing, he c'n ask you. I guess he's goin' to ask Andy an' Tyler, an' he's already tried for Carval, an' then – or in between – he's goin' to therapize you, an' you'll have to take it, because Kent ordered it."

Casey turned away, staring through the trees as if she could see the river. She couldn't, of course. Not from the middle of Sakura Park in summer. The leaves didn't provide her with any comfort. Carval slid an arm around her, but the hug didn't help either. Silence stretched out as they finished the last remnants of their lunches.

"We'd better get back," she decided.

"Okay," the others agreed.

"An' Renfrew?"

Casey shrugged. "I can't stop him annoying us. Let's solve the case and have our vacations. He can't follow us there. Let him ask his dumb questions. He can't do anything and he won't help, but we have to put up with it." Her calm, almost bored tone didn't reflect the bitter twist of her mouth or the despair in her eyes.

The group heaved themselves up and plodded back towards the precinct, Carval peeling off at the subway to return to shooting construction sites.

***

"Captain Lewin?" Kent said. "Kent here, from the Thirty-Sixth."

"Yes?"

"You can collect Officers Grendon and Estrolla any time you like. I want to finish dealing with Estrolla about the harassment relating to Clement's father, but by the time everything's in order, I'll be done."

"Okay." Lewin paused. "You realise, even after I've interrogated them, until they're formally dealt with, they'll still be in your bullpen?"

"Yeah," Kent rasped. "They have to have a fair chance. I know. Unless they do something truly dumb – like Birkett did, falsifying evidence – when we can charge them, they stay." He emitted a *pah!* "Unfortunately, putting press clippings on desks – where I have no admissible evidence – or intimidating others – which could be spun lots of different ways – doesn't count. Yet."

"If they're tied to this leak, though, it'll be enough to suspend them."

"If," Kent stressed. "If."

"Yeah. IA only wants the truth. The rest – it's your precinct and your problem. I'll send a couple of guys down to get them."

"Thanks."

Kent cut the call, and marched back down to Interrogation, to finish with Estrolla.

***

The team had barely re-entered the bullpen when Agent Bergen descended upon them. "We got something." He hustled them to the FBI's annexed room.

"What?" Casey asked.

"We got something useful from the wiretap. They're talking in code" –

Andy broke in. "After Casey went after them, they've likely guessed someone's listening in" –

"For sure. But," Glencross noted, "we put together what we knew and managed to extract some information, and once we had that, we did a bit of analysis and profiling – the gang as a whole, not Dr Renfrew's usual person-by-person – and we came up with the three most likely spots for the delivery."

Casey waited.

"From your point of view," Dani said, "we think Grappano might be there, though he might be backing off."

"From ours," Glencross added, "we have the chance to disrupt the Tarticcas and the Pagliaccis, and with a little luck and Agent Bergen's tracking of Paddy Hocking, maybe the Yarrabees too."

"When?" Casey asked.

Glencross, Dani, Bergen and Renfrew all made unhappy faces. "That's the problem," Glencross said. "We don't know. We're hoping Bergen's wiretaps will throw up something about timing, but it hasn't yet."

"Surveillance?"

"Not the best plan," Dani said, with Glencross nodding. "We're known. There's a serious risk we'd be recognised."

"Aren't there any officers or rookies in Narcotics you could use?" Andy asked. "All of ours were out there finding the chip readers, and even the dumbest Yarrabee or Tarticca might spot a familiar face."

Dani's phone rang. "Handjiev." Her face blanked. "Sir? Yes, sir. When? I see, sir." She glowered at the screen as the call was cut.

"What's wrong?" Casey asked.

"That was my captain. He knows we've wiretapped the gangs. He says they found information DEA needs to have." Her eyes skittered around the group. "I had to keep him informed when he asked about progress, but I didn't tell him the taps threw up anything – how could I? I've been with you since we found out."

Casey's stomach twisted with ominous foreknowledge. "He's sent Marcol over, hasn't he?"

"Waal, *shit*," O'Leary accurately summed up.

"He has done what?" Dr Renfrew asked icily. "Without first referring to Captain Kent, Agent Glencross, or me?" Renfrew's glacial precision didn't prevent a single person from noticing his fury.

"He sure didn't tell me," Glencross snapped. "This should have been done by phone, so nobody spots a man from Narcotics arriving here." Suddenly, something struck him. "What's your beef with Marcol, Casey?"

"We didn't get on at the Academy," she replied, and said no more. Glencross's piercing glance conveyed far louder than words that he knew there was more to it, but Casey wasn't opening that can of worms. Unobtrusively, her team had closed around her.

"Agent Bergen," Renfrew rapped, "please find Captain Kent and ask him to see me at his earliest convenience." He paused. Bergen ran out of the room. "Detective Handjiev, when did your captain – please remind me of his name? – send Detective Marcol?"

"Captain Travers. I don't know when he sent him." Dani drooped. "I'm sorry."

"This has nothing to do with you," Casey bit. "So stop with the apologising already. *My* captain assured me Marcol wouldn't be involved, and he doesn't lie. Someone's set this up. So what? Dr Renfrew and Agent Glencross can deal with it, and if I can put up with Marcol in case he has some useful information, I'm damn sure the rest of you can. Sure, I'm not happy about it," she directed at Renfrew's searching gaze, "but he's not involved in my murder case and you need to take these gangs out. Personal doesn't matter when we've got crimes to solve."

"Casey," O'Leary began.

"No, Detective," Renfrew interrupted. "If Detective Clement is content, we will deal with this unwarranted interference and discourtesy." He nodded politely at Casey, and once, far more sharply, at a thought he did not intend to share. "I am impressed by your professionalism. We shall ensure that Detective Marcol does not impinge on your part of this investigation."

Bergen hurried back in. "Dr Renfrew, Captain Kent is in Interrogation with one of his officers. I left a message with the sergeant and a note on his desk" – Renfrew nodded once in approval – "to ask him to join us as soon as he's free."

"That will suffice. Thank you."

***

"Officer Estrolla. We have established that you have been interfering with my management of my precinct. I required you to think about your answer to the question of whose idea sparring with Clement's team was. Was it you?"

"Yes," Estrolla admitted.

"Why?"

"Some of the other officers were saying they'd dropped them, and we wanted a go. It'd look great if we could beat O'Leary, sir."

"So it was about personal pride?"

"Yeah. Who wouldn't want to beat him? It'd improve our promotion chances, sir."

Kent, no fool, recognised Estrolla's tactic, and decided that the ground could usefully be cut from under his feet. "I don't think so. I don't promote anyone who can't see beyond the obvious."

"Sir?" Estrolla managed.

"Did it not occur to you to question how any officer was able to beat Detective O'Leary or Detective Tyler, both of whom have been consistently at the top of the NYPD's sparring standings? Did it not, at any point, occur to you that they might have been training those officers and that the falls they took were simply to allow the officers to practice a manoeuvre? Or did you rush in without considering all the possibilities? Because, Officer Estrolla, it does not appear that you considered any of those possibilities." Kent's expression would have skinned oxen.

"However, stupidity is not why we're here. Nor are we here because the shots of the sparring session show quite clearly that you and your colleagues were hoping to inflict damage on Detective Clement and her team. Physical discomfort is a necessary concomitant of sparring, which you experienced in full."

Estrolla stayed quiet, sensibly, though his face darkened at the contemptuous reminder.

Kent returned to his real objective. "We're here to discuss the distribution of articles relating to the death of Detective Clement's father. Explain why you informed Officer Bartlett that Detective Clement would take receiving copies of those articles as a *joke?*"

Estrolla looked blankly at Kent – but not blankly enough. Something unpleasant had slithered through his eyes. "I didn't say that."

"So Officer Bartlett was lying to me?" Kent asked softly.

"Must'a been, sir."

"Mm," Kent hummed. "He told me you told him Officer Birkett of the 112th Precinct had been at the Academy with Detective Clement."

"Yes, sir."

"You agree?"

"Yes, sir."

"He admitted you had told him that Officer Birkett and Detective Clement were friends."

Estrolla paused. "Uh…"

"How did you know they were friends from the Academy? You weren't in their class, and you weren't at the Third when Detective Clement was a rookie. Nor were you at any precinct where Officer Birkett has been stationed. So, Estrolla, who told you?"

"Officer Henegan, sir."

"Officer Henegan has never served at the Third, the 112th or indeed with Officer Birkett, and wasn't at the Academy with Detective Clement, being considerably younger. Did this not give you cause for concern, or for further investigation, before relying on his information?"

Estrolla looked hunted.

"Surely you see that it's entirely implausible that Henegan would know about Detective Clement's friendships."

"Cops don't lie to other cops," Estrolla tried.

Kent dropped any vestige of pleasantness. "You say that to me? You've been lying to me outright since the moment I re-entered. I know you instructed Officer Bartlett, and, I have no doubt, others, the names of whom Sergeant Tully is already establishing, to harass Detective Clement. You are well aware that she and Officer Birkett are not now, and never have been, friendly. You have two options. You can tell the whole truth to me, and face disciplinary proceedings with the possibility of some leniency, or you can continue in this vein, I will prove you are lying, and there will be no prospect whatsoever of leniency." Kent stood up. "Think about it. You don't have long." He exited.

By the time the IA officers arrived, Estrolla had not requested Kent to return. Kent couldn't say he regretted it.

***

"Before we deal with Marcol," Glencross said, in an arid tone which suggested he already knew of Marcol and didn't like him, "let's fix up how we'll deal with our three possibilities."

"Long-range surveillance," Tyler suggested.

"Detective Tyler was a sniper," Renfrew observed.

Glencross regarded Tyler with appreciation. "Small details from a distance? We can work with that." He tapped the printed street map in front of him. "Here are the three sites we think are most likely."

Tyler leaned down, and considered. "Street view?"

"Sure." Andy whipped off and returned with his laptop open, already pulling up the street view of the first site. "It's a couple of months out of date, though."

"Go see, after."

"Sure," Glencross said. "Is there anyone else who could survey like you?"

The other three shook their heads. "We can't," Casey said, "and I don't know if any of our officers have an Army background, let alone sniping."

"No," Tyler said. "Know it."

"Okay. We can ask Tully." Casey eyed Glencross. "Sergeant Tully. He'll know if anyone has the right background."

"We don't need any others," Andy pointed out. Everyone stared at him. "All we need is Tyler to do recon, and tell us where to put some of those nice neat little cameras Bergen and I used for the models – with a longer range. We can hook them up to a computer, and watch, and we'll record it as well. That way we'll know what's going on and we can put people near but out of view, ready to swoop in."

Bergen grinned. "Yep. Tyler can scope it out, Andy and I'll place the cameras, and off we go. Always on, no blinking, nothing missed, and we free up people to be ready when you say go."

"Okay." Glencross approved, impressed. "We'll do it your way."

"Do you have any idea where Grappano is?" Casey inquired.

Glencross shook his head. "Not yet."

Casey made a face. "Okay. The last we saw was him going into Tarticca HQ?"

"Yeah," Andy confirmed. "I've put in a request for street cam footage around there, but I haven't gotten it yet."

"Time for recon." Tyler turned to the door – and stopped in disgusted recognition.

"Hey. I'm Detective Marcol." A self-assured blond man entered. "Captain Travers sent me to join the team." His eyes latched on to Casey, while obtrusively ignoring Tyler, Andy and O'Leary.

"I beg your pardon?" Dr Renfrew queried coldly. "This is a federal investigation, in which your captain has no authority whatsoever."

Marcol blinked. "But" –

"There are no buts. Your captain has grossly overstepped his authority. You will provide me with your information, after which you will leave. I shall talk to your captain myself."

"Who are you?"

"I am Dr Renfrew, the ranking FBI agent in this investigation. This is Agent Glencross, the ranking DEA agent. Your captain has not had the courtesy to discuss your presence with either of us. Had he done so, he would have been informed that a short call to provide your information would have been sufficient. You may deliver your report in person, immediately."

Marcol's mouth dropped open unattractively. As he was about to speak, a stentorian bellow preceded Captain Kent into the room.

"Detective Marcol? Why are you in my precinct, interfering with an investigation for which I have responsibility – the murder of two men and the severe injury to a woman – without anybody requesting my permission? Did you not think it would be courteous to contact me first?"

"Courtesy does not feature in explaining Detective Marcol's presence. Neither I nor Agent Glencross were notified," Renfrew said frigidly. "I intend to discuss *courtesy* with Detective Marcol's captain in the exceedingly near future."

"As will I," added Glencross.

Marcol flicked his gaze from one to the other, then at Kent.

"Clement, you and your team may leave," Kent rapped.

"Agent Bergen, please go with them."

"Detective Handjiev, would you go too?" Glencross requested.

They all left, O'Leary shutting the door firmly behind them. "That don't sound good," he said.

"Nope," Bergen concurred.

Dani didn't say anything.

"'Tain't your fault," O'Leary reassured her.

"He's from my precinct, though. Saw a chance to look good and muscle in on a key investigation."

"How'd he know?" Andy asked the air. "You don't report to him, you report to your captain."

"Travers'll do anything Marcol asks, 'cause the family has pull." Dani's face was pale and crumpled. "It's never gotten in the way of my job before."

Casey didn't say anything. Marcol had gotten in the way of her job.

"Can't he stand seeing a woman get kudos?" Bergen asked.

Five cops stared at him. "How'd you know that?" Casey whipped.

"I work for the best profiler in law enforcement. Just because I'm great at tech, doesn't mean I haven't learned a lot from Dr Renfrew – and I know Marcol's not fond of you since you beat him to the top of the Academy." Casey glared, and Bergen, far too late, didn't continue down that line.

"You did?" Dani squawked.

"She did," three cops confirmed.

"Hold on. You're *that* Clement?" Dani looked around the team. "You're – I never made the connection. You're the ones on all the trophies?" She stared, stunned. "But you're *normal.* The way they talk about you in the Academy…"

"We put our pants on one leg at a time, just like anyone else." Andy grinned wryly.

"But" –

"It doesn't matter a damn," Casey overrode her, "once you're on the job. We're cops, same as you. No better, no worse."

Dani's face screeched *who the hell do you think you're kidding?* Agent Bergen's face echoed her. Neither of their mouths were stupid enough to open.

"We're the same guys you were comfortable with an hour ago," Andy added. "Don't spoil it now."

"They're fun to work with," Bergen said. "C'mon, Handjiev. They don't bite."

"'Cept doughnuts," O'Leary suggested happily. "I like doughnuts. Let's go get some while the bosses're feedin' on live prey."

Casey squirmed. "This won't be good," she mumbled.

"'Tain't our problem," O'Leary replied. "Our problem is that I ain't got no doughnuts."

"I guess we'd better get you some," Dani said, a touch weakly, and led them out.

CHAPTER TWENTY THREE

Renfrew, Glencross, and Kent fixed frigid gazes on Marcol.

"Explain your presence in my precinct," Kent opened. "It is normal and courteous – a concept which I commend to your attention" – Marcol cringed, and failed to conceal it – "for the Captain in charge of a precinct to be informed when personnel from other precincts are involving themselves in live cases, invited or not."

"In addition," Renfrew added, "you are also expected to seek the permission of the ranking federal agents before interfering in an ongoing federal investigation, so that you do not compromise the investigation." He raised his brows. "Surely you are aware of this, since you must previously have worked with DEA?" He waited. "You have worked with DEA?" Another pause. "I require an answer, Detective Marcol."

"Yes."

"And in each case, your involvement has been by prior arrangement between DEA and your captain?"

"Yes." Marcol finally registered the icy glares directed at him. "Uh, sir."

"As it should be," Glencross stated.

"So why has Travers" – Kent didn't bother with his rank – "not contacted any of us?"

"I believe we should ask him," Renfrew said, "since it is perfectly clear that Detective Marcol should not be here for one single moment longer than it takes him to provide us with his information."

"Report, Marcol," Kent rapped.

"You purport to have vital information. Disclose it."

"We might as well get some value from you being foisted on us." Glencross glared at Marcol. "You're an adequate Narcotics detective, but you have no role in this investigation."

Marcol clamped his mouth shut, though his eyes flashed at Glencross's dismissal of his ability.

"Report. We have an investigation with which we must proceed. You are delaying us."

Marcol produced a report which added nothing to the investigators' knowledge.

"Is that it?" Renfrew asked incredulously. "Your captain sent you here for *that?*"

"Did Travers know that was the total of your information?" Glencross snapped. "If so, I'll be having a long chat with my colleagues about the reliance to be placed on him."

Marcol stared at them all. "But…but I'm telling you there's a delivery due."

"We know." Glencross's words fell like stones. "We *also* know the three most likely places for it to take place, the gangs involved, the key personnel, and how they'll identify each other. In addition, we know the Yarrabees will try to disrupt it."

"We have Federico Tarticca in custody, thanks to Detective Clement and her team," Kent added. "In fact, the vast majority of the information we have gathered has been thanks to Detective Clement, her team, and Detective Handjiev."

"Their work has bought us sufficient time to reconnoitre and place surveillance," Renfrew noted. "Unlike your redundant information, Detective Clement's work, and that of her outstanding team, has added considerable value to our operation."

"Detective Handjiev has also been outstanding," Glencross pointed out.

Marcol's face contorted.

"Dismissed," Kent ordered. "You will not speak to anyone on your way out, and if you should see Clement or any of her team anywhere" –

"Or Detective Handjiev or Agent Bergen," Renfrew supplemented.

"– you will not speak to them. We are aware of your issues with Detective Clement, her team, and Carval. 1PP is exceedingly pleased with the exhibition, and their performance."

Both Kent and Renfrew scrutinised Marcol. The blankness of Marcol's expression screamed guilty knowledge. Kent would have loved to have shoved Marcol into Interrogation, but he'd leave that to IA. Come to think of it…

"You will *also* not discuss any matters relating to this operation with anyone. That, Detective Marcol," Glencross instructed, dangerously quietly, "means you will not seek information from Detective Handjiev. If your Captain instructs you to do so, you will refer him to me and tell him that Detective Handjiev has been ordered by both DEA and the FBI – *federal* agencies – not to speak to anyone without my explicit authority, given in advance. If I should hear of any retaliation against Detective Handjiev for obeying our orders" – Renfrew and Kent nodded approvingly – "I will, personally, take action against that person for interfering with a federal investigation."

Marcol's mouth opened and closed again.

"Dismissed," Kent repeated, and withdrew his attention from Marcol to meet Renfrew's and Glencross's eyes. "I have business to deal with. Excuse me, gentlemen."

Kent marched out of the conference room without a further glance at Marcol, and went straight to his office, shutting the door behind him.

"Lewin? Kent. Travers of Narcotics sent Marcol here to – quote – join the investigation team led by Dr Renfrew of the FBI and Agent Glencross of DEA. Travers failed to contact either agent, or me, but simply told the Narcotics detective who *is* part of the team, after Marcol was already on his way. The Feds aren't happy," he added with considerable understatement. "I'm about to ask Travers what the *hell* he was playing at."

"I see. Thank you." Lewin added nothing more.

Kent tapped in Garrett's number, and had shortly arranged for soothing beers and a chance to complain bitterly to an equally senior friend, the following night. Before he could unleash his ire on Travers, he was informed that the IA officers had arrived.

***

Back in the conference room, Glencross shut the door behind Marcol with a decided snap, and frowned at Renfrew. "How about explaining Kent's commentary?"

Renfrew peered over his pince-nez at Glencross, who held his gaze.

"Look, it's obvious there's far more to Marcol showing up than simply wanting to be in on a big case, and I'm the only person in the room who doesn't know what's going on. Will it affect this investigation?"

"Not if Detective Marcol and Captain Travers take heed of our commentary," Renfrew said. "If it should transpire otherwise, I will brief you. For now, I do not see the point of troubling any of us with further discourteous behaviour on the part of the Narcotics division." He paused. "I would suggest, however, that it might be advisable to make it clear to Detective Handjiev that no blame or criticism will attach to her. She has been treated with discourtesy as well."

"Don't worry. I'll reassure her."

"And Captain Travers?"

"We could both question him."

"That would be most satisfactory, at a suitable point."

"After we've completed this operation. We can leave him to Kent for now."

"I entirely concur."

***

"Officer Grendon," Kent rapped.

"Sir!"

"You will go with Officers Loudon and Yarley."

"Sir?" Grendon clearly didn't understand.

"These officers are from Internal Affairs," Kent said with relish. "IA has some questions for you. I suggest you do not lie, obfuscate or temporise as you have done with me."

Grendon's blood vacated his face. His hands shook.

"But, sir" –

"You are a person of interest in IA's investigations. I have no authority to interfere." Kent gestured the two IA officers forward. "He's all yours." They marched Grendon out.

Kent waited, and when they returned, took them to Estrolla. From Estrolla's suffused face, he'd never expected his actions, and his lack of explanation to Kent after being offered the chance, to have consequences. Kent was delighted to prove him wrong.

***

"How many doughnuts?"

"Lots," O'Leary warbled in a bone-shaking bass.

"I don't want any," Casey demurred. "I'm not hungry." O'Leary flashed her a glance, but said nothing. Casey knew he'd fuss at her, but fussing would come later. She'd eaten lunch. Okay, a small lunch, but lunch.

Tyler picked up two boxes of mixed doughnuts, paid, and started back to the precinct. "Coming?" he asked, and didn't wait to watch them follow. They trailed after him like a gaggle of goslings.

Dani lagged behind, and after a minute, Casey hung back to join her. "It's not you," she explained. "Marcol's after me. You're just…collateral damage. None of us blame you." She forced cheerfulness. "We like you," she teased. "Can we keep you?"

"Glencross might complain," Dani managed. "I like Narcotics. I don't like Homicide."

"Glencross, not Travers?" Casey inquired.

"I'm under his command until he says this case is done," Dani clarified. "Assuming," she added bitterly, "he doesn't throw me back to Travers after today's fiasco."

"It's still not your fault. If he tries to blame you, I'll say so."

"So will I." Agent Bergen ghosted back to them. He shooed them up to the others. "Let's allow Tyler to work out sightlines for my tech."

"*My* tech," Andy complained.

198

"Our tech," Bergen suggested. "After *my* doughnut."

When they reached the bullpen, Marcol was absent, to everybody's relief. Andy pulled up street views again, and he, Bergen and Tyler discussed sightlines and camera angles.

"Detective Handjiev?" Glencross poked his head out of the conference room. "A moment, please?" His mild expression didn't reassure Dani, who marched in as if she were going to the guillotine. Casey put her head down to work.

Sadly, putting her head down didn't help.

"Detective Clement," Renfrew requested, "might I have a moment of your time, please?"

Casey stood up reluctantly, and followed Renfrew to a separate room.

"Agent Glencross is reassuring Detective Handjiev that no blame attaches to her for Captain Travers' or Detective Marcol's regrettable behaviour, and informing her that on his, and my, order, she is not to discuss this operation with any person outside this team whatsoever, without DEA's explicit authority." he stated. Casey goggled. She had *not* expected that statement. "Nor does their discourtesy reflect on you or your team."

Casey gaped for a moment, but recovered. "I didn't think it did. I'm not responsible for Marcol's ideas."

Dr Renfrew was more relieved than he should have been that Detective Clement was not suffering guilt over another issue for which she was not to blame. He examined her, and decided he should not probe her feelings around her father's death or the shooting of her suspect at this time. "Thank you. That is all."

Casey left rapidly before Renfrew could open any other conversation, noting Kent's closed office door with alarm.

***

"Travers. Captain Kent here. Why did you not inform me, the FBI or DEA before attempting to foist Marcol on to the team – which I had already told you would be firmly rejected?"

"He had urgent information necessary to the case."

"Really? Nothing he said added anything to what we already knew. We're well beyond that stage. Had you had any concept of proper behaviour, you'd have called one of us, and saved your detective a wasted trip. All you've done is prove he isn't nearly as good as you think he is to two federal agencies, and shown to those same agencies and to me that you are incapable of managing your precinct appropriately. Your support of Marcol has gone beyond acceptable bounds. Should he appear in this precinct again without me, *personally*, requesting his presence, I will report him and you to IA for harassment of Detective Clement. Do you understand me?"

Travers gibbered. "You can't stop me managing my team."

"*I* cannot. However, consider this your formal notification that Detective Handjiev has been ordered by both DEA and the FBI not to discuss anything to do with this operation with anyone. I shall put that in writing, so there can be no misunderstandings, with Agent Glencross and Dr Renfrew copied in."

Travers' gibbering reached new heights.

Kent smacked the phone down, sent Travers the confirmatory e-mail, and tried to recover his own temper, which he only achieved by remembering that IA would be dealing with the issue.

***

"Casey," Andy called, "come see this."

"What?"

O'Leary ambled up, then Dani. Everyone looked at the street views and Bergen's map of Paddy Hocking's movements, after which Andy overlaid the map of the RFID readers.

"Wow." Casey traced overlapping lines. "*That's* interesting."

"Sure is. Funny how the highest concentrations of readers and Hocking's movements are gathered around the three sites we're betting on, isn't it?"

"Ain't that what we call clues?" O'Leary joshed.

"Usually," Casey said. "Tyler, are you going off with Andy to place cameras?"

"Yep." He turned to the stairs.

"Let's go get eyes on these sites," Andy proposed. "Bergen, you coming?"

"Sure." Bergen, wise in the ways of the team, simply accepted his inclusion.

Casey, now that the others had gone, glanced at Dani. "Okay?" she asked.

"Yeah."

"Good."

"Are we goin' to interrogate Tarticca?" O'Leary hoped.

"Not yet. Let's get him good and riled before we start. We don't have to do anything till tomorrow morning, so let's use every minute."

"Sounds good. What'll we do instead?"

"I'll talk to Evan. CSU must have found something in Wiedecz's car by now. Then I wanna get my gun back."

200

"You won't get it back today, Casey. You'll be lucky to get it early tomorrow," O'Leary pointed out. "Three days. Most likely tomorrow, but it might be Wednesday."

Casey scowled. "What if I need it 'cause we're ready to go on the raid?"

"You c'n ask Kent. He don't want you goin' out unprotected either."

Casey humphed at O'Leary, who merely smiled back at her. "Go harass Evan," he suggested. "Harassin' makes you happy."

***

"Where do you want to start?" Andy asked Tyler.

"Don't mind. Nearest."

Andy parked a couple of blocks from the first option for the drug delivery. "Do you need to have us with you, or do you want to work it out and we'll place the cameras once you're happy?"

"When I'm sure. Three of us stick out." Tyler dismissed Andy and Bergen with a gesture. Andy cast a glance at his partner, but didn't insist he took one of them along. "Call you."

"Okay."

Tyler strode off, every line of his burly body suggesting he didn't want any company.

"Problem?" Bergen tried.

"Nope." Andy shut it down. Tyler wasn't fond of Marcol, and had been protective of Casey when Marcol had hit on her previously. "He knows what he's doing. There's a café around here somewhere. Let's get some tea, and wait."

Two and a half cups of tea later, Andy's phone rang. "Tyler? You ready for us?"

"Yeah."

"Okay. First site?"

"Yeah."

Andy swiped off. "Playtime," he said to Bergen.

A couple of hours later, all three sites had been thoroughly reconnoitred and cameras placed everywhere necessary to cover the approach routes and the sites. Bergen patted the last one into place, and sighed with satisfaction.

"All done," he said. "Nice to work efficiently."

Tyler nodded.

"Time to get back."

Tyler nodded again, contented with the reconnaissance operation.

***

"Hook up your cameras," O'Leary wheedled. "I wanna see."

"See what?" Carval asked, ambling up from a long afternoon spent wandering around construction sites.

201

"Sightlines," Tyler said, which meant nothing.

"We've put eyes on the sites where we expect our perp to show up," Casey expanded, leaving out a whole mass of detail around drug raids.

"I see. Can I shoot when you go to take him down?"

Everyone looked at each other, hoping someone else would answer.

"It's complicated," Casey eventually said. "It's likely to be part of a drug raid, led by Agent Glencross of DEA with support from the FBI, Narcotics, and us – but we're there to get our perp, not take down drug dealers and gangs."

Carval searched around for Glencross. "I wanna shoot it. Where's this Glencross so I can ask him?"

"Ask?" Casey exclaimed. "You're *asking*, not *telling* him you'll tag along?"

Carval pouted at her. "I can be polite."

"You can?" O'Leary grinned. "Can't say as I'd noticed."

"You can ask him," Casey said. "But if he says no, that's the end of it."

Carval wasn't listening. He was sure he could persuade Glencross to let him follow along. It wasn't like he wanted to be part of the raid or arrests, he simply wanted to shoot it. He had to shoot it. He hurried off to find Glencross before anyone could stop him.

Carval found Glencross in the federal lair and bounced in. "I'm Carval. I wanna shoot when you raid these sites and Casey arrests her perp."

Glencross whipped his gaze up. "*Who* are you?"

"I'm *Carval*," Carval said. "Photographer."

"Ah."

"What do you mean, *ah*? Everyone knows about my shots. I wanna shoot your raid for *Murder Two*."

"Do you? Why should I let you? Raids aren't like taking snaps on the beach."

Carval bridled – then examined Glencross closely, whipped up his camera and took six shots without a pause. "I know that, and *you* know exactly who I am." He lowered the camera. "You're messing with me to see if I mean it. I do. I'll stay back or to the side or wherever's safe-ish – I don't want to be hurt or dead – but I have to shoot the raid."

"I'll consider it."

"Prior to deciding," Renfrew's prim tones intervened, "I suggest you visit Mr Carval's exhibition, in order to make an informed judgement."

"Good plan – if I get any time," Glencross said.

Carval departed, before Renfrew could grill him.

"Is he for real?" Glencross asked Renfrew.

"Yes. He is obsessed with taking photographs. I am most surprised he remembered to ask your permission." Renfrew steepled his fingers. "However, should you give permission, he will undoubtedly portray you in the best possible light. I commend his current exhibition to you."

Carval sauntered back out of the federal room, perfectly certain he'd be allowed to shoot the raid. He examined Casey, who was pale, but not obviously upset. "How're you doing?"

"I want my gun back," she grumbled.

"They took your gun away?"

"Yeah. Until they confirm it was a legitimate shot. It could've been desk duty too, but Kent allowed me to keep investigating."

"Oh." Carval gazed around. "If nothing's happening, I'll go save a table in the Abbey. It's almost shift end."

"'Kay."

He strolled off.

CHAPTER TWENTY FOUR

"Come look at this," Andy called. "We've hooked up the feeds, and see, here's our perp."

"Grappano?" Casey hurried over to Andy and Tyler.

"Yep."

"Which site?"

"Two."

O'Leary was already striding towards the federal room. "We got a hit on Grappano already," he announced from six feet away. The agents surged past him to Andy's desk.

"What are you seeing?" Glencross opened.

"Here." Andy pointed. "But it's only Grappano. No-one else is there."

"Scouting," Tyler stated.

"I agree," Renfrew and Glencross said together.

"I don't think they'll decide on a site till the last minute," Glencross mused. "We'll need to have people at all of them."

"I want to pick Grappano up," Casey groused, "but if we do we blow your raid." She scowled. "I don't like leaving murderers out on the street."

"Your view is entirely understandable, but leaving this particular man on the street, for only a short time further, will enable us to remove far more murderers from society." Renfrew's face chilled. "The damage done by criminal organisations peddling opioids is greater than any single homicide."

"We know," Casey muttered. Glencross muffled a cough, eyes glinting, crinkling at the corners.

"No harm comes from reminding us of our mutual goals," Renfrew pontificated. "However, Grappano is but one small piece of our jigsaw. I suggest we utilise your four officers to keep watch over these feeds, with Agent Bergen and, if she agrees, Detective Handjiev, available to consult."

"Sure," Dani said. Casey heard *I don't want to go back to Narcotics tonight.*

"Okay," Bergen agreed. "One more overnight won't kill me."

"I'll go find them." O'Leary tromped off. Shortly, he returned with the four officers.

"Sirs, ma'ams?" Fremont asked.

"Meet Agent Glencross of DEA." Casey waved towards him. "You know Dr Renfrew and Agent Bergen – oh. Henegan, Adamo – they're FBI. You know Detective Handjiev is from Narcotics. Agent Glencross, they're all yours."

"Listen up," Glencross began. The four officers riveted their attention to him. "We have a major drug deal going down. Detective Clement's perpetrator is a key part of the delivery. Detectives Tyler and Chee, with Agent Bergen, have put eyes on the three sites we've identified as most likely to be the drop point. Those eyes are linked to these computers. You'll watch the feeds for any activity, all night. Spell each other – you can't watch carefully for more than an hour at a time, so work out a rota and stick to it. Take naps. Eat and drink."

The four officers hadn't taken their eyes off him. "How do you define activity – and when do we call you?" Fremont asked.

"Anyone going near the sites is activity – note it with exact times, so we can go straight to the right footage. If it's more than four people, call me." He caught Fremont's look at Larson. "And call Detective Clement's team. The FBI – Agent Bergen here, and Detective Handjiev – will be around, for anything else interesting." Glencross paused. "If you see this man" – he put a photo of Grappano on the desk – "make sure you have all the details of what he does, even if he doesn't go inside."

"He's our homicide perp," Casey said.

"Yes, sir. Ma'am."

"If you see this one" – Glencross put a shot of Paddy Hocking down – "call me immediately."

"Sir?"

"He's from a rival gang, trying to work out where the drop will be. We're tracking him." Glencross turned to Casey. "Anything you want to add?"

"No." She caught the officers' gazes. "This is as important as interrogating. Taking these gangs off the streets makes a difference."

"Yes'm!" they chorused.

"I wish to brief each of our good officers individually," Renfrew said. The good officers paled. "Officer Fremont, I will begin with you. Please accompany me."

"Before he does," Casey intervened, "is there anything more we should discuss tonight?"

"I do not think so."

"Nope," Glencross said. "You're obviously letting Tarticca stew, and after you've had a go at him tomorrow, I'll have a turn." He bared his teeth. "I'll be good cop."

"I'll be starting at eight, if you want to watch from Observation."

"Yep. Thanks. Go get some rest. You've done good work already."

Casey turned to her team, back in the bullpen. "Let's debrief," she said, "'cause I think we're done for the day. I spoke to Evan, and they're still running the data they got from Wiedecz's vehicle. He'll ping me as soon as anything pops. I haven't heard from the shooting team," she added with rigid control. "I don't like this hurry-up-and-wait."

"We all know about the eyes," Andy said. "Nothing else."

"We know who, we know where," O'Leary hummed. "Wish we could go get him, but screwin' with a federal investigation ain't goin' to win us any points."

"In that case – and since it's after six – let's quit and get a beer."

"Yeah. Carval's already there."

"Before you go, Detectives," Kent said ominously from behind them, "a word in my office."

***

"Officer Fremont," Dr Renfrew opened, "I wish to brief you on the operation as a whole, and the role of the Thirty-Sixth precinct." Officer Fremont eased fractionally as Dr Renfrew explained.

"Thank you, sir."

"You may know I am researching team dynamics. In pursuit of this research, I wish to question you about your relationship with Detective Clement's team."

Officer Fremont's eyes narrowed, but he said nothing. Dr Renfrew noted the flash of caution, and changed his approach.

"It is my understanding that Detective Clement's team do not admit outsiders. Yet you and Officer Larson appear to have become their preferred officers. Why?"

Officer Fremont held Dr Renfrew's gaze with a firm look. "We work hard and don't mess around," he said mildly. "We know their style and I guess we fit with it."

"I see. Thank you."

Dr Renfrew made a short note. He had developed a theory, but he would have more evidence once he had been able to interview Officers Larson and Henegan.

***

"Come in," Kent said when Casey had knocked. "Close the door." The four cops stood at parade attention as Kent surveyed their apprehensive

206

demeanours. "I will explain exactly as much as I need to. You will not ask questions, and anyway they won't be answered. Understood?"

"Sir," they replied in perfect unison.

"The same unpleasant behaviour that tried to upset Clement's success at the Academy has culminated in an Internal Affairs investigation, which began with Officer Birkett on Thursday. Various other members of the NYPD will be interviewed." Kent didn't say *and potentially charged*, but the team understood it. "You may be interviewed as witnesses. If so, I expect you to co-operate fully and honestly. You are not to conceal anything, including your respective histories before you joined the NYPD – that includes your childhoods. Understood?"

"Sir."

"Clement."

"Sir?"

"More than one officer has been involved in harassing you with press cuttings. There is now surveillance covering your desk." Tyler, Andy and O'Leary tensed. "It is not admissible evidence. However, it will be used informally, by me, to warn off any other officers who attempt to harass you. I will not have this behaviour in my precinct. I will *also* take an exceptionally dim view of any retaliation against those people, either by your team or by the officers you've adopted. Keep them reined in. Their behaviour will reflect on you."

"Sir."

"Dismissed. I expect you all to have left the precinct within five minutes. Go."

They went, at speed.

***

"Detective Handjiev?" Fremont said, a few minutes after he'd spelled Larson, "we got movement around Site Three, ma'am."

"Yes?" Dani came to full attention. "What's up?"

"Two men went in, but they're not the ones you left mugshots of. Another two went in just now, so that's four. Thought you'd want to know."

"Sure do. Good call. Let's see?"

Fremont ran the section again, on his own computer.

"Mmm." Dani frowned at it. "They're not carrying anything. No boxes. They came on foot."

"D'you mean they aren't planning to take anything out, ma'am?"

"Yep."

"So it's a diversion?"

"Maybe. Or maybe they're making sure nobody else slips in."

"Like us?"

"Exactly. Keep watching, and give the other officers the heads-up. If anything looks weird, or other guys turn up, let me know immediately – even if it's one man. I'll bring Agent Bergen up to speed. Nice work."

***

"Officer Larson," Dr Renfrew began, having summoned the officer after he had completed his short interview with Officer Fremont. "Allow me to brief you on the full details of our operation."

"Thank you, sir."

Dr Renfrew explained. "Now, I wish to discuss another matter. You may be aware that I am conducting research into how the NYPD teams are constructed, in order to improve team selection across law enforcement agencies."

"Sir."

"In pursuit of my research, I should be grateful if you would answer some questions."

"Yes, sir." Officer Larson's brow creased, but he waited calmly.

"You and Officer Fremont have been working for Detective Clement's team for some months now."

"Yes, sir."

"How did that arise?"

"Sergeant Tully assigned us, sir."

"They didn't ask for you?"

"No, sir. Well, maybe Fremont. Not me."

"What impression did Detective Clement's team originally have of you, personally, and your work?"

Officer Larson winced, then swallowed. "Uh…not good. Sir," he added.

"You need not add the honorific every time, Officer Larson. You are respectful enough without it. Expand."

"Uh…"

"This interview is confidential."

Officer Larson blinked. "Uh, um…I didn't realise they needed to know about the rifle results" – he stopped and recalibrated – "on the runner who was shot" –

"Ah, yes. I recall, although I was not involved."

"Well, uh…anyways, I didn't tell Detective Clement fast enough and she was mad. And I…" Officer Larson acquired a shamefaced blush. "Uh, I wasn't comfortable around Detective O'Leary. I'd heard about them at the Third…"

"Clearly you are perfectly comfortable now, and, since you are still working with the team, Detective Clement and the others must be satisfied with your work. How did this transpire?"

Officer Larson squirmed again. "The team – Detective Clement – ripped me a new one. Fremont kicked my ass. I thought I was done." He met Dr Renfrew's eyes. "I made a good suggestion, and she *accepted* it. She listened, even though I knew she thought I was a total dumbass. They – Detective Clement, 'cause they'd never have done it if she hadn't agreed – gave me another chance."

Dr Renfrew's eyes bored into Officer Larson. "I was under the impression that Detective Clement's team did not give second chances."

"They're real hard-asses – uh, er" –

"I comprehend."

"They got a reputation. Great detectives, but they don't care about anyone else."

"Yet, they gave you a second chance."

"Yes, sir. I don't know why, just for one suggestion, but I'm glad they did. Detective Chee's training me in tech work."

Dr Renfrew thought for an instant. "There are four of you, and four detectives. Has each detective taken on one of you?"

Officer Larson thought in turn, for longer. "I guess," he said slowly, "but I don't think they decided it. It just…sorta happened. I knew a little about social media so Detective Chee pulled me out. Detective Tyler's taken on Adamo, and Detective O'Leary took Henegan, though that's because he was big enough to deal with him if" – Officer Larson stopped.

"If Officer Henegan's motives proved to be malign," Dr Renfrew said blandly.

"Uh, yessir."

"By elimination, Detective Clement must have taken Officer Fremont."

"Yeah. He's quick and smart. She doesn't accept dumb. He wants to go for detective, and I think they know it."

"You say Detective Clement does not 'accept dumb'. Has working with her team made you a better police officer?"

"Yes." Officer Larson squirmed some more. He appeared to be embarrassed by his previous performance, which was, of course, an exceedingly important datum. Detective Clement's team had, it seemed, shamed him into working more effectively. "I don't wanna disappoint them. They gave me another chance." Ah. *Not* shame, but the far more powerful force of gratitude.

"I see." Dr Renfrew pushed up his pince-nez, then steepled his fingers on his desk. "Thank you." He determined to take a break before interviewing Officer Henegan, and further decided he should eat while little was occurring. He endeavoured always to be prepared.

***

"Back to the Abbey," Casey said. "I want to hear about this *surveillance*."

209

The team looked at each other.

"C'mon. Now!" she ordered.

Ten minutes later they were in the Abbey, where Carval bought the round, and Casey fixed each team member with a basilisk stare.

"Carval knew nothin' about it," O'Leary said easily. "So you c'n stop givin' him the evil eye."

"She could stop giving it to us, too," Andy suggested.

"Surveillance?"

"Just a camera, so we could see who was leavin' you li'l love letters."

Casey snorted, which was exactly what O'Leary had intended. "And what did your covert" – she put a nasty edge on the word – "surveillance bring up?"

"Waal," O'Leary began, "uh…Grendon."

"Reported to Kent," Tyler said. "Left it to him."

"He approved of this little camera? Don't tell me you asked him for permission first, 'cause I won't believe you."

"He didn't *not* approve," Andy pointed out.

"Scowled. Growled. Didn't say scrap it."

Casey sighed. "Just don't tell our pet officers. We'll have enough trouble making it clear to them first thing tomorrow that there'll be no more attitude adjusting." Her face crumpled slightly. "Why can't they all leave us alone? They always did before. If this is fame, I don't want it."

"Naw, this ain't fame, nor anythin' like it. This is bad people doin' crappy thin's to upset you 'cause they're jealous, like they always were. Iffen you think it's anythin' to do with fame, you're wrong."

"I guess," Casey said exhaustedly, hands around her beer bottle. "I'm tired."

"Waal, go home an' get some rest, 'cause it's all goin' to be fun, games, an' raids pretty soon."

"Yeah. I want this case to be done."

"You want to take vacation."

"I'll get one whether I want it or not," Casey pointed out, without mentioning that she did want to take vacation or saying it was already planned. Under the table, she put her hand on Carval's knee, reassuring him.

***

"Agent Bergen?"

"Yes, Officer – Henegan, isn't it?"

"Yes, sir."

"What've you got?" Agent Bergen's forgettable face invited Henegan to expand.

"It's Site One, sir. Four men have gone in."

"Interesting." Bergen's brow creased. "A bit less than half an hour ago four men went into Site Three – two, then two more. This was four at once?"

"Yes, sir. Fremont told me about the Site Three men, sir." Henegan wriggled a little. "Um…these men were on foot too, and they weren't carrying boxes, same as Site Three."

Bergen adopted mild enthusiasm, looking at the feed, and Henegan relaxed slightly.

"Weird," the agent said. "They're wearing coats, but it's seventy degrees out. Okay, it's raining, but it's a bit odd." He frowned at the screen.

"Officer Fremont, could you pull up your feed of the four guys at Site Three?"

"Yessir."

"Henegan, go find Detective Handjiev, please." Despite Bergen's *please*, it was clearly an order. Henegan jumped to it.

"What is it?" Dani asked, hurrying up.

"Look at these guys at Site One – all with coats on. Site Three, same. Why would they be wearing long coats if it's seventy degrees?"

Dani's face scrunched in thought. "You're right. Hiding something under them?"

"Yep. Best guess? I'm going for weapons."

"Yeah – but why? There's no way for them to have a delivery anywhere tonight, and they've no transport in place. Four men in one place isn't enough for what we've heard, even if they split it over all three sites." She frowned intensely, matching Bergen's wrinkling brow.

"Do you think they're trying to provoke something?" Bergen suddenly said. "Deliberately taunting the Yarrabees? This footage should be good enough for running facial recognition."

"Let's do it." Dani turned to the two officers, and summoned Adamo. "Who's up watching?"

"Me," Henegan admitted.

"Okay, you keep going with the feeds. You two, come learn how we do facial rec, and Henegan, we'll make sure you and Larson get a turn later." She left Henegan staring at the screens, and took the other two off with Bergen, who was delighted to instruct them.

A quarter-hour later, Bergen straightened up from his computer and beamed at the two officers. "So that's how we do it. Now we let the facial recognition programs run – shame it's not as quick as on TV, or as definite – and in a little while we'll come back and see if anything's popped. Who's next up on watch duty? Officer Henegan's had his hour, so if there's anything more he's found, he gets a turn finding out about faces."

Henegan's slumped shoulders indicated nothing more interesting than a rainy night in Manhattan, and he gratefully sloped off to the break room for refreshments.

"Who's next?"

"Me." Larson, who'd exited the conference room a moment before, sat down. Adamo trotted off to whatever pursuits would keep him occupied, but Fremont stayed put.

***

"Officer Henegan," Dr Renfrew said, an hour after he had finished with Officer Larson. "I wish to brief you on the operation." Officer Henegan followed him to his conference room.

"Sir." The officer looked at the floor as Dr Renfrew provided the necessary information for the third time. "Thank you."

"Now, I wish to ask you why you are assisting Detective Clement's team." Dr Renfrew met Officer Henegan's shocked gaze. "I am well aware of your previous behaviour towards her. I am also aware of her intolerance of discourtesy and refusal to work with those who are not acceptable to the team. So, Officer, why have they allowed you to work with them?"

"Sergeant ordered it, sir."

Dr Renfrew rapidly deduced that Captain Kent had ensured that Henegan would have to 'face his fears', in the form of Detective Clement. "Continue."

"They had to take me. They all told me I had one chance, and if I messed up or upset Detective Clement, I'd be gone."

"When was this?"

"The case before this one."

"Mm." Dr Renfrew pushed up his glasses, then steepled his fingers. "How did you convince them to accept you on a second case?"

"They – Detective O'Leary, mostly – explained. Showed me what to do, sir. Even though I'd been, uh…"

"You need not specify. I understand."

"They put it aside to solve the case. They weren't trying to catch me out, or bully me, or trap me into something. They played straight with me, even though it was clear they didn't want me and likely didn't trust me. They gave me a chance. Detective Clement listened to me as well as Fremont, even though we can all see she's impressed with Fremont, but she didn't play favourites. She wanted to know what I thought, and she *agreed*."

"How heartening." Dr Renfrew made a mental note that, again, Detective Clement would not allow any personal prejudices to interfere with solving cases.

"It sure was. I never expected it. Larson told me they'd given him a second chance, so, uh…I came clean about, uh…"

212

"I am aware of the other officers who were involved in harassing Detective Clement."

"Uh…yessir, that…and Detective Clement wasn't happy, but she said I had guts to come clean, then she said I had to make a choice and I still only got one chance. She was totally honest about it. But she *believed* me. I didn't think she would. She believed me. They let me do proper work like the other three as if I'd never fucked up – uh, sorry, sir."

"I am not offended."

"…and she told me I did well if I did. Nobody did before." Henegan squirmed. "I don't think I did good before. She must have asked for me this time, because the Sergeant wouldn't have put me with them if they hadn't said it was okay."

"In fact, you have been given the second chance for which you hoped, and you have performed well."

Henegan coloured, embarrassed.

CHAPTER TWENTY FIVE

"Home time," O'Leary said parentally, draining his beer. "We all need to get some sleep, 'specially iffen our good officers wake us up for int'restin' events in the middle of the night."

"You trying to be Mommy again?"

"Someone has to be. We don't got no other moms here." Casey made a small noise, and O'Leary wriggled. "Didn't mean you." He patted her. "You know that. Now, off you go home an' get some rest. Likely we'll be a bit busy tomorrow."

"Before we go," Andy stopped them, "why's Marcol trying to push into our case?"

"He wants to look good in front of the Feds," Casey said cynically.

"Naw. That's not all. He wants to show he c'n work with you, to prove none of this was him. He's playin' all friendly an' helpful, an' hopin' the Feds'll believe his play-actin' an' not the history. He's pretendin' he's a good guy."

"In front of the best profiler they have? He's totally dumb." Carval slugged his beer back. "Renfrew'll never believe him."

"He ain't happy Marcol shoved in, though if I was Marcol or his Captain I'd be worryin' more about blowin' up DEA's goodwill. Glencross wasn't happy with them, an' he's a lot closer to home than the FBI."

"Still, it fits with him not being involved with this latest mess."

"Yeah." Casey made another horrible face. "Shame. If he was, we might get rid of him for good."

I don't think he'll be botherin' us for a while. Glencross an' Renfrew'll make sure of it." O'Leary plonked his empty beer bottle down. "Now, it's time for me to go home. Don't stay up too late."

***

214

"Do you believe that crap about team bonding the FBI guy gave out?" Fremont's voice was low as he spoke to Larson, and his eyes scanned their vicinity to ensure no-one else was listening.

"I believe it more'n I believe he wanted to brief us." Larson's eyes stayed firmly on the screen. "He was digging into why I'd smartened up."

"Didn't ask me that."

"Didn't need to. You were doing good before – they asked for you, not me. I was just... dead weight."

"Not now." Fremont gently punched Larson's shoulder. "They ask for both of us now." He paused. "Did you mention those clippings Bartlett and the others were leaving around?"

"Nope."

"Good call. Wish we could do some" – he made air quotes – "attitude adjusting, but they'll" –

"No, Casey will," – Larson corrected.

"– have our balls."

"Yeah – look! Another four guys going into Site Two. That's all three, now. Long coats and all. Just like Henegan saw." A coat flapped in a sudden gust of wind. "There's a gun!"

"Handjiev and Bergen thought they might be trying to provoke the Yarrabees into making an early move." Fremont was already halfway to the federal conference room as he spoke. "Detective, Agent, we got the same movement on Site Two *and* Larson thinks he saw a gun."

"Gun?" Dani was already striding towards Larson. "We were right. Show us."

"And we'll add another round of facial recognition." Bergen added, following her. "Henegan and Larson's turns to learn. Go find him, would you?"

Fremont located Henegan in the break room and almost had to run after him as Henegan hurried towards Bergen.

"Sir?" Henegan said.

"Okay." Everyone's attention landed on Dani. "That definitely looks like a gun. We can assume everyone took guns in under those coats."

"Should we call Detective Clement?"

Dani considered Fremont's question. "Not yet. We haven't seen Grappano, and we haven't had more than four in each site. Besides, she hasn't been cleared to get her gun back, so..." She trailed off.

"Let them get some rest. We haven't seen that Hocking guy either, so I don't think anyone'll start shooting yet."

"I'll brief Glencross, in case he wants something else done, but keep watching."

"The facial rec should be nearly done by now. Henegan, Larson, you come with me to put these four in, and we'll have a look at the results from the first batch."

"Sir."

"Well, well, well." Bergen almost rubbed his hands together with glee as the first set of results arrived. "What have we here? This looks like a nice even split between Tarticcas and Pagliaccis, all best friends together, plotting to take out the Yarrabees. Handjiev and Glencross will *love* this."

***

"Do you really think it isn't Marcol?" Carval asked, on the way back to Casey's apartment.

"I'd like it to be, but yeah. O'Leary's right – again." She fell silent until they reached her home, where she flopped on to the couch.

Carval dropped down next to her, and hugged her. "You okay?"

"Tired," she drooped, and curled in. "There's too much going on. It's okay when I'm at work because there's something to concentrate on, but as soon as the case is quieter it's all there waiting for me." She stopped, hands knotting. "And Renfrew's trying to *therapize* me," she added bitterly, which Carval already knew. "As if he wasn't bad enough."

"But you've got the team."

"Yeah, but Kent ordered it. Part of the post-shooting protocol – well, it's not compulsory, but Kent's made it a requirement."

"He's worried about you." Carval failed to engage his brain before opening his mouth.

"Kent?" Casey exclaimed. "Kent, *worried* about us? You're kidding."

"Nope," Carval contradicted. "I can see it in my lens. He worries about you. And the others, but right now it's you."

"I don't need to be *worried* about, especially not by Kent. He should leave us to it."

Carval considered, shuffling his arm around Casey's small shoulders. "I don't think that's how he does it."

"And you know this how?" she snarked.

"I told you; I can see it in my camera," Carval said equably. "I see far more through it than without it – you know this. You've *seen* the exhibition. And what I see right now is that Kent thinks you're right on the edge and he wants to stop you from falling off."

Casey's jaw passed her knees on the way to the floor.

"Now, maybe it's 'cause he likes your solve rate, but I didn't get the impression he was too happy about all the harassment either."

"I don't need him trying to fix me. I can fix myself, with the team," Casey spat. "I don't want anyone to interfere."

"Sure you can."

216

"Of course I can!" she yelled. "I don't need to have that damn profiler or Kent prying into my life. I'm not *on the edge* and anyone who says I am can go to hell."

Carval kept quiet. Casey suddenly slumped. "That doesn't sound like I'm okay, does it?" she admitted.

"Nope." He cuddled her. "We had this conversation already. You're allowed to be upset. It's not like you're losing it in the bullpen." Cuddling turned to careful, unobtrusive petting. "But…even Tyler said you should talk to someone, and if he did, there's no shame in it."

"I guess," dribbled out after a long pause. "I don't like Renfrew. Pompous, patronising prick."

"Can't you see someone else?"

"Kent ordered Renfrew. Ordered me to see Renfrew, I mean."

"Oh. That sucks." Carval carefully didn't say *Renfrew's seen a lot about you that you wouldn't necessarily tell a different shrink.*

"Yeah."

Psychiatrists weren't exactly Carval's speciality, since he'd never doubted anything about his abilities, personality or life. As far as he was concerned, his life was pretty perfect, and if he was a little obsessed with taking brilliant photographs, well, it was the same obsession as any world-class performer had in any walk of life.

"You could take the initiative," he offered.

"Huh?"

"Get in first. Renfrew expects you to do everything you can to avoid him, so if you take the first step – like Tyler said – he'll be defensive, and you can control where it goes." He grinned wryly. "You don't want it to come back and bite you. If you deal with the shooting, it's one problem out of the way."

"And with Estrolla and Grendon in trouble, Birkett out of the way and Marcol squashed, the others'll stop. Dad…" She sniffed. "O'Leary said it would take time. I know that. I've been here before."

"He was right. But with the other stuff gone, you'll be able to deal with it."

Casey sat up straight. "Yes," she decided. "That'll work. Get it all out of the way... Yeah."

"Going on vacation'll help too. Somewhere away from Manhattan."

"Yeah." She slumped back again.

"Okay," Carval said. "Do you want to have dinner, or just coffee?"

"No. I'm too tired. I'll go to bed."

"Want me to stay?"

"If you want to."

He looked at her drawn face, a hint of grey under the cream of her skin, the dark circles under her eyes. "Yep," he replied.

Casey hoisted herself up and dragged into her bedroom. Carval gave her privacy for her night-time routine: only joining her after he'd heard the small sounds of Casey sliding under the bed covers. He sat on the edge of the bed, and stroked. It was barely ten, and he was nowhere near sleepy. Casey went out like a blown candle, though she was curled tightly into herself, buried in the quilt and pillows, as if she were cold.

Carval left her to sleep, knowing he'd be next to her later, and went back to his thoughts and a coffee to help those thoughts along. He didn't like Renfrew, and he didn't like the idea of Casey, the team, and by extension his exhibition, being dissected – but Casey couldn't carry on without something breaking, and even the unstinting support of her team wouldn't be enough to solve all the issues around her. If there had been one issue fewer…they might have gotten through it. But everything together, and having to wait before arresting a known perp… Even Casey had a breaking point, and she was about one inch away from it.

He backed away from any idea that he might talk to Renfrew without being specifically asked to, however. He was firmly on Casey's side, and he had no reason to support Renfrew, Renfrew's psychiatric practices, or Renfrew's research. He only wanted to support Casey.

That established, he drank his coffee, made himself a sandwich, and used his phone to research various photographic techniques which he might use in future. Later, he washed and slid into Casey's bed, spooning around her. She gave a sleepy little noise, and relaxed against him.

***

"Anything interesting overnight?" Casey asked the yawning officers, horrifically early on Tuesday.

"People went in, ma'am, then they came out, but nothing happened yet." Larson yawned again.

"Okay. Debrief with everyone, and you can all go home and get some sleep. We'll need you to be alert when it does go down."

"I'll catch some sleep too." Dani nodded at Bergen. "And so should you."

"Both of you get gone," Glencross ordered. "I've cleared it with Dr Renfrew." He turned to Casey. "I'm up to speed. Let's make sure we're all fully briefed, then you have an appointment with Tarticca and Tarrant." He bared his teeth. "Then I do."

Casey nodded. "Yep. I'll stick firmly to the murders and baby-killing. Anything else is yours."

"Sounds good."

Briefing over, with no new leads to follow, Casey and O'Leary left Andy chasing up more camera footage in the hope of finding where Grappano had gone, and Tyler reviewing the feed to try to identify the type of guns

218

being carried in – and whether they'd been carried out. They sauntered to Interrogation, where Tarrant awaited them. Casey had received some extremely interesting information from CSU, which she was looking forward to using.

"Time for some nice intimidatin'." O'Leary chuckled at the thought. "Ready?" he added seriously.

"Yep."

She pushed the door open, and gazed contemptuously at Tarrant. "We'd better make sure he's properly informed. I wouldn't want a baby-killing gangster to get off on a technicality."

O'Leary administered the preliminaries for the recording and the Miranda warning with a tinge of menace. Tarrant, regarding him as a mouse would regard a hungry tiger, shuddered.

"Jeffrey Tarrant." Tarrant's attention whipped to Casey. "I arrested you for obstruction."

"I didn't."

"You lied to me. That's obstruction. You told me you didn't know this man." She shoved the photo of Grappano across the table. "You told me he hadn't been in" – disbelief dripped from her words – "all day. Yeah, right." She paused. Tarrant kept his mouth shut. "You're the Tarticca doorkeeper. You know *everyone* who comes in."

"I'm a barman."

"And all good barmen notice customers. It wasn't busy."

"How would you know? Our bar's busy all the time."

"On a Saturday afternoon when everyone wants to watch the ball game later and you don't even have a big screen for them to see it?" O'Leary growled.

"Not everyone likes baseball." Tarrant tried to stay calm, but his eyes were jerking away from the cops.

"Guess that's why Andrew Grappano went into your bar on Saturday afternoon."

"I told you; I don't know who you're talking about!"

"Have a look at this picture." Casey tapped the still from the street camera. "This man is the same one who's in the photo I put right under your lying nose. He's going into your bar. He's the only person who went in for two hours." Tarrant's shoulders shivered. Silence stretched out in the interrogation room. Casey broke it. "Still want to tell me you didn't see him? It's a slam-dunk charge against you."

Tarrant stayed silent. "I want a lawyer," he finally demanded.

"Sure," Casey said casually. "Anyone in particular? I'm pretty sure the Tarticcas have a few on retainer."

And it's always good to know who they are, the thought passed between the two cops.

"I'll call them. I've got a right to call."

"You do. We'll leave you to it."

Casey and O'Leary exited.

"I guess we'll go for Tarticca now?" O'Leary enquired.

"Yeah. Do you think he's arrogant enough not to lawyer up first off?"

"Depends how often you call him a baby-killer."

***

"Federico Tarticca." Casey ran a slow, disgusted gaze over him. "Or should it be Babykiller Tarticca?"

"Federico Babykiller," O'Leary corrected. "That's what he is. Murderin' innocent unborn babies. That'll go down good in gangland."

"Pretty sure all the other organised crime families'll *love* to know Babykiller Tarticca's the reason the FBI's hunting them down even harder."

"Ain't that a shame."

"Still, I'm sure he'll be safe in prison." Casey smiled viciously, then returned her gaze to Tarticca. "So. Why'd you kill a baby?"

"I didn't."

"Conspiracy to murder is murder," Casey pointed out, still smiling viciously. "So you did. Even if you didn't do the deed yourself."

"I have no idea what you're talking about. I haven't killed or conspired to kill anyone."

"Let's talk about that. You told me you had no idea who Pieter Wiedecz was."

"I don't."

"Your DNA's all over his car."

Tarticca froze for an instant. "I get plenty of Ubers." It wasn't convincing.

"We can check if Pieter was drivin' for Uber," O'Leary said casually. "It won't take long."

"No. While we wait, Tarticca Babykiller here'll be back in a cell."

"You only got twenty-four hours" –

"Not if I charge you. And I can charge you with obstruction, because you lied to me, so I can keep you in a cell as long as I want to."

"I didn't lie," Tarticca argued.

"You told me you had no idea who Pieter Wiedecz was. You denied knowing Andrew Grappano. I know you knew Pieter, because I have direct witness evidence of your connection."

"Ooops," O'Leary drew out.

"I know Grappano went into your bar, and didn't come out for hours. Either Tarrant saw him, or he slipped through to somewhere Tarrant wasn't. You trying to tell me you allow random barflies past the door of the bar?"

220

"No!" Tarticca shut his mouth, quickly.

"So why did you let Grappano through? You've already admitted he wasn't a random customer in the bar."

Tension stretched through the air. Tarticca's hands had stayed below the table throughout, though Casey would have bet they were clenched into fists, and that he would have loved to have hit her. She waited, and when the atmosphere was suffocatingly intense, spoke again.

"Tarrant's next door. He's as badly off as you, and he doesn't have your resources. Of course, neither will you when I walk out of here. We'll freeze everything because you're pushing drugs."

"I don't."

"Liar." Casey leaned forward. "You lied about Pieter Wiedecz, and we can prove it. You lied about the drugs, because the same car that's got your DNA all over it, the same one that was filmed doing the shooting by a hundred passers-by – that'd be the shooting that killed two men, injured an innocent bystander and murdered her unborn baby – has enough traces of opioids that I have more than enough probable cause. Oh, and the man who did the shooting and the driver were also caught on film, and the shooter's the same Andrew Grappano who walked into your bar and stayed there."

Silence.

"Pieter Wiedecz tried to shoot us. What do you know about that?"

"I want a lawyer." Tarticca's face remained entirely still, though the muscles in his arms tightened as if his hands were clenching and unclenching.

"Sure. Don't forget to tell them all your assets are frozen, so they'll have to represent you on credit."

Casey and O'Leary left on her excellent exit line.

***

"They both lawyered up," Casey grumped to Glencross.

"What did you expect?"

"Them to lawyer up." She made a sulky face. "Still, they didn't have to."

"Yeah," Glencross sympathised. "I wish they wouldn't too."

"I want Grappano."

"He didn't come up on the feeds last night, unfortunately, after the first view."

"He went back to Tarticca HQ," Andy said.

"Back there?" Casey complained. "Sure, we arrested Tarticca and Tarrant, but if Grappano's back in HQ, how can I arrest him? I can't execute my warrant without blowing up your raid."

"No, and the federal investigation trumps yours."

221

"Casey," Andy intervened. "I've got the rest of the footage and I've been through it – around Tarticca HQ. If Grappano came out, he didn't do it on any street with a camera. There's only one other option, an alley, and I've asked for the footage at the end of it."

"You don't think he came out?"

"No. I think he's still in there."

Casey grimaced. "I want Grappano." She stopped. "I mean, sure I want gangs off the streets too, but I want Grappano. He killed two men and a baby. Potential baby. And…" she stopped again.

"And what?"

"Just…he deserves to pay." Which wasn't what she had been thinking, which had been *and Tania Hercliffe's husband is too fond of booze already, so what will this blow do?* Fortunately, though it was clear from his expression Glencross didn't believe her, he dropped it.

"Yes," was all he said.

Andy turned around from his chair, where he'd been clicking on his computer. "I'm setting up a feed so we can see Tarticca HQ real-time."

"Lot of feeds," Tyler commented. His burly frame hunched, and he blinked several times, as if he was trying to watch all of them at once.

"Lots of us to watch 'em," O'Leary pointed out.

"The officers have all been sent home to sleep." Casey flicked a glance at Tyler. "You wanna take a break?"

"No."

Casey left it. Tyler knew his limits, and if he didn't need to take a break, it was his business. "I want my gun," she carped. "Kent said there was no doubt, so I want it back."

"Give 'em till lunchtime, an' call afterwards. Iffen they're difficult, tell Kent we could be out raidin' drug dealers any moment, an' likely he'll help." O'Leary's homely face crinkled. "Now, are we goin' to watch these here feeds?"

"Yeah. We can't do anything else anyway."

"If I might intrude," Dr Renfrew interrupted, in a way which made it clear he would, whether Casey liked it or not, "may I take some of your time, Detective Clement?"

Casey acquired a *leave-me-alone* expression which she didn't even try to hide, but nodded.

"I suggest our discussions would benefit from your most excellent coffee."

"I guess." Casey couldn't have been less gracious if she had tried. Dr Renfrew remained impervious to the atmosphere, and indicated that she should precede him to the break room.

CHAPTER TWENTY SIX

Coffee brewed, Dr Renfrew conducted Detective Clement to his borrowed conference room, from which he had already requested Agent Bergen to depart. Detective Clement sat without invitation, clearly deciding permission need not be requested in her own precinct. Dr Renfrew steepled his fingers, and assessed her signs of stress and tiredness. He was about to speak, when Detective Clement forestalled him.

"Stop trying to find out things from my team and ask me directly instead," she snapped. "If I have to do this, you shouldn't be going behind my back."

"I take it you have spoken to Detective O'Leary."

"You had no right to speak to him. If you want answers about me, you ask me."

Dr Renfrew blinked. Detective Clement's tone had acquired the same quality as, he imagined, Ghengis Khan addressing his Horde. Disobedience was not an option. However, Dr Renfrew was not feeble enough to succumb to psychological pressure, even from such an expert in intimidation as Detective Clement.

"You fail to understand the methods that any psychiatrist must employ," he rebuked, and received a look that should have scorched his skin to ashes.

"Explain those methods," Detective Clement bit. "*Now.*"

Dr Renfrew succumbed, having instantly determined that appearing to concede to Detective Clement's anger would provide far more information and co-operation than an unnecessary conflict, undoubtedly provoked by the circumstances which had occasioned her overwhelming stress. Adding further tension to her state would assist nobody. Dr Renfrew did not admit, even to himself, his profound relief that Detective Clement had stayed sitting, and had not released her tension in an unhelpful fashion, such as an emotional explosion. From his previous observations, such an explosion would result in Detective Clement withdrawing from her team and Mr Carval, which at this time would be the most damaging action of which Dr Renfrew could conceive.

"Just as you would not rely on a single piece of uncorroborated evidence, nor a single witness, without investigating further, nor would I, or any other competent professional. Your own words are but one part of the whole. Others provide a different view, which assists in establishing the whole picture." He steepled his fingers again. "Those others include your team, Mr Carval, and the four officers whom you have taken under your wing."

Detective Clement's face set still and hard. "I see." She emitted nothing more while she sipped her espresso. Dr Renfrew concluded that she was considering his explanation, and did not intrude upon her thoughts.

Some moments later, Detective Clement finished her coffee and regarded Dr Renfrew with a coldly cynical expression. "How will you separate your research on team building from the *therapy* that Captain Kent has ordered me to undergo?"

"Nothing identifiable related to you, or indeed to any other person within your ambit, will be in my paper. I am interested, for those purposes, in interpersonal dynamics, not specific actions or inactions leading to those dynamics. Nor is your background relevant. I will be discussing the general, not the particular." He paused. "It would be impossible to replicate the dynamic between the four of you, which arises from specific circumstances. However," he continued, having decided a small revelation would reassure, "the way in which the team has improved the behaviour and performance of Officers Larson and Henegan is extremely relevant to my work, and requires no knowledge of your specific issues."

Detective Clement frankly gaped. "Say what?" Her hostility had disintegrated.

Dr Renfrew elucidated, based on his conversations with the two officers. Detective Clement appeared to be unable to find a single word, and, as their admiration of her was revealed, blushed fiercely.

"I didn't do anything any good cop wouldn't have done."

Dr Renfrew decided not to point out that no other team had taken the time or trouble to improve the officers. "Perhaps not. However, my point is that the way in which the officers have improved is part of the team dynamics paper, whereas the discussion I should like to have with you following Captain Kent's suggestion" –

"Order," Detective Clement corrected.

"It was a suggestion to me, though he may have ordered you to avail yourself of my agreement."

"Sophistry," she muttered.

"In any event, discussions relating to your necessary shooting of Pieter Wiedecz – I have reviewed your statement, which is a model of lucidity" – Detective Clement did not appear to appreciate the compliment – "the publicity surrounding Mr Carval's exhibition, which is universally favourable" – Detective Clement's face contorted in a most unattractive fashion – "and the alcohol induced death of your father, which certain elements of the NYPD are attempting to leverage against you, do not impact the team dynamic."

"Is there a point to this?"

"Your therapy will not form part of my paper on team dynamics," Dr Renfrew summarised.

Detective Clement muttered something. Dr Renfrew believed it to be *it had better not.*

"May we now begin?"

***

"Waal, this is more borin' than watchin' sand an' tumbleweed in the desert." O'Leary scowled theatrically at the feeds. "Can't they do somethin'? At least last night the officers said they went in an' out again. We don't even get that."

"Nope." Andy yawned. "Think Casey's murdered Renfrew yet? She's been in there more than fifteen minutes."

"Naw." O'Leary chortled. "No gun."

"Hope they get it back to her quickly. If there's movement, I don't see her staying behind."

"She'll have to. Nobody's goin' to let her out on a drugs bust with no gun."

They watched the feeds for another few minutes in which the most exciting occurrence was a large dog taking its tiny, elderly owner for a walk, at speed.

"Where is Clement?" Kent enquired, regarding the team with disfavour.

"With Dr Renfrew, sir," Andy replied.

"I see." Kent departed, producing a wave of relief. They returned to watching the feeds, in which nothing continued to happen.

"They only come out at night, like vampires," O'Leary suggested. "They don't want to be seen."

"Yeah." Tyler didn't look away from the screen. "Already caught out by guys filming on phones. Won't want it again. Shapes aren't clear in the dark."

"You mean people are less likely to notice they're carrying weapons."

Tyler nodded.

"Okay," Andy decided, "let's get some uniforms to spell us – anyone who's not busy – and think about what we know."

"Bein' Casey? You ain't got the hair an' eyes to be her."

Andy ignored the teasing. "Yep. Let's make some progress, and maybe she won't spit fire and venom at us." He stood up, and tapped at the murder board. "We still haven't seen Grappano come out again."

"Nothing on the feed." Tyler glowered at the relevant screen. "Other exits?"

"Who'd know?"

"Tarticca, not that he'll tell us, or mebbe Tarrant. Glencross is interrogatin' Tarticca, though I don't think he's gettin' too far since there's a lawyer in there, but we could have a go at Tarrant. Me 'n' Tyler. We c'n do scary almost as good as Casey."

"Tarrant asked for a lawyer too," Andy reminded O'Leary. "Can't go interrogate again till his lawyer's present."

"Oh," the big man mourned.

"Rooms." Tyler looked at the others, who looked back hoping for more words.

"What you mean," Andy said patiently, being the best at Tyler-expansion, "is that there might be rooms attached to the bar and Tarticca HQ."

"Said so."

"Mebbe."

"The city should have blueprints for the bar, at least. Building records. Let's get them, and see what the footprint looks like." Andy made a short call, and put his phone down with a smug smile thereafter. "I'll have them in an hour. I bet we find there are rooms."

"No bet." O'Leary declined the offer. Tyler managed a half-grin.

"Sir?" An officer hurried up to them. "There's movement on one of the feeds. He's got a baseball cap on, but it looks like the man you wanted to know about."

All three detectives whisked after the officer.

"Hocking." Tyler identified him first, a beat ahead of the others, staring at the feed on screen.

"What's he doin' at Site One?"

"Recon," Andy suggested. "What's going on at Two and Three?"

"Nothing, sir," the officer said. "There hasn't been any movement since we took over from you."

Tyler hadn't taken his gaze from the feed. "Looking for something."

"You or Hocking?"

"Hocking."

"Yeah," Andy said. "See that in his hand? Let's blow it up and get a good look. Andy tapped, and brought up the relevant portion of the recording on his laptop, letting the live feed run.

"I'm guessing it's a driver's licence."

"Looks like it." Andy and Tyler squinted at the magnification.

"Bigger?" Tyler asked.

Andy tried, but it didn't help. "I wanted to see if we could tell whose it was, but I can barely see that it's a licence."

"Yeah, but if he's carryin' it, he must be expectin' it'll do somethin'. Question is, what?"

"Open doors," Tyler said.

"Of course!" Andy exclaimed. "He's trying to see which doors the chip will open."

"Then what? There's only one of him."

"Yeah, but if he works out that the chip opens it" –

"They still only got one licence, far as we know, 'cause we got the other two from Buster and Crusher," O'Leary reminded everyone. "We ain't seen another shootin', so I guess they don't got no other missin' licences."

"Or they haven't noticed," Andy said cynically.

"Look!" O'Leary exclaimed. "He opened the door."

"Uh-oh."

"He's not going in. He's just closed it again."

"Testing," Tyler said brusquely.

"Yeah." Andy frowned. "I guess he'll be off to Sites Two and Three." He turned to the watching officers. "Keep your eyes open for movement there. If there is any, call one of us immediately."

"Yes, sir."

Andy turned to the other two. "Should we wake up Bergen and Dani?"

"Let's see if Hocking goes to Two or Three – or both – first." O'Leary grinned. "We might even hafta haul Casey outta her therapy session. Think she'll be tetchy with me iffen we do?"

"She's more likely to kiss you," Andy pointed out, "but she'll have to get in line. At this point, Renfrew'll kiss you first, for taking her away."

O'Leary snorted. "I don't wanna kiss him. He couldn't reach, anyway."

"And on that horrible thought," Andy shuddered, "the blueprints have come through. Let's see what we have here."

***

"May we start with your emotions relating to shooting Pieter Wiedecz? You have described your actions, and the effect on our investigations, but you did not mention your emotions. Please now do so."

Casey would rather eat a live mouse. Discussing feelings and emotions wasn't her thing. Showing them was also not her thing.

Take the initiative, Carval's voice whispered in her ear.

"I didn't feel anything while I shot him," she dragged out. "He was trying to shoot both of us, and training took over. I took the shot."

Dr Renfrew waited, careful not to project his own emotions into the room. Detective Clement's words did not entirely surprise him. Her devotion to duty would undoubtedly have prevented her emotions interfering with the necessity to shoot. He waited for her to continue.

"There wasn't any blood…"

"Mm?" Dr Renfrew steepled his fingers, and waited some more. Speaking would be entirely the wrong path to take. Detective Clement had to decide for herself what she would say, or not say. Haste would serve both of them ill.

Casey stared at her own hands, knotted together in her lap, below the level of the desk. She had no confidence that Dr Renfrew couldn't see their betrayal of her tension. She forced her thoughts from her father's blood-splattered apartment, to the pinpoint-sharp memory of Pieter Wiedecz, dead on his apartment floor at the muzzle of her gun.

"When you're training," she started, and stopped. "All the movies show blood from their mouth, but there wasn't any," she mumbled, after a moment. "It wasn't like the movies or cop shows. Not that cop shows are anything like reality," she added, for an instant returning to her normal, acerbic tones, "but…there was hardly any blood, only a trickle on his chest, and there he was dead." She swallowed hard. "I never shot anyone dead before." Another convulsive swallow, and shiver. "I've never been shot at before."

"He shot at you?" Dr Renfrew asked.

"He creased O'Leary, then he took another shot at me, but he missed, and I shot him."

Detective Clement's tone and words were entirely different from her first relation of this incident, in which she had not mentioned that she had also been targeted. He tried to recall her report. Ah, yes. She had included it, but she had minimised it. She still stared at her hands, and the floor.

"I wasn't scared when I shot him. There wasn't time. I had to wait for the shooting team. Fremont stayed. Preserve the scene. Larson took O'Leary to the ER to get patched up, and Carval went with them."

"He did not stay with you?"

"No."

Detective Clement's single word indicated that this was not an avenue she wished to discuss, which, of course, meant that it had some importance.

"He had observed the events?"

"Yes."

Her statement was, Dr Renfrew observed, equally clipped off. "What was his reaction to the shooting?"

"How is that relevant?"

"I shall explain, after you have answered the question." Dr Renfrew adopted a bland demeanour.

"He shot the whole thing, from the moment we went in. He ran out right after. He said he threw up. He was upset because he'd shot until it was all over."

"What did you do?"

"Sent him with O'Leary, and waited for the shooting team."

"Did Mr Carval ask you to go with him, or ask to stay?"

"No."

"Did you want him to stay?"

"No."

"Why not?"

Casey stopped hard. "What?"

"You are in an intimate relationship. Did you not wish for his support at a stressful time?"

Dr Renfrew immediately comprehended that he had discovered an extremely sensitive topic. He expected Detective Clement to obfuscate and outright deny.

"Yes."

Dr Renfrew confined the evidence of his astonishment to a blink.

"But it wouldn't have been appropriate."

"No," Dr Renfrew agreed, considering that Detective Clement should be encouraged to expand through his assent to her thesis.

***

"Sirs?" The same officer as previously dashed up. "We got movement at Site Two. Looks like the same guy from five minutes ago."

"Let's see." O'Leary took three giant strides to the feeds. "Oh, boy. There he is again. Ain't he cute? He's openin' the door, an' shuttin' it after. I guess we know where he's goin' next."

Andy tapped for a second. "It should take him about fifteen minutes to get to Site Three. Time to speak to Glencross, and wake up Bergen and Dani."

"I'll take Glencross," O'Leary whipped out.

"Dani," Tyler said.

"So I get Bergen." Andy completed the roster.

"Let's move," O'Leary said. "Put the calls in, an' I'll get Casey out."

Five minutes later all the calls had been made, and O'Leary had extracted Glencross from interviewing Tarticca. From Glencross's frustrated expression, he'd gotten nowhere, slowly. O'Leary explained, and Glencross perked up immediately.

"Bergen and Dani are on their way," Andy told them.

"I'll get Casey," O'Leary said.

***

Dr Renfrew observed Detective Clement carefully.

"There's a procedure to follow after a shooting. Carval couldn't help, and wouldn't be allowed to stay anyway. Better for him to be away from the scene."

Dr Renfrew was about to ask Detective Clement whether she would have *preferred* Mr Carval to be able to stay, when someone knocked on the door. He was initially annoyed at the ill-timed intervention, but he swiftly realised that only significant progress on the case would have necessitated such an interruption. "Come in."

Detective O'Leary appeared. "Casey, Dr Renfrew, Paddy Hocking's been to all three sites, used one of them chipped licences to open up each time, an' we're gatherin' to discuss the next steps an' what it means."

"Have any of the Tarticcas shown up at the sites yet?" Casey asked, already standing and heading for the door.

"Naw, but I don't guess it'll take long. Depends if they're monitorin' the doors or not."

"If they are, they will shortly know of the unauthorised entry," Dr Renfrew pontificated.

Casey and O'Leary exchanged an unimpressed glance, and aimed straight for the assembled group.

"Where are Bergen and Dani?" she asked.

"On the way." Andy didn't take his eyes from the feed. "Uh-oh. Look at that."

On the screen, three men were converging on Site One. They went in, and a moment later came out again. One of them made a phone call.

"Get someone down to Processing's personal effects storage area to see if Tarticca's phone's ringing. Stay there till I call you back." Casey rapped out the order. The nearest officer ran to obey.

"You think they're tryin' to warn him somethin's goin' down?"

"Yep." She stared at the screen. "Bets on them checking Two and Three in the next few minutes?"

"No bet," chorused everyone.

It took fifteen minutes for two different groups of three men to show up at Sites Two and Three.

"Let's check if we can match these guys up to the ones who went in and out last night," Andy said. He looked up as Bergen arrived, barely pausing to dump his sweater on a desk before leaning over Andy's shoulder. "You got some of your clever facial recognition tech?"

"Sure I do. Recognition – or matching?"

"Matching. There are nine guys – three at each site – who we need to check against the overnight movements."

"Okay. Let's go play."

"Set it running and come back," Casey ordered.

Andy and Bergen disappeared off, gabbling techno-speak which nobody else understood. Casey sent another officer off to find the one she'd dispatched to the storage area.

The officer, clearly having run back from the storage area, stared at Casey. "How did you know?" he panted. "Tarticca's phone was ringing."

"How often?"

"One missed call – I didn't hear it but it was still on the screen – then another call, and another. Then it stopped and Levon here came to get me."

"Mm," O'Leary hummed. "Not conclusive, but pretty significant."

"Yeah. Now, what'll they do when they can't get instructions?"

"Initiative," Tyler offered.

"You think they'll show initiative?" Casey queried. "I guess they're brighter than the Yarrabees, but – okay, what would *you* do?"

Tyler thought. "If I was a Yarrabee, get eyes on all the sites. Wouldn't go in till the delivery arrived, take 'em all out in one go."

"Okay," Casey said. The others, including Glencross and Renfrew, stayed quiet. Dani, who'd arrived as the officer ran back, watched intently, comparing Casey's style to that of other detectives. "If you were a Tarticca?"

"Get inside. Stay there. Wait. Hit 'em as they came in."

"Guard it?" O'Leary tried.

"Yep."

"So why haven't they?" Casey asked. The team – minus Andy – had entirely forgotten there were others present as they tossed ideas around. "The Tarticcas aren't dumb, so why aren't they staying in place? There's been enough of them around."

"Decoy. If they stayed, the Yarrabees know it's important. Bluffing."

"So where does that leave us? Nothing's happening yet, we don't know the details of the delivery, so we're stuck." Casey scowled.

CHAPTER TWENTY SEVEN

"Maybe not stuck," Glencross intervened. "We're out of time to charge Tarticca or Tarrant. I propose we release them – for now," he added hastily at Casey's appalled look, "and let Tarticca arrange the drug delivery."

"I could charge them," Casey griped, adding grudgingly, "But...okay. If it's necessary for your operation."

"It is," Glencross confirmed. "We'll keep monitoring Bergen's ears and Andy's eyes, and be ready to pick up any communication that might help us. Let's get them out of custody and able to make their plans."

A few moments later, the two Tarticcas had been cleared for release, and Glencross and Casey returned to the bullpen.

"Done," Glencross said. "Everyone needs to be ready to roll, so let's work out our strategy when we know which site they'll use for the delivery."

"Don't need to be different," Tyler commented. "All the same terrain. Warehouse, off street entrance, alley. Same tactics, whichever site. Need to know which one."

"Agent Glencross, do you think they'll be moving product tonight?" Dani asked. "'Cause I don't. It's already almost one, and we only released Tarticca a few minutes ago. I don't think he can fix it up by nightfall."

"Not unless it's already out there." Glencross frowned. "It could be, but it can't be that close."

"Should we check with the Coastguard?"

"I'll do it," Glencross decided. "It'll be quicker if it's someone they're used to talking to." He made a call. "Nope, nothing on their radar. Let's think about tactics."

"Okay," Casey said. "Four of us, Dani, Agent Glencross, Agent Bergen, and Dr Renfrew, plus our four usual officers." She added up on her fingers. "Twelve. If we're walking into a firefight – and it sounds from Tyler's summary that's pretty likely – we want a SWAT team."

"Vests, guns. Casey, if you don't have your gun back, you can't go. No place for unarmed cops." Tyler held Casey's aggrieved gaze. "No. No gun, no go."

"He's right," O'Leary decreed. "No gun, no go. I'm not havin' you gettin' shot. 'S not good for us iffen you're hurt. Your temper's bad enough already without addin' pain to it."

Casey muttered something incomprehensible, then cast a black look around. "If Kent'll give it back to me," she grumbled. Nobody commented. She refocused. "So. SWAT team, twelve of us. Tyler, raids are your area – you've got insights the rest of us don't have. How would you play it?"

"Before that," O'Leary rumbled, "Bergen's got a dinky li'l track of Hockin's movements. Let's have a look an' see where he's goin' now he's tested out all the sites."

"Yarrabee HQ." Tyler said.

"You'd think," Casey agreed. "Let's check anyway, and keep an eye on him – I'm sure Andy's tech can do it in real time if it isn't already."

"I'll go an' bring Andy an' Bergen back." O'Leary clumped away.

"Hocking might go back to the sites," Dani thought aloud.

"With some pals," Casey added. "Like Tyler said. Go back with a team, keep eyes on the sites, be ready."

"Exactly what we are doing," Renfrew noted, "with the key difference that we are intending to preserve law and order."

Everyone else rolled their eyes behind Renfrew's back.

"Where's Hocking going?" Casey asked, as soon as Andy was within ten feet.

"Yarrabee HQ."

"We're tracking in real time," Bergen added, "but he went straight back there and hasn't moved out since."

"We need to keep monitoring. Andy, put an officer on it, till we get our four back – they should be back late afternoon?" Andy nodded and found a victim, who didn't look happy to be picked up for the Misfit Team's business.

Half an hour later, everyone had taken a short, late lunch break before the hard thinking began again. Hocking hadn't moved from Yarrabee HQ, which simplified matters.

"Let's focus on how we do this raid," Casey opened, taking charge as if by right and ignoring the federal status and seniority of Renfrew and Glencross, both of whom raised eyebrows wryly but didn't interfere. "Tyler, you're up."

Tyler took a moment to collect his thoughts, stood at ease, and spoke as if he were still in the Army. "Two options. Be inside first, or wait outside. Inside, control the field. Could mess with the lights. Catch the first gang in, take them in, pick up the others, take *them* in. Disadvantage, if the enemy spots us, they'll go to a different site. Lose everything."

"Not if we were in all three sites," O'Leary mused. "Them Feds c'n produce enough agents to do that." It had taken less than three minutes for the team to forget the existence of the Feds, who didn't remind the cops of their presence.

"How do we get in without tripping the Tarticcas' entry warning system?"

Tyler wrinkled his brow. "Don't know yet. Andy, you know?"

"Before Andy starts technogeeking, let's get all the options out there. We've talked about going in," Casey said. "How about not going in?"

"Can't alert the system. Less risk of warning them, not none. SWAT teams aren't invisible. Risk level depends on light levels. Could pick up Yarrabees as they get there. Tarticcas or Yarrabees – whoever's inside first – would have the terrain. Could surround the site. Get the drugs for sure. Gangs might open fire on each other, we're walking into a hot firefight. Not optimal. Could let them kill each other, pick up the survivors. Gang inside might open fire on us. Also not optimal."

Tyler stood down.

"'Kay. We got Tyler's two options, but I got another - sorta halfway house – what if we had people inside an' outside?" O'Leary waited.

"Twice the chance of being spotted," Tyler noted. "Too many men. Friendly fire."

"Translation," Andy said dryly, "if the inside team and the outside team don't have perfect communication – and we all know no plan survives first contact with the enemy – there's a high risk we shoot each other, not the bad guys."

"Not optimal," Tyler noted with considerable understatement.

"'Kay," rumbled the big man. "I didn't think it was a go, but we gotta cover all the bases."

"Okay," Casey said. "Andy, you're up. We can only go with the inside one if you and Bergen can fix the system, so it doesn't notice us going in."

"Or if it thinks we're a Tarticca going in and out. What we *want*, rather than hoping that deactivating those readers won't flag up somewhere, is to go in on a Tarticca chip, then leave again." Andy's forehead creased.

"We have a Tarticca chip, remember?" Casey pointed out. "We still have Maria's driver's licence – she didn't come down to get it yet."

"No, that won't work." Andy frowned horribly at his own stupidity. "Hocking had a Tarticca licence, and they still went to check." His eyes suddenly lit up in technogeek delight. "We could cook up a jammer."

"Jam the frequency, you mean?" Casey clarified.

In the background, Bergen's eyes lit to match Andy's. Renfrew and Glencross watched as the team continued to outline a full plan without a pause.

"Yeah. If we go look at a system, if it's wired I can reroute the wires, if it's a radio signal we know the RFID frequency, so we can jam it."

"Back door." Tyler suggested. Everyone gaped.

"What?"

"Blueprints. Second entry point. Might not be monitored. Fire door. Window. Back door. Got to be one. Access."

The collective team gaped at him. "Breaking and entering?" Casey gasped.

"Feds can fix up a warrant."

The Feds in question blinked, as they weren't even consulted: their co-operation simply assumed. "Are they always like this?" Glencross whispered to Renfrew.

"Yes," Renfrew murmured. "It is most impressive, but they are not inclusive. I believe the phrase is 'they do not play well with others.' Detective Clement took charge without consulting me on our previous joint cases."

"I'd say they don't play with others at all," Glencross noted. "Still, they're doing all my work for me, so I'm cool with it."

"Okay." Casey didn't notice the whispers. "We – hang on. Why worry about tipping the Tarticcas off? Why can't we *use* the monitoring, instead?"

"Yeah?" Tyler invited her to continue.

"Well, we want to arrest them all, so if we tip them off at our convenience, they'll turn up, and we can take them from inside, as you suggested. This way *we* force the timing on them. We're in the driver's seat."

Andy chimed in. "We'd need to know the drugs were on the way and couldn't be rerouted, before we went in, so the timing has to be exact..." he mused, "but..." His brow creased as he considered the options. "Tyler, could it work?"

After a moment, Tyler nodded. "Yeah," he confirmed. "Timing. Know when, have them scrambling. Disorganised, panicking enemy. Best situation." Tyler bared teeth in a vicious not-smile.

"We should secure the product as it comes in." Dani glanced at Glencross, who nodded. "DEA should stay out of the firefight inside – if any – and make sure they get the shipment into custody; the FBI and Casey's team, with SWAT as needed, take the gang – both gangs – down. That way Casey gets Grappano and Tarticca and we get the drugs off the street."

The team blinked, noticing the others' existence for the first time in nearly an hour, and finally remembered there were three Feds and one

Narcotics detective, who, up until Dani's comment, hadn't been allowed to get a word in edgewise as the team planned the raid.

Casey looked unapologetically at Glencross and Renfrew.

"A masterly summary of the three options," Renfrew opined. "All have advantages and disadvantages, but my opinion is that *if* – he stressed the conditional word – "we can enter safely, we should be the first to the site. It would be better if we could establish which site is to be used, but if we cannot, I concur with you, Agent Glencross, that we have sufficient personnel to cover all three sites."

"I agree." Glencross developed an arid twist to his mouth. "However, this is a drug raid. I know we have three different strands here – the drugs, which are my business; organised crime, which is Dr Renfrew's; and the shootings and murders, which are the NYPD's problem. However, the drug raid is what we're discussing, and although I won't turn down any sensible suggestions or any assistance – and I agree with the three options – we all need to understand that this is DEA's operation and I make the final decisions." He focused on Casey, then Renfrew.

"Fine by me." Casey missed the subtext. "I just want to get my hands on Grappano."

"I agree," Renfrew assented.

"Andy, Bergen, could you go play with your tech and see what you can come up with? If you need to go inspect the actual sites, talk to me first."

"'Kay," they said to Glencross, and departed.

"Dr Renfrew, could you deal with the blueprints and the warrant?"

"Of course. Detective Clement, may I request the assistance of one of your officers?"

"Sure. I'll send Fremont in."

"Tyler, you, me, and Dani need to work out the tactics of the raid – inside or out, on all three sites."

Tyler nodded. "Yes, sir," Dani assented.

"Casey, I understand you've already got the blueprints of Tarticca HQ?"

"Yes."

"Could you plan how we arrest Grappano and Tarticca, if they aren't part of the site raid?" He noticed her expression. "We won't need to do that till after we take down the site, because if you can arrest Grappano for murder and the injuries to Mrs Hercliffe on site, that's fine, and we'll arrest Tarticca for the drugs. By the time we know which site it is, we'll have enough to get him too."

Casey eased. For a moment, she'd thought she would be left out of the main action, and had wondered whether Renfrew or Kent had suggested that she should be kept on desk duty and away from any live-fire action.

"When should your gun be returned to you?" Renfrew asked, before the group separated.

"Today if I'm lucky, but definitely by tomorrow. There's no problem with the shooting, so I don't see why I can't have it back now."

"Psych clearance." Tyler became the latest recipient of the Casey nuclear glare.

"I can provide that," Renfrew said, to general surprise and approval. "I will so advise Captain Kent, and he can take the necessary steps. I see no problem with your attitude to the necessary and proportionate shooting of a criminal who had already shot at you and Detective O'Leary." He didn't mention Casey's commentary on the amount — or lack — of bleeding, for which she was thankful.

"Okay," Glencross wound up. "Casey, thanks. Let's get to it, people."

***

Casey sent Fremont, who manfully concealed most of his worry, towards Renfrew, and settled down to pore over the blueprints of Tarticca HQ. Shortly, O'Leary wandered up to help.

"You okay?" he enquired in a sub-woofed whisper.

"I guess. I thought they'd leave me out entirely."

"Mm. Renfrew's givin' you psych clearance, so he thinks you c'n cope." The big man looked at the top of her head. "Ain't no-one goin' to think less of you iffen you don't wanna go into a firefight this week."

"It's not shooting criminals that bothers me," Casey explained, "though I don't like it and I don't want to do it if I don't absolutely have to. It's the blood. It wasn't like Dad..." She trailed off, and stared blindly at the blueprint, blinking hard. "So much blood..."

O'Leary discreetly patted her. "Isn't your boy around?" He gazed around the bullpen. "Where is he?"

"I don't know. I left before he woke up."

"Thought you'd been told not to do overtime?"

"I got coffee till Kent wouldn't notice."

"'Kay. Let's look at these here drawin's." He bent over, blocking both the light and anyone from noticing Casey's overflowing emotions. "Waal, ain't that somethin'? There's a whole bunch of rooms on this plan that we didn't see." He stretched up. "I'll fix us some coffee an' we'll plan." Ambling off to the break room, he didn't scruple to message Carval to suggest he show up, then ambled back with the coffee.

"Thanks." Casey slugged back her espresso in one scalding gulp. "I needed that." She peered at the blueprint of Tarticca HQ. "If this is still accurate" —

"'Cause we all know criminals get the proper permits to make changes, don't we?"

"Yeah — *if* this is right, here's where we went in, and here's" — her finger traced a route — "where we crashed through and down to spoil Tarticca's party. Where's Andy's footage?" She tapped her computer. "Okay. Grappano went in same way we did, here." Her nail moved back to the door and bar area. "He didn't – as far as we know – come out." The nail tapped. "So, from the bar there was only one door – I don't remember anything else."

"Restrooms. Gotta have restrooms in a bar."

"Did you notice where they were? I didn't."

"Iffen I had to guess; I'd say they were here." O'Leary's sausage-fingers pointed, "but I don't remember either." He chortled. "We could go back an' look."

"We could get arrested by Glencross or Renfrew for messing up their operation, too," Casey said sourly, "so I don't think it's worth it."

"Naw. Mebbe not. Anyways, iffen they're here, there still ain't no way out except down to Tarticca's office. Lookee here," he pointed, "there's a door off into these rooms."

"Yeah…" Casey's fingers tapped again. "Bergen wasn't with us. Shame, He might've remembered." She shut her eyes, and tried to visualise the bar and office. O'Leary, following her ideas, did the same.

"Nope," she eventually grumbled. "I don't remember anything more. I guess we'll go with the blueprints, and hope there weren't major changes. We've already got a search warrant, but we can't execute it till Glencross gives the go."

"Yup. I don't remember nothing more either. Grappano's likely in these rooms here."

"Yeah, but there could be any number of unknown exits from them."

"Naw, we'd have seen him on camera. Andy covered the whole area."

Casey's irritated expression lightened a touch, and her fingers stopped their drumroll on the desk. "Okay, so we don't think – no, there must be a fire exit." She glared at the plans. "Where is it?" Her nose almost touched the paper as she searched. "Got it." She straightened up. "Let's review Andy's footage, and let's get eyes specifically on that door."

"We don't want our bad guys sneakin' outta the back, do we?" O'Leary agreed. "Who'll we dress up as a panhandler?"

"Who don't we like today?"

"You could have Marcol," Dani spat, marching up. "With a little luck, someone might accidentally shoot him."

"Shouldn't we put him in the front of any raid?" O'Leary sniggered. "He's a brave NYPD detective, ain't he?"

Dani made an annoyed noise, and scowled.

Casey tapped her fingers on the plans. "Let's not worry about Marcol. He's someone else's problem. Can we talk about this raid now?"

"Sure."

Tyler, ghosting up, nodded.

***

Carval had spent most of the day prowling around theatres, talking his way into them by mentioning the Finisterres' authority, and photographing non-stop. He failed to pause for lunch, and only came out of his photographic haze when his phone, otherwise silent (largely due to Allan's absence), buzzed annoyingly. His first instinct was to ignore it and keep shooting, but he hoped it might be Casey.

O'Leary. Hm – oh. He tapped the message and read the sparse words, checked his watch, found it was mid-afternoon, and decided that, since the rehearsal seemed to be wrapping up, he could happily go home to download, then to the precinct to shoot there. He had no idea what this group had been rehearsing, and didn't care. All he'd wanted were the shots, the light and shade, the expressions, the work.

As he bounded up to his studio, he remembered there would likely be a raid, and he would shoot it. The minor little detail that, as yet, Glencross hadn't agreed he could tag along was entirely irrelevant to Carval's obsession with the next great sequence. It would go perfectly with the Wiedecz shots. He pushed away any idea that he'd be as upset by the raid as by Wiedecz's death at Casey's gun, and concentrated on the various ways to shoot a raid all the way to the precinct.

"Hey," he said happily to Casey and O'Leary. "What's the plan for the raid? I need to make sure I use the right lenses, and assess the likely light levels depending what time you're starting."

The cops stared at him. "Hi?" Casey snipped, with a sarcastic inflection. "Nice to see you?"

"He don't see nothin' but his snaps," O'Leary pointed out. "Who said you were comin' on the raid with us?"

"I have to!" Carval exclaimed. "I have to shoot it. It's vital to *Murder Two*."

"It's Glencross's decision," Casey pointed out. "If he hasn't said you can go, you're not going."

"I spoke to him."

"Did he say you could go?"

Carval shuffled. "He didn't say I couldn't."

"That's not good enough. We can't have stray people around a likely firefight." She knew that was a mistake as soon as it left her mouth.

Carval's eyes lit up. "Firefight? Wow! I have to shoot it. Nobody's ever done that before."

"Movies," O'Leary said blandly to the air.

"That's nothing like the same!" Carval squawked. "It's all faked for the cameras. This'll be real. I have to do it."

239

"War photography," Andy pointed out.

"That's war. This is cop work. Totally different."

"You'd better go ask Glencross again. We're not taking you if he doesn't explicitly say yes."

"We don't want you hurt," O'Leary said, "much." Casey raised cynical eyebrows, and didn't comment, though mirth flirted at her lips.

Carval glared. "You're no help." He gazed around, trying to spot Glencross.

CHAPTER TWENTY EIGHT

"Agent Glencross!" Carval called, spotting his quarry and, amazingly, remembering some manners and formality.

"You," Glencross groaned. "Yes?"

"I need to shoot this raid. I have to. It's the key sequence in *Murder Two*. You have to let me follow you."

"Me?" Glencross managed before Carval barrelled on.

"Not you personally, all of you. Dani, Renfrew, my cops, the officers, Bergen – everyone. I'll blur the bad guys – Casey always makes me blur them and the witnesses – but I have to shoot it."

"And if I say no?"

"Casey won't let me go with them if you say no, but you can't stop me shooting in public so I'll be there anyway and you won't have any control."

"Say what?" Glencross turned an interesting shade of furious red.

Carval, who'd lost any concept of diplomacy as he saw a brilliant sequence disappearing over the horizon, stampeded on. "I'll be exercising my constitutional rights to shoot in public, and since I won't be obstructing your raid you can't stop me. Let me, and I'll capture everything to show how great you are, just like I did in *Murder One*."

Glencross gaped, lost for words. Renfrew descended on the scene. "Agent Glencross, let us discuss this – *without* the unhelpful commentary of Mr Carval or indeed anyone else." Renfrew paused. "Mr Carval, I suggest you return to your studio" –

"What the *hell?*"

"– and acquire a selection of the best shots from your present exhibitions. Those shots should include Detectives Tyler and O'Leary clasping hands; the centrepiece of Detective Clement; and any of your shots of the team as a group. Further examples of your craft are up to you. Go."

Carval, dumbfounded, went. Renfrew directed Glencross into his conference room, watched by the team, Bergen, and Dani.

"Waal, ain't that somethin'?" O'Leary chuckled. "Your boy ain't got no sense."

"His funeral," Casey flipped back, and winced as she realised what she'd said.

"Iffen he keeps rilin' up DEA, he'll be in a cell."

Renfrew re-emerged, went to the break room, in which action not one of the cops followed him, and returned to his room with two cups.

"Dr Renfrew'll calm him down. Agent Glencross is feeling a touch steamrollered," Bergen said, "what with you four ignoring all of us to plan *his* raid for him and Carval bulldozing him. You know, we Feds quite like being included."

"Yeah," Dani agreed. "We fellow cops do too."

The four Homicide detectives wriggled, exchanging embarrassed glances. "Uh...okay, sorry," Casey managed. "We, uh..."

"Don't play well with others," Bergen suggested gently. "We know. We don't bite."

"We might," O'Leary joshed.

"You know us. You know we know what we're doing."

Casey sighed. "I'll go talk to Glencross when he's had his coffee and a chance to calm down."

Bergen smiled. "Good plan. The coffee'll smooth him down a bit."

Casey spent a further few minutes poring over the blueprints of Tarticca HQ, without finding anything except a large helping of embarrassment. She loathed apologising, especially when she knew the team – which meant her, as its leader – had to. If they hadn't had the Feds around, she grumped, there wouldn't have been any need to include them.

"You know, he's right," O'Leary rumbled.

"Who?"

"Bergen. We hafta be a little better at lettin' them play too. We can't keep all the fun to ourselves."

"Don't see why not," she complained.

"It's not chocolate," O'Leary teased. "We all know you don't share chocolate."

"Nope." Casey dragged herself out of her chair. "I guess I'd better go see Glencross. Ugh." She trudged off across the bullpen to Glencross's borrowed home, where he was discussing DEA tactics with Dani.

"Agent Glencross," she asked, "could I have a moment, please? Privately?"

"Sure. Excuse us, Handjiev."

Dani left, shutting the door behind her.

"Uh, Agent Glencross, we…We want to apologise for excluding you all from the planning." She stopped; scarlet faced.

Glencross gazed straight back at her, silently. Casey held his eyes, still hot-faced, but not giving way. Suddenly, he relaxed his stare. "Thanks. Your team isn't used to letting others go first, is it?"

"No. We – well, we tend to work alone."

"Mm. Wonder why?"

Casey's blush leaped back to scorching life.

Glencross gave a short laugh. "If I'd thought you were going wrong I'd have stepped in. It would have been nice if you'd tried to include us," he rebuked gently, "and the next time you're working with any of us, I'll expect you to do so, but no harm, no foul. This time."

Casey eased. Glencross's correction bit, but he had been kinder than her Captain, who would have scarified her.

"However," he added, and her heart sank. "Since we have a chance for a private discussion, I have two questions for you. The first is: why should I let Carval follow us on the raid?"

"He's shot some of our more exciting arrests," Casey said slowly. "I don't like being the subject of his photos, but I won't tell you to stop him. That's between you and him. All I can say is: he didn't get in our way at any point. He isn't interested in being involved; he only wants to shoot. He's not trying to be a cop. He stayed well out of the way when we went to arrest Wiedecz and had to drop him. Same when we took down a nasty rapist-murderer gang."

"I see. Thanks. Now, what's between you and Detective Mark Marcol?"

"Nothing," Casey declared.

Glencross's scepticism was patent. "Maybe I should rephrase. Why did Detective Marcol want to be a part of this specific investigation and operation, and why did Captain Kent order him not to speak to you or your team?"

Casey inhaled slowly and collected her thoughts, desperately trying to work out what she could say to Glencross without disobeying Kent. Not saying anything would raise even more questions. "We were in the same class at the Academy. I did better than him." Which covered an awful lot of ground. "He wasn't happy. I didn't see him again till last October, when we had a horrible case." Her mouth twisted. "I just mentioned it. Three men were kidnapping, drugging and raping girls for snuff movies on-line." Glencross's face curdled. "Narcotics sent over Marcol about the drug issues. He asked me on a date. I turned him down. He didn't like it, but Captain Kent shut it down. I have no idea why he would want to get on to this investigation." She left out any mention of photographs, slander, or IA. If Glencross wanted more dirt, he could dig it up someplace else.

"I see. Well, he won't be on this operation. I'm in charge and I'll decide who's on the team." His tone softened. "That includes your team and your four officers. From here on in, though, I'll run the raid briefings and strategy discussions. Thank you. Dismissed."

Casey left, musing that the last comment had been rebuking them as painfully as, but more quietly than, Kent would have done. She aimed for the break room and a soothing espresso.

"Still alive?" O'Leary asked.

"Yeah. Most of my skin's still on. We'd better not do that again."

"Naw." O'Leary grinned. "But it sure was fun seein' their faces while you did."

Casey made an indeterminately unpleasant noise.

"Now, no call for grumbling."

"He asked me about Marcol."

"Oh. That ain't great."

"No," she bit off. "When do I get my gun back?" she complained. "I wanna get out there and arrest Grappano so DEA can do their thing and all the Feds can go back to their own shops. I want this case *done*."

"We all need to take vacation," O'Leary rumbled.

"I want it *done*," Casey reiterated. "I want to have my gun back and I want to do this raid and take them all down and I want everything to be over." She sniffed mightily.

O'Leary considered his partner, handed her a Kleenex, and put a monstrous arm around her shoulders. "You need to sleep for about a week, an' to eat properly, not those tiny li'l meals that wouldn't feed a canary. You ain't any bigger than a canary, but you need to eat more an' sleep more."

"Than a canary?" Casey snorted soggily.

"Than you're doin'. You'll get sick, an' then what?" He patted, cautiously. "Now, blow your nose, dry your eyes, an' we'll go finish workin' out where Grappano's hidin' while your boy deals with Glencross."

"Carval's back already?"

"Yup. He musta hurried. He really wants them snaps, don't he?"

***

Carval had raced home, taken almost no time to select the best of *Murder One* and *Hands*, and catapulted back to the precinct. He *wouldn't* let the chance to shoot a multi-agency raid with possible live fire slip away. He was entirely oblivious to any personal risk, and though he hoped his cops wouldn't be hurt, he was confident they'd avoid it. They had to avoid it. He couldn't bear it if Casey were injured again. He pushed that horrible thought away, and strode into the bullpen, rapping assertively on Glencross's door. A small semblance of sense told him not to burst in.

"Come," Glencross called. He looked blandly at Carval. "Dr Renfrew and I have had a discussion. He, and, separately, Detective Clement, informs me you haven't impeded previous arrests. Dr Renfrew also told me you've shown the NYPD in an extraordinarily good light. Obviously, my priority wasn't visiting exhibitions." He grimaced wryly. "I have a raid to plan."

Carval, sensibly, stayed silent.

"Dr Renfrew suggested that you show me – as he put it – the highlights of your two current exhibitions." The wry expression dried to Saharan aridity. "So, impress me."

"Let me plug into your laptop," Carval said. "You'll see what I can do."

"Be my guest."

Carval, stung by the dismissive tone, plugged in the thumb drive, set the slide show to an interval which would force Glencross to study each shot, and pressed *Play*. "Watch," he bit. "When you're finished, let me know." He walked out, thwacking the door shut behind him.

***

"What's he doing in there?" Carval griped. "Anyone can see how brilliant the shots are. He shouldn't take this long." It was at least the fifth repetition of his complaint.

"Mebbe he doesn't think you're a genius," O'Leary teased.

"Well, he'll be wrong, won't he?" Carval bit.

"Now, no call to be snappin' at me."

"He's got to see. He can't miss how good they are. What's keeping him?"

"Can you *chill?*" Casey complained. "I'm trying to work here. Go make coffee. Go *get* coffee, if it'll calm you down."

"He has to let me shoot!" Carval insisted.

Casey opened her mouth, but O'Leary forestalled a looming fight. "Coffee," he instructed, landing a meaty paw on Carval's back and pushing him towards the break room.

"I don't want coffee. I want Glencross to get off his" – O'Leary shoved one paw across Carval's mouth.

"You want banned? 'Cause iffen you finish your sentence the way I think you're goin' to, you'll be out." He hustled Carval into the break room and shut the door. "Now you c'n rant as much as you like, for two minutes. I'm timin' you. Then drink your coffee an' pipe down till Glencross comes out. Casey don't need no more stress today. She already had to go apologise to him 'cause we forgot to let the Feds play *let's-plan-a-drug-raid* with us."

***

"Clement," Kent summoned her to his office.

245

"Sir?"

"You've been cleared. Here's your gun." He passed it over.

"Thank you, sir." Casey kept it pointed downward, where it would stay until she could retrieve its holster from her desk.

"I understand you and your team will be part of DEA's operation." He handed over a piece of paper. "Approval for Tyler and Fremont to use special weapons, as requested by DEA. None of the rest of you are qualified, so don't bother asking."

"Yes, sir. Thank you, sir."

"Keep clear of bullets. I don't have time for more injuries to your team." He scowled. "And make sure you get your man."

"We'll do our best, sir."

"Don't do your best. Succeed. Dismissed."

***

O'Leary's huge hands expertly made the coffee, while Carval complained and criticised Glencross's apparent lack of appreciation.

"Time's up," the giant said. "Drink your coffee, an' stop complainin'. Iffen you won't do it for you, do it for Casey." His light eyes scanned Carval. "She needs to take vacation, somewhere away from here."

"We are," Carval blurted before he thought about it.

O'Leary blinked. "You are? Waal, ain't that somethin'? Good." He laughed, then drank his coffee without saying more, though his eyes twinkled. His massive mug drained and rinsed, he stretched. "You calmed down now? We better go back."

Carval followed O'Leary, failing to spot Glencross, but noticing that the conference room door remained firmly closed. He didn't care to knock.

"Renfrew's in there again," Casey noted.

"Yeah?"

"Bergen went in, Glencross came out, found Renfrew, went back. They've been in there with the door shut ever since."

Carval's relaxation disappeared in an instant. "They can't stop me shooting!"

"*Chill*," Casey snapped.

Fortunately, Glencross appeared a moment later. "You can shoot," he threw at Carval. "Find an unmarked vest. I don't want you inadvertently injured." He disappeared again. The door clunked shut behind him.

"He ain't full of sunshine suddenly." O'Leary frowned. "You got what you wanted, but I'd lay low for a while iffen I was you. Somethin's goin' on." He looked at Casey.

"I got my gun back."

Ten minutes later, Bergen exited. "Casey, get your team and your officers. We got something." He dashed off in search of Dani. Tyler rounded up the four officers, who'd only just returned to the bullpen.

Carval had his camera up and clicking before Bergen had taken more than half a step. Casey's expression had shifted to a hard ferocity that he'd last seen as she eviscerated Caveman Bill, a construction worker twice her size and three times her weight, suspected of murdering an African American runner. O'Leary's face had set into frightening lines. They rose as one, and marched to the room.

"Let's *get* these bastards," Casey bit. Tyler, Andy, Dani and Bergen fell in behind her. Carval whipped ahead of them and kept shooting: a further sequence of one single team, one leader, one goal. He only stopped to allow Casey to lead them into the conference room, then slid in behind them, still shooting.

Glencross raised his eyes, spotted the camera, sighed, and ignored it. Beside him, Renfrew smiled thinly, and also ignored it.

"Okay," Glencross said, when everyone had squeezed into the room and Adamo, last in, had closed the door. "We've gotten lucky with the wiretaps. The drugs are on their way in, and they'll be delivering to Site Two tonight – so they think. I'm amazed they got it fixed up in time, but the wiretaps are clear. Bergen's still listening, even though he's in here." Everyone noted Bergen's small earpiece. "We'll take the drugs at the same time you enter the site – I'll tell you all when to enter. We're trying to narrow down the time. However, this meeting is to reiterate our earlier planning, so we're all sure of who is taking which actions. There's no room for error. SWAT will be involved to take down the drugs, but this group includes everyone who'll be inside the warehouse. Let's go over it one more time."

***

An hour later, the team marched out of the Feds' room, having been instructed to get some rest and a meal before the operation, which wouldn't begin for at least another two hours.

"Quick meal," Casey said. "Something filling that won't put us to sleep."

"No beer." O'Leary pouted, monstrously, then grinned.

"No. Drink tea, instead. Better for your insides." Andy smirked. O'Leary groaned.

Dinner took only forty minutes, during which time there was little conversation. Casey, not hungry, satisfied herself with a small, plain burger and soda. O'Leary and Carval flicked concerned glances at her when she declined dessert, but didn't comment.

Back in the precinct, they settled down to wait. Their four officers arranged themselves nearby. Dani and Bergen reappeared, having dined elsewhere, and joined them. Nobody spoke. Everyone pretended to be working on cold cases. Carval drifted around, taking photographs.

"We better find Carval a plain vest," Casey said. "I know he didn't have one any other time, but this operation's different."

Tyler beckoned to Carval. "Vest." He led him away.

Shortly after Tyler and Carval returned, Kent emerged from his office once more, and stumped over to the team. "My office." He spotted the four officers. "You too."

Nine people (Carval had assumed his inclusion) squeezed into Kent's office, which wasn't designed for eight normal size people and one giant. Kent glared impartially at all of them. "You will obey Agent Glencross's orders as if he were me."

"Sir," they rapped.

"There will be no heroics. No death-defying exploits. This is not a movie. The bullets are real. You all know this, but I'm reminding you." His eye fell on Casey. "Clement, you will not take unnecessary risks."

"Sir."

"Carval."

"Yeah?"

Kent fixed him with a pitch-black stare. Carval looked amiably back at him, and resisted the suicidal temptation to whip out his camera and shoot Kent.

"Stay out of the professionals' way," he eventually instructed.

"Yes."

"Dismissed." Kent didn't bother with any words of encouragement.

Once the team had left, Kent stared at the space they'd vacated and hoped like hell he'd made the correct call on Clement. He'd thought deeply before allowing her to stay on the operation, and he still wasn't sure he'd been right. Renfrew might have given her psych clearance, but Kent was still unsure about everything else. However, forbidding her to participate would have been even more damaging to her morale, which had been damaged enough by the unpleasant antics led by Estrolla. At least that weasel was off shift for another day. The raid would be done and Clement on leave when he returned.

On balance, especially given Glencross's commentary on the raid planning (Kent snorted: his team had shown those Feds how to do it), she was up to it. When this case was done, though, they'd have one shift to put the papers in order before he benched the whole bunch.

***

"Everybody ready?" Glencross asked. Everyone nodded. "Okay. Move out, as we discussed. Get in place and wait for my order."

The team nodded, and split up. The four officers with them had been ordered to change into plain clothes, dressed as if they were meeting in a sports bar.

"Henegan, Adamo – with Tyler and Andy." Her face hardened. "Don't screw up. If the Feds don't deal with you, I will. If they do, I still will." She eased. "Andy, try to look as if you cared about baseball." Andy humphed at her. "Think of it as cultural heritage," she added.

The four of them left, to park themselves in a sports bar as if they were any four guys on a night out.

"Fremont, Larson – follow O'Leary and me. We'll see you in our bar – join us as if we're all good pals. Don't freak if O'Leary hugs you – or if I do." Casey grinned, though it carried shadows behind it. "It's for the case. Similarly, if O'Leary's pretending to be my boyfriend, go with it. Fremont – special weapon locked in the trunk, now."

"Yes'm."

She changed focus to Carval. "You can be with us, but don't take your camera out until Glencross tells us it's a go."

"Okay."

"Five more minutes before we move," O'Leary rumbled. "Five after that, you pair follow us three."

"Yes, Detective."

Fremont and Larson drifted off.

"Casey," O'Leary asked, "you're good, yeah?"

"Yes." They exchanged looks. "I wouldn't go if I didn't think I could do it. You know that."

"I do. 'Kay. Let's go."

"You and me."

"Me an' you," O'Leary gave back with a fist bump.

Carval watched as Casey and O'Leary reinforced their bonds, until they had the same fixed, united focus as they'd had the instant before they'd hit the warehouse where Yarland and his pals had been drugging, raping and killing girls. Inadvertently, he shivered. O'Leary's eyes were hard. Casey's – were adamantine.

"Showtime," Casey grated.

CHAPTER TWENTY NINE

"Clement – go!"

"Night's over, boys." Casey manufactured an end-of-evening wave. "See you soon." O'Leary joined her, and they hugged the others. As soon as they exited the bar, they ran for O'Leary's SUV, Carval right behind them. Five minutes later they were at the warehouse, thirty seconds later Fremont and Larson joined them; Andy, Tyler, Henegan and Adamo pulling up as the first four pulled their vests on, looping their night vision goggles around their necks.

"Carval! Get your vest on!" Carval, shooting every movement, had forgotten, but Casey's sharp order pulled him back to common sense. He struggled into the unfamiliar body armour as fast as he could, and went back to his shots.

"Ready? In." The detectives moved in as one unit; the officers following.

The warehouse was dark, with few windows. The huge doors opened so silently that it was clear they'd recently been greased. When O'Leary turned the lights on, there was plenty of racking, but most of it was empty.

"No cover," Tyler said: his voice echoing in the vast space.

"Andy. Set your night-eyes up. Tyler – scope out our positions. You're good at terrain. Find us some cover if you can. O'Leary, you're on the lights and fuse box. We want to kill the lights as soon as we know the Tarticcas are on their way." She listened. "Dani says they're moving."

"We don't want them to be able to switch on an' see us, for sure."

"No. Not after they've come in. You'll plunge them into darkness if they don't surrender right away. Go do magic with the fuses. Henegan, with O'Leary. Tyler, you're in charge."

"Got it."

Carval stayed well clear of the instruction zone, simply shooting everything and going where he was told. He focused on the expressions of all eight cops, catching small nuances. He'd call it *Stalking*, he thought, or maybe *Pause before Action*. Even while the harsh fluorescent lights were still on, there were deep shadows in the corners; odd reflections in the racking. Grimy windows showed only sludgy, orange streetlights, the concrete floor had sticky patches, gripping at the soles of his sneakers.

"Carval. When I tell you, go to that spot." Tyler gestured. "Don't move. Shoot, but *do not move*."

"Yes." Carval barely avoided adding *Sir*. He set his camera for night shooting, and made sure of his fields of view from his safe nook. He had no intention of disobeying Tyler. He liked living. He took another set of shots of the cops' intent, hard faces: catching their tension, their fingers at their guns.

Casey's neck prickled as she assessed the territory and waited for Tyler to confirm their positions. She didn't like the scrabbling noises in the shadows, and with every minute that Glencross didn't confirm they'd captured the drug shipment, her nerves twanged. She forced herself not to think about Wiedecz, dead on his floor, and repetitively checked that her vest was tight and her Glock ready. She could see Andy, as motionless as a statue, focused inward; O'Leary alert, looming out of the gloom.

"Tarticcas five minutes away. Yarrabees moving, maybe two minutes behind them," Dani clipped in every earpiece, adding sharply, "We're on the shipment. Be ready."

"Five minutes," Tyler stated. "Carval, corner, now! Places! Goggles stay *off*. Lights *out*. Don't kill the fuses till they're here!"

The warehouse went dark and silent; the cops barely breathing, tension heavy in the dusty air.

Vehicles stopped outside. Andy switched on his spy cameras. Holsters were undone, guns drawn and ready.

"We're taking down the shipment now. No more comms till it's done. You're on." Dani's voice went silent, though Casey heard someone yelling *Federal agents, hands up!* and shots.

The doors eased slowly open. Nobody inside moved: pressed flat against walls, taking as much cover from the shadows and racking as they could. Tiny sounds of someone moving softly towards the light switch were the only clue that the Tarticcas had entered. Casey shut her eyes as Tyler had told them –

Light blazed. Federico Tarticca shouted, "We got you, Yarrabee dumbfucks!" and raised his semi-automatic as five others slammed in behind him.

"NYPD! Drop your weapon! Hands on your head!"

"No fucking way!" His finger tightened on the trigger, aiming for Tyler, the only cop in clear view.

Tyler put one shot from his assault rifle through Tarticca's calf as Tarticca fired. He screamed, and fell. Someone shrieked in pain as Tarticca's bullet flew wide. "Lights!" Tyler yelled. O'Leary killed the fuse, whipping on his night vision goggles. Outside, another gang came roaring in, yelling at the gang members inside, already firing. Muzzle flash, noise and chaos filled the space.

Pressed as far into his corner as he could manage, Carval kept clicking, trying not to duck or flinch; hoping his reactions didn't block his sightlines. The whole warehouse had gone to hot lead and hell, and he was terrified. It didn't stop him photographing.

"NYPD!" O'Leary bellowed. "Drop your weapons! Hands on your head!"

"No way, muthafucker!"

Tyler fired again, aiming at the voice, and was rewarded with a howl.

"Hands on your head!" the giant bellowed again. "NYPD Police!" He flicked the fuse. Every cop had their eyes shut and pushed their goggles down at the code phrase as the lights came on again, blinding the Tarticcas and Yarrabees. Shots flew wildly.

"NYPD! Drop your weapons!"

The staccato firing of semi-automatics continued. Tyler expertly put bullets into non-fatal areas of any gangsters aiming for the cops: his face peaceful, his body entirely still. One shot, one man hit, every time. Carval didn't have a moment to marvel at it; turning his focus on to Andy, almost as still, aiming his handgun to scare, not wound; O'Leary, grim-faced; and finally Casey, shooting as accurately as the others, but under her concentration, belying her steady hands, Carval caught suppressed horror.

"NYPD! Drop your weapons!"

"Drugs are secured," Dani confirmed into the earpieces.

The rattle of fire finally died away. Carval, still photographing as fast as he could click, didn't move. The cops moved in to cuff the uninjured gangsters, and to take stock of the injuries to those left alive. Three gangsters didn't move, dead.

"We got 'em all?" O'Leary asked.

"Yeah." Tyler looked around. "All good?"

"Yeah," Andy confirmed.

"Yeah." Casey swallowed hard at the sight of spots of blood on the concrete and the few corpses, turning her back on them. "Call ambulances for the injured. Larson, Henegan – you go with them, and we'll round up a few more officers to go with you."

Andy called the precinct, and arranged for more officers to arrive asap.

"Cuff them to the beds," Casey continued, while Andy organised back-up. "You know the drill. Larson – you're in charge. Henegan, call me when they're safely stowed."

"Yes'm."

"Now, who's hurt?" Casey asked. "Someone yelled."

"Ma'am…" little Adamo forced out. "I…"

"Aw, hell." O'Leary frowned at a long, bleeding score down Adamo's right arm. "Okay, let's patch you up. We'll have matchin' scars. We'll be twins." Adamo, no more than a slim five-ten against O'Leary's barrel-chested six-ten, managed a painful huff. "You c'n go with Larson an' Henegan to the hospital, an' don't let them get over-enthusiastic an' cuff you along with all them naughty types. That'd be embarrassin'."

Adamo, considerably paler than his normal colouring, nodded, then sat down on the ground, faster than he might have done. Fremont knelt next to him, murmuring something and tying a handkerchief around his upper arm. Henegan called for ambulances.

Casey, meaning to reassure Adamo, couldn't force out a single word. She couldn't look at the blood flowing sluggishly from Tarticca's leg. She turned her eyes away, staring high up on the dingy walls. "Did we get Grappano?" she rapped, but there was a tremor lurking below the words.

"No."

She swore sulphurously. "Why wasn't he here? The wiretap said he'd be here. Now we'll have to go get him." Her face curdled, fingers tapping angrily on her holster. "Fremont, get CSU in to process this mess. Wait here for them." She tapped her earpiece. "Dani? We got Tarticca but not Grappano. We'll want to go straight to Tarticca HQ. Can someone review the footage from around there to see if Grappano came out?"

"Yeah. Bergen's on it."

"Casey," Bergen interjected. "I've been watching, but I'll recheck while you're moving. I'm guessing you don't intend to go in till I confirm?"

"Nope. I'm not raiding an empty site."

"Okay. Give me a few minutes."

Casey kept her back turned to the corpses and injured men. She couldn't bear to look at them. "So CSU and a bunch of officers are on their way. Fremont, you deal with them. Andy, how long will they be?" Her foot tapped.

"They should be here in ten."

"Okay." She considered. "Everyone who can move is cuffed," she murmured to the team, "but I don't want to leave them with only Fremont. It would only take one idiot and it's gone to hell. We'll have to stay here until the reinforcements turn up."

"Tyler and I can wait," Andy murmured back again. "You and O'Leary go on, and take Carval with you. He's no help here and he probably doesn't want to stay. He hasn't moved from his safe space yet."

Tyler marched over, exchanged two words with Carval, and brought him back. Casey noted his pallor, and badly wanted to reassure him, but couldn't while they were still in the middle of a major operation. Her foot tapped again. She wanted the back-up here, right *now*, so they could take down their killer. She ruthlessly suppressed any idea that she didn't want to be anywhere near blood or dead men.

"I better call Kent," she said. "Live shooting...I don't think *we* shot anyone dead, but we still have to report." She swallowed. "Here we go."

"Kent."

"Sir, it's Clement. We've completed the takedown of the Tarticcas and Yarrabees, and DEA has secured the drug shipment."

"I see."

"The two gangs each came in shooting – semi-automatics. Three gang members were killed, but we didn't shoot to kill. We did injure some of them, but only if they were shooting at us. I think it was the gangs that killed each other. CSU is on the way, and they'll look for that specifically. However, sir, our murderer isn't here. We're checking, but he may still be at Tarticca HQ. We'd like to go and pick him up. I have a warrant to enter."

"I see. Injuries have been inflicted?"

"Yes, sir. We've called ambulances for the wounded, to take them to the hospital, with officers in attendance. Adamo was injured, but not seriously. We'll send him to the hospital as well."

"I see," Kent repeated.

"We had cameras recording the whole operation," Casey added. "Sir, I want to go get Grappano – our killer. Fremont will wait for CSU."

"I'll send down a shooting team to secure the cameras. You may complete the operation – it's still ongoing until DEA says it's done. Report to me as soon as you have secured the killer and handed him over to Processing."

"Thank you, sir."

"Get him, Clement," Kent ordered, and cut the call on Casey.

"We can get Grappano," Casey said, "but then it's report to Kent. Fremont can deal with the shooting team when they get here – Andy, they'll take your cameras." She sighed, relieved. "Nearly there." She made a face. "Where are those ambulances and the officers?"

Before she exploded in frustration at the delay, the ambulances arrived, swiftly followed by more officers. "Okay. O'Leary, let's go. Tyler, Andy, you follow once you've dealt with all of this. Fremont, you do exactly what CSU and the shooting team tell you. Go back to the precinct when you're done, and wait for us there."

"Yes'm," Fremont said.

"You all did good."

"Thank you, ma'am."

***

Before O'Leary could unlock his SUV, Casey turned aside, leaning on the hood, swallowing hard. Carval came around to her.

"Give me a minute."

"But" –

"*Give me a minute*," she snapped.

Carval retreated, hurt. O'Leary pulled him further away. "Leave her be. Iffen she's throwin' up – an' it's possible – she don't want either of us watchin'."

"I wanted" –

"Yeah, but she don't want it. Don't push. Casey's got enough to be dealin' with. You follow her lead, an' take her off on vacation. We're all goin' to be benched as soon as we've arrested Grappano, so iffen I were you I'd be thinkin' about that, not worryin' about bein' told to leave her be when she's pullin' herself together." The big man smiled. "Anyways, how're you doin'? It was pretty lively in there. You okay?"

"It was scary." Carval massively understated his total terror. "How do you all *do* it?"

"Trainin', experience, an' sometimes downright dumbness, iffen you call standin' your ground dumb."

"I wouldn't say it's dumb near you four," Carval said, thinking that this sequence would highlight the courage of the best of the NYPD.

Casey came back around the car, pallid skin tinged grey-green, still swallowing.

"You look like shit," O'Leary commented. "I should take you back to the precinct."

"Let's finish this. I can do it." Her eyes were hard, no emotion in her face, though her hands trembled. "Grappano killed three people, including an unborn baby, and injured its mother. I want him in a cell. I want to tell Tania Hercliffe we got him." She didn't say that she hoped the news would shock *Matthew* Hercliffe off the booze train he was boarding.

"Let's go make it happen," O'Leary assented.

Casey tapped her earpiece. "Bergen, did you find anything on your recheck?"

"Nope. Almost done. Nothing to show he's moved. Give me five more minutes."

"Okay. We'll move towards Tarticca HQ."

"Yeah." Bergen sounded distracted, as if he were – as he should be, Casey thought – giving all his attention to the camera feeds.

255

Exactly five minutes later, Bergen spoke again. "Nothing. If he left, he didn't do it through any exit we can see."

"Okay. Tyler and Andy are following us in. Tell them too." The flat tone robbed her words of all courtesy, but she didn't notice, and Bergen didn't quibble.

"We're on the way," Andy's light tenor announced cheerfully. "We're not letting you have all the fun."

"Okay. We'll go through this place like Ex-Lax. Everyone gets arrested. No exceptions."

"Need more officers."

"You handle that, Tyler."

"'Kay."

"See you there," O'Leary said.

The remainder of the journey took place in silence. Casey drifted, lost in her own head, and her pallor didn't lift in the slightest. O'Leary didn't disturb her, and Carval, both hurt and remembering O'Leary's advice, followed suit.

O'Leary drew up a block away from their goal, and waited in the SUV until Tyler and Andy arrived.

"Where are the officers?" Casey rapped.

"Coming." Tyler frowned at her. "You okay?"

"Yes. Will you all *stop* asking me that every five minutes? I'm *fine*. I want this operation over and done, finish with the shooting team, and wrap up the paperwork."

"Don't we all," Andy soothed. "I'll use my vacation to catch up on all the exhibitions and culture I haven't had a chance to see."

Tyler made a derisive noise.

"I'm goin' to foreign parts," O'Leary beamed. "Me an' Pete are goin' to Niagara."

"Out of the USA?" Andy gasped. "I didn't know you had a passport."

"I do." O'Leary pouted. "I go places. I don't tell you about it, 'cause you'd envy me my jetsettin' lifestyle."

"Can we focus on the job?" Casey snipped. "Braid each other's hair on your own time." She scowled at the street. "Where are those officers? They should be here by now."

"Relax. If Grappano tries to leave, Bergen'll tell us."

Casey retreated into silence again. She didn't want to talk. She wanted some time to glue herself back together for long enough to get through the last of the evening, then she could tell Tania they'd arrested her baby's killer and finally go home and rest. (*Throw up till you see your toenails,* an unpleasant little voice suggested. She squashed it back down. If she hadn't thrown up by now, she wouldn't.) She didn't have the headspace for anything except bringing Grappano in.

"Finally," she growled when the latest batch of officers turned up. "Tyler, brief them." He did, without a wasted word or second.

O'Leary tapped Andy on the shoulder. "Keep an eye on Casey," he whispered. "She's wired."

Andy blinked: the only indication of astonishment. "Stand her down?"

"Naw. Not yet. She's managin'."

"So why're you worrying?"

"Intuition."

Andy blinked again. "Up to you. You're the only one who can make the call."

"Yeah," O'Leary said heavily. "That's what I'm worryin' about."

"Kent approved her."

"Kent didn't see her before we got into the car to come here. Iffen she wasn't throwin' up; she was right on the edge."

Andy flicked a glance at Casey. "She looks okay now. Touch pale, but together."

"Keep an eye out," O'Leary reiterated, as Tyler ended his briefing. "Good to go?" he asked Casey.

"Yeah. Keep your vests on." She added a hard stare at Carval, who was adjusting his camera for normal light levels inside a bar. "Ready?" Everyone nodded. "Arrest them all. We'll sort them out later. Go!"

O'Leary and Tyler hit the door as Andy touched Maria Montelucci's chipped driver's licence to the reader on the wall, bursting through. Casey followed them.

"What the *fuck?*"

"Jeff Tarrant, you are under arrest." She turned to the nearest officer. "Cuff him and take him in. The charge is conspiracy to murder, but the Feds'll have more."

Tarrant tried to make for the door down to Tarticca's office, but one huge stride by O'Leary stopped him cold. "Cuff him," the giant repeated Casey's words, a ham-hand preventing Tarrant going anywhere. Behind Casey, Andy, Tyler and a few of the officers arrested the three or four men in the bar. They didn't resist.

O'Leary took point as they barged through the door marked *Employees Only* and into Tarticca's office. It was empty. This time, having scrutinised the plans, Casey could see the other door, painted to match the wall. "That way," she pointed.

"Me first." O'Leary's bulk blocked any possibility of Casey leading the way.

Carval kept shooting, abruptly reminded of his very first case, with Casey on the hunt through a dark lab. He hoped, below the surface of his mind, it wouldn't end with Casey back in the ER. He could see the biting tension in her back through his lens, and knew he couldn't do anything about it. Her job came first.

O'Leary stopped. "I c'n hear somethin'," he whispered. Casey made a *go-on* gesture. "Sounded like a gun bein' cocked." She pointed to herself, gestured to the left of the door, and moved there. O'Leary took the other side. They drew their guns without hesitation. Carval stayed well back, and out of the sightline when the door was opened. Tyler and Andy arrived, Tyler going left, Andy right. Carval caught Casey's face as Tyler stepped in front of her, but though she grimaced horribly, she didn't argue. A swift flash of relief crossed O'Leary's face.

Tyler took command again: a gesture to O'Leary indicating he should kick the door open; his hand raised, counting down fingers: three...two...one –

O'Leary's massive boot smashed the door open. A man fired and missed, as Tyler fired back, dropping the shooter instantly, screaming in pain, his shoulder bleeding and misshapen. Andy kicked the man's gun away.

"Andrew Grappano," Casey ground out. "You are under arrest for the murders of Beau Resorge and Carson Williams, serious injuries to Tania Hercliffe, and the murder of her unborn baby. You will be escorted to a hospital where you will be guarded until you can be brought to a cell." Her face twisted. "Babykiller," she spat, and turned away, leaving the others to deal with him.

Carval focused on her drawn, cold face; her gun held slackly at her hip, pointed downward in automatic safety; then switched to the activity around Grappano. When he turned back, Casey was missing.

CHAPTER THIRTY

"Where's Casey?" O'Leary asked, once Grappano was safely subdued and removed.

Tyler shrugged. "Disappeared."

"I'll go back to the other room," Andy said. He searched around the empty room: all the gang members arrested and taken away, and finally spotted Casey slumped in a corner, head down. He went over, and sat down next to her. He didn't say anything, but put a slim-fingered hand on her arm and waited. She didn't shake it off, but she didn't look at him either. After a moment, he slipped away to find O'Leary and Carval.

Casey, once Grappano had been secured, crashed. Every drop of adrenaline, everything that had allowed her to finish the operation, drained. She couldn't look at Grappano's blood any longer without disgracing herself. She slipped out without fanfare, needing to be alone to pull herself back together for long enough to get through the next hour. She stared blankly at her watch, finally understanding it was close to midnight. Andy ghosted up to her, but she couldn't summon the energy to acknowledge him. He ghosted off again, and shortly O'Leary's tread shook the floor.

"Tyler an' Andy are takin' him to the hospital."

Casey didn't look up. Carval sat down and slung an arm around her.

"One last thin', an' we c'n all go home."

"I have to tell Tania we got him," she dragged.

"Not at nearly midnight, you don't. We're goin' back to hand off to the shootin' team, an' we're all goin' home. Carval's takin' *you* home, 'cause you're done." O'Leary pulled her up. "Let's go."

Casey trudged out, not arguing when O'Leary simply hoisted her into his SUV. Carval, now worried, scrambled into the back, but when he put a hand on Casey's shoulder she didn't react, just as she hadn't reacted in the Tarticcas' bar.

259

Parking at the precinct, O'Leary nudged Casey, who hadn't opened her mouth the whole way. "C'mon." He steered her into the building, up to the Homicide floor.

"Detectives," Kent rapped, looking as if he would rather be at home asleep. "My office." They trailed after him.

In his office, Renfrew and Glencross were already waiting.

"A most successful operation," Renfrew said, as the detectives entered. "My congratulations."

"We captured the whole shipment, and you've arrested the main players. Well done. A successful multi-agency venture," Glencross's face lit with pride. "It doesn't happen often."

Where Casey would normally have spoken, there was silence. Andy nudged her. "You're welcome," she dragged, after half a beat.

Kent looked up sharply. "Clement?"

"Sir?" She tried to cover a yawn.

"All of you, hand over your service weapons, and get home. You're all dismissed until twelve noon tomorrow, when you'll see the shooting team."

One minute later his office was empty of the team.

"Detective Clement does not look well," Renfrew observed.

"You cleared her," Kent pointed out.

"She got the job done," Glencross noted. "However she feels now, it's been a huge success, and her team had a lot to do with it. We've taken a huge opioid shipment off the street, and disrupted at least two of the major players."

"Yeah." Kent scowled. "They're still right in the middle of a mess, but at least now I can bench the whole pack of them for ten days, starting as soon as I send them home tomorrow. They can give their statements to the shooting team and get gone."

"Very wise," Renfrew approved. "Agent Bergen and Detective Handjiev have already left. I will ensure Agent Bergen is here by noon tomorrow."

"I'll do the same for Handjiev. We'll want a team debrief, and then" – Glencross smiled viciously – "we'll have a little chat with Travers of Narcotics. He needs to be, hm, *reminded* of my favourable view of Handjiev."

"Okay. Let's quit. I didn't want to be here this late, but I couldn't go before your operation was complete."

***

"Home time," O'Leary said avuncularly. "Get some sleep. Casey, I'll give you an' Carval a ride. You shouldn't drive."

"'Kay," she muzzed. Sleep was the most desirable thing in the world right then. She barely noticed Carval helping her into the back of the SUV, following her and wrapping her in. Her eyes were already closing as O'Leary pulled away.

Casey reluctantly roused when O'Leary dropped them off at her apartment. Carval steered her upstairs and straight into her bedroom, undressed her as if she were a child and tucked her into bed. She was asleep again before he'd smoothed the quilt over her. He thought for a moment, found her keys, scrawled a quick note, and hurried back to his own apartment to download. He couldn't risk these shots being lost, and he'd only be half an hour.

He downloaded as fast as he could, and almost ran back out to catch a cab and race back to Casey's. He didn't want her to wake and find him gone, even though he'd left her a note. He sighed, relieved, when he heard only the soft whisper of her sleep, stripped and slid in beside her, and fell asleep instantly.

He was woken when Casey sat bolt upright, gasping, grabbed him and buried her face in his chest, sobbing.

"What's wrong?"

She didn't answer, pressing as close as she could, emitting gulping sobs and gasping for air, trying to burrow under his skin. "All the blood and corpses," she whispered.

"Did you have a nightmare?"

"Dad…"

He cuddled her in, and didn't try to talk.

"I dreamed about Dad…there was so much blood. I thought I'd gotten past it…"

"In two weeks? What are you *on?* You've been running a major operation where everyone was shooting each other with blood all over the floor and you think you *won't* have nightmares?" He sat up. "Of course it'll upset you. You're not a robot." She shuddered against him. "You can't get past it all at once."

He jammed his mouth shut before he voiced *you shouldn't have gone out on the raid.* She'd throw him out if he did, and he'd deserve it. The job had been the only thing holding her together.

"When will you finish tomorrow?" he asked instead. "Now that the case is done, we'll go to San Francisco like we agreed, and if you're done tomorrow I'll fix up flights and a hotel for Thursday."

"'Kay."

He didn't push her to enthuse or celebrate. Agreement was enough. He'd have it all arranged by lunchtime. "Snuggle in and go back to sleep. I'll be here. Keep the nightmares away." He wriggled back down, taking her with him, and dropped back into slumber without letting go.

Casey didn't fall asleep again. She stared into the dark, held against Carval's wide chest, and tried not to cry again. More. At least she hadn't thrown up, but tomorrow she'd have to talk to Tania Hercliffe, and right now she didn't think she could face it.

She could do it, she told herself firmly. She was a cop, and she could do it. Do the job. Tania must have been released from the hospital by now, so there would be no memories to interfere. She'd do it as soon as she'd made her statement to the shooting team. She'd go message Fremont to make sure Tania wasn't still in the hospital.

She carefully detached herself from Carval, slipped silently out of bed and into her robe, and went to send her message. When she was done, she sat on the couch, hitching the oversize garment around her to keep herself warm. It might be June, but she was chilled to the bone. Still, she didn't go back to bed; simply stared into the dark, alone, trying to push away the nightmare. Maybe, she thought, maybe she'd sleep peacefully now.

She knew she was lying to herself.

***

Casey finally fell asleep properly as the sun rose; having tossed and turned, woken from inchoate nightmare – nothing definite, nothing she remembered, only a vague impression of horror and a pounding heart. She hadn't slept this badly since...since about a month after she'd met Carval. She'd been drained last night, and she'd plunged into sleep – then the nightmares had begun and no matter how exhausted she had been, she couldn't find rest. Now, with the light brightening (*chasing away the nightmare*) she finally succumbed.

Carval, waking around eight, was slightly surprised to find Casey sound asleep beside him, but when he levered himself up on an elbow and looked at her face, she was no more rested than she had been when he'd tucked her into bed. He crept out of the bed, leaving her there, and made himself coffee and some toast. They didn't have to be at the precinct until noon, but Casey had left her vehicle there. She could sleep for another couple of hours, before he'd think about waking her. If, of course, she hadn't woken already, naturally or chased by nightmares.

Just as he thought he'd better waken her, Casey trailed out of her bedroom, swathed in her enormous robe, and went straight to her coffee machine. She made her espresso automatically, tipped it down and made another: chain-caffeinating until she could grind into gear.

"Urgh."

"Toast?"

"Urgh." She tipped back a third espresso, and faint intelligence finally flickered in her eyes. "What time izzit?"

"Ten."

"Ugh." She flopped on to the couch.

"Kent told you twelve noon. You've time."

Her grimace would have broken rocks. "I guess."

Carval plonked down next to her and gave her a hug. "We're flying out mid-morning tomorrow. You'll need to pack. Or I can pack for you."

"I can do it. I'm *fine*." She abruptly flipped around and stared at him. "Tomorrow mid-morning? To San Francisco?"

"Yep." He grinned. "All fixed up. We're staying near Union Square, so we're central."

"I know."

"Yeah." He bent and plopped a kiss on the tip of her nose. "Go fix yourself up."

"Are you coming to the precinct too?" An unusual note of neediness inflected her question.

"Sure. I need to take more shots of Glencross and Dani." He did, but it wasn't his only, or even main, reason for going. He strongly suspected that Casey was wobbling on the precipice of total crash, and he wanted to be there to catch her. "I better go home and clean up. I'll see you at the precinct."

He didn't want to leave, but in his hurry to download and return, he'd forgotten to bring a change of clothes and a wash bag.

Carval gone, Casey pulled herself together with the aid of an entirely justifiable fourth espresso, packed, and dragged off to the precinct. She assembled her papers for the district attorney, wrote her statement for the shooting team, tidied up her desk, and waited for noon. Carval appeared, and occupied himself ambling around and carping about Glencross's absence.

"Where is he?" Carval asked for the fifth time.

"You sound like a five-year-old, asking if we're nearly there yet," Andy gibed.

"He should be here," Carval insisted. "I need to close out this sequence."

"Mebbe he's got better thin's to do than be snapped," O'Leary suggested. Carval muttered. Casey fiddled with a pen, and paid no attention to anyone until twelve o'clock arrived.

"Time to see Kent," she pointed out. Trailed by the whole team, she tapped at Kent's door.

"Come in."

None of Bergen, Dani, Dr Renfrew or Glencross were present.

"Shut the door."

That wasn't normally good. Kent's stern, choleric face gave nothing away. Andy shut the door, and the team drew closer together, Casey, unwillingly, at the front. Kent allowed the silence to continue for another long moment.

"You've scored another success with the FBI," he said aridly, "and added DEA to your fans." He paused.

"Sir," Casey acknowledged, with no idea where Kent was going.

"Your performance has been exceptional. However, you are all exhausted." He gave a hard stare to O'Leary, whose shirt bulged over the dressing on his arm. "No arguments. I ordered earlier that when this case was done you were all to take ten days' leave. You will see the shooting team, hand over your statements and weapons, and leave."

"Sir," Casey said, "I ought to tell the innocent bystander we've caught her shooter."

Kent's mouth pursed. "You may," he allowed. "Do it immediately after you've seen the shooting team. I don't want anything left until tomorrow. If I find any of you anywhere near cop work before July 3rd – a Monday: you wouldn't be on shift that weekend anyway – you'll be in trouble."

"Sir."

"Well done. Wait here. Dr Renfrew and Agent Glencross want to speak to you." Kent exited, and shortly returned with Renfrew, Glencross, Bergen and Dani, all cramming into Kent's office.

Renfrew and Glencross exchanged glances. Dani stood with the team; Bergen took a position at their side but slightly separate.

"You first," Glencross invited Renfrew.

"Thank you." Renfrew steepled his fingers in front of his chest, and looked down his patrician nose, over his pince-nez glasses, at the team, Dani, and Bergen. "Thank you for your outstanding efforts throughout this case and, in particular, your execution of the operation yesterday. I am most impressed with your actions." He smiled. "Should any of you ever wish to apply to the FBI, I will be pleased to recommend you. I shall, as I have said before, be delighted to work with you on future cases, as will Agent Bergen."

In the background, Kent spluttered, his face suffused.

"Your acceptance of him has done much to aid our federal efforts." Bergen blushed, to the amusement of the four detectives. "We are very grateful."

"Thank you," Casey said, after a short pause, in which the team, who didn't like overt praise and had no intention of joining the FBI, squirmed embarrassedly.

Renfrew made a gesture to Glencross.

"I agree with Dr Renfrew. You've done an excellent job. I'll be happy to work with all of you again. Detective Handjiev, I've sent a commendation to your captain. Captain Kent, the same is in your inbox for your detectives." He smiled wryly. "You're a bit unorthodox, but you do the job. Thank you."

"Thank you," Casey repeated.

"Dismissed, Detectives, Detective Handjiev, Agent Bergen. The shooting team is waiting for you. Please close the door." Kent managed an approving nod as they left.

"I seem to remember, Glencross, you suggested a chat with Captain Travers might be...interesting." Kent exposed his teeth.

"So I did." Glencross's expression also showed his teeth. Neither was smiling.

"I anticipate that this will be an enjoyable discussion," Renfrew added. "Shall we proceed, gentlemen?"

Kent dialled, and put the phone on speaker.

"Captain Travers, Narcotics."

"Travers. Captain Kent here. You are on speaker, as I have Dr Renfrew of the FBI and Agent Glencross of DEA present."

Ugly silence fell. "Why are you calling?"

"We are calling, Captain Travers," Renfrew enunciated with exquisitely frigid precision, "to discuss your actions in sending Detective Marcol, a known Narcotics detective, to Captain Kent's precinct, without the courtesy to contact any of Captain Kent, Agent Glencross or me beforehand."

"Glencross here. By failing to contact me, and openly sending a Narcotics detective into the middle of an ongoing operation, you put that operation at risk. Did it not occur to you that it was likely that either, or both, of the gangs involved would be watching the Thirty-Sixth Precinct to obtain information about our plans?"

Silence.

"Were you aware," Renfrew took up again, "that Detective Marcol *informed* – not, note, requested – us that he was to join the team?"

Another ugly silence.

"Was that at your order?" Travers still failed to answer. "I must, therefore, presume that it was. On what possible grounds did you think that you, a junior captain of the NYPD, had any authority whatsoever to interfere with a federal operation, or to instruct its leaders as to the composition of their team?"

"You already had NYPD" –

"We chose that NYPD team," Glencross corrected, "because they had *already* uncovered the problem and called us in, as they should do." He exchanged a quick glance with Renfrew. "Their conduct was professional and appropriate, as was that of Captain Kent. We took over the case from them, and requested they stay involved to minimise disruption. As it happens, we could not have asked for a better group. Why do you think you knew better than us?"

"Marcol is my best" –

"Really?" Glencross queried. "Not from where I'm standing. Detective Handjiev has performed outstandingly well, and a commendation for her work is in your inbox. I'll be checking to ensure it is on her file. If it is not, I will resend it – to your superior."

"You dare suggest" –

"Captain Travers," Renfrew interjected, "please explain why you sent Detective Marcol, a man who you know has harassed Detective Clement? I am deeply interested to know why you condone such behaviour, and why you took an action which you must have known would risk disrupting Detective Clement and her team, and by implication a federal investigation."

Glencross stared, then raised his eyebrows at Kent, who nodded and made a *tell-you-after* gesture.

"He had relevant information."

"Which should have been conveyed by telephone, as you have been told. I find it difficult to believe that a competent captain in the Narcotics Division would not know that."

Kent smiled sharply in appreciation of Renfrew's comment.

"I am waiting, Captain Travers."

"You have no right to ask me about my staffing decisions. I don't have to listen to your unfounded accusations. This call is over." The crash of Travers' receiver could probably have been heard in the nearby subway station.

"Fascinating," Renfrew said blandly. "I consider, Agent Glencross, that Captain Travers' misjudgements give rise to considerable doubt over his ability to command his precinct in alignment with DEA's federal obligations."

"Yeah. Before we get into that, how about someone clues me into the Clement position? She didn't mention any harassment."

"Clement was told not to discuss certain matters."

"She didn't. I asked her flat out, and she simply said she did better at the Academy" –

"That is one way of putting it," Renfrew opined –

"And he'd asked her out, she'd declined, and you, Kent, had stepped in. I need to know if there's anything that can mess up our collective case."

"That was all she said?"

"Yep."

"Mm."

Glencross looked from Renfrew to Kent and back again. "Is there anything that can mess up the case?"

"No," Renfrew stated.

"No," Kent agreed.

"I'll drop it. There's clearly something going on, but if you're not able" – he regarded them closely, and nodded in comprehension – "to tell me, I don't want to spoil anything else. I'll make sure Travers' behaviour on this case is noted at DEA. He won't be on my list of guys to call if I have an option."

Kent refrained from comment, which was as good as an open statement.

"Nor mine," Renfrew confirmed.

"Okay. I'd better get back to my shop and make sure the drugs case is cut and dried – a bit like the drugs." Glencross laughed. "I'll be headhunting your team, Kent."

"Paws off. I'm keeping those closure stats for me."

Glencross gone, Kent scrutinised Renfrew. "You cleared Clement."

"Only because I determined, as, I believe, did you, that being forbidden to participate in the operation would be significantly more detrimental to her than allowing it. Had you not already mandated ten days' leave, I should have recommended it."

"Has she consulted you? I'm not asking for any details, and you won't provide any, but is she properly engaging?"

"Yes."

"Good. Thank you."

"My pleasure. I look forward to my next interactions with the whole team."

More than I do, thought Kent bitterly.

CHAPTER THIRTY ONE

"We're done with the shootin' team," O'Leary said. "You want some lunch before you talk to Tania Hercliffe?"

Casey looked up from where she was numbly straightening papers and clearing her desk. "No," she replied. "Let's get it done. Fremont says she's been released from hospital."

"Iffen you faint from not eatin', I won't carry you home."

"Same to you."

O'Leary guffawed.

"Been nice working with you." Dani strode up. "We could go get a drink some time."

"Okay," Casey agreed. "Message me."

"Will do." She swung off.

Four men looked at Casey. "What?" she snipped. "I'm ready when you are."

"Before we go see the Hercliffes," O'Leary said, "even iffen you don't want lunch, I do. Let's do it an' we c'n all go home."

"We don't all have to go."

"We're only coming as far as lunch," Andy pointed out.

"I wanna shoot," Carval said. "I've never seen you delivering the news that you got the guy to the victim's family."

"Would you have shot me straight after Dad died?" she snapped.

"Casey…" O'Leary murmured.

"It's the same thing. Grief is grief. She lost someone. I lost someone." Her eyes dropped to the desk top; her whole demeanour defeated. "Ask first," she sighed. "I don't think shooting grief's appropriate, but it's up to Tania."

Carval opened his mouth – then abruptly shut it again as he thought. "Uh…yeah. Not this time."

"You *don't* want to shoot?" O'Leary gasped.

"Sure I want to, but this isn't the time. It's…it would be brilliant, and I'd die to shoot it, but it's far too raw for her. And if I have to ask, she wouldn't be natural anyway, so they'd be useless. It only works if people don't notice me."

"And there's the obsessive photographer we're used to," Andy said sardonically. "I didn't think you'd suddenly had an injection of tact."

Carval ignored Andy. He could do tact. He hadn't shot Casey's father's funeral, or indeed Casey's father, never mind her grief. "So, I better not come with you. I'll have lunch and go back to the studio." He met Casey's weary eyes. "Come over when you're done?"

"I'll call you."

Which, Carval noticed, wasn't *yes*. Or *no*, he supposed, so it wasn't awful. He didn't like the dragging tone in Casey's voice, or the black circles under her dark eyes, or the downturn to her mouth – but there wasn't anything he could do about it here and now.

"C'mon," O'Leary cajoled. "Your desk's all tidy, an' Tyler isn't goin' to mess it up till we're all back from vacation." Tyler muttered at O'Leary. "I'm hungry," the big man continued. "Lunch time."

Casey put her last few papers in order, locked her desk, and trailed out, following the others to the nearest sandwich bar. She only meant to buy a soda, but O'Leary's questioning glance prodded her into adding a brownie. She could always feed it to the pigeons if she didn't eat it, and O'Leary could keep his nannying looks to himself.

By the end of lunchtime, sitting in the sunshine at Sakura Park, Casey had eaten far less brownie than two mice would have. She stared O'Leary down when he thought about commenting, and contributed less conversation than those same mice. She could tell Tania the good news, but it wouldn't bring her baby back. Nothing brought back the dead. Her mouth twisted.

"Let's go," she said to O'Leary, who was munching on a large piece of apple pie.

"Lemme finish." He swallowed and picked up the last piece. Casey tapped her fingers fretfully on the grass, and stood as soon as he'd chewed.

"Come on," she hurried him. "It won't get any better for waiting."

"I'll have indigestion, an' it'll all be your fault, rushin' me like this," he grumbled.

"She deserves to know as soon as possible. She shouldn't have to wait." Casey stopped, rubbing a toe into the turf. "We should've gone this morning before we saw Kent."

"Naw, we shouldn't," O'Leary corrected gently, one syllable ahead of Tyler's likely rebuke. "You needed a rest, an' I sure did, an' you wouldn't've been no good to Tania iffen you're yawning. Looks rude, an' you don't want to be lookin' rude. Better to've had some sleep an' go do it now, since I've finished my pie."

"You know he's right," Andy said, Tyler nodding firmly. Carval stayed extremely quiet. Interfering with the team bonds, when Casey was teetering on the edge of exploding, would be dumb.

"You need to take a break," O'Leary continued. "You wouldn't take bereavement leave when you should've, and now you're sayin' you should've gone an' exhausted yourself for no good reason when we c'n go do it now an' do it right. Anyways, if you'd gone this mornin' an' Kent found out, you'd've been in trouble for it, so…don't be dumb. You already did plenty findin' Grappano."

"We all did that."

"Yup, an' the important words there are *We all*. Means you too. Unless you're tryin' to tell us you're goin' to go work for the FBI."

"No!"

"Well." O'Leary let that hang, hoisting his massive form up from the grass to tower over her. "Team."

The others stood up as well, dusting off crumbs. "Vacation time," Andy said. "I've made a list of exhibitions already."

Tyler groaned.

"I'm goin' to Niagara, like I told you. Where're you goin', Casey? Tyler's goin' to the gym. Says he's unfit."

Tyler growled. "See who's unfit when you're back."

"Sure." O'Leary flexed a bicep. Tyler flexed one back. "Where're you goin'?" he repeated to Casey.

"San Francisco," she forced out.

Three men turned their gazes on Carval, who merely smiled, and declined to comment.

"Good. You need to take vacation. Let's go."

The remaining men watched Casey trudge out of the park alongside O'Leary.

"I hear San Francisco's pretty nice this time of year," Andy smirked.

"So do I," Carval replied blandly. "You should go."

Tyler snorted. "Staying here."

"I heard you'd developed a taste for culture," Andy carried on. "Senior recital, wasn't it?"

Tyler shrugged. "See you after vacation." He marched off.

"Take care of her," Andy instructed.

"Have a nice vacation." Carval gave nothing away. It didn't stop Andy's knowing look.

***

"You don't hafta do this," O'Leary said. "I c'n tell Tania, an' you could go home, or see your pal Kayla, or somethin'. Or you could'a called her."

"I'm fine. Tania deserves to hear it from me in person."

270

"Okay."

"Stop looking at me like I'm breaking. I'm *fine*."

"Never said anythin' different." O'Leary took the next right.

"You don't have to say it. It's written all over your face."

"Just don't promise anythin' that it'll hurt you to give – an' I don't mean gettin' beat up, neither. You got enough goin' on without addin' another layer."

"I hear you."

O'Leary pulled up at the Hercliffes' block. "You hear me, but are you listenin'?"

"Yes."

O'Leary cast her a glance, but said nothing, deafeningly. Casey said nothing right back at him, all the way to the Hercliffes' door, rapping assertively.

"Yes?" Matthew Hercliffe peered around the door. "Uh…oh, you're the detectives."

"Yes. Detectives Clement and O'Leary," she reminded him. "Is your wife here too? We have some news for you both."

"I don't want her to be upset." A faint whiff of whiskey suggested that he'd muffled his own upset.

"We've caught your wife's assailant," O'Leary rumbled softly.

"Oh – come in. Tania will want to know. I hope it helps her. She's devastated."

Tania half-lay on the couch, wrapped in a cherry-red robe. Her unstyled hair hung loosely, and her haggard face bore no make-up.

"Tania," Casey murmured, noticing the glass of water by her side – and the dregs of whiskey in the glass on the table at the other side of the couch. "How are you feeling?"

Tania's mouth twisted. "How do you think?"

"We caught the guy who did it." Prolonging the conversation would help nobody, and pleasantries weren't what Tania wanted or needed. "He was injured in the takedown."

Bitter satisfaction flashed through Tania's drawn face. "Good. He deserves as much pain as he gets." Her eyes brimmed. "I wish you'd killed him like he killed *my baby*." Matthew put a hand on her arm, but she shook it off. "I wish he was dead! I wish he'd suffered and died like my baby did. I want him to *rot*." Her hands knotted, unknotted, twisted hard together around her stomach.

Matthew tried once more to comfort her, but she shook him off again. "You don't get it," she cried. "It wasn't you who had it all until it was taken away *by mistake*. I wasn't even a target, and that sonofabitch killed my baby. I wanted my baby and *don't* tell me we can try again. It doesn't help, and I don't even know if I *can* try again." Sobs ripped through her chest. Matthew blinked hard, white-faced, and drained his glass.

"We should leave," Casey suggested. She couldn't bear to watch as Tania tore herself apart.

"Don't go. You get it. You lost someone. You *understand*."

Behind Casey, O'Leary beckoned Matthew, whose bemusement didn't stop him following the big man's summons. Casey sat next to Tania, passing her a box of Kleenex. The men disappeared, and Tania collapsed into tempestuous tears. "I wanted my baby so badly. I hadn't known…we weren't trying…but when I knew I couldn't wait to meet her."

Casey gave a small, sympathetic noise. Words weren't appropriate, even if she could have found any. *You weren't this devastated*, a small voice in her head pointed out. *You were relieved. Weren't you?* She concentrated on Tania.

"I can't stop crying," Tania wept. "And Matthew keeps saying we can try again but I don't want a *new* baby, I want *my* baby." Further words drowned in her furious grief.

Casey gave her an awkward, embarrassed pat, and waited.

"How do I keep going?" Sodden eyes turned to Casey. "How can you be working? How aren't you as upset as me? You said you lost your father. How do you do it? How can you?"

Casey heard *How do I do it?* right alongside *Are you that cold and heartless?*

"I can't deal with it now, like I told you. I'm working so I don't think about it."

"If you were as upset as me, you wouldn't be able to work. Maybe you didn't care like I do" – Tania stopped dead, staring at Casey's bloodless face as she jerked from the couch. "I'm sorry. I didn't mean it. I'm so *sorry*. Don't go. I can't…"

"I have to go. I only came to tell you we caught the man who injured you." Casey was already three steps towards the door. "O'Leary, we have to go." Her voice caught on the lump in her throat.

"Please don't go." Tania stumbled off the couch and caught at Casey's shoulder. "Please. I can't think straight and I didn't mean it. Of course you cared."

She had. She *had* cared. But the more she told herself so, the less she believed it.

"Don't go."

"Tania? Tania, you shouldn't be standing up. You have to rest, honey. You have to get better." Matthew held her close, worry on his face, fingers unbearably gentle, encouraging her back to the couch. "Come on, honey. Sit back down." He glanced at his empty glass, then away, settling Tania, making sure her robe was comfortably wrapped around her. "Do you want any more water?"

"No, thanks."

"Can I get you something?" Matthew asked Casey, still fussing over his wife. "Your colleague wanted to get a coffee."

"No, thank you. We have to go."

"Don't go, *please*." Tania sobbed.

Casey looked helplessly at the mess in front of her, and chose the least awful option. "If you wouldn't mind…a coffee would be good."

"Sure. Sure. I'll get it now. Just…stay with Tania, please?" Desperation coloured his jerky movements, flicking glances from Casey to his empty glass to his weeping wife.

"Okay." She wanted to go. Her stomach twisted; her chest hurt. She could take the few steps out of the door and go home – but Matthew was already in the kitchen and she couldn't walk away from Tania's distress until he returned. She could toss back the coffee and leave. It would only be a few more minutes. She could cope, the same as she'd coped until now.

When Matthew returned with a mug of black coffee – O'Leary must have intervened – Tania was still fitfully sobbing, interspersed with desperate apologies. Casey hoped, equally desperately, for the coffee to cool enough that she wouldn't scald her throat, and produced as many meaningless, sympathetic-sounding platitudes as she could manage through her own, better-hidden, upset.

Finally, the coffee had cooled enough to drink. Casey tipped it back, and waited for a pause in Tania's misery.

"We have to go now," she inserted into the gap.

"But…You'll still be there if I want to ask you anything?"

"Yes. You can call me if you need to." Casey could sense O'Leary struggling not to say anything about her offer from a dozen feet away.

"Thank you."

Casey made her escape, exhaling relief with every foot of the elevator's descent. Beside her, O'Leary loomed, ominously silent.

"I'll get the subway," she said as they left the building.

"Naw, I'll take you home. Seein' as you're doin' dumb thin's, I better make sure you ain't doin' more of 'em."

"What was I supposed to say? No? How would *that* look? You couldn't have told her *no* either."

Uncomfortable silence filled the SUV.

"See? You couldn't have. Stop with the *dumb*. Anyway, what'll she call me about? We got Grappano. There's nothing more."

"'Cept Matthew's drinkin'."

"She won't call me about that."

"You hope. So do I, 'cause it won't do you no good. You need to take vacation an' not think about anythin' but havin' a nice time an' fixin' your head so's you c'n stop feelin' guilty about your dad."

Casey stared straight ahead. O'Leary patted her knee with a giant paw. "Anyways, we're here."

"This isn't my block."

"Nup, it's your boy's. You need a hug, an' I ain't got time. I gotta pack."

"You really are going to Niagara?" Casey gaped. O'Leary never went anywhere outside the USA, and complained about Philadelphia being foreign. The team teased him about never going further than the Bronx.

"Yup." O'Leary grinned widely. "It's goin' to be great."

"Yeah."

"Now, go see your boy. Make sure you get a hug."

"Have a good vacation."

"You too."

Casey slid out of the SUV. She thought about going to the subway, but O'Leary was blatantly watching. She buzzed the door, and went in. O'Leary nodded approvingly at the space on the sidewalk where she'd been, and drove off.

***

"I didn't expect you," Carval said. "I thought you were going home?"

"O'Leary dumped me here and watched to make sure I came in." She scowled at Carval, who ignored it.

"Are you packed?"

"Yeah."

"Great!" Carval also ignored the dull tone, complete lack of any enthusiasm, and hard blinking. He hugged her. "It'll be amazing. You can show me all the places you used to go, and I'll do the same."

Casey extracted herself from his shirt. "You?"

"I spent some time there – you know that, it's how I took the photo of you at graduation."

"I didn't know you'd spent more than a day or two."

"Sure I did. I tried shooting wildlife in the Don Edwards refuge, but I didn't enjoy it. The animals didn't appear, and it wasn't anything like the TV shows, so I came up to San Francisco and Palo Alto."

"You mean you had no patience."

Carval pouted. "I have plenty of patience, just not for animals." He hugged her again. "Let me finish tidying up the studio, before I tell you tomorrow's timings."

"Okay." Casey perched on the corner of the desk and marvelled at how rapidly Carval reduced the chaos to order. Every other time she'd been in the studio, it had been a mess only exceeded by O'Leary's desk (which was reputed to have coal seams in the lower strata of the paperwork), though Carval always seemed to know exactly where everything was. Casey would have gone crazy in half an hour. *Her* desk was tidy to the point of pristine, and she kept it neat. She couldn't think when it was in a mess. She hated mess.

Her father's apartment had been a bloodstained mess. She'd had it cleaned…and hadn't been in it since. If only she'd heard from the probate attorney, she could sell it: push it away with the horrible memories of his last days; push away the knowledge that, on the day of his death, her anger and resentment had outweighed her love for him. Tania's unthinking, pain-driven words returned. *Maybe you didn't care like I do.*

Maybe she hadn't.

She sniffed, found a Kleenex, wiped her eyes and nose; repeated it, staring at the pine floor, turning away from Carval. She heard paper shuffling, drawers opening and closing, and a small sound of satisfaction.

"Done," he announced. "Casey?" He cuddled her in. "Don't cry. What's wrong?"

"Nothing."

"Sure. You normally cry all over the place, so how on earth would I guess something's wrong?" He paused. "Was Tania upset? Was that why O'Leary dropped you here, not at your apartment?"

"I don't want to talk about it." She blew her nose. "I'm going on vacation and that's the only thing I'm thinking about. What are the timings?" She met his eyes defiantly, still perched on the corner of the desk.

"Nine a.m. from JFK."

"Ugh. Early."

"Not too bad." He didn't mention the priority boarding or that they'd be in the comfy seats. He didn't see the point of squashing himself into no-leg-room seats if he didn't have to, and he wouldn't get into an argument with Casey about it. She might offer to pay her way, and he'd already told her she couldn't. She wriggled out of his arms. "Where are you going?"

"When are we coming back?" she asked. "I need to give Kayla a date, so she doesn't think I ghosted her. The case closure'll be all over the media because it was a big drug bust, and they'll all still be feeding off your show." She managed to extract her phone. Carval leaned on the desk next to her and slung one arm back around her.

"A week from tomorrow – Thursday the 25th."

"'Kay." She swiped open, and found the previous messages, reading through with still-red eyes then tapping the reply icon.

Hi. How about coffee Friday the 26th? Can't do sooner – holiday with my boyfriend.

She tapped *send*, and only afterwards looked back up into Carval's utterly shocked face. "What?"

"You actually admitted it. You admitted I'm your boyfriend to someone who didn't already know." He grabbed her and kissed her hard. "You're really into this." He kissed her again. "Vacation'll be *great*."

Fin.

ABOUT THE AUTHOR

SR Garrae grew up in Scotland and then worked in international finance in London until her retirement. She lives in the UK with her family, who are somewhat bemused by but supportive of her complete change of career.

She always loved books, but didn't start to write original fiction until after she retired. She now balances writing with travel, reluctant but very necessary gym visits, and designing her own book covers.

Modern, romantic cop stories are the stories she had always turned to as a go-to read, and always loved.